EARHART KENTWORTH

Beatrice

An Alarming Tale of British Murder and Woe

Copyright © 2022 by Earhart Kentworth

All rights reserved. No part of this publication may be reproduced, stored or transmitted in any form or by any means, electronic, mechanical, photocopying, recording, scanning, or otherwise without written permission from the publisher. It is illegal to copy this book, post it to a website, or distribute it by any other means without permission.

This novel is entirely a work of fiction. The names, characters and incidents portrayed in it are the work of the author's imagination. Any resemblance to actual persons, living or dead, events or localities is entirely coincidental.

First edition

ISBN: 978-1-7365059-1-5

Editing by Tedd Hawks

This book was professionally typeset on Reedsy. Find out more at reedsy.com

Contents

Dedication	v
Cast of Characters	vi
A Note from the Author	viii
A Note on the Author's Note	x
A Note on the Note about the Author's Note	xii
Prologue: The Complex History of the Hawsfeffers	xiii
1 The Solicitor and His Assistant	1
2 Beatrice	11
3 A Suspicion	22
4 The Last Arrivals	32
5 Lucinda's Last Words	41
6 An Indigent and a Lady	49
7 A Voice in the Dark	56
8 The Pot Boils	64
9 A Perfect Night for Murder	74
10 The Aftermath	86
11 The Vault	95
12 A Prime Suspect	106
13 Sleuthing	114
14 May's Secret	125
15 A Shot in the Dark	134
16 Detective Lucian Lucretian Pimento	149
17 Tick Tock	158
18 Portraits of Death	169
19 Toward the Climax	179
20 Bixby Ex Machina	189

21	Pimento, Triumphant	198
22	Brontë at the Brink	207
23	Crockett's Confession	215
24	A Murderer's Monologue	220
25	The Battle of the Tiddlymouth	233
26	Martha	242
27	The End of the Affair	249
28	The Danube Mob	259
An Afterword and Apology		272

Dedication

For JJ, who is always wonderful enough to ask,
and my dad, who encouraged me to laugh.

Cast of Characters

Crockett Cook—19-year-old junior solicitor, anxious around danger and the female sex

Petrarch Bluster—master solicitor, rotund and joyful

The Von Bunsons

The Baron (deceased)—created the estate which fell to the Hawsfeffer family, died mysteriously

Gladys (deceased)—classically pale and sickly Victorian, (also) died mysteriously

Bixby (ex-patriated)—theatrical and garish, moved to the United States to seek his fortune

The Hawsfeffers

Bixby (deceased)—patriarch of the Hawsfeffers, recently died in a boating incident

Lucinda (deceased)—first wife of Bixby Hawsfeffer, (also) died in a boating incident

Pip (Bixby Hawsfeffer, Jr.)—homosexual son from Bixby's first marriage, now in Paris

Corinthiana—second wife of Bixby Hawsfeffer, classist, loves prolonged vowels

May—youngest daughter of Corinthiana and Bixby Hawsfeffer, failed nun

Robert Edward Harrington—second cousin of Bixby Hawsfeffer, odd face and accent

The Winterbournes

August—married to June, family is known for dying under non-nefarious circumstances

June—eldest daughter of Corinthiana and Bixby Hawsfeffer, really quite ordinary

Brontë—eldest daughter of June and August, prone to wearing trousers, speaking her mind

Kordelia—youngest daughter of June and August, arsonist, dramatist, oddball

The Hawsfeffer Staff

Martha Smith—family maid, served the house since Bixby Hawsfeffer's first marriage to Lucinda

Dexter Fletcher—family groundskeeper, prone to theatrics and being forgotten

A Note from the Author

14 January 1913

To Whomsoever It May Concern:

It behooves the author to warn the reader that the following is based on entirely almost-true events. There was an encounter with Mrs. W——'s barrister which led to the "almost" portion as select occurrences had to be altered to protect the identities of certain persons. If the true nature of the crime were to be public, it could tarnish the reputation of the W—— and H—— families forever. As their position in West Hampminstershireshire society is rather tortured as is, I have agreed to write this almost account on behalf of Mrs. W—— and her family. The family's need for total privacy was overshadowed by the hope that the following text would generate a small income, enough to provide for their youngest daughter at her new French finishing school, as opposed to the Swiss institution which had made her almost entirely unbearable on the subject of cheeses.

But that aside, certain events are absolutely true.

There was a grisly murder.

There was a love story.

There was, indeed, a plot of much cunning to conceal all.

I have recorded as much of the incident as truthfully as possible. When Mrs. W—— appeared at my door, weeping about the loss of her dear friend and asking how much a good mystery book could earn a fair, gentle, middle-aged woman, I promptly assured her that it directly correlated to the amount of gruesome details that could be included therein. Between sobs she assured me that there was a *large* amount of such things and that, if needed, additional, tasteful gore could be added in order to heighten tensions.

That was the beginning of our story, the adventure. I write this to you at the end of it all, the barrister's extensive notes taken into account ("Does blood really 'burst with geyser-like zest' from a papercut?"). I present to you the, henceforth named, Windham and Hogsdish families and the death of their dear friend. It is not for the faint of heart, or those afraid of lawyers as there are several included in the following pages, but I sincerely hope that I do the whole complicated debacle justice.

Your servant,
Earhart Kentworth

A Note on the Author's Note

17 March 2020

Dear Reader,

It also may behoove you (in a rare instance of double behoovement) to know that this text was discovered by dumb luck while I was visiting a bookshop in London.

I mentioned to the store owner that I was working on my third book, a mystery novel. His interest was immediately piqued, and he told me about his distant cousin, who had written a draft of a novel a long time ago based on events which occurred in a large family. The story he described included deaths, betrayals, fallen nuns, and ghosts. He said that his cousin who wrote the novel was prone to drink and flights of fancy and that he only sold one novel to a publisher during his entire career, a romance about a pirate and a mermaid. The book in question sold only forty-five copies, thirty-seven to the author's mother, Adelaide Earhart, and one to Ms. Kordelia Hawsfeffer, who went on to recommend the author to her mother to tell their family's story.

As the shopkeeper told me more about this unsuccessful writer, I couldn't help but feel a certain connection. I, too, was an unsuccessful writer who was prone to flights of fancy and drink.

After a long chat, the owner agreed to give me the manuscript to clean up and publish. I have to say that Earhart did (mostly) an excellent job on the initial draft. My main contribution was toning down scenes of horrific violence that, from the previous note, seem to be a device used for increasing sales. There were some questionable pieces added which I have largely edited out, but for the most part, I think the text is fine in its own right and his characterizations are actually very good. In the end it took two bad writers to get this text to the public, but we hope that you will find the time well spent.

Sincerely,
Tedd Hawks

A Note on the Note about the Author's Note

2 January 2021

Reader,

The complexity of the given case makes it important to mention that the H—— and W—— family, upon discovering that their story was going to be published so many years after the initial crimes were committed, have reneged upon their first request for anonymity. At this point in time, they are grateful for any attention or publicity sent their way.

They kindly asked for their real names to be restored to the text, which is presented before you as the Hawsfeffer and Winterbourne families. The heiress of what little fortune remains, Ms. Kinzay Sprout née Winterbourne, also asks that you follow her Instagram @badgrrlKinzay47.

Sincerely,
Herman Schloop, Esq.

Prologue: The Complex History of the Hawsfeffers

Hawsfeffer Manor sits in stately, smug assurance at the edge of the Tiddlymouth River. The house was built in the middle of the nineteenth century, the great Baron Von Bunson constructing it for his new wife, the sickly and pale Gladys. The two had only one child, Bixby, who chose to move to America rather than keep the grounds and heritage of his family. The estate then fell to his cousin Bixby Hawsfeffer (the author apologizes, there are several Bixbys, but the name was the rage of the time), who would make it his family home.

It is important to note that the fate of Baron Von Bunson is the subject of much local myth. After Gladys' death and his own late-life ailments, he turned over his estate to Bixby Hawsfeffer, who, local rumor conjects, kept his uncle locked in the attic until the poor man's death. To this day there are legends that the ghost of Baron Von Bunson roams the grounds at night. It is a common pastime for youths from the area to set up a camp at the edge of the Tiddlymouth and see if the Baron's ghost flits over the surface of the water during the midnight hour. Many have claimed to have seen him floating over the waves, singing an old German nursery rhyme, which roughly translates to "Duck Man of the Old Hat."[1]

Bixby Hawsfeffer made the most of his uncle's fortune, investing in ventures in America via his cousin, Bixby Von Bunson, who went into

---

[1] The editor has looked for references to this rhyme in contemporary texts but has only found reference to an old German song "Mallard Man Who Eats Hats." He conjects that Earhart was unfamiliar with German and did not do sufficient research.

the American West. Gold was struck and both Bixbys reaped the benefits. Hawsfeffer Manor went from a ten-room, two-story mansion to a twenty-room, double-winged monstrosity. The locals looked on in wonder as the once subtle, stately home turned into "an Americanized terror." All over the house, Bixby Hawsfeffer put Western-themed memorabilia, inspired by the stories told by his American ex-patriot cousin Bixby Von Bunson during Von Bunson's visit back to the Hawsfeffer estate in 1869. The ballroom is still decorated with murals of cowboys, Indians, and covered wagons.

The Hawsfeffer family went from condescended-upon middle class to egregiously pompous upper class in a matter of months. With the new money, Bixby's son Bixby, Jr. (another Bixby, yes; for the sake of the reader, however, this Bixby shall be referred to by his childhood nickname, "Pip") was sent to a private school in France, where he took a liking to powdered wigs and other men. Shortly after this disgrace came out to the family, Bixby the elder's wife, Lucinda, passed away. The countryside was filled with gossip on whether she took her own life, died by accident, or was murdered. She vanished into the river just as the Baron had many years before. Local children are also said to camp at the river to watch for her ghost, who sings a beautiful harmony of "Duck Man of the Old Hat" with Baron Von Bunson.

Our story centers on Bixby Hawsfeffer, who received the manor and estate (not his son, the homosexual French Pip-Bixby, or his cousin, the American ex-patriated Bixby Von Bunson). His eldest daughter (from his second wife, Corinthiana, whom he married after Lucinda's death), June Hawsfeffer, stayed in the mansion with her mother and father into her adulthood. In the spring of 1887, she married another local, landed gentleman, Mr. August Winterbourne, who agreed to cede his less monstrous mansion to live on his wife's family's estate. They had two daughters, Brontë and Kordelia, who were raised as best they could be, despite the disappearances, ghostly harmonies, and general malfeasance manifest in the house.

Our story begins at the foot of this gnarled family tree, its branches so twisted it's difficult to tell a Hawsfeffer from a Von Bunson from a Winterbourne.

After the remodeling of the family home, the death of Lucinda, and the birth of the two girls, the Hawsfeffers lived in relative ease. There were no new tragedies and no additional German nursery rhymes sung by ghosts on the edge of the river.

But in 1912, the patriarch, Bixby Hawsfeffer, died, leaving his will and his grief-stricken second wife, Corinthiana, to deal with his entombment. There was no body, the elder Bixby having lost his balance and plunged into the Tiddlymouth River.[2] The river itself is a tributary to the nearby Blustenwich River, which eventually leads farther out to the deeper and bluer waters of the English Channel. The hope of ever finding his body was gone when Corinthiana sat down at her small secretary and began writing notes, the first to her solicitor, Petrarch Bluster, the second to her youngest, childless daughter, May. A third letter was sent late the same day, the contents a mystery to all, even to the old maid, Martha, who slipped out in the middle of the night to post it under the cover of darkness.

This is all very confusing but necessary information. The author humbly suggests if one has questions as to the lineage of the Hawsfeffers or the number of Bixbys, they please direct their inquiries to the character list at the beginning of this text.

In most cases a cliffhanger of sorts would now be suspended before the reader to keep momentum into the next chapter, but after ghosts, two possible murders, correspondence delivered under the cover of night, and several drownings, it may be best to leave just a moment of solace before moving into the horrific details of the death which is the subject of this novel.

---

[2] The editor does wonder why no one built a fence or, at the very least, prioritized swimming proficiency.

1

The Solicitor and His Assistant

The carriage was stuck a mile from Hawsfeffer Manor. Petrarch Bluster, not yet having emerged from the interior of the coach, was already slick with sweat—neat, fat droplets covering his large, moon-like face. Beads of perspiration had accumulated in his thick, bushy eyebrows, so that his vision was slightly blurred. Dabbing his forehead, he called to his young assistant, Crockett Cook, who was assessing the wheel buried in mud.

"Crockett, how is it looking, my boy?"

Crockett pushed back his bowler and scratched his head. "Petrarch,[3] it doesn't look good. Any more pressure and it could break all together."

"Oi!" The carriage owner hobbled around the back of the vehicle to get a better look at Petrarch. He shook his fist up at the old man. "Think it was yer fat arse that buried it in the mud. Ther's not even a lot of muck, but it's stuck like I'm haulin' 'round a whale."

Petrarch laughed. "You and my late wife would likely have a thorough conversation about that. She liked to call me 'King Arser, the Knight of the

---

[3] Please note, in an editorial decision, it has been decided to rely on Christian names throughout the text. Although in the period there would have been more decorum around such things, for modern audiences, having a character called William Little and referring to him as Mr. Little, Will, Bill, Billy, Billiam, Willbob, etc. would be taxing. In this novel, the number of Miss Hawsfeffers alone is troublesome.

Round.'"

The carriage owner was not amused. "Well, it's too late for you to be unwhalin' yerself, so I suggist you walk on from 'ere or wait with me for the nixt passing cart for some hilp."

Crockett looked up at his master, his gaze full of concern. "Petrarch, it's a mile. Do you think you can walk with all your luggage?"

Petrarch steeled himself. "Of course! If I can still work, then I can still walk!" He quickly reached out to grab the door of the carriage.

What followed was a chaotic moment, the rotund solicitor pitching forward and falling out of the carriage into the mud. Crockett and the carriage owner looked at each other uncomfortably as the old man rolled back and forth trying to fetch his balance.

"I'm all right! Fine here! Be up in a moment," Petrarch gasped. "This actually is a bit of my morning calisthenics routine."

Crockett hesitated a few moments before gingerly stepping forward and extending a hand. Petrarch's great girth, however, was too much for the young law clerk. He ended up hurtling forward, sliding headfirst through the mud, his bowler launching under the carriage. The carriage owner sighed and crossed his arms as the two adult men embraced and flailed in the muck.

It took Crockett sitting on his knees, placing his hands firmly on Petrarch's buttocks, and pushing with all his might, to get the old lawyer back onto his feet. Once he was stable, Crockett nimbly raised himself up and tried his best to wipe off the grime from the roadside and locate his hat.

"This whole routine part o' yer service?" the old carriage master asked. "I'd laugh if yer girth'ness hadn't broken my means of livin'."

Crockett and Petrarch, rivulets of mud running down their faces, shrugged politely.

"We'll give you a touch more compensation to make amends," Petrarch said. "We're on the way to Hawsfeffer Manor, and it should prove to be a lucrative job for my assistant and me. It's a will reading, marking the death of the family patriarch."

"Oi!" The carriage master's mood immediately altered. "Old Hawsfeffer is *dead*?" He ran a hand through his slicked back, gray hair. "You think the mistress, Lady Hawsfeffer, is lookin' for a new man o' the house? I once cleaned out the horse stables for 'em when ther houseman, Dexter, was under th' weather. While I was shovelin' shit into the rubbish, she said I looked rather 'gratesquen.' She was always makin' eyes at me, she was."

"I think she may have said 'grotesque,'" Crockett posited, eyeing the growth on the carriage master's neck.

"Ha ha!" Petrarch interjected. "Well, we can put in a good word for you, my man. Corinthiana and I have long been friends. Mark my words, I'll find out her interests toward you and your unpalatable societal position." As he finished the insult, he winked at the carriage master and slipped a bank note into his hand.

"Ah!" The carriage master grew docile. "No need to lie about me being unpa'tatoed socialistically, sir. I have plenty o' compleyments on me 'tatoes."

Crockett lost all direction in the conversation and feigned looking at a bird flying in the distance. Petrarch continued using words easily mistaken for compliments until the carriage master unloaded their things and waved an enthusiastic good-bye.

As they moved away from the carriage on the muddy path toward the manor, Crockett grew inquisitive.

"What are tatoes, Petrarch? I was lost immediately after it was brought up."

"I'm prone to guess he was talking about his potatoes, but to be honest, your guess is as good as mine. In general, as you've just witnessed, a very important skill in human relationships is being able to level insults with great gusto. If you keep a smile and use a clever word, most people assume it's something complimentary. I've had numerous clients in my office who I have insulted egregiously, but they have left paying me my full bill and a handsome tip. Directness with some panache feels honest and satisfying. There is nothing wrong with a little candor."

"Candor, yes…"

Petrarch patted his great belly in approval.

The road was long and unpleasant; between the mud and the rolling hills, both Petrarch and Crockett were winded halfway to the mansion. Crockett was surprised that, in spite of his great spherical appearance, Petrarch was quite nimble in his old age, the heaviness of his physique giving him increased momentum on their journeys down hills. It was he who resumed conversation between them.

"Now, Crockett, let's go over the details again, at the very least, names. It's always very flattering to know everyone's name."

"Candor and names."

"My boy!" Petrarch glowed. "Now, the matriarch, what do we know?"

"Corinthiana Hawsfeffer, second wife to the late Bixby Hawsfeffer. She is known to always be dressed as if ready for conference with King George, and she absolutely adores hanging onto her vowels.[4] Her beloved pet herring, Beatrice, is her pride and joy."

"Most excellent."

"Petrarch…" Crockett faltered.

"Yes, my boy."

"Could we…discuss again why she has a pet fish? I don't see how it could drive the grandiose emotional attachment which you said it brings her."

"Well, Crockett, you have to remember she was raised as a shy, country girl. It may remind her of her childhood paddling in ponds or," Petrarch stroked his beard, "it could be the general eccentricities of the wealthy. Once you get into certain circles, inbreeding does complex things. Even though Corinthiana isn't from the upper classes herself, it could be a kind of aspirational incoherence."

"Perhaps I should be grateful for my own austere upbringing."

"Indeed." Petrarch nearly tripped over a deep rut in the road. "Regardless, since Corinthiana has ascended in rank, she tends to have an even more classist view of the world than most. For some reason, those who come

---

[4] The editor does apologize for the grueling, awkward quotations throughout the text from Corinthiana. They were going to be edited, however a phonograph recording of Mrs. Hawsfeffer did reveal she actually spoke as if she were an owl with a mouth full of large plums. If one is in private, it is beneficial to speak the words out loud. Phonetically, it is more comprehensible than in its written form.

from nothing are the most judgmental of the lower classes. Corinthiana was originally Lizzie Crankship before marrying Bixby Hawsfeffer. Her jewels and garbled speech try to conceal her very inauspicious beginnings."

"I'll refrain from speaking about my time on the London streets, then." Crockett smirked.

Petrarch's eye sparkled. "Indeed, an intelligent course to take! Now, what can you tell me about the daughters of Corinthiana?"

"June and May. May has never married and was going to become a nun until unknown circumstances arose."

"Get thee *away* from a nunnery."

Crockett laughed.

He held a deep admiration for Petrarch's wit and joyful presence. It was this that drew the young solicitor to him when he was homeless in his early teenage years. They met at a fortuitous time; the thirteen-year-old Crockett, in his attempt at joining a wild street gang, intersected with the old lawyer. He had been tasked to rob the old man as part of his initiation, but after shadowing him for a few hours and finding him charming and disarmingly humorous, he decided to not pilfer from him, the two sharing a cup of tea instead. The old man, caring for his sick wife, and the young Crockett, who had never had a home or family, found an immediate esprit de corps which bound them together. Crockett, always more of a lover than a fighter, gave up street shenanigans for books and began his tutelage under the old solicitor.

"The other daughter, June," the young man continued, "is the mother of two daughters, Brontë and Kordelia. She is the most level-headed of the lot, married to August Winterbourne, who agreed to move into Hawsfeffer Manor."

"And August?" Petrarch asked.

"Loves going shooting in his free time. He is also widely reputed to be boastful, arrogant, and obnoxious."

"Well done, my boy! I knew you had talent, but even I am still impressed by your memory at times."

"I try." Crockett tipped his hat.

"There is one last matter I want you to be cognizant of during this affair. It's not gossip, of course, but I think something to be very tactful about." Petrarch pulled out a handkerchief to dab his brow. "I'm sorry to bring it up, but I know that a few times you have been caught by surprise and reacted rather rashly because of it."

"I am still very sorry for throwing that cat from the window," Crockett said sadly. "But I didn't expect him in the office, and he did rather look like a tiger."

"I suppose after the amount of gin we had that evening, even a barstool would look like a tiger—forgive and forget!" Petrarch gently patted Crockett on the back. "In this case, there are no domestic feral cats, however there is a domestic secret. When I went over the will with Master Hawsfeffer just a fortnight ago, there, shall we say, were not many things to leave to the family."

"You mean, perhaps, a bad investment?"

Petrarch sighed. "*Many* bad investments. Additionally, their wealth connection to America with Bixby Von Bunson deteriorated."

"You know, I have never heard the name Bixby until you brought me onto this particular case."

"It was common for a brief moment. I myself have four cousins named Bixby or Bixbiana. You, having no family, perhaps missed having Bixby connections."

"Very plausible."

"Very—but!—returning to the family, all the money is dried up. The America connection is gone, and they have made a number of poor investments, one in a diamond mine under a French bakery and another in searching for the Loch Ness Monster after John Macleod's sighting in 1908."[5]

"They had no help managing the money?"

---

[5] @badgrrlkinzay47 took after her ancestor in regard to both capital investment and entrepreneurship. She owns nearly one-quarter of a strip mall in Idaho, the stores of which include a nail salon, a tanning studio, a nail salon with a tanning studio, a tanning studio that does nails, as well as a joint dermatology/podiatry office.

"Bixby Hawsfeffer was…shall we say…hard-headed. He made a plan and stuck to it, regardless of how intelligent or plausible it was."

"In some ways that is a trait to admire."

"Indeed. I complimented him on it the day he was in my office." Petrarch tried to suppress a smile.

"So, there's no money?"

"All that's really left are physical items—the jewels, the family heirlooms, the house. If anyone asks you about anything in the will, we are, of course, to keep it confidential, but tensions may rise. I'm honestly surprised the family doesn't know; the only staff kept in the house are the maid and groundskeeper, both, most likely, kept on due to the length of their tenure in the house. I've also heard rumors that the family hasn't taken a holiday or made expenditures more than the hiring of a roofer or cobbler in years. Either way, the family, aside from Corinthiana, appears to be in the dark about the lack of any inheritance. Bixby took that secret with him to the bottom of the river."

"Drownings really are such tragedies. There is never closure."

"And this family is full of them. There was Baron Von Bunson, who mysteriously died near the river, Bixby Hawsfeffer's first wife, who also vanished into the water, and now Bixby himself."

"Perhaps the rumors of a haunting are true. There is a long list of foreboding incidents in this place."

Petrarch let out a loud, emphatic laugh. "Crockett, trust me, there is nothing supernatural to worry you. You're new to the eccentric-country-folk part of our business, but, more often than not in these places, you simply have a number of odd characters with large, ugly houses. Ghosts are merely open windows; rattling chains are shaken by bored housekeepers; and the local townsfolk, heads full of vivid images from gothic novels, impose a haunted history based entirely on conjecture."

At that moment, as if kismet, the house appeared before them. The local descriptions of its monstrous nature were not embellished; it was clear it could elicit a number of wild theories and stories based on its incongruous construction. In the center, the original house glowed in classical glory—large and white with Corinthian columns lining its entrance. The wings extending to the east and west, however, were uneven, an odd smattering of architectural styles. On the west was a large brick structure that collided with what looked like a sad version of the American White House. The east wing appeared completely unfinished, a rickety, wooden structure leading to a large folly, the castle turret halfway completed, the brick on the top raw, and undulating like jagged teeth.

"You can look and see as the money went away." Petrarch sighed. "That wooden plankway on the east side leading to the folly was supposed to be beautiful stone and masonry work. Bixby Hawsfeffer was still talking about completing it when he was in my office two weeks ago."

Crockett looked on in stupefied wonder. It was hideous, to be sure, but there was something about its attempt at greatness which had to be admired.

"It is a gaudy mess, but it has character."

"Indeed," said Petrarch. "It is one of the most well-known houses in West Hampminstershireshire."

Crockett sighed. "I'll never get used to the naming conventions out this way."

"Yes, it was all the rural areas outside of London fighting for tourism money. There was quite the naming war to prove just how arcadian they could sound. That's what got us East Shelfsheepminstead, North Joyfuncharmington, and, of course, East-Westward Portminstershiresh iresheadheath."

"My fingers are cramping thinking of writing that on an envelope."

The two carried on in silence farther up the private lane to the house. The track was not well worn, with chunks of grass spread intermittently throughout the gravel. As Crockett assessed the shoddy groundskeeping work, he suddenly remembered a question.

"You said we had to be tactful about the lack of money," he said, "but why does it matter? I assume Bixby's funeral has already taken place or will very soon. I can keep my mouth shut for a day, Petrarch."

Petrarch shook his head. "Just before we left, I received another letter from Corinthiana. Had I gotten it sooner, I would have delayed our trip."

THE SOLICITOR AND HIS ASSISTANT

"What did it say?"

"Well, she admitted that full funeral arrangements have not been made. She is still holding out hope the local police will be able to find the body—or, at the very least, it will wash ashore." Petrarch patted his large belly, as was his reaction when discussing something that provoked joy or thought. "She implied we should delay coming. The whole family will be gathered, and she isn't precisely sure when the entombment will take place. It is imperative she have Bixby's casket stowed away before they talk of money—she's very superstitious, you know—so she said she wanted him at peace before they discussed how little of everything was left."

"Oh, dear," Crockett said, "so we may be in the middle of a large, raucous family gathering with no entombment date in sight."

"Precisely."

"And the longer we are there the more questions will arise about the will and the assumed fortune of Bixby Hawsfeffer."

"Indeed."

Crockett, again, looked at the large mansion, deep in thought. They had made it to the main boulevard approaching the home, a mere twenty yards from the main entrance.

Out of the corner of his eye, he saw something odd. A figure emerged from nearby shrubbery, large pruning shears in their grasp. The person, however, met no description of male or female that he had ever encountered. From the neck up, he would guess male, a grizzled, masculine face, topped with a large, American cowboy hat. But from the neck down the individual wore a mix of odd garments including a leather, Western-style jacket on their torso and (what could only be described as) a woman's head scarf around their legs.

"Petrarch..." he muttered. "What—who?"

The old solicitor looked up and squinted his eyes. The figure, sensing being watched, bolted into the shrubbery and vanished from view.

"I believe," said Petrarch, "that is the groundskeeper, Mr. Dexter Fletcher. Both he and the head of house, Mrs. Martha Smith, are said to be senile. They are about the age of the departed Master Hawsfeffer, old, that is to say—in or near their seventh decade of life. Dexter is said to enjoy wearing outfits of varying styles. Martha is regarded as just plain batty."

"And," Crockett said slowly, "we may be spending several *days* with everyone in this house—the oft-disguised groundskeeper, the two, maybe three, lake ghosts, the arrogant father, the insane housekeeper, and the rejected nun."

Petrarch laughed loudly. "Now, Crockett! Aren't you tired of the usual office solicitor paperwork? This is a chance to have an adventure. There aren't many of these in the law field."

Crockett was about to respond, however his train of thought was interrupted by the sound of a gun and shattering glass.

2

Beatrice

Petrarch, in a continued display of his amazing, girthy nimbleness, dropped to the ground directly. His apprentice, meanwhile, froze so severely that he toppled backwards like a stunned goat.

"Crockett!" Petrarch rolled over to his assistant and shook him. "My dear boy!"

The young man came to his senses quickly, but his face was pale, his pupils the size of saucers. "Petrarch! What was it? It wasn't another house tiger, was it?"

But before his master could respond, another figure emerged from the shrubbery. This was not Mr. Fletcher, the groundskeeper, but a well-kept gentleman of important bearing. His hair was pomaded and shone black with streaks of gray in the late morning light. One of the most impressive mustaches Crockett had ever seen bedecked his face.

"Hullo," he said curtly. "Just missed."

Petrarch, trying to regain some professional standing, was rolling himself back up to a standing position. Crockett pulled himself up and blinked several times before responding to the mysterious gentleman.

"What were…you missing?" he asked.

"You didn't see it?" The man's mustache shook as if of its own free will. "Londoners probably wouldn't. A beautiful thrush just flew in the line of my gun." He crossed his arms and thrust out his chin. "You must be the solicitor and his poor assistant."

"Poor...?" Crockett pondered to himself.

The man extended his hand to Petrarch (who had successfully risen to his feet). To Crockett, he did a haphazard salute.

"Au*güst* Winterbourne, at your service."

"August," Petrarch said, "delighted to meet you."

"No, Au*güst*."

"Awwwgust?"

"Au*güst*," the man said matter-of-factly.

Petrarch threw a confused glance at Crockett.

August looked more closely at Crockett and Petrarch, his mustache dancing amusedly. "Seems you've had trouble on the road. Unless mud is now couture in the city."

Both men had forgotten the earlier entanglement in the muck.

"Indeed. Our carriage was stuck and then, you know, there was an incident."

"Well, I suggest you come inside then. You will have rooms in the east wing turret set up to receive you."

Crockett looked sadly up at the crumbling tower.

"It looks deplorable in a very cozy way. Thank you very much," Petrarch said, his eyes twinkling.

August looked at Petrarch in confusion before turning toward the house.

They walked in silence up the front walk, a cobblestone pathway very poorly kept. Weeds poked through the stones and shook in the warm summer breeze. Crockett took in the scene with morbid curiosity. In general, the bizarre groundskeeper seemed to have shirked his duties, the front walk not the only part of the mansion grounds in disrepair. Large chunks of the shrubs surrounding the front entrance were dead or yellowed. A large tree near the folly, where he and Petrarch would be housed, was dead, its branches extending like the claws of an old crone.

Just visible, directly west of the house, Crockett saw, what appeared to be, a tomb. It was made of dark green marble and far larger than any he had ever seen. The heavy metal doors looked as if they led into a large underground cellar.

"AwwwGOOST?" he asked their host. "Is that the tomb over there?"

"It's Augüst, but yes. That is where we will lay the remains, or, more appropriately, the imaginary remains of our dear patriarch." His mustache made an erratic, almost angry movement. "It hasn't been opened for years, since the death of his first wife, Lucinda."

Petrarch's eyebrows rose. "That long? How very interesting." He looked to his suitcase, as if gathering his thoughts, then continued, "It seems that your family has been the center of a number of shocking tragedies through the years."

"Well," August boomed, "not *my* family. My *wife's*. My family is perfectly normal, and no one has died under mysterious circumstances for generations."

"You must be very proud," Crockett said.

"We are! It's on our family crest—*Winterbourne, we die naturally, naturally.*" August's mustache emphatically punctuated this with a side-to-side jaunty dance.

Nearer the house, Crockett was able to see beyond the tomb to the ripple of the Tiddlymouth, which ran behind the dilapidated mansion. It was brown and greasy, an unsettling, disgusting ribbon cutting through the countryside. He felt an odd sensation looking to the house's east and west sides—the river seemingly ran through the mansion, as if the crumbling home was a broken heart and the river a quivering artery.

Crockett contemplated the ramshackle, disconcerting nature of their residence and its river as they arrived at the front door. August leaned forward to open it, however the great wooden portal flew open on its own accord just as his hand lifted to push it. Not expecting the door handle to disappear, August toppled forward sprawling into the entry foyer.

Crockett was relieved to see that the door had not opened by magic but rather by the hand of the homely housekeeper, Martha Smith. Homely is perhaps generous, as the older woman could have been a relative of Victor Hugo's beloved hunchback. She was stooped low, wearing a blue and white striped dress and apron. Her hair skewed in an innumerable number of directions—had someone divulged that she had been hit by a lightning bolt that afternoon, it would have been more probable than her hair naturally falling in the way it did. The most shocking part of her appearance, however, was the bulging left eye, the iris of which appeared to spin slowly with the reliability of a clock.

"Ehhh," the woman said, assessing the two men with disdain. She took just a moment, her iris doing one full rotation around her eye, before turning her back to them and trudging out of the foyer.

Crockett watched her amble away then threw his gaze on August whose mustache was twitching fitfully.

"Is everyone here fit for a Shakespeare play?" Crockett asked Petrarch in a strained whisper. "We have Richard II as the maid and a man in women's clothing as the groundskeeper…" But he was unable to finish his assessment, as the great, looming frame of the house's matriarch appeared on the stairs.

To describe her as dripping with jewels was an understatement—it was a deluge of glittering white diamonds which hung from her neck and wrist, and danced along golden threads in her high, white hair. Her face was pleasant, wrinkled, and white as freshly floured dough, the red slice of her lips a garish stroke in her alabaster countenance.

"Hellooo!" she called down to them. "Hellooo, Petraaarch!"

Melodramatic was the only way to describe her approach toward them. She waved slowly as her stockinged feet gently stepped down the large, twisting staircase. The motion was slow, painfully so. Crockett wondered if there was perhaps something wrong with her knees, the steps were so tiny, so deliberate, so theatrical. As she came toward them, no one moved. It was as if all gathered were sucked into the vortex of her entrance—the momentum of the morning impossible to accelerate until Corinthiana was present. The only lively thing about her entrance was the small bowl she kept cradled in her left hand, the contents, her beloved fish Beatrice, swimming happily in a small circle; her right hand deliberately and grandiosely waved back and forth in slow time like a half-broken metronome.

It was a dozen or more minutes before she took her final step off the staircase. When she settled her feet on the tiles of the entryway, she moved forward, like a great, drunken bear, her right hand clawing for an embrace from Petrarch.

"My deeear! How lovely tooo seee yooou—not under theeese circumstaaances, ooobviously, but yooou know I dooo love our chaaats, Petraaarch!"

Petrarch returned the embrace warmly. "My dear, how are you? It's always a shock—even at his age—a drowning!"

"AWRK!"

Crockett stumbled backwards. The sound, the verbal explosion of Corinthiana's "AWRK!" stupefied him.

"It is terrible. TEEERRIBLE!" Great heaving sobs came from the grieving woman. Just as with the "AWRK" her vocalizations resembled that of a seal with asthma. Corinthiana's outburst had led Beatrice to thrash slightly, her bowl throwing water to the floor. "Ooohhh! Ooooh!"

August came forward and gently lifted the fishbowl from her arms. The fish, despite having no capacity to register emotion, somehow looked upset. Its dead eyes appeared perturbed.

"The constabulary came out and had a look at the scene," August said. "Their chief inspector is a bit of a dolt, if you ask me. They've been parading up and down the river looking for a body. Since they've found none, the inspector is grasping at incoherent theories."

"Tooo beee true," Corinthiana wailed. "They suggested Bixby haaad beeen kidnaaapped by nefaaarious caaarnival folk."[6]

"Which is ridiculous, obviously." August's face turned red. "The carnival hasn't been here in years!"

"Well, these small-town constables often prove too overzealous in their investigations, I believe," Petrarch said.

---

[6] In his research, the editor found that West Hampminstershireshire did have a string of carnival kidnappings in the spring and fall of 1898. The chief constable at the time caught the kidnapping ring by sheer accident, his affair with one of the carnies (the strongwoman) the reason for the discovery more than detective work. From that time onward, the constabulary blamed carnival folk for most crimes in the province, leading to an exodus of the carnival performers and a local distrust and embarrassment of the area's law enforcement.

August snorted in agreement as he turned and carried Beatrice out of the room.

It was then that Crockett saw her.

The young lady stood in the doorway to the dining room, her long, brown hair shimmering in the morning light. Her eyes sparked, two orbs of hazel fire; her face, somehow both angular and soft, smiled, not at him, but at something distant, just out of sight.

"Grandmother putting on her grief show for you all?" Her voice rang out like a bell. "She does this every so often to make sure we know she's grieving."

Corinthiana responded with an emphatic "AWRK!"

"Um…" Crockett couldn't avert his gaze from the young woman as she came closer. "Hello," he said softly. "Hello. Hello."

"Good morning and good morning," she said. Her eyes scanned Crockett's mud-stained suit, a flash of amusement expressing itself in the slight upturn of her mouth.

Crockett was not handsome, not in the general, accepted sense of the word. Everything about him was just slightly off-center, yet the features of his face connected together in such a manner as to make them interesting, if not pleasant, despite the fact that on anyone else they would have been completely hideous. His large nose stood out against his long, thin face, drawing attention away from his tiny, bowlike mouth. A lack of testosterone rendered it impossible for him to grow anything like a beard or mustache, but his eyebrows were thick, curious, like caterpillars in a constant state of motion upon his brow. His eyes were perhaps the most distinguishing feature, one blue, one green.

Brontë, the young woman in question, could not quite decide what to think of Crockett as he stood, awkwardly, awaiting her approach.

"Has anyone caught you up on the family's current state?" she asked.

"You may have to be more specific about the term *state*," Petrarch said warmly.

"Brontë, pleeease," Corinthiana bellowed, "with your sister praaacticing her haaalf-baaaked Aaaustro-Hungaaariaaan draaama and your mother's uneeemotional reeeaction tooo your graaandfaaather's death, the laaast thing weee neeed is yooou stirring up Mr. Bluster and his impooooverished friend."

"I'm sorry, Mrs. Hawsfeffer," Crockett said, "but I'd appreciate if we could exclude the pejorative statements about my financial status moving forward."

"Oh deeear!" Corinthiana put her hand to her mouth, the jewels on her wrist tinkling merrily. "I thought I waaas uuusing theee correct nomenclaaature. Dooo yooou preeefer finaaancially copitulaaated?"

"I believe the term, Grandmummy, is *müllesser*, the German. It is more accepted." This was uttered by another household member, a waifish, spritely girl, who had entered unseen. Her wide unblinking eyes danced between Petrarch and Crockett.

"Awrk!" Corinthiana uttered softly. "Thaaat does sound better."

"And if it sounds better, inevitably it is better. That's why people, at large, prefer the sound of cows over the laughter of spiders," the girl said resolutely.

Petrarch blinked twice. His mouth moved to speak but then settled, confounded and open, looking at the young girl.

Brontë swiftly took the arms of Crockett and Petrarch and led them out of the room. "I'll catch them up, Grandmother. I don't want you to worry about it."

"I'll gooo check on deeear Beeeatrice then with your mother. Herring dooo grow aaagitaaated when guests aaare present."

Brontë sighed and led Petrarch and Crockett into a formal sitting room adjoining the foyer.

The room itself was cozy, a large pink couch serving as the centerpiece, turned so it faced a marble fireplace. Crockett let out an accidental laugh as he gazed upon a large portrait of the beloved Beatrice hanging over the mantle. It was a painting of the fish's face. No emotion or anthropomorphic features had been given to the aquatic creature, so that it was just a large fish head with empty eyes staring upward. Had the room been less colorful, it may have created an ominous feeling but, combined with the hues of pink and blue, the effect was simply bizarre and humorous.

As Crockett continued his inspection, he also noted that everything had a patina of dust over it; it all seemed aged and forgotten, despite the opulent fixtures scattered throughout—silver candelabras, a soaring crystal chandelier, and a colorful, enormous vase full of fresh flowers. Another incongruous item was a large elephant gun hanging over the fireplace—the violence of the weapon at odds with the floral, rose-colored hues which surrounded them.

The oddest piece, however, was a large, opulent cage placed in the corner of the room. Instead of bars, strings of jewels skirted the outside, while inside there were thick, lush satin pillows and a long, silk bedsheet.

"What is that?" Crockett asked pointing to the magnificent monstrosity.

Brontë threw a cursory glance to the corner and then shrugged her shoulders. "Beatrice's bed," she said. "Grandmother had a shaman come into the house who suggested Beatrice's dyspepsia was caused by sleeping next to Grandmother and her assortment of perfumes and powders."

"Fish get dyspepsia?" Crockett scratched his head, looking into the coal-like eyes of Beatrice's portrait.

"Honestly," Brontë said, "when it comes to Beatrice, I don't ask too many questions. They tend to confuse rather than clarify."

Crockett turned from the painting and looked at Brontë with warmth. "In most families that's probably generally true of questions."

A smile flashed on the young woman's face; her eyes shone with a gentle intelligence. "Anyway, I'm sorry that the family is so out of sorts. Grandfather's death has exacerbated all of our family foibles—Grandmother is more opulent and overbearing, Kordelia more idiotic, and Mother and Father as clueless as ever." She paused and turned away from Crockett. "There is always an undercurrent of discontent in this house, whether it's my mother fighting with her sister, Grandfather fighting with Father, or Martha and Dexter skulking in the shadows—there isn't peace here usually, but now it's worse than it has been in years."

Crockett couldn't find words to respond. Everything about the young woman in front of him had him transfixed, the most shocking of which was her choice of trousers instead of a dress. But, unlike the gun, it was not incongruous with her demeanor—if anything, it seemed that she wore it all perfectly, or as if the clothes wore her, the effect was so complimentary.

"Brontë, I very much appreciate you taking us out of the chaos," Petrarch said jovially. "Can you tell us a bit about the funeral? Has it commenced?"

"I'm afraid not. Grandmother wants everyone here, and Robert Edward and Aunt May have yet to arrive."

"Robert Edward?"

"Robert Edward Harrington. He is our grandfather's second cousin, only recently come from the European continent."

"Your father never mentioned him to me."

"He's from abroad and turned up at the house a few days before grandfather died. He told us that he has gypsy blood and felt a horrible premonition about Grandfather; he wrote to him to ask if he could come, and Grandfather welcomed him. He's not here for any claim to the money."

"How can you be sure?" Crockett asked.

"He told Grandmother 'I'm not here for ze money.'"

"Self-explanatory." Petrarch winked at Crockett. "And your Aunt May?"

"She was supposed to arrive this afternoon, but we haven't had any word." Brontë looked quickly to the entrance of the room before turning back to Petrarch and lowering her voice. "To be honest…I think…"

Before she could finish, August's booming voice broke the calm. "Brontë? What are you doing with the guests?"

Brontë raised her eyebrows at Petrarch and Crockett. "I took them away to alleviate stress for Grandmother. I was just telling them that we're waiting for Mr. Harrington and Aunt May."

"Fine, fine." August entered the room, his mustache shaking irritably. "Go help your mother in the east tower. She's preparing the rooms for these gentlemen."

"Father, I don't think—"

Before she could finish the thought, August's neck swelled and his face flushed red. "I said GO! Ingrate, go!"

Brontë turned her eyes to the floor and left the room.

Crockett and Petrarch glanced quickly at each other. Crockett's caterpillar eyebrows knitted together in concern.

"Children!" August ranted as he crossed to the fireplace. "You pour your lifeblood into them and then they betray you. BETRAY! Brontë is dressing like a man and Kordelia, my god, the girl barely utters anything sensical since we sent her to Switzerland. The corrupting forces of boarding school." He rapidly turned to Crockett. "Be glad your status as a gutterslug didn't allow you to be corrupted in such a fashion—poverty can be a blessing."

"Could you perhaps…" Crockett started.

"A blessing!" August picked up the gun from the mantle and pointed it out of the room, in the exact direction Brontë had exited. "Sometimes you want to brain them."

Slowly, he dropped the gun. His chest swelled with a large, dramatic breath. "But that's only occasionally."

August then went on for the better part of a half hour comparing raising children to shooting thrush. The complex analogy never fully bore fruit.

"And that is, of course," he said in summation, "why a gun is like your daughter's wedding day."

Petrarch and Crockett nodded enthusiastically but had nothing to add. The soft ticking of a distant clock filled the quiet.

Feeling enough time had passed to transition topics, Crockett spoke. "Awwgist?"

"Augüst. Yes?"

"Could I trouble you for water? I think both Petrarch and I could use a drink after the journey."

"The kitchen is through there," August said, his voice returning to a calmer timbre. "Martha should be about. She can get you some refreshment. Apologies we haven't offered anything. It's…" he sighed heavily, "it's been a terrible week."

Crockett fled the room anxious to leave August's stifling presence.

The transition from the warm pinks of the living room to the shadowy, dark-paneled corridor to the kitchen was stark. It was in this darkness, out of sight, that he took a moment to lean against the wall and reflect on their arrival. The day had been a monumental disaster, from the stuck cart, to the gunshot, to the irritable explosion of August Winterbourne. The household appeared to be a pot, simmering, the temperature climbing higher. Even the spritely girl, Kordelia, seemed out of place in this house, a fairy light in a room full of long shadows. Brontë alone stood as if she belonged in the mansion, as if she wore her position here as strongly, as confidently, as she wore her slacks that morning.

He took a deep breath, the Hawsfeffer and Winterbourne characters dancing through his mind's eye.

"Who are these people?" Crockett muttered softly to himself in the dark hall.

"Who indeed?" A croaky voice came from the shadows. "Ask yourself who are they really—what are they really."

Crockett slowly turned and saw her standing in the doorway. In the half-light she looked even more menacing, the glint of her spinning eye sparkling as it turned in the maid's wrinkled face. It took all the young man's resolve to stay upright, resisting the need to shamelessly collapse for the second time in an hour.

"Be careful in this house. It's swallowed many a secret," she said, spittle flying from her contorted mouth. "Nothing is quite what it seems."

3

A Suspicion

Crockett watched Martha drift backward, out of the hall and into the darkness of the kitchen. His heart pounded in his chest; his hands grew wet, beads of sweat forming on his palms.

"Sorry, my dear," a soft voice sounded behind him.

He turned to see a beautiful, blonde woman in her autumn years smiling at him from the lighted doorway.

"You'll have to forgive Martha. She gets…ominous around guests. She adds a mélange of supernatural charm to the house, but I can assure you that we are a very ordinary, aristocratic family with nothing to hide."

Crockett blinked. "Thank you for that…assurance." He leaned forward and extended his hand. "I'm Crockett Cook. I'm assisting Mr. Bluster."

"Charmed, my dear." The woman said grandly. "I'm June Winterbourne, the deceased Mr. Hawsfeffer's eldest." After gently dropping Crockett's hand, she studied his face. "Kordelia said you looked a bit like a destitute horse with variegated eyes."

"How…" Crockett searched for something candorous Petrarch may say. He finally settled on "Thoughtful."

"She can be. Switzerland ruined her, but she was expelled from English schools, so we had to do something."

"How…thoughtful."

"Aren't we?"

Crockett shifted on his feet and looked toward the kitchen.

"I'm sorry, dear, did I interrupt you in the middle of something?"

"I was just going to get a drink for myself and Mr. Bluster."

"Ah! Yes, I'm sorry we haven't been more hospitable. We're not used to having guests in the house. To be honest, Martha and Dexter have perhaps rested a bit too much on their laurels in the past few decades. My father preferred doing everything himself, and there weren't guests, so things have fallen into a bit of disrepair."

"You've been wonderful, Mrs. Winterbourne, but if you could direct me to the kitchen, I'll prepare us something cold."

"You'll do none of that!" Mrs. Winterbourne bustled quickly by him. "I'll fetch Martha and have it brought out to you. You and Mr. Bluster should go relax on the patio while I get refreshments."

The hall empty, Crockett took another moment to breathe. Something seemed—to say the very least—off-kilter. The family was in a frantic state, the house in disrepair, even though their arrival was known in advance. The maid was senile and the groundskeeper wildly eccentric. How had the house managed for so many years? What had caused the degradation of the construction of the folly and the west wing?

"You look like you're thinking far too intensely."

Brontë appeared, now wearing a dress, her hair pinned back from her face. Crockett again lost himself in her beautiful eyes, his lip twitching with nervousness as she drew closer.

"I went to help my mother with the beds and ended up being scolded by my grandmother and told to change. No hat or parasol, but I hope that the dress will make them happy."

Crockett suddenly jerked as if waking from a dream. He ran a hand through his hair and pondered a response. The seconds elongated, sweat forming along his high forehead. "I uhhh," he stuttered, "I'm sure it do do that."

"Do do?"

"The dress doos—does it. It makes them happy, I'm sure."

Brontë looked interestedly at Crockett's face. A ghost of a smile appeared then vanished.

"Do do aside," Crockett continued earnestly, "is everything all right? It seems...it seems as if no one knows quite what is going on. And before your father entered the sitting room earlier, you were going to say something." Crockett's thick eyebrows went up in thought. "He is quite the conversationalist," he continued, employing Petrarch's skill of slight euphemisms. "He held us for nearly half an hour discussing how you were like a gun."

Brontë fidgeted for the first time since his and Petrarch's arrival. Her hand went nervously to her arm.

Crockett, concerned he'd offended her, went on, "I'm sorry if that upset you; if you are at all like a gun, I'd say it's a petite, very feminine pistol."[7]

"No, it's not that...It's about the general state of the house you mentioned." Brontë paused. When she resumed speaking her voice was very low. "Can I trust you, Crockett?"

"Of—of course!"

With a whirl of her skirts, Brontë flew down the hall. She turned to him and beckoned him to follow.

Crockett pursued her, his long legs moving with nervous energy generated by the need for escape and the burning emotion he felt in Brontë's presence. He tailed her out of the hallway, through the main sitting room, now abandoned, and onto the patio.

"Where's Petrarch?" he asked as they came outside.

Brontë said nothing, instead flitting to the door and closing it softly behind her. When she had peered through the glass and confirmed no one was following them, she spoke rapidly.

"Something's not right, Crockett. Grandfather just disappeared. He knew how to swim, and despite his age, he was in very good shape."

Crockett scratched his head. "The police did an inquest, I'm sure."

Brontë sighed and said, "Crockett, the law enforcement here is a nightmare.

---

[7] In some parts of England during this time, it was high praise to refer to a woman as "decorated as an aristocrat's pistol grip."

They said it was either a drowning or perhaps a wayward bearded woman who kidnapped him for beard oil."

"I'm sorry?" Crockett asked.

"The constabulary always blames carnival folk—a historical oddity—but they didn't do any due diligence."

"The policemen in London aren't much better."

"Well for our family, it's downright offensive. My cousin in America is part of the carnival circle; we don't appreciate the stereotyping."

"Of course." Crockett's head spun. In an effort to return to more fact-based findings, he asked, "How did your family come to find out…that he was missing?"

"Dexter."

"Dexter?"

"He heard someone fall in the river and scoured the water from the bank, but he saw no one. Because he knew Grandfather was in the boat, he immediately assumed there was trouble and went into the house where he encountered Grandmother and Martha. Grandmother grew intensely hysterical, so it was Martha who went out with him to investigate further."

"Those two…"

"Exactly." Brontë's eyes burned brightly. "They couldn't have saved him even if he was in trouble. It's true—it is a swim from the middle of the river, especially with the current from the spring rains, but I can't help but think he could have made it."

"Where were your mother and father?"

"Mother and I were in the east wing going through an assortment of old boxes and trunks as part of our spring-cleaning ritual—we had nothing to do with it. Kordelia, home for the summer from her boarding school, was out reading, and father was shooting."

"Could your father have shot him?" Crockett asked, between the intrigue and Brontë's flushed cheeks, he was fully invested in the conspiracy theories.

"To what end?"

Crockett tapped his index finger to his mouth, pensively. "Did anyone hear a gunshot? Kordelia was out reading, you said."

Brontë rolled her eyes. "Of course, there were gunshots, Crockett. He was shooting."

"But any interruptions? Any shots more sporadic than others?"

"Kordelia is cryptic as always. She's stone silent on everything that happened."

"Could she have…?"

Brontë's eyes flicked to the ground. She offered a terse "I don't think so" in response.

"Hmmm…" Crockett tried his best to recall the smattering of detective novels he had read. From the depths of his mind, he pulled out words, which he believed made him seem authoritative. "In terms of your local police…They weren't able to find the body of your grandfather? Was there any *physical evidence?*" He said this with a flourish, impressed with his own knowledge.

Brontë sighed. "None at all. Even despite their incompetence, there was nothing to catch. He drowned from the boat. The boat was found floating in isolation. There were no notes, no letters left, nothing incriminating in any degree—"

The eldest Winterbourne daughter jumped slightly as the patio door opened and Mrs. Winterbourne appeared with a tray of drinks.

"I see you chose to look like a lady for our guests," she barked setting down the drinks on a small metal table. "Between the two of you, I really don't know which daughter is more of an embarrassment."

"It's me." Kordelia appeared from the yard. Twigs decorated her hair. Her eyes retained the glossy, distant look she had at her and Crockett's first meeting.

"Darling…" Mrs. Winterbourne edged forward, very much resembling a younger version of the drunken bear Corinthiana was likened to earlier. "You know I don't mean…"

Mrs. Winterbourne embraced Kordelia. The young girl tried to delicately slip away, but her mother kept a firm grip.

"Mummy, I think it's very fair to say I'm the embarrassment," Kordelia said, continuing to pull away from her mother's show of affection. "Brontë looks as if she's always ready to ride a horse, but I've been expelled from several schools and have halitosis. I once even made a score card for us on the subject, and I was the worse daughter by nearly forty-three points."

"Only forty-three?" Brontë asked.

Mrs. Winterbourne refused to let Kordelia go; the youngest daughter then gave up her resistance and sat lifelessly in her mother's embrace. "You see!" Mrs. Winterbourne called to Crockett. "It's the Swiss-German influence, this coldness. Before Switzerland she was so much more affectionate."

"And an arsonist," Brontë said.

"That was the largest reason for the deficit," Kordelia said matter-of-factly. "Halitosis was a close second."

"Arsonist?" Crockett squeaked the question.

"I think witch is more apt." Kordelia finally pulled free of June's grasp with a sudden movement. "I'd gotten into one of Grandmummy's superstition books and was trying to summon the ghost of a boy whom I'd had some affection for, one who died of tuberculosis. It was just a children's game, but it was during Michaelmas term and when our dormitory cat went up in flames[8] and carried them into a dry bush, things escalated."

"As they do," Mrs. Winterbourne said quickly. "The headmaster was not as understanding as we would have liked."

"And I couldn't quite articulate what had happened, another reason for the deficit between myself and my elder sister," she said quickly, "so I ended up in Switzerland."

Crockett looked between them, unsure what the reaction to the family yarn should be. The moment of awkwardness was broken by August Winterbourne peeking his head out from inside the house.

"Darling," he said, "Petrarch is settled. Do you want to take the necessitous lad to his room? I'd do it myself, but your mother gave me the vault key and wants me to go down and bring some things up for the impending funeral."

"Of course, my duck."

---

[8] Earhart inserted a rather grisly description of the feline fire, which has been omitted in this draft.

August's plump face disappeared from the doorway with a faint flutter of his mustache.

"Well then, Crockett, let's get you settled in."

#

Crockett's quarters resembled one of the many flophouses he frequented as a child. Once it may have been a grand place, but in the present, it was a ramshackle assortment of broken furniture, damp rugs, and drafty windows. His view of the house grounds consisted of a dusty vantage point overlooking a number of dead or half-alive trees in the side garden.

Petrarch's room was better—there were no holes in the windows and velvet drapes flanked the glass. He also had a large, comfortable feather bed to relax into at the end of the day. Crockett had only a bed that sagged heavily in the middle, which stood beneath a dripping roof. The stained divan in the corner, quickly displaced it as the location where he would sleep. It smelled of livestock, but at least it didn't have a pool of water in its center.

"This should be something someone from your caste will enjoy," Mrs. Winterbourne said, kicking an old newspaper to the side. "If you need anything, you can always ask Martha."

Since there was not much to do in the way of getting comfortable, Crockett changed out of his muddy clothes and set aside his hat for safekeeping. To refresh himself, he washed his face in a basin full of dun-colored water. He then went to visit Petrarch and discuss the mysterious conversation he had with Brontë.

When he entered Petrarch's room, the old man was stripped down to his undergarments, doing calisthenics in the middle of the room.

"Keeping limber, Petrarch?"

"Always, my boy." The old man tipped to his left side; his arm extended in a crescent over his head. "After I made sure all my things were whole after our topple in the mud—you'll be very happy to know my thinking pipe is in top condition!—I went immediately to my exercises. One must make sure the body stays as agile as the mind. I may look like a sphere, but I roll like a ball!"

"Did the late Mr. Hawsfeffer keep himself fit as well?" Crockett asked.

"He did, indeed," Petrarch said, his breath growing a bit shorter. "We often talked about our exercise regimen. You know Bixby ran a mile every day around the grounds. In a suit. He always kept things very decorous."

"That's very interesting."

"I wouldn't say *very*, dear boy. Many men of the upper class take to exercising in their Sunday best. Mr. Gerald in London swims every morning in his wedding formals."

"Now, relatively, that is *far* more interesting."

Petrarch winked at his protégé as he bent over, his protruding belly hindering him from dipping too low to the ground.

"Do you think it odd, Petrarch, that Bixby drowned? He seems to have been in very good shape…"

Petrarch lifted slightly. "My boy, even men in the best shape, once they get to be my age, are prone to accidents. Bixby Hawsfeffer was a very excitable man. When I first heard that he had died, I thought it may have been an issue with his heart."

Crockett nodded gravely. "You can't swim if your heart goes out, even if you're the best swimmer in the world." He thought for a moment, the bizarre past of the family emerging to the forefront of his consciousness. "It's so odd about the river; it's swallowed so many of the family."

"Hmmm." Petrarch remained leaned over, his voice a slight grunt. "There does seem to be a malevolent force in the house with the power to expel things from inside itself. But," Petrarch lifted up before dipping back down over his toes, "I assure you Crockett, it's nothing supernatural or out of the ordinary for these upper classes. I once worked for a family that had a narrow attic stair that killed the maid, the matriarch, and several dozen rats.

People were quick to blame specters, but it was simply shoddy carpentry."[9]

"I suppose if you have a lot of money you can be as eccentric and reckless as you like." Crockett shrugged his shoulders. "I don't think I'll ever quite get used to monied people."

"They're very unpredictable. Indeed, when Bixby visited me in my office he was in a very odd, excitable state."

"Really?" Crockett unwittingly took a step forward. "Why?"

Petrarch lifted himself up. His eyes twinkled. "Crockett, you're letting your imagination run away with you. It was family business that had him upset, not a fear of murder or a diabolical plot. Trust me, when you've been a solicitor as long as I have, you know the ordinary from the extraordinary, and this was a number of very ordinary concerns. The house isn't haunted; the river simply hosts a truculent current. And the attic stairs seem to be in very fine condition."

Crockett shook his head. "I'm sorry, Petrarch. You're absolutely right. Brontë swept me up in her wild conjectures."

"I feel that she would have the power to sweep you into a great many situations you usually wouldn't fall prey to. It brings to mind the incident with Mrs. Brettwick, the day you forgot to draft her father's will."

Crockett's face grew red. "I don't know what you mean."

"My boy, I *know* what it means when a face lights up like yours did when Miss Hawsfeffer entered the room. Don't be embarrassed. Those sparks of infatuation *are* extraordinary. But as I've told you before, in these circumstances, they are to be kept to yourself."

Crockett turned toward the window. He said nothing.

The two men settled into a comfortable silence. As Petrarch counted out his jumping jacks, his bulbous body lurching up and down a few inches with every jump, Crockett assessed the room. Outside the windows the sky was growing darker. The warm afternoon light was disappearing under a

---

[9] @badgrrlKinzay47, inspired by the manuscript, briefly developed a "side hustle" of selling intricate, portable stairs that were designed to make rats fall down them as a form of pest control. The hosts of Shark Tank were unimpressed.

shroud of gray clouds. Under the bed, he saw a small speck of white. He moved directly to the object, lifting it up and examining it.

It was a small, white glove.

"Petrarch, look at this."

"Heh." Petrarch was beginning to wheeze. "Looks—like—a woman's."

"It does. I'll ask after it when we join the rest of the family."

At that moment, Kordelia, the youngest daughter, appeared at the door. She looked terrified, her face the color of milk. Petrarch turned to her, concern immediately registering in his eyes.

"My dear, are you all right?"

Kordelia trembled. She raised a hand to her pale brow. Her eyes, which had always been glossy, were coated with tears.

"Kordelia..." Crockett moved closer to her.

"She's..." Kordelia's voice shook. "She's dead...mother's dead."

4

The Last Arrivals

Crockett collapsed whilst Petrarch clucked like an exasperated chicken.

"Well—cuck—I—just—cuck…"

"She fell in the well," Kordelia continued. As she did, she deftly grabbed a glass of water from Petrarch's nightstand and threw it on Crockett; she then tossed it aside and went to the center of the room. "It was…the fault of the ram in the garden." She ran dramatically to the window. "Do you think it's the baron?!" Her voice lifted upward, its tone growing hysterical. "Was it the baron's ram?!"

Crockett, covered in water, stood and pulled his thoughts together. He was unsure whether his confusion was due to his shaken mental state or the mere act of being in Kordelia's presence. He also noted that, even across the room from the young woman, the halitosis which had lost her points to her sister was very noticeable. "I…I'm sorry, does a baron own a ram here?"

Kordelia's face changed quickly. The dreamy stare returned; she did a small bow.

"Was that too much?" she asked.

"Too much?" Petrarch had begun to sweat even more profusely. He dabbed his forehead with a handkerchief.

"The scene," Kordelia said, "do you think it was too dramatic? My teacher says that I should elevate the dramatics, but she's French, you know, and you can't trust them."

"I'm…thinking that your mother isn't actually dead," Crockett posited.

"Oh!" Kordelia said shocked. "I don't know. Do you know something?"

"What?" Crockett asked.

"Is mother okay? I mean with Grandfather…I knew she wasn't too well, but dead!"

"No, no!" Crockett looked at Petrarch for help. "She's perfectly fine—as far as we know."

Kordelia sighed heavily. "Well, Mr. Cook, you really shouldn't frighten people like that."

"Miss Winterbourne," Petrarch said slowly, "why…did you say those things when you entered the room?"

"For the play of course," Kordelia said.

"Of course." Crockett looked at Petrarch, completely lost.

"I guess you aren't familiar. It's a famous French play called *Mère, Bélier, Mort, Chapeau*. You may just not recognize it. We're performing the German-language version of the French translated into English. The Swiss do things in unique ways. The English version is called *The Viscount's Ram*, which you may be more familiar with."

Crockett shook his head. "I…haven't heard of that production."

"It's wonderful, even if it is rather French." Kordelia's voice had a habit of rising and falling at incoherent moments, causing declarative phrases to sound like questions. "There are four scenes where people just eat croissants, which was changed to meat pies for the English version."

"It sounds complex," Petrarch jumped in.

"Very much so," Kordelia responded. "Then, of course, people outside of Vienna always have trouble with the Danube Mob."

Crockett fell onto Petrarch's bed out of sheer intellectual exhaustion. As a perfunctory response he asked, "And what is the Danube Mob?"

"Well, a long time ago, an instructor was teaching his Austrian literature class about the concept of the French *dénouement*, the ending phase of a story."

Petrarch patted his belly, his face a mix of confusion, amusement, and intrigue. "Now," he said slowly, "do you mean Austrian or Hungarian? I am always confused with the Austria-Hungary dual monarchy."

"Why would Austria be hungry?" Kordelia asked startled. "What do countries eat?"

"He means," Crockett interjected, "would the writer consider himself Austrian, Hungarian, or Austro-Hungarian?"

Kordelia scrunched her eyes, deep in thought. "Well, my Swiss teacher said Austrian. He never mentioned anything about Ostrich-Hungarians, which I don't think would have enough dexterity in their wings to actually do any writing—"

"Yes!" Petrarch said quickly. "Austrian it is. We will call this writer Austrian." He gave Crockett a look of fatigue.

"Yes, very good," Kordelia continued. "Well, one of the brightest students in the class was confused, you see, so he thought the instructor had said 'Danube Mob.' In his befuddlement, he misunderstood the dénouement to be a mob of Austrians who enter a story and set things right at the end. Like a *deus ex machina*, but specifically Austrian, German-speaking, and more interested in blackmail and gambling."[10]

Crockett opened his mouth to change the subject, but Petrarch, riveted, asked her to continue.

"So, this student, Henreick Gruber, wrote a play which became famous all over Austria and Germany—and now I suppose must also have found an audience with hungry ostriches—and the Danube Mob became a very common ending to comedies in the region." Kordelia took a deep breath. "All that is to say that when *Mère, Bélier, Mort, Chapeau* was translated into German, the translator inserted the Mob, which has continued to confuse modern readers and performers."

"I should say *I* am very confused," said Crockett.

"I do love literary history, though," Petrarch smiled. "But, my dear, after

---

[10] In the editor's research, the Danube Mob isn't, as a millennial might say, "a thing." There was a literal Austrian Mob at work in New York during the late 1890s, but this seems to be unrelated. As Earhart did interview Kordelia for this book, it could simply be a literary fact taught only in Swiss learning institutions during that time period.

the lesson and the confusion about your dear mother, can we help you with anything else?"

"Oh, yes! Grandmummy sent me up to tell you it's best to pull your beds and lamps away from the walls. A storm is coming, and the windows don't keep out the water."

At that moment, a clap of thunder burst from the sky. Crockett, again exhibiting his penchant for overreaction, fell to the floor out of fear. The white glove he had held since its discovery under Petrarch's bed dropped at Kordelia's feet.

"My glove!" Kordelia knelt down and picked it up, nudging the frozen solicitor's assistant out of the way. As she rose, she looked bemusedly at the collapsed Crockett. "Are you easily scared, Mr. Cook?" Her glazed stare took on a more focused look. "If so, I may suggest you move out of this wing."

"Why is that, my dear?" Petrarch narrowed his gaze.

"This is the haunted wing." She looked to the exposed beams suspended above them. "I'm sure you've heard of the ghosts around this house. Children from the local village come to see the river, but there are phantoms who occupy the dark corners of the manor. They particularly like the folly." Her musical voice lowered slightly. "I've heard screams in the night coming from your room, Mr. Cook."

Crockett, now recovered, rose to his feet. He shivered as he looked upon Kordelia.

Petrarch cleared his throat. "My dear, I think the fantasy of the play is toying with your imagination."

Kordelia turned, her eyes glittering. "Mr. Bluster, I'm young, but this house has taught me that the truth is often much stranger than fiction." Another peal of thunder shook the windows. "I think the estate is very unhappy Grandfather hasn't been returned to it yet. I know Grandmother is trying, but I think the house, the river, the family needs there to be closure. There is no body, but there can be peace."

An eerie silence settled. Crockett appraised the young girl with a wary eye. "We should...perhaps go get some lamps. Dark is coming quickly with the storm."

Kordelia had already left the room. Her voice rang like a bell from the hallway. "The dark is already here."

#

When the storm broke and rain thrashed the windows of the house, the family and houseguests settled into the main sitting room. Martha lit a number of candles and started the fire so that, despite the gloom of the outdoors, the room took on a festive air, the pinks and blues of the furniture and Beatrice's absurd painting glowing in the soft light. Corinthiana sat in the center of the couch, alone, Beatrice in her after-dinner fishbowl at her side. The aquatic creature floated, nearly lifeless, staring into the flames dancing in the fireplace.

August and Petrarch spoke of news from London, while Kordelia sat with her play script in the corner of the room. In keeping with her odd demeanor, she sat just out of the firelight, a slice of shadow cutting her off from the rest of those gathered.

Crockett sat in a chair near Petrarch and August. He appeared to be listening to their conversation but, in actuality, was ideating conversation topics to bring up with Brontë, who was reading quietly on the smaller sofa. As he pondered asking her favorite shape of tea leaf,[11] he let his interest in the conversation of the two older gentlemen fade completely. In his reverie, he focused fully on Brontë, memorizing the lines of her face as she looked downward at her book. She, however, had felt his attention and looked up, her hazel eyes boring into him. He jumped slightly, mistaking the pounding coming from the front door for his own excited heartbeat.

"Awrk!" Corinthiana exclaimed. "Thaaat must beee deeear Maaay or Robert Edwaaard. They must haaave gotten caaaught in theee storm."

---

[11] Although an English stereotype, many Edwardian romances began with the discussion of the favorite shape of a tea leaf. It often segued into innuendo, as the butt leaf and the clitoral frond were two of the most popular leaf shapes of the period.

It was, in fact, both of the expected guests arrived at once. Martha showed them into the sitting room, grunting and pointing at the odd pair then stomping off toward the kitchen. Their arrival darkened the room—the storm outside suddenly reaching into their pleasant, firelit existence in the form of the dripping, shadowy man and woman who joined the party.

May Hawsfeffer, the youngest daughter of Corinthiana, looked exactly as Crockett expected, fully embracing her role as the rejected nun. She wore a black dress that flowed down her thin body and came to her feet in a dense pool of fabric. Despite the intense warmth of the day, she had wrapped her shoulders in a cape of black fur which covered her pencil-thin neck. Her countenance was a mix of bright white and shadow, the bags under her eyes and the recesses of her hollow cheeks contrasting with the milky white skin that tightly wrapped her face. Small spectacles flashed on her nose, like two search lamps going before the dark tunnels of her small, beady eyes. She was an almost perfectly inverted image of her sister. Whereas June carried an air of blonde, quaffed, pastel lightness, May occupied a diametrical pole of frigid, brunette malfeasance.[12]

Her companion, Robert Edward Harrington, the unknown (until recently) second cousin of the deceased, was even more villainous in appearance. He also wore all black, but his clothing was ominously contrasted with dark red in the form of his handkerchief, tie, and cape lining, which gave the impression that his insides were covered in blood. He appeared to be unkempt, a dense black-and-gray beard on his face merging with the wild silver locks of hair that tumbled onto his shoulders. Crockett squinted, noting some peculiarities of his face, as if parts of it were both too large and too small; it gave the impression that he had been struck by a shovel or cooking pan which had scrambled its features so that everything was marred and bent.

Corinthiana rose and slowly crept toward the guests. Crockett observed that, even though she had to go but a few yards, she proceeded with the

---

[12] The editor does apologize to brunettes. There is nothing in Earhart's journals which gives any insight into this bias.

same theatrical gait and wave she used when coming down the stairs.

"My deeears!" she cried as she tiptoed toward them, Beatrice's bowl firmly in tow. "Our paaarty is aaat laaast compleeete."

May Hawsfeffer didn't move, but Robert Edward threw back his cape and slunk toward the hostess, crying in a thick, continental accent, "Darling, Corinziana. Please excuse my tardiness."

He planted what Crockett perceived as two very aggressive kisses on her cheeks, Corinthiana blushing profoundly.

"Hello, Mother," May said coldly.

Crockett turned his attention to Petrarch, who, he noted, was shrewdly examining the expressions of all those gathered. Crockett followed his glance and saw that everyone had registered dramatic changes in appearance since the arrival. Brontë's gaze was fixed on Robert, an expression of distaste not hidden on her beautiful face. August also looked disgusted, not with Robert, but rather with his mother-in-law and her labored greeting of the new guests. June's eyes were filled with worry, locked specifically on May, whose gaze was turned resolutely on the flames dancing in the fireplace. Only Kordelia appeared unaffected, her mouth moving slightly as she continued to review lines from her script.

"Sorry ve are late," Robert said. "This storm! From novhere it seems." Crockett cringed at the way Robert's nose and jowls flapped as he spoke.

"I walked," May said abruptly. "I got caught in the rain and had to run."

"My carriage came up behind my dear cousin, but she refused ze offered ride."

"I don't trust him," May said looking at Corinthiana. "Mother, you know how I feel about you including him in all this."

Corinthiana clasped her hands. "It is best not tooo bring it up. Robert is paaart of theee faaamily."

"Speaking of, Corinthiana," August stood and moved to the center of the room, "let's get going with the will. Tensions are palpable, and I don't know if it's going to be…" his mustache twitched uncomfortably, "*pleasant* to keep all of us together."

"Au*güst* has a point," June said. "Now that we're all present, we should take care of the messy bits quickly."

All eyes were on Corinthiana, who had grown so nervous she had plunged her hand into Beatrice's bowl and begun stroking the fish erratically. Even under her powdered complexion, Crockett detected a red flush.

"This is aaabrupt and veeery uncivilized." She coughed into her fist. "Weee caaan't simply reeead theee will when Robert aaand Maaay haaave only aaarrived. It's uncoooth. Whaaat would your deeear graaandfaaather saaay?"

"He'd say get on with it," Brontë said with a laugh. "Grandmother, he'd be more interested in the service and all the attention he's going to get. How many people are coming for it? I assume everyone in West Hampminstershireshire is aware."

"Well," Corinthiana's voice grew shrill, "yes. Of course." Beatrice, sensing her human mother's agitation, began to thrash in her hand.

Silence fell. June turned, her skirt rustling. "Mother, you have contacted the vicar and sent on the information about the service, haven't you? It was supposed to be done last Sunday when we went to church."

Corinthiana grew extremely uncomfortable. She emitted several unintelligible sounds, adjacent in timbre to her *awrk*s, but none that revealed any coherent thought. Her cheeks turned a fiery red and her jewels tinkled as she waved her hands in the air, attempting to draw some excuse from the air around her.

"You haven't…?" Robert asked quickly. "You haven't begun ze preparations? Ze tomb isn't opened…"

Corinthiana began to weep. Large tears plopped onto her gown and into Beatrice's bowl. "I haaaven't!" she said quickly. "It is…" She wiped her eyes with a ringed finger. "It's, just…"

"If I may, Corinthiana?" Petrarch stepped forward.

Corinthiana, her eyes flooded with relief, nodded.

"Everyone, Corinthiana notified me that preparations are…delayed." Petrarch put his hands behind his back and rocked slowly on his feet. "She very much wants the funerary services to take place before the will is read—it's a sense of propriety…respect. The arrangements were delayed due to some logistical problems, complications with the vicar and the arrival of the family, but we should be able to move forward tomorrow, once the weather lightens. Crockett and I were going to go to the vicar this afternoon, but we were held up by the weather."

Crockett looked suspiciously at Petrarch.

"Yes," Corinthiana said softly. "It's truuue. Very truuue."

"But we don't want to delay you, even with this delightfully volcanic family dynamic," Petrarch said, winking at Crockett. "Corinthiana, Crockett, and I are going to discuss some final items in the will and get ready to move forward with the entombment and services in the next few days."

May, August, and Robert appeared perturbed at the news but nodded in agreement. Brontë looked amused. She put her finger to her mouth to suppress a smile.

"Mother," June said softly, "why didn't you tell me? Why didn't you tell me it was going to be delayed? I thought we were moving forward with the plan we established for this weekend."

"Let her be, my dear," Robert said warmly. "She has been zrough much."

Corinthiana looked to Robert with great affection.

"Death is the great discombobulator," Kordelia said speaking up from her dark corner of the room.

"It is, deeear," Corinthiana said loudly. "But weee shaaall get baaack on traaack. Petraaarch!" she barked at the old man. "We haaave much tooo discuss. Up to theee study!"

5

Lucinda's Last Words

Corinthiana sent Crockett and Petrarch to the second floor so she could take time to re-powder her nose. The two men sat in large leather chairs in the study; Crockett, arms crossed, looked at Petrarch with an expression of deep annoyance.

"I just wish you had told me," he said quietly. "I thought the family knew of the delays but not about the money. I didn't know we were co-conspirators."

"I didn't either, my boy. Corinthiana caught me before May and Robert arrived. This is a bit of a mess—an old-fashioned kerfuffle." Petrarch patted his belly. "Corinthiana hasn't told anyone anything. She's trapped in a number of escalating lies."

"Can it move forward? We shouldn't be helping her negotiate these family problems."

At that moment, Corinthiana entered the room. Grandiosely, she spun and shut the door, then marched, dramatically, across the room to the large oak desk which sat near the far west wall. Crockett sighed as he watched the old woman step with overpronounced elegance to her seat. She didn't fully sit down until she had pulled out the seat and assumed a pose of grief, hand to her forehead, eyes screwed shut and lifted to the ceiling.

"It is a mess," she said slowly.

"It would appear so, Madame," Petrarch said.

"I lied to you, Petrarch." In the confines of the study, Corinthiana's theatricality shed like the skin of a snake. Her vowels compressed, shrunk to normal. Her regal pose evaporated as she slumped into her seat. Suddenly, Crockett clearly saw the farm girl, Lizzie Crankship, that Bixby Hawsfeffer married all those years before. He heard her country lilt re-enter the relaxed tones of her voice.

"I know." Petrarch sighed.

"Many times."

"Yes."

"So," Crockett said slowly, "can we hear the truth now? All of it?"

Corinthiana turned to Crockett, her eyes bright. A lilt returned to her voice. "Awrk! Is thaaat how theee underclaaass haaandles such measures?"

"I'm sorry Corinthiana," Petrarch said softly. "I think in light of the situation it may be best to handle this discussion with more lower-class precision. I know you usually like to air grievances a bit more dramatically."

"Must we, really?" Corinthiana asked sadly. "I had prepared a speech."

"Perhaps there will be time later. I'm sure it's very good."

"It is. You'll hear an abbreviated version during the eulogy for dear Bixby—I reused parts. You can't always re-invent the wheel."

Corinthiana slunk further into her chair. Her jewels dimmed in the melancholy atmosphere, their usual garish luster thrown into shadow by the bent posture of their mistress. "There's no money. There's nothing."

"That we know," Petrarch said.

"I don't think you realize the extent," Corinthiana said softly. She put her head in her bejeweled hands. "Bixby liked to be cavalier about it. He told you there was nothing, but there's less than that. We owe thousands of pounds. These," she said pointing to the diamonds in her massive necklace, "are fake. The real ones sold off, one by one, to pay off Bixby's debts."

In all his years working for Petrarch, he had never seen such shock on the old man's face. His expression contorted as if he had been struck in the stomach.

"There's less than nothing…" he said quietly.

"Less than," Corinthiana nodded.

"But the will…it—"

"Is a fake," Corinthiana said. Nimbly, she opened a desk drawer and retrieved a single sheet of paper. She pushed it across the table to Petrarch.

The old man scanned the sheet. "When was this made?"

"Just after he went to see you. He was too humiliated to tell you the truth. He had a local solicitor to do this work."[13]

Petrarch read the document carefully.

"Why did Petrarch even need to come?" Crockett asked. "If the local solicitor did the work, we don't need to be here for the reading. There can't be legal disputes over less than nothing." Crockett smiled, his mismatched eyes looking at Corinthiana humbly.

The old woman did not appreciate the joke. She awrk'ed and threw her head back. When she returned her gaze forward, she gave Crockett one last glare of hostility before turning her attention to Petrarch.

"He loved you, Petrarch; you are such old friends," she said massaging her temples. "He needed to make sure it all ran smoothly. Bixby said you were indispensable."

"More than that," Petrarch leaned back in his chair. "I know something more. When Bixby visited me, we discussed his late wife's letter. It was to be read when he passed away."

Corinthiana cringed. "Lucindaaa?"

Petrarch looked at her warily. "Yes—"

"Whaaat would sheee haaave tooo dooo with aaany of it?" Corinthiana asked, nearly rabid with suppressed anger. Her vowels swelled alongside her feelings of consternation.

Petrarch reached across the table and took Corinthiana's hand. "My dear, it's the rather sensitive subject of Lucinda and Bixby's son, Bixby, Jr.—Pip. It's nothing more. No secret affair, just a letter to her son."

"To be read when Bixby the elder died?" Crockett asked. "Why?" He tried to suppress the agitation in his voice; he was irritated Petrarch kept this and

---

[13] Interestingly enough, @badgrrlkinzay47 shares this penchant for manipulating the legal system. She was on the reality show *I Faked My Death and Got Pregnant*, a bizarre cable program about those who not only fake their death to claim insurance money, but also sleep with and bear the child of the insurance agent they defrauded.

the knowledge that the family did not know of the delay of the entombment from him.

"She had hoped Bixby Hawsfeffer and Pip would reconcile, but it was made in case they didn't. She penned it when he went to France. She assumed his homosexual proclivities would pass like a cold, but they didn't. This letter was to be a last chance of family amicability upon the death of his father."

Corinthiana immediately became tame. Her eyes grew wet with tears. "I'm sorry for my reaction, Petrarch. Humiliation or not, Pip is family. Lucinda was trying to be a good mother."

Petrarch patted her pudgy hand. "Corinthiana, no apology necessary. We all know you are very protective of your Bixby."

The old woman's eyes flashed. "Indeed. Haaad it beeen a letter tooo Maaarthaaa, yooou maaay haaave seeen quite theee theeeatrics." To add emphasis to the statement, the old woman swelled out her bosom, just as a cobra would show its hood when threatened.

Crockett's agitation transformed to thoughtfulness. He steepled his fingers and leaned forward. "Petrarch, do you have a copy of the letter?"

"Of course, my boy. Just a moment." The old man reached into his leather attaché case and dug through a number of crème-colored papers.[14] For all Petrarch's admirable qualities, his organization skills left much to be desired. After several moments, he had to give up merely flipping through his belongings and lifted the whole case onto his lap. A jangling of keys, a rustle, and the clunk of some unknown objects followed. Corinthiana looked briefly at Crockett with a questioning look. Crockett smiled and shrugged his shoulders. He held up his index finger to indicate it would just be a moment. In the end, the letter came out, crumpled with a torn corner.

"Sorry about that," Petrarch said jovially. "It slipped into a dark corner, but here you are."

Crockett lifted the paper. His eyes scanned the neat handwriting.

---

[14] This was the scene of the papercut and geyser-like spray of blood mentioned in the introduction.

My Dearest Child,

It would appear that my fears were realized. In this event, I hope this letter finds you and that history has not made the contents less precious.

If your father is dead, you must come home. Find me where I rest and sing, like we used to, the old rhyme of "Duck Man of the Old Hat," and think of the games we played when you were young.

Although time is not kind, there is always a chance to make amends for past wrongs. I hope you will have the insights and the ability to do so for myself and your father.

Love always,

Mummy

"It's rather sad," Crockett said reading it again. He now realized the deeply personal nature of the letter. The epistle was out of the realm of their business dealings—it was no wonder Petrarch did not feel the need to share it. "But you're right. There's nothing odd about it at all. Lucinda was a mother who wanted her family to forgive past wrongs and celebrate their history."

"I tried to find some hidden meaning." Petrarch flipped over the piece of parchment, as if expecting some secret to be written on the other side. "However, nothing was out of the ordinary. She simply asks him to forgive and go see her sarcophagus in the tomb."

"Do you remember what she said when she left it Petrarch? Was there any urgency to it?"

Petrarch gently patted his belly. "It was so long ago…She was distressed, but I assumed it was simply due to the nature of the letter. Having a homosexual family member is extremely indecorous and their activities illegal. When I was a child, we had a sheep that was oriented that way, and we had to put it down due to the stress it was causing the chickens."

"We had a dandy sheep as well," Corinthiana said quietly. "They did always give the best wool."

Crockett, never having encountered sheep or chickens predisposed to attachments to their own sex, stayed silent.

"She did," Petrarch began after a short pause, "say that I should be careful who I told about the letter." He threw a quick apologetic glance at Crockett. "I, however, assumed it was for the same reason. She didn't want people to know about her son's inclinations." After some thought, the old lawyer continued, "If we wanted to look into the tomb, could we be let in to do so, Corinthiana?"

Corinthiana looked pensive. Her red mouth twitched, as if she was going to say something, but then closed tightly.

"Could we, Mrs. Hawsfeffer?" Crockett dipped his neck forward, suddenly very interested in the old woman's response.

Corinthiana, however, said nothing; she stared toward the corner nervously drumming her fingers on the desk. After a tense minute of quiet, she shook off her torpor and spoke slowly, "We must get in the tomb, yes," she said with finality. "I've been a coward about ending all this. I didn't want to reveal the truth about the fortune."

"That is very understandable," Petrarch said reassuringly.

The old woman let out an enormous sigh. "And, to answer your question, I can't find the key. Even if we wanted to put the coffin in it, we'd have to crash it through the side."

Petrarch stroked his beard. "There is no key…" he said softly.

"But there must be another," Crockett said quickly. "There must be some way in."

"Weee will find a waaay!" Corinthiana jerked up, toppling the chair as she stood. It appeared as if her opulent manner had returned with full force; the sparkle returned to her jewels. "Theee truth must beee told! Weee shaaall find theee keeey!"

Crockett looked to Petrarch for an explanation of Corinthiana's sudden, dramatic shift in resolve, but the old man was distracted, his gaze fixed out the window. He responded to the matriarch with idle prattle. "Yes, my dear," he said. "We'll find the key…"

"Tooomorrow I shaaall send June and Maaay tooo theee vicaaar, and theee finaaal prepaaaraaations will beeegin," she said resolutely.

With her head held high, she slowly and dramatically made her way to the door of the study.

Out of curiosity, Crockett looked down at his watch to gain a measure of how long the exit took.

It was roughly two minutes.

When she had gone, Crockett turned his attention to Petrarch and sighed.

"Petrarch, this is a very curious affair, but I think you were correct about Brontë. She is imagining foul play where there is none."

"Perhaps, yes," Petrarch said with a faint smile. "The key business is interesting…"

"It's an old key to an old tomb, Petrarch. I'd be surprised if it *wasn't* lost."

Petrarch's face brightened. "My boy, when there is a surprise death, any of us can be swept up in crazed ideas!" The gusto returned fully to the old man's voice as he continued. "Everything from ghosts and thwarted lovers to angry children and lost keys can take the blame, but in the end it's always a mundane event. No one killed Bixby Hawsfeffer." His voice broke briefly as he said this, his resolve dipping momentarily before returning. "My guess, from the beginning, was that the event was a cardiac issue which landed him in the river. The murderer is simply an irascible current."

Crockett nodded. Outside the halo of Brontë's warm smile, he was thinking more clearly, his logical-thinking facilities restored. "And you did know Bixby very well, Petrarch? I didn't realize you were so close as to share personal confidences."

"Our relationship grew closer through the years. To be honest, after the first visit from him all those years ago, we didn't see each other for a long period of time. When he came in to talk about land agreements, I had even forgotten what he looked like. But, after that, we met at least once a year. Often, we'd just get a pint or have a meal. He had a very large presence, I think something he aged into, probably under the theatrics of Corinthiana."

Crockett smiled. The old woman was truly unique, unlike anyone he had met before. He suddenly thought of her anger directed at Martha. "Speaking of Corinthiana, why was she so upset about Martha? Did she imagine an affair between her and Bixby?"

"Martha has served here for nearly fifty years, Crockett. She used to be a comely young woman. She and Bixby shared an intimacy. Corinthiana was nervous about it, but it was nothing of note. Their history went back to his first wife, so it's no wonder he wanted someone around who remembered her. But jealous eyes see a great many things which simply aren't there."

6

An Indigent and a Lady

It was still dark when Crockett's eyes fluttered open. Upon going to sleep, his mind was filled with the hilarity of Corinthiana's theatricality and her imagined feud with Martha, but in his dreams, the terror-inducing warnings of the old maid and Kordelia seeped into his unconscious. There, they caused a number of distressing nightmares. The one that stirred him awake involved the old carriage master, who drove them to the estate, riding a large canary whilst playing an out-of-tune harpsichord.[15]

Restless, Crockett rose and dressed, deciding a stroll around the grounds of the house would at least calm his nerves. It was nearly five o'clock, so the sun would be coming up shortly; he could watch it rise and, hopefully, forget the terrors of the night.

As he dressed, his mind wandered from oversized canaries to murderous humans, piecing together the string of bizarre occurrences he and Petrarch had seen in the last twenty-four hours—Brontë's fears about a murder, the odd dressing of both May and Robert Edward, and, of course, the note left by Bixby Hawsfeffer's first wife decades earlier. There was no clear connection between any of these things, and he still felt as he had the previous evening that none of it could be connected to a nefarious, homicidal act. However,

---

[15] Out-of-tune harpsichords are a terror in all time periods but especially so in the Edwardian era.

their combination created a feeling of mystery he couldn't shake from his mind, especially freshly awakened from a nightmare in the early hours of the morning. Was there something going on at Hawsfeffer Manor? Was Brontë's intuition correct? Or, perhaps, it was simply the gathering of a very queer, irritable, and curious family. Petrarch said the house was only a house and contained no nefarious presence…but what if it did?

Crockett searched through his bag, becoming keenly aware that his wardrobe would soon be all worn or covered in mud. This tedious detail, as well as the crisp air felt as he exited the house, calmed his wild, imaginative musings. His mind turned from a brooding state to one of relative tranquility. This was aided by the arrival of the sun, which brought with it a thin strip of rosy light, giving the air a tint of beauty and solemnity.

Crockett let his eyes close and took a deep breath. He enjoyed a moment of calm, before he heard a stirring behind him. Immediately his hyper-reactive tendencies went into effect, the mysterious noises eliciting a high-pitched, feminine shriek from the young lawyer.

Brontë, the source of the stirring, tried to suppress her laughter as she attempted to calm Crockett.

"My goodness! Crockett, it's me! I'm not here to harm you."

"Oh, dear," Crockett's heart raced. Despite the embarrassment of the scream, he counted his reaction to this surprise as a victory, seeing as he didn't completely goat-faint as he had when he'd met August the previous day or collapse as he had twice in the presence of Kordelia. To add some additional context to his shocked reaction, Brontë was wearing a yellow, fringed housecoat, so that, from the corner of his eye, it appeared that she was a very large bird. "I thought you were a canary," he said.

"Do you fear them?" Brontë asked.

"Only since last night…It's very similar to a fear I had a few months ago about a small, housecat, which resembled a tiger."

"Well, I am firmly not feline nor avian." Brontë said reassuringly. She cautiously crept forward and stood next to Crockett.

"I'm very sorry that my alarm alarmed you." Crockett's heart slowed. "I'm never good under pressure, so to speak, but last night I was restless.

Kordelia and Martha both said some things that stirred the darker side of my imagination."

"Hmmm. This house has long shadows. I'm sorry it stirred your fear, but I understand. The wing you're currently in has a rather macabre air to it."

"I'm glad my shriek at least earned your sympathy." Crockett's ears turned red. "Not that I'm trying to earn anything," he said quickly, "I just, I hope that you think not too awfully, terribly, badly of me, you know…as a client of Petrarch's."

Brontë looked intently at Crockett. A small lopsided smile formed at the edge of her mouth. "You are certainly very nervous, Mr. Cook."

"I can get that way." Crockett took a deep breath. "As I mentioned, I tend to overreact in certain situations, take the most foolish course of action." Crockett cringed. "I don't know why I said that. I'm sorry, I'm just…a bit… you know, I think I didn't get enough sleep because of the canary."

"Well, I'll do my best to present as less birdlike, so please, feel free to regain your nerves. And don't be afraid of sharing with me. In this house, feuds and secrets are a way of life, but I don't agree with that ideology. There's no good hiding and squirreling away the different parts of yourself."

"I feel the same." Crockett did his best to resist the tugging on his heart strings Brontë called forth. In the dawn, she resembled a brunette, hazel-eyed angel. "I feel," he continued slowly, "we have similar ideas, Miss Hawsfeffer. We share some propensities."

"I would agree to that sentiment."

Crockett smiled.

Brontë ran a hand through her hair. A feeling of heat ran up the back of her neck. She turned and took a tentative step away from her companion.

"Mrs. Brettwick," Crockett said quickly, feeling her unease and desiring the conversation to continue.

"Sorry?" Brontë's eyes again focused on Crockett. "Who is Mrs. Brettwick?"

"Petrarch and I were drafting the will of Mrs. Brettwick's father. There was an issue, and it got lost in Petrarch's papers, so we missed the date it was to be completed. She arrived at the front door, she's a beautiful wo—"

Crockett stopped abruptly; his ears again flushed.

Brontë tried to hide her mirth by covering her smile.

Crockett stuttered. "It's—sorry—no, I mean…I just…She's…"

"You can find women beautiful, Crockett," Brontë said into her fist, attempting to tame the last of her grin. "I find some men handsome, if you can believe it."

Crockett's eyes grew wide. His lips pursed. For a brief moment, he and Brontë stared at each other, neither sure what to name the emotion passing between them.

Crockett kept his eyes fixed on Brontë as he breathlessly continued, "So, I said he was dead."

"You what?" Brontë's eyes bulged.

"When Mrs. Brettwick showed up at the door and the will wasn't completed, I hated to disappoint her. And I hated to disappoint Petrarch; it was really my fault. So, I…well, I said Petrarch was dead, and that's why it wasn't done."

"What did she say?"

"She was speechless, naturally. But, before she could respond, Petrarch entered the room, the picture of health, and then it got *worse…*"

"Worse?" Brontë's expression shifted between joy and confusion.

Crocket was also pulled between two emotions—both the relived horror of his encounter with Mrs. Brettwick and the rising pleasure from Brontë's reactions. Perhaps all feelings could be redeemed if he could simply filter them through Miss Winterbourne's smile. "So," Crockett continued, "then I said, 'I said he's deb! As in deblightful.'"

"Deblightful?"

"I lied and said I had a speech impediment. So, to this day when Mrs. Brettwick comes in, I randomly insert *b*'s into words." Crockett thrust his hands into his pockets. "She's a rather good sport about it. She often asks how me how I enjoy the 'weaber.'"

Brontë said nothing for a moment. The sound of the birds waking in the first light of day filled the silence. Then, softly, she said,

"That's unbeliebable."

The morning stillness exploded as both the lady and the apprentice lawyer broke into frantic, unbridled laughter. Tears rolled down Crockett's cheeks. Brontë doubled over so that the sleeves of her housecoat slipped into the mud. A few times they tried to gather themselves together, but it proved futile. In the end, both of them had dry throats and wet cheeks. They panted as the rosy light of morning turned golden.

"Thank you," Crockett finally rasped, "for taking it well, not…making me feel like I was incompetent."

"Well, we all can act rashly and irresponsibly." Brontë crossed her arms. "I often treat my poor sister like a leper. She's just so frustrating, but I immediately regret it. She's sweet and has so much imagination. Sometimes I think I may be jealous, you know. Grandmother likes her better because of her creative tendencies. She says she has an opal spirit."

"Is that good?" Crockett's eyebrows raised.

"I assume so. She says it's better than being amethyst."[16]

"I'll take your lady's word on the matter," Crockett said uncertainly.

Noises from the house alerted them others were waking. Crockett reached for something to say, but nothing came to his mind. Phrases started to form on his tongue, but the moment he lifted his face and gazed upon Brontë, they vanished like dew in sunlight.

It was she who finally broke the silence.

"I miss him."

"Who?"

"Grandfather. He was an odd man." She thought to herself for a moment then smiled broadly. "For example, he once told Kordelia and me that one should never be painted before their hair turns white, because it makes portraits less regal." She laughed quietly to herself. "He stayed true to his word—there's not a single image of him as a young man."

"I suppose it's little use to remember youth."

---

[16] A book entitled *What Colour Is Your Spirit?* was very popular at the time of Earhart's writing. In it, Miss Divina Q. Wellesley enumerates the color of spirits based on an abstract (and largely arbitrary) number of things, including the kind of shoes one likes, the color of one's nasal hair, and the number of shepherd's pies one can eat in a fortnight.

"I think I'd like to," Brontë smiled warmly. "I can't imagine not having a picture with my children or from my wedding."

Crockett flushed at the word wedding. Brontë appeared not to notice, turning her glance to the house, where Robert Edward and Dexter (or who Crockett assumed to be Dexter; that morning he was wearing a coonskin hat and American Indian–styled leather breeches) came out the front door.

"You were lucky to have him, even if it was a short time," Crockett said, his voice sullen. "I never had anyone—a mother, father, or grandfather. Petrarch's been like a father to me. His wife died shortly after we met; it caused a unique bond for us, a family formed from the ashes. I suppose that's why I try so desperately to impress him," Crockett sighed, "why I try so desperately to impress *anyone* with some authority or who inspires a passion in me."

Crockett's gaze had fallen to the ground, but when he looked up, he found Brontë's eyes fixed on him. Her expression was melancholy; she appeared to want to reach out and lay a hand on his arm, but she refrained. A warmth, separate from the rays of the sun, radiated from them both. Without fear, nervousness, or compunction, Crockett smiled.

Brontë turned to the house, her gaze settling briefly on Robert Edward and Dexter. "Family is always interesting, whether it's something destined by birth or a found object encountered later in life."

"Your family has its share of unique found objects," Crockett said. "Robert Edward is—well…"

"As I mentioned before, I try not to ask questions, as they tend not to clarify."

"His face…" searching for the word, Crockett made a swirling motion around his own countenance to express the confusion of Robert Edward's facial arrangement. "It's…not aligned, I guess I would say."

"Well, it could be an expression of his amethyst spirit." Brontë winked at Crockett. "I would like to ask about its ugliness, but it would be indecorous, I believe."

"Sorry," Crockett spoke quickly. "I didn't mean—your family is lovely. Kordelia is very unique. We have spoken a few times…She is sometimes lightness and sometimes so very leaden with sorrow."

Brontë pulled a strand of hair from her face. "That's the general story of our family. It's an odd tension."

More voices erupted from the house, what sounded like August making a comment about eggs.

"I suppose we should go in," Brontë said.

"Yes, we'll be missed if we wander about much longer."

"Well," Brontë said beginning to walk toward the house, "this chat was wonderful. It is a true deblight getting to know you, Mr. Cook."

Crockett concealed his face. His smile spanned ear to ear. "The feeling," he said quietly, "is mutubull."

7

A Voice in the Dark

When Crockett returned to his room, the warm June sun flashed through the windows in bright white beams. He was in abnormally high spirits and couldn't help but whistle a tune from his childhood[17] as he put on a fresh shirt and combed his hair. His thoughts strayed to Brontë and the magnetic nature of her smile during their conversation. It felt as if something changed in their little talk; he believed her thorny exterior had bent or even broken.

"Hullo."

Crockett leapt upward. He had been in the middle of an especially aggressive stroke through his hair and nearly pulled out a clump due to the surprise.[18]

"I'm terribly sorry. I didn't mean to startle you." It was Kordelia, oddly clothed in a long silk housecoat, her fine blonde hair wrapped in a turban. In the center of the headwrap, a glittering, red jewel glinted in the morning light.

"Kordelia..." Crockett said slowly. "Are you practicing for the play?"

---

[17] Earhart had inserted the whole song, however since it was from Crockett's days as a pickpocket, most of the lyrics were about "clubbing gadabouts" and other acts of assault.

[18] The original text included the description of a piece of Crockett's scalp being torn "from his head with the ease of a peel stripped from a banana"—for a scene which takes place on a bright June morning, this page was phenomenally violent.

"Why would you say that?"

"Your…clothing seems out of place for a day in a country manor."

"Your clothing seems out of place for a séance," she said, an edge to her bell-like voice.

"I'm sorry—a séance?"

But Kordelia had fled. Crockett, again, was left with nothing to say in response to the spritely apparition that was the Hawsfeffers' youngest granddaughter.

He finished combing his hair and went into the corridor. Petrarch was waiting outside his room, looking out the hazy, cracked windows that faced the front courtyard.

"Kordelia was just here. She mentioned a séance," Crocket said.

Petrarch laughed. "At least she told you in plain English. She invited me to join her fortune teller's tongue. '*Abbiminy jugtildamesztch*' were the words, I believe."

"Petrarch, I don't think it's out of place for me to mention that that girl confounds me."

"It's the Swiss influence, Crockett. I think the cheeses and clocks are affecting her. I'm hoping her mother, June, pulls her back into a good, staunch English finishing school, where there are no plays, just some good embroidery courses and less dairy, of course." As Petrarch said this, he spun with a flourish and marched away.

In the dining room, Martha had put out a simple breakfast. Brontë sat at the head of the table tapping a soft-boiled egg with a spoon. When Crockett entered, she started. Her face flushed, and she nervously played with her hair.

"Hullo, Miss Winterbourne," Crockett said dreamily. Brontë suppressed a smile into her napkin.

Petrarch tsk'd quietly viewing the interaction. He took a seat and gave Crockett a look, which he hoped reminded him of the futility of his flirtations. Crockett, however, failed to notice. His gaze remained fixed upon Brontë.

The only other person in the room was May, whose expression was, if possible, even more pinched in than when she appeared the previous evening.

"If you'd like to join the séance, you better eat quickly," May said, judgment dripping from her tone.

"Grandmother has already taken up the biscuits she keeps exclusively for the ghosts," Brontë added.

May snorted with contempt. "Mother used to be religious; she was the one who coerced us to attend services and taught us from the Holy Book. I don't understand her new propensities for the occult. It's diabolical—absolutely wicked."

"Well, according to her, she's *heard* things during the night which indicate a spiritual presence," Brontë said.

Crockett nervously played with his napkin, the reverie born of his attraction for Brontë replaced by his fear of the occult. "I told you Kordelia mentioned ghosts yesterday. She said Petrarch and my rooms are full of them."

Brontë looked at him, her eyes smiling. "Crockett, have you seen the windows in those rooms? Even a gentle spring breeze would howl through them like a screaming banshee." The mirth in her eyes faded. "To be honest, it's Grandmother who got Kordelia into all that ghost nonsense, hence the arson and now her exile on the continent."

"Well, I would much rather enjoy breakfast than talk to ghosts, even if they do have good taste in biscuits." Petrarch said, ladling a heaping mound of porridge into his bowl to punctuate this statement.

Crockett was about to reach for some jam, when he suddenly thought the better of it. He had never been to a séance and, even with the wily Kordelia leading it, the experience would be novel.

"You know, I would like to join," he said. "Where are they gathered?"

May groaned. "In the study. Be careful when you barge in; they lit enough candles to be seen from the moon."

#

May's remark on the candles was not exaggerated. They were arranged on every empty space in the study—the desk, the carpet, the couches, the window ledge. They had not pulled the drapes over the large window; it was needless as an expansive oak tree grew outside. Its long shadow fell through the clear panes, keeping the room deep in shadow. In the center of the room, the participants gathered around a circular table draped in a blood-red cloth. Corinthiana wore a similar costume to Kordelia, a silk dressing gown but with a more ostentatious turban. Beside her, swimming happily in her bowl, was Beatrice (a tiny, flamboyant headpiece matching Corinthiana's placed on top of her transparent home). June and August looked disinterested but nevertheless occupied spaces next to Kordelia. Facing them, across the table, were Robert and, to Crockett's surprise, Martha. In the center of the small group was Kordelia, a large book with yellowed pages open before her.

"Welcome, our beggaaarly friend. They haaad saaaid yooou maaay aaarrive." Although Corinthiana spoke to Crockett, her gaze was fixed on a point above his head.

"They?" Crockett asked.

"The spirits," Kordelia said. Her eyes sparkled in the candlelight.

"Mummy was in touch with them this morning, evidently." June threw an embarrassed glance at her mother.

"Zey have been very chatty recently vith ze passing of Master Hawsfeffer." Robert looked over at Crockett and smiled. Something about the gesture was off, the rising of his mouth delayed just a moment too long after speaking. Although he wore a new set of clothes, a pinstripe suit of black and gray, it retained the gothic-horror tones of the previous evening. On his neck he wore a tie covered in ugly skulls, while a chain hung from his jacket pocket. In the nascent morning light, he looked even more haggard than Crockett previously thought, his beard ragged and unkempt, almost as if the hairs had all twisted in his sleep. His face resembled a child's painting, the nose slightly off-center and his eyebrow at a bizarre forty-five-degree angle above his right eye.

"I'm sorry I've been remiss as to not comment on how very stylish you are," Crockett said, employing Petrarch's lesson from the previous day of insulting compliments.

Robert's eyes flashed.

"Get on with it!" Martha grunted, munching on one of the biscuits reserved for ghosts.

Corinthiana reached out and swatted it from her hand. Her vowels plumped with rage. "Steeealing whaaat is not yours aaagaaain as aaalwaaays, Maaarthaaa."

A proper row would have erupted had the table not jumped beneath them.

Terror seized the gathered party. June clutched August. Martha's mouth dropped open, biscuit crumbs falling onto her lap. Crockett goat-froze, as he was wont to do under duress; being at the table, however, kept him from fully collapsing.

"What was…" August looked around nervously.

"The dead." Kordelia said softly.

"I told yooou! Weee must entooomb deeear Bixby or weee will continu-aaally faaace theeese terrors!"

A pregnant silence filled the room. In the quiet, the group noticed a great number of sounds they had not hearkened upon entering—the slight, eerie twitter of a bird outside the window; the wraithlike mutter of an unseen draft; the crackle and hiss of the candles, so many lit that it sounded as if they were surrounded by snakes.

"Very interesting," Robert said, the chain on his suit rattling.

"*Jumbiminy jumocha maraxes twiddle haux*," Kordelia muttered as she read from the tome before her.

"Silence," Corinthiana said in a low tone, which shook with a rising fear. "Kordeliaaa will now reeead from theee aaancient texts." She paused for a moment, then quickly added, "Yooou maaay leeean in closer. I haaave given her some herbs for her haaalitosis."

Everyone was very pleased by this effort to make the young girl's breath more bearable.

"What are we hoping to learn?" August asked, his mustache lightly shaking in terror.

"We are attempting to speak with Grandfather." Kordelia's eyes did not lift from the book. "It is hoped he'll tell us where his body is."

What followed was a long reading from the shadowy book before Kordelia. Although at first Crockett was filled with terror, as the reading went on and questionable words arose in the ancient tongue ("pettifogerry," "tea cozie," and "philanderer" all sprinkled in), the fear subsided. August joined Crockett in renewed skepticism, along with June and Martha who exchanged suspicious glances across the table.

Finishing the speech, Kordelia threw up her hands. Corinthiana looked up to the sky, her fingers clutching a large, gold necklace that was around her throat.

"Theee gaaatewaaay of theee dead is opened." Her voice shook. "Weee caaan now aaask theee phaaantaaasms whaaat they know."

The candles continued to hiss. An elongated moan came from the draft flowing through the room.

June was the first to speak. "Daddy…" she asked warily, "are you here with us?"

Martha tensed. Her wild eyes scanned the room. Robert was intently focused on Corinthiana, his knotted hands stroking his wild beard. From outside the room a clock chimed.

"Bixby Hawsfeffer is not here," Kordelia said slowly. "Who else would like to address the undead?"

"Lucinda?" Martha asked softly. "Lucinda…do you wish to speak?"

At that moment, a great thud was heard in the room. Corinthiana and June both shrieked. Robert fell back from the table. Even Kordelia lost her composure, her turban slipping from her brow. Only Beatrice was unperturbed, her dead fish eyes revealing no emotion.

"Sheee is heeere!" Corinthiana gasped. "Lucindaaa! Speeeak tooo us!"

"Missus," Martha said softly.

"Silence!" Corinthiana whispered. "Lucindaaa speeeaks!"

Martha crossed her arms, her face filled with abject loathing. Crockett, heart racing, hands braced on the table, followed Martha's vindictive gaze and saw that she was looking to the window, which was covered in blood.

"Mrs. Hawsfeffer," he said softly, "Martha was pointing out that a bird crashed into the window...It may not have been the voice of the dead."

Martha grumpily interjected, "Poor thing was probably confused by the number of candles in here. He thought we were signaling to him."

"Martha is correct," Kordelia said softly. "Lucinda is not present, but that bird is dead." There was a collective sigh of relief. Kordelia closed her eyes and put her fingers together. "Who else would like to ask something of the dead? Address the name of a lost one, and they may respond."

"Bixby Von Bunson?" Corinthiana asked.

Silence.

"Aunt Merriwether?" August amusedly set this name forward.

Nothing.

"Hercule Poirot?" Kordelia posed.

A sound was heard, but it was merely Martha knocking over a candle while reaching for another biscuit; the disturbance was quickly classified as a very living sound.

"Recently dead bird?" Crockett asked sadly, looking to the window.

No contact from the bird; Kordelia then explained to the group that the dead (even birds) do not communicate until after a full moon phase has passed.

A prolonged silence filled the space. Each of the gathered looked tentatively between Kordelia and Corinthiana.

"Perhaaaps," Corinthiana began apprehensively, "theee voices I heard this morning were not signs of theee dead." She gingerly placed her finger into Beatrice's bowl, stroking the fish's silver-blue scales. "But, I just," her voice tremored, "I waaanted some sign. In theee river...of aaall plaaaces, where sooo much traaagedy haaas haaappened tooo this faaamily...Caaan weee never haaave closure? Must it aaall be mystery and murder?"

Crockett's heart felt for the old woman. For the first time he saw all the trappings of Corinthiana stripped away—her accents, her garish garments, her posturing—all gone, and in their wake only infinite ripples of grief. The young country girl, who found a handsome, landed gentleman who promised her a fuller life, merged with the gaudy, outré matriarch to shape the anguished figure before them. The rest of the family felt similarly, their faces conveying empathy and grief—the squabbling, the blaming, the desire for money, and the old grudges evaporated in the dim candlelight. August gently reached out and gripped June's hand. Even Martha looked on Corinthiana with a (tepid) look of understanding.

But it was then that the table jumped once more. The door to the study flew open, and a strong breeze whipped through the room making the pages of Kordelia's book dance. A large proportion of the candles blew out, leaving the corners of the room dark.

Then it started slowly, mournfully. It was a tune played from some unseen place. In the darkness, it felt as if it was coming from each shadowed corner. The twitching silhouette of the oak tree danced eerily along with the lilting notes.

The voice that joined was distant, muffled.

The Duck Man, the Duck Man he creeps along the lake.
Thunder hides his footsteps; shadows hide his face.

Corinthiana, her face so pale her rouge glowed against the white of her cheeks, gripped Beatrice's bowl tightly. Martha leapt into Robert's arms, while June jumped away from the table, a scream erupting from her mouth. Crockett held the table, his knuckles turning white. He felt himself tense, start to lose control, but for the first time, a spark of courage resisted the urge to collapse. An odd feeling of calm collided with his fears and kept his body fully erect.

Children hear his heartbeat; they follow after him.
Disappear into the darkness, their own life growing dim.
With the children missing, the parents follow quick.
But nothing is left of boys and girls but Duck Man's battered hat.

The music stopped suddenly. Crockett looked to August, who was quaking in fear.

"Kordelia," August asked quickly, "what was that?"

The young girl shook her head, pearl-sized tears forming at the edge of her eyes. "It's the old song," she said quietly. "'Duck Man of the Old Hat.'" She took a deep breath, trying to keep her composure. "It's the song the ghosts sing along the river."

8

The Pot Boils

The room was evacuated. August and Crockett helped the women flee, then immediately opened all doors to fill it with warmer, brighter light. August took the great book from the center table and threw it into the desk, slamming the drawer and locking it with the key.

Brontë, Petrarch, and May came to the bottom of the stairs, all wearing looks of wonder.

"What's happened?"

"We heard noises—a scream."

"Was that music?"

Petrarch, and a reluctant May, took the women into the sitting room, while the shocked Martha sought out Dexter to help prepare tea.

Brontë alone climbed the stairs and peaked in on August and Crockett. Even her arrogant smile had faded.

"Are you all right?" she asked tentatively. "Father?"

"Fine," August said brusquely. "It may have just been a coincidence."

"What happened exactly?" She looked between her father and Crockett.

However, August was already running down the corridor. "I'll get to the bottom of it!" he yelled, disappearing down the hallway, manic footsteps trailing into the distance.

Crockett went to the window. He gazed on the blood of the bird, still freshly smeared on the glass. He shuddered slightly and then turned, his variegated eyes falling on Brontë.

"That song..." he said softly.

"Which song?"

"You didn't hear?"

Brontë shook her head. "May and I were on the patio—it's such a beautiful morning. Petrarch left us a few minutes before the chaos to do some work in his room. As soon as we heard the shrieking, we ran inside. Petrarch arrived at the stair the same moment as May and I."

"The scream was your mother," Crockett said. "Once the music stopped, she let out a terrified shriek."

"What *happened*?" Both concern and excitement were fused in Brontë's tone.

"It was extremely tense—we were all afraid. A bird crashed into the window, but that was probably due to the candles. But...then at the end..."

"Yes?"

"Someone played 'The Duck Man of the Old Hat.' It's about a man who steals children? I never knew that." Crockett dabbed his brow thinking of the odd nursery rhyme. "Isn't it a bit macabre for a children's song?"

"Well, it's German," Brontë said.

This seemed to settle the matter.

The house grew quiet once more. The only sound that disrupted the peace was a slight banging coming from near them, which was August looking for the source of the wind and song. The séance had shifted the atmosphere from murderous conjecture to active malfeasance. Everyone, in the light of the new events, had become a suspect in some way, the questions about their characters more pressing than before.

Feeling this transformation, Crockett turned to Brontë. "Do you get scared in this house?" he asked. "I know you teased me earlier this morning about how fearful I was, but is there anything that makes you uncomfortable here?"

Brontë leaned back against the wall. Her eyes looked skyward. Again, just as in the dawn light, the image of a hazel-eyed angel filled his imagination.

Her voice softened. "I wouldn't call it fear," she began, "but it feels as if the house has always been on the precipice of disaster. It's not scary in the way of ghosts and spirits, rather the more mundane horror of some malignant sadness." She looked directly at Crockett; every trace of irony in her expression was gone. "Everyone in the house has been volatile for as long as I can remember. Father didn't want to live here, but grandmother put on such a production of tears that she convinced my parents to stay. So, father has been unhappy, my grandmother is constantly watching Martha, sure that some decades-long affair is going on, all this while Dexter parades the grounds in costumes from his days in America. Even he is trapped here. After our cousin Bixby returned to America, Dexter had no money to go back, so he was forced to stay in England. Anger and resentment stew here—I have tried to resist its pull, but Kordelia was affected. I don't think she'd be quite as wily if we had a normal, healthy upbringing. Grandfather was terrible to her, disgusted by her peculiarities. I know I said I missed him this morning, but I don't know if it's true emotion or a kind of grief, a nostalgia that accompanies loss. He was always a mystery; sometimes he was very kind, taking Kordelia and me on his knee to tell us a funny little story about the house, but then he could be frightening." Her eyes closed in frustration. "It's not supernatural but very terrestrial, an emotional burden…" Her voice faded like the resonance after a bell rings.

Crockett felt the compunction to reach out and give her hand a squeeze but resisted. Instead, he offered his voice in sympathy. "I grew up on the London streets, pickpocketing and sleeping wherever I could find respite. I lived through a lot of anger and resentment, just in a different way and a different place."

Brontë took a deep breath and opened her eyes. "I can only imagine. If it helps at all, Grandfather was also terrible to the local farmers. He often picked their pockets with his rental agreements, so I think the distinction of what is criminal and what isn't is rather gray."

They both felt the return of the effusive, golden feeling which passed between them in their morning conversation. Although they didn't look directly at each other, they both harbored small, satisfied smiles.

"Mr. Cook, it's been very nice to have you here the last few days," Brontë said. "I often feel that I can talk to people for hours, days, and weeks and not know a pinprick's worth of their true character. That's not the case with you."

Crockett heart lifted his chest skyward. "I would agree, Miss Hawsfeffer. It's been a true pleasure."

The exchange was a brief moment of reprieve before the ominous feeling of threat and suspicion returned. June brought it with her when she suggested they clear the study of the candles. She made Crockett do a precursory ghost check before she and Brontë felt comfortable taking up the work themselves.

Once relieved of ghost duties, Crockett returned to the formal sitting room. As he predicted, the atmosphere was altered. Every person he saw appeared to be on edge, flighty. Outside, the day did its best to dispel the malignant feeling. By the noon hour, the warmth of summer fully blanketed the countryside and the fragrant scent of blooming flowers rolled through the open windows.

August solved most of the mystery by the time lunch was served. He surmised that the door being thrown open was attributed to Crockett not closing it tightly, a wind gust at the right moment pushing it ajar. The music was generated by a phonograph he discovered in a closet close to the study. All was credited to a simple prank, but the perpetrator did not come forward. In the end, August tongue lashed Kordelia, blaming her for the events, as one of her white gloves was found near the closet where the phonograph was kept. The prim girl said very little at lunch as her formidable father ranted, his mustache bobbing rapidly.

Brontë did not agree with August blaming Kordelia, so a second row erupted, even larger than the first.

Crockett, using the basic rubric supplied by his detective novels, tried to logically piece together the events, thinking of who would have access to the phonograph and was near enough to start it. There appeared to be no contraption tied to the device to make it move a certain time, so the culprit had to be in close vicinity to make the song begin to play. The only individuals not in the séance, however, were May, Brontë, Petrarch, and

Dexter. May and Brontë were on the patio; Dexter was found by Martha in the back lawn after the events; and Petrarch was headed for the folly wing, his plan to review some papers for his next clients, the Mayweathers in East Fletchfordtownhampsonvilleshire. There was no logical explanation for any of it. A ghost was a more plausible solution than one of the persons in Hawsfeffer Manor.

By mid-afternoon, a state of normalcy returned. August went to shoot, and May went with Kordelia to attend to Corinthiana rather than going to the vicar. In the main sitting room, Crockett's eyes grew heavy watching light ripple off the strands of jewels in Beatrice's bed. His eyelids fluttered open and closed as he heard Petrarch's warm baritone speaking to Brontë over a hand of gin rummy. The image of Beatrice above the fireplace, its hues of pink and periwinkle, added to the dreamlike state of the afternoon.

The moment of peace was broken with the slamming of the patio door. Robert spoke quickly to himself as he rushed inside.

"It is getting ridiculous," he said savagely.

June followed after him, her dress rustling behind her. "Robert, it *is* getting ridiculous. We're all exhausted and want this to end, but mother isn't well."

"It is ze child's fault." Robert's eyes were wild. "Kordelia's subterfuge zis morning destroyed Corinziana's nerves."

"Now, now, old boy..." said August, freshly returned from shooting, as he overheard the conversation. His neck bulged like an angry sea bird. "You aren't close family, and if you feel the need to leave, you are more than welcome."

June looked appreciatively at her husband.

Robert's teeth grated. His uneven eyebrows rustled menacingly.

There was a moment of hostile silence.

Crockett looked to Petrarch, who sat with an amused expression on his doughy face. It was May who broke the tension as she entered from the main hall.

"Mother is feeling better," she said with her usual coldness. "She says she will decide whether to move forward with the funeral tomorrow or wait another day. The stress of the past few weeks has been overwhelming for her."

"Zis I understand," Robert said, attempting to warm his chilled tone, "but I must return to home soon. I have very much appreciated ze varmz of our beneficent hostess, Mrs. Havsfeffer, hovever, my vife vill be missing me, and I have ze vork to do."

August grew red. "Sir, you are not wanted or needed here, so if this family affair is upsetting you, you are free to leave this house."

"August, I do not like ze tone –"

"It is Augüst."

"Regardless, I do not mean to offend." Robert raised his hands as if surrendering. "I only zink zat for all parties it is best to end zis affair qvickly."

"I, for one," Petrarch said lightly, "will also be happy to return to my own bed."

Crockett was grateful for his master's candor at that moment. The bubbling of anger lightened to a simmer. Robert left the room, and everyone else resumed idle tasks—reading, card playing, or talking. When the sleepy malaise returned, Petrarch lightly tapped Crockett's shoulder and motioned toward the main hall.

Brontë, who had been reading, watched them leave with keen interest. Smiling, she mouthed, "Are you being scolded?" before she disappeared from Crockett's line of sight.

"We must be ready for Corinthiana when she asks us to read the will, my dear boy," Petrarch said loudly as they left the room. "We can at least try to abbreviate the duration of this family tragedy."

Crockett followed closely behind his master down the wooden hall, toward the folly, making idle conversation. It was a relief to get to the cooler stone structure, even if it was drafty and allegedly haunted.

To Crockett's surprise, Petrarch did not stop at his chambers or Crockett's; he kept moving until they came to small, wooden door. He looked back and then slid inside. Crockett went after nervously.

He had led them into a small servants' quarters which was unfinished. There was a rug on the floor and a small, wooden stool, but, otherwise, it was spartan. The walls were all stone; there were no windows to offer any light. Petrarch handed Crockett a book of matches and pointed to a lamp on the stool.

As Crockett lit the lamp, Petrarch gently closed the door. When he turned to face his apprentice, his normally calm demeanor was absent, replaced with an uncharacteristic anxiousness.

"Crockett," he said softly, "sorry to act so conspiratorially, but I am beginning to think you and Brontë may have been correct in your assumption of some sort of plot being afoot."

"You think there is something going on?" Crockett's thick eyebrows rose.

"There is a swelling, ominous atmosphere of suspicion...I've felt it growing since the séance."

"Indeed. I feel something as well."

"What could it be?"

"*Everything* going on is very odd."

"Everyone here is very odd; the things may simply be symptoms."

Petrarch allowed a small smile. "Perhaps."

"Perhaps symptoms or perhaps conspiracy?"

"Maybe both." Petrarch took a deep breath. "Did you notice anything strange during the séance?"

"Everything was strange. The fish was wearing a hat."[19]

"I mean, anything compounding off the general strangeness."

Crockett thought for a moment. "Some of the persons present were odd. Why was August—Aaghoost?—there? He seems very logical. He wouldn't support contacting the dead."

"Unless his wife made him."

"That's true. But what about Martha and Robert Edward? Martha won't even get someone a cup of tea, why would she sit through a séance?"

---

[19] The editor feels compelled to add that, in addition to the blood and gore of the first draft of this book, Mr. Earhart also had an absurd number of hats on Beatrice's fishbowl in that initial draft—bonnets, bowlers, top hats, even an American-style campaign hat. Although in places humorous, accompanying many of the hats were diatribes into the state of English fashion, which were, to be honest, poorly informed and overly loquacious.

Petrarch nodded. "When you were in the actual séance, before I left their company, May and Brontë both said very interesting things."

"You don't say."

"Brontë asked May about Robert. She wanted to know if they had ever met before. May responded that she had never heard of him until his arrival at the manor, but she said they all deserved each other. Then she said something ominous, quite like 'Soon everyone will get what they deserve.'"

Crockett frowned. "Why would she say that?"

"I don't know. Then, when the séance occurred with that odd trick, it seemed, well, interesting." Petrarch paused. His eyes sparkled as he looked to Crockett. "Speaking of, I was very proud of your candor during the aftermath. A year ago, you would have fainted like a goat or screamed like a laundress[20] and run to the lavatory." Petrarch gripped Crockett's shoulder with warmth. "You've grown up a lot, my boy."

Crockett was so overwhelmed with emotion that he felt tears form at the edge of his eyes. Quickly, he wiped them away. He nodded at Petrarch, acknowledging the compliment, but then charged forward, returning to the subject at hand.

"In terms of the séance, you don't think Kordelia did it, do you?" he asked, still trying to suppress a smile.

"No." Petrarch tapped his forehead with his index finger. "But I don't see any real, concrete motives for anyone else. Kordelia has been convicted of arson, but that wasn't intentional." He scratched his beard as he attempted to pull the threads of disparate thought together. "Why would someone be trying to scare those people in the room? To what end? Is it to get to some conclusion—to scare someone into something?"

Crockett shook his head. "I've mentally run through the logistics of it, and there's no explanation. Everyone has an alibi, and someone had to be in the actual room to start the phonograph. My main suspect is Robert Edward,

---

[20] This simile caused many questions for the editor, but, after much research, it was discovered vis-a-vis Earhart's diaries that his neighbor was a laundress who shrieked loudly when she and her husband were intimate. This was a major pain point for the author, as it often occurred at four o'clock when he liked to have tea.

and that's mostly due to his galling ugliness."

Petrarch thoughtfully rubbed his protruding belly. "In terms of logic, Dexter and I are the main suspects; although, the women saw me go toward my bedroom, and Martha found Dexter on the back lawn practicing an American square dance."

"None of it makes logical sense." Crockett rubbed his eyes in frustration. "Brontë said she had a terrible feeling in this house…not fear, but she called it a 'malignant sadness.'"

Petrarch frowned. "That was the strange thing she said to May and me. She said the house was like a pot, and she thought things were beginning to boil."

For a moment, they both contemplated the strange events of the day. Eerie shadows danced on the walls of the small room. In the silence, Crockett shivered, remembering Kordelia's warnings from the previous day.

"Crockett," Petrarch finally said softly, "why don't you find out more from Brontë. See if you can draw out any reasons Bixby Hawsfeffer may have been dispatched or why anyone would be trying to frighten Corinthiana. We are getting ahead of ourselves. I think this house is deluding us with its dark history and suspicious characters, but we should start to think through this as men of science with sound logic." He paused for a moment, then said quickly. "And be careful, my boy. I've sensed the growing affection between you and Miss Hawsfeffer. I'm sympathetic to the budding emotions, but I ask you to be on guard. Despite the state of their finances, the Hawsfeffers are of a higher caste than yourself, and I don't want you leaving here heartbroken."

Crockett's eyebrows went up in surprise. "Yes…er…yes, Petrarch. Thank you for saying so…" The young man tried to conceal his disappointment. "I…I will…er…I will find out what I can from Brontë. And," he said sadly, "will be careful in the process."

Petrarch smiled knowingly in the half-dark. "It's for the best, Crockett. We'll find you a nice girl when we return to London and have this mess behind us. You're nineteen, in the prime of life, with an excellent career ahead of you." He, again, reached out and gripped his assistant's shoulder. "On a lighter note, in terms of business, I am very proud of you. Having been your master for these long years, I should know when to trust your intuition, especially on a case like this where the incoherence is rapidly compounding." He sighed and shook his head. "Even if it's not murder, there is something amiss in this house. It hides some secret, some malice that must be rooted out."

9

A Perfect Night for Murder

Crockett left Petrarch's room flush with pride from the praise of his mentor. He intended to go directly to interrogate Brontë about her thoughts on the events of the day; however, his mission was delayed by dinner.

In the dining room, Corinthiana joined the party for the evening meal, the potatoes growing cold as she marched from the south end of the table to the north. The entrance took longer than usual due to the old woman's mix of fear and anxiety.

Rather than dissipate, the tension swelled at dinner. The explanation of the phonograph incident being caused by Kordelia was unsatisfactory to everyone but August. Few words were exchanged during the course of dining—the room was filled with the sounds of cutlery and the occasional indecorous belch from Robert.

The long-lost cousin did finally speak up, gently wiping his mouth with his napkin before proceeding, "Allo' me to apologize again for ze earlier moment vith you, August."

"Au*güst*, yes."

"I vas terribly out of ze line. Corinziana may memorialize her husband however she desires."

"That's very nice of you to say." June gave Robert a cold smile before turning her eyes to her plate.

August said nothing, but his mustache slightly jostled to the left, which most took as a sign of understanding.

"While we're speaking," Kordelia said softly. "I'd also like to re-assert that I had nothing to do with the earlier séance incident. I hope whoever is guilty will have the courage to speak up."

There was a lengthy silence. Eyes moved around the room, most of them reflected sympathy for the young girl.

"Darling, now is not the time," June said looking empathetically at her daughter. "We can discuss this later."

Brontë threw a glance at Crockett to convey irritation with her mother's response.

"Everyone, a moooment pleeease." Corinthiana was exhausted. The mammoth earrings that decorated her ears pulled her head to the table. In truth, since the séance, a great deal of energy had gone out of the previously vivacious woman. Beatrice matched her mood, sitting stock-still in her bowl, staring into space. "Theee entooombment will commence in twooo daaays time. I neeeded a moment of rest. I aaam sorry I haaave kept yooou here." She smiled at Robert. "I haaaven't beeen myself laaately, but with a quiet daaay, yooou caaan beee sure thaaat things will beeegin moooving briskly."

"And the will reading?" May's dark eyes fixed on her mother. Her mouth twitched.

"Theee daaay aaafter." Corinthiana sighed.

"Why not the same day?" May said it lightly, but even Crockett saw the direct challenge it presented.

"Rest." August's neck turned purple. "She needs rest, May. It's best to let this sleeping dog lie."

"Lie," May said forcefully. "What an interesting choice of word." The austere woman swiftly rose and left the room, her black heels echoing in the main foyer.

Corinthiana put her head between her hands and groaned, a slight, wavering "Awrk." Before long the table emptied—June took Corinthiana to her room, Kordelia disappeared like a fine mist, a white glove left in her place, and Robert left to go enjoy a cigarette on the front lawn.

Petrarch gave Crockett a knowing look before quietly asking August if he would take a walk with him on the grounds.

As Martha began taking the plates away, Brontë turned to Crockett with a sigh.

"Well, at least we know what day the whole thing will end," she said.

Crockett watched Martha leave the room before leaning toward Brontë. When he was sure that Martha was gone and couldn't overhear their conversation, he said quietly, "Petrarch pulled me aside today." He paused for dramatic effect. "Well, he thinks you're right."

"About what?" Brontë's eyebrows jumped on her smooth face.

"He thinks something is afoot. He described it as 'some malice.'"

"The séance convinced him?"

"Not fully but it played a part." Crockett and Brontë were inches away from each other. The earnestness of the conversation forced them to lean closely together. Crockett could feel her warm, potato-tinged breath on his face. He stopped short of continuing his speech, the amount of perspiration accumulating on his palms and forehead causing him to grow self-conscious.

Brontë also found herself speechless, staring into the multi-colored eyes of Crockett. While their amicable bond had grown over the past two days, this conspiratorial moment raised the emotional stakes exponentially.

It was a distant gunshot that brought them to their senses. Crockett leapt up, backing against the wall. Brontë turned her head, taking a deep, shaking breath to calm her nerves.

"It's Father," she said quickly. "I bet he's showing Petrarch his toys."

Crockett put his hand to his heart. "I'm never good under pressure, but this house is testing every fiber of my resolve."

"Are you afraid of more canaries, Mr. Cook?" Brontë rose from the table, an ironic smile returning to her face. "If you let all these small pressures get to you, you'll be in a mountain of troubouble."

Crockett laughed. "I did expect at least a modicum of sympathy from you." For some reason, an insult from Brontë meant more than one thousand compliments from others. "And, if you must know, guns I'm actually quite stable around, but, in this house, they seem to mean something more."

"Neither ghosts nor canaries can shoot, as far as I know," Brontë laughed uneasily. "But…" She looked toward the door to see if Martha was close. When she was sure the old maid had not returned, she continued, "Well, if you and Petrarch also have a suspicion—" She stopped when she heard Martha's footsteps returning. She mimed for Crockett to stay quiet and pointed to the south exit.

Once out of the dining room, both paused in the main foyer.

The color of the twilight sky took their breath away. It was a magic, if foreboding moment, the front windows, half black, half the color of blood.

"It's so ominous," Brontë said softly. "It's not the peaceful sensation twilight usually brings but something like violence, the sky rent in two."

"But beautiful," Crockett said mesmerized. Below the sky, and visible through the lower two windows of the two-story façade, Crockett saw Dexter and Robert somberly speaking. The wispy smoke of Robert's cigarette circled them. They, too, seemed lost in the spell of twilight.

It was Brontë who shook them from the daydream. She touched Crockett's arm, sending an electric shock through his whole person. The graze appeared to be accidental, the young woman not acknowledging the breach of propriety. She instead turned and moved quickly into the sitting room. Crockett regained his senses before following after her.

Entering the sitting room, they found it empty. The only sounds were hushed voices coming from the patio and the old clock chiming, signaling the eight o'clock hour. Crockett noted the gun, usually ominously hung over the fireplace, was missing.

"Does your father shoot with that gun?" Crockett asked. "I thought it was more a decorative piece."

"He takes it when he would like to make a statement for a guest. He most likely wanted to give Petrarch a thrill."

Brontë casually looked around the room, checking the back hallways and looking out onto the patio to see if anyone was nearby. When she was sure no one noticed their entrance, she sped to the card table and took out a deck of worn cards. Carelessly, she threw out an arbitrary number, then flipped one up on the top. She took a seat and motioned for Crockett to sit across from her.

"What are we playing?" Crockett kept his voice low.

"It doesn't matter, but it would be best not to draw attention to this conversation. If someone comes in quickly, it looks like we are preoccupied."

Crockett fanned his cards and was glad no game was being played; he had one jack and a handful of low-numbered spades and hearts.

"Now that we have some privacy, let's return to the subject from earlier." Her gaze lifted; the lights reflected in her eyes quivered with excitement. "Petrarch thinks there is something odd?" While still staring intently at Crockett, she flipped a card and discarded one of those from her hand with a casual grace.

"He does," Crockett said, admiring Brontë's natural inclination to play-acting; between her current performance and Kordelia's German-French-English play rehearsals, the family was very strong in the arts.[21] "The séance was bizarre, but he doesn't necessarily believe anyone is in danger. He thinks there may be some foul play somewhere, though."

"But he thinks Grandfather died naturally?" The door in the main foyer opened. A clacking of gentleman's shoes filled the hall as Robert walked toward the stairs. When he was gone, Brontë continued, "He was in such good health. And I feel the circumstances are strange, to say the least. There are a great many people here who hated Grandfather."

"Really?" Crockett had been pretending to look at his cards, but this statement pulled his eyes upward to focus on Brontë. She scolded him with an annoyed look and motioned for him to pick up a card from the draw pile.

"My father has never liked anyone in the family," she said. "He resented moving into Hawsfeffer Manor, but my grandfather said that his residence here was a requirement to receive Grandfather's blessing to marry my

---

[21] In Earhart's notes, the author wrote lengthy, unnecessary details of Brontë's character that included the information that she played both Juliet and Juliet's nurse in the same production of the Bard's famous play; additionally, her fourth toe was 3.2 mm longer than her second.

mother."

"Why?"

"He said it's because my mother is Grandmother's favorite. He couldn't bear to see them separated."

"Which gives cause for May to hate him as well." Crockett threw down a card haphazardly. "No child likes to be the least favorite."

Brontë nodded. "May left the house as soon as she could to go to the convent."

"But she never finished."

"No."

"Why?"

Brontë shook her head. "I don't know. I think my grandmother and mother know, but it's never been told to us."

"Your grandfather was a bizarre presence of chaos in the house—he caused disruption for Kordelia, your mother, August…May…" Crockett absentmindedly looked through his cards. "What about Robert Edward? Does he have a story?"

"We don't know. He simply appeared one day."

"After your grandfather died?"

"Before. Grandfather was in London on business; after meeting with Petrarch about the will he was home for a short time before returning to the city. Robert arrived during his absence claiming his familial connection. Although he appeared to be a bizarre villain from a gothic novel, he was kind. Before that, however, no one had spoken of him."

"Where's he from?"

"Some odd country near mountains. He pronounced it once, but I'd never heard of it. He claims to be a cousin."

"And his story was his gypsy blood told him to come here?"

"Yes, he claimed 'a premonition.' He sent a letter to Grandfather in regard to this fear, and Grandfather invited him to come see that everything was perfectly fine."

Crockett again forgot about the card game. "That is very suspicious."

Brontë shrugged her shoulders. "He brought a letter of introduction from my grandfather, written in Grandfather's own hand."

Crockett let out an exasperated breath, frustrated that the handful of threads they unspooled the past few days all lead to dead ends.

"Then, of course," Brontë continued, "there are Martha and Dexter."

Crockett coughed. *"They* have something against your grandfather?"

"They've been part of the family for a long time. Martha and Grandfather were always seen talking on the grounds, often privately. My mother claims there was never an affair, but one can never know. Martha has always been very unhappy, whether that's from being a jilted lover or something else, I can't say." Brontë paused, her hand holding a card just above the table. "The very interesting thing is that Martha and Grandfather's meetings increased in frequency and intensity as his death approached."

Crockett's eyes widened. "You don't say."

"I did just say it."

The two forgot about the fake card game, both looking to the middle distance, collecting their thoughts.

"And what," Crockett asked distantly, "is Dexter's connection? Would he have motive?"

"Dexter is a very odd case. He keeps to himself, aside from my grandfather, for whom he showed infrequent but consistent affection. He came over with Cousin Bixby from America. When our cousin fought with Grandfather, they separated. Dexter had no money. Supposedly, he was also swindled by Cousin Bixby and forced to stay on as groundskeeper because he didn't have the funds to return to America."

"So," Crockett said, "if anything, he would be the most loyal to your grandfather."

"Honestly, he and my grandmother are the most blameless in all this." She then added, "And, of course, Kordelia is a peculiarity, but she means no harm to anyone. Grandfather didn't care much for her, but I hardly think she's capable of murder."

Crockett tapped a card on the table. "That still leaves quite a number of others with motive to get rid of him."

Brontë laughed softly. "Beatrice even has cause, if we're being honest.

Grandfather hated the poor scaly thing. To be fair, Grandmother treated her better than she did anyone in the family."

Crockett shook his head. "I still don't understand the fish…Why does your grandmother love it so much?"

"There's nothing to understand. Most often things we love find us by accident. It doesn't mean anything more than what it is—it's a connection—intangible, magnetic." Brontë abruptly stopped speaking.

The layer of perspiration reformed on Crockett's hands and forehead. Both young people felt overwhelmed, hot with an anticipation they didn't fully comprehend.

Unable to make eye contact with Brontë, Crockett set aside his cards and placed both hands on his temples. He cleared his throat. "If we…ummm…if we…are being pragmatic about this, though,"—the word *pragmatic*, taken from one of his detective novels, offered the young apprentice renewed grounding—"pragmatic…yes, if we are that, then the day your grandfather died, the only individuals in the house were Dexter, Martha, you, your sister, your mother, grandmother, and father, correct?"

"Yes." Brontë kept her eyes fixed at a point in the hallway to the kitchen. She appreciated Crockett's return to natural discourse. "Well, and Beatrice, of course."

Brontë's eyes met his, the tension dispelled. Crockett chuckled softly, "And Beatrice." He took a moment to think, his eyes closing. "There's no proof your grandfather was murdered, but if there was, those gathered in the house, aquatic creatures included, would be the culprits."

Brontë pondered a moment. "I think we must add Aunt May to that list. Although she wasn't present in the house, she does live near. It could have been a plot."

"Very good. So, the only ones truly free from suspicion in that regard are Petrarch, Robert, and I."

"It would seem. You and Petrarch were in London and Robert was as well. After his visit here he went into the city for business. When he returned to the house to say good-bye to Grandfather… well, he found out he was deceased."

"This shakes the conviction in my mind that the séance scheme is in any way related. The only two individuals who could have possibly executed it were Dexter and Petrarch, both of whom for which it seems impractical that they could hurtle to the second floor, turn on the phonograph, then sprint downstairs to get to their respective positions in the bedroom and the back lawn."

Brontë bit her lip. "It seems as if nothing is connected at all."

"So," Crockett said resignedly, "we have no suspects and no concrete motives for any of it." He thought briefly of Lucinda's note; he decided it best not to address, as it also only muddied their current understanding of events rather than clarify it. "There's also no physical evidence," he continued. "The body is gone and Kordelia's glove is hardly a clue because… well, they are everywhere."

Brontë suddenly started and looked toward Crockett. She leaned so closely to him that he could see the small, individual lines of color in her eyes. "What if there is someone else?" she asked breathlessly. "We're thinking too small, Crockett. Is there anyone else who could have a reason, and the means, to get rid of Grandfather? Perhaps the séance is a practical joke, but what if there is someone secret, someone hidden from us who would want to enact violence on him?"

She finished quickly, her face radiating excitement. Crockett sat for a moment, caught up in her earnest energy. Her beauty filled the room, clouding his comprehension of the facts of the case.

This was the first time in his life he'd shared such intimate confidences with a woman. He never truly became acquainted with other feminine figures in his life; they always were at some distance. But here was Brontë, fully before him, her beautiful complexities causing his heart to flutter.

In the intrigue, neither Brontë nor Crockett noticed Kordelia enter and stand beside them, her dainty hands placed behind her back.

"Looks like an intriguing game," she said in her ethereal voice. "You both appear enraptured."

Brontë looked to her sister. Her face was flushed. She spoke airily as if waking from a dream. "We were…We were just talking about Grandfather…

about how he died."

"Why in the river, of course." Kordelia's wide eyes looked innocently at her sister. "If you fall in the warmer season, it's difficult to get back out. Nothing floats—ghosts, bones, and keys or stones."

"Ghosts, bones, and keys or stones…" But before Crockett could ponder this further, Kordelia danced off to the corner.

"As I told you this morning, she has a powerful imagination," Brontë said, an edge of fright to her voice. "If she's still keeping points on our status with the family, I hope she gave herself scores for the phantasms that fill her brain."

#

The rest of the night passed uneventfully. Everyone eventually made it to the sitting room, except for May and Corinthiana. Corinthiana went to sleep early, while May had taken her righteous indignation and gone to read the Bible in the study; she hoped to dispel any residual spirits from the séance. Any fears held by the rest of the party faded as more lamps were lighted and the conversation turned away from family drama. Even Beatrice, placed early by Corinthiana in her grand bed, had a wonderful evening. She swam jovially watching the lively gathering.

Petrarch held the crowd in rapt attention during the latter hours of the evening, regaling them with a number of stories of his clients and cases in London. His last tale primarily concerned how he met Crockett, how the young boy had been sent to rob him but was unsuccessful.

"One of the sharpest boys I'd ever met," Petrarch said beaming at Crockett. "He went out to rob me and followed me to a public house by my office. Inside I caught him in his pilfering and scolded him. I soon discovered he was quite a smart boy. I eventually offered him a job if he wanted."

"That was very brave of you," August said brusquely. "Most of the poor draw their intelligence from being impoverished, you know. He could have swindled you in that game."

No one quite knew what he meant, but it put an end to the night's discussion rather handily.

Before bed Crockett told Petrarch about his conversation with Brontë. The old man laughed heartily when Crockett finished his explanation that there were no suspects, no motives, and no physical evidence. He pooh-poohed Crockett and Brontë's thoughts of there being some other mysterious presence responsible for Mr. Hawsfeffer's murder and the otherworldly séance trick.

"I think, perhaps, we're all forgetting our heads," Petrarch said. "After the séance, I was also ready to round up everyone and send them to jail, but I've since regained my equilibrium. If a review of the facts only makes us go further into conjecture and fantasy, then it would appear we are losing sight of the real, current state of affairs."

Crockett went to bed hearing Petrarch counting out his exercises. Despite the chilling sunset of blood-red and black, the night turned calm. The velvet sky was dotted with sparkling stars. A brisk chill ran through the windows of Crockett's room. He went to sleep on his tiny couch with the soft howl of the wind in his ears.

Compared to the first night when he'd had nightmares of terrifying canaries and grating harpsichords, his dreams were so calming that he didn't hear the scream.

It was Brontë who woke him. Her thundering footsteps in the corridor pulled him from his slumber before the door opened.

"Come," she said, her voice like a knife in the dark. It was pain and panic joined horribly together, a forceful word, edged with a shriek. "When we arrive in the foyer you may not want to look…"

Petrarch rose and joined them in the hall. As they ran down the corridor, Crockett felt a slight surge of pride in the midst of his terror; the new courage again collided with overwhelming fear to keep him upright. Not even the threat of a faint preoccupied him. He was quite functional despite all this frenetic movement.

This flash of joy and pride failed, however, as he, Petrarch, and Brontë entered the main foyer.

Gathered around some dark object, suspended over the front door, the household stared upon a scene of horror. All faces were aghast, trying to assign meaning to the chaos before them. It struck Crockett that his fear of the nursery rhyme that morning was made absurd by the corpse, which took shape before his eyes in the dim candlelight. No one uttered a sound except Corinthiana, whose shrieks rebounded against the high ceiling.

It was Beatrice—or what once was the small aquatic companion—horribly eviscerated. The animal's entrails were loosed and slung across the wall. The object of defilement appeared to be a blade, which had been forced through the pet's eye. In the dim light of the lamps, the fresh pink and white innards shone like evil, glittering jewels. Crockett watched the streaks of gore drip. The effect grew even more sinister as time elapsed, the fish's viscera transforming into a demonic paint, shimmering in the glow of their lamps' dim flames.

10

The Aftermath

As they examined Beatrice's entrails,[22] August broke the silence.

"You know," he started, stroking his mustache, "it seems to me a trout or Atlantic salmon would be a much more robust pet, definitely could have survived this kind of flaying or at least put up a better fight."

Corinthiana wasn't comforted. The old woman responded with a prolonged, doleful "AWWWWRRRRRKKKKKKK!"

"Darling, now is not the time." June shook her head at August as she held her mother. "Stiff upper lips are sometimes a bit *too* stiff and *too* upper, if you catch my insinuation."

"I rather liked Beatrice, Grandmummy," Kordelia slid beside her grandmother and gently gripped the old woman's hand. "We always had wonderful conversations."

Crockett, again at a loss after an interjection by Kordelia, said nothing. His most useful tool at the current moment was investigative prowess; he looked around the room, assessing reactions to the sordid scene. The escalation in chicanery and violence cemented the fact that a foul game was afoot;

---

[22] The original description of Beatrice's death was roughly three and one-half pages of violence with a great (and frankly admirable) number of synonyms for fish entrails and innards. Although skimping on other research for the rest of the novel, he heavily invested in the anatomy of herring, spending three paragraphs describing the fish's "pyloric caeca."

perhaps only in the Hawsfeffer house would a fish being filleted constitute an inhuman, nefarious transgression, but—here they were.

His examination, however, brought no clarity. If anything, his chief suspect, Robert Edward, appeared the most distraught. His eyes were averted from the gore and settled on the grieving Corinthiana. May was the most indifferent. In her black nightgown she looked smug as the light of pale flames danced across her face.

"I think someone should fetch Dexter and Martha," June said to Brontë. She flicked her eyes to Crockett. "Perhaps two should go—it's a bad night to wander alone in the house." She extended her hand so that Crockett could take her light.

Brontë sighed. She turned to Crockett and signaled toward the stairs.

During their ascent to the second floor, the young lawyer leaned close to Brontë.

"This seems entirely—"

The young woman silenced Crockett with a severe look. "Not tonight, Crockett. Tonight, we just get through this. Poor Grandmother. Losing Grandfather was bad, but Beatrice…She loved that pet more than anything in the world."

They both moved cautiously down the hall toward Martha's quarters. She occupied a small chamber close to Corinthiana's own large bedroom. This was a recent arrangement. Prior to Bixby Hawsfeffer's death, she stayed in the servants' quarters attached to the kitchen. When the patriarch died, Corinthiana asked her to move into the house. The force of grief was evident to everyone, as Martha was the last person she ever wanted close to her while Bixby was alive. It was thought she wanted to make amends or bury hatchets, as the arrangement was the first white flag Corinthiana had waved in all her years at Hawsfeffer Manor.

Upon entering Martha's chamber, they found her snoring loudly. The screams and chaos had not reached her old ears. Crockett moved close to the old woman and gently shook her. Even though he tried to wake her calmly with a soft touch, the old woman still sat up in a panic.

"I MUST PROTECT THEM!" she screamed. A glob of spittle splashed on

Crockett, which he subtly shook off.

Brontë, not particularly fond of Martha for a number of reasons, put out a hand to soothe her. The effort was so lackluster it appeared she was swatting a lethargic fly.

"Martha," Crockett whispered, "we're all fine."

"Well..." Brontë said playing with a strand of her hair.

"All the people...are fine," Crockett started again, "but we need you downstairs."

"Is it him?" Her voice quavered. Crockett saw a deep terror in her eyes.

"Who?" he asked leaning closer. "Is it who?"

She did not answer. She jumped up as quickly as her aged years would allow and tottered into the hall.

Crockett and Brontë exchanged worried glances before following behind.

When they arrived downstairs, things were mildly less chaotic. More candles were lighted, and most of the party had retreated into the sitting room to regain their calm. Only Corinthiana and June were absent, having gone to the kitchen to fetch tea for the family and a cup of sherry for Corinthiana.

Dexter arrived during their absence. The old man was, for the first time, wearing normal clothes. His bald head shone in the candlelight. It was the first time Crockett saw him up close—what struck him as most remarkable was how unremarkable the groundskeeper was. Stripped of his normally bizarre costume, he could have been any man, or no man, for that matter. His countenance was of so little consequence Crockett found when he turned away, he had to look back again to remember any small detail. The banal housemaster stood close to August, receiving orders on what to do with the fish's corpse.

"We'll need to save it—Corinthiana will want to have it put in the family tomb with Bixby and herself."

"Yessir," was all Dexter said as he approached the lanced herring.

Crockett took the moment to attend to the corpse. It truly was ghastly, the entrails of Beatrice ripped out and smeared on the wall. Whoever had done the work had a precise hand. It wasn't entirely slashed and mutilated but cleanly opened with an expert cut. The sword which did the work was still driven into the animal's eye. To Crockett's surprise, it wasn't a hunting knife but looked as if it was an heirloom, a long rapier, slightly discolored with age.

"It looks as if a madman did this," Crockett said turning away.

Dexter wiped his nose with the sleeve of his coat. "Better the fish than someone in the house, I suppose," he said in his clanging, American accent. "The house has gone after bigger prey before."

Crockett shuddered thinking of a person gorily suspended as Beatrice was now. For his part, however, Dexter was correct—Lucinda Hawsfeffer, Baron Von Bunson, and Bixby Hawsfeffer were all victims of the house's malice and the river's terrifying current.

Crockett shook his head and turned away. He made his way to the sitting room to join the rest of the party in mourning.

Immediately upon entering the room, his eyes met the piercing gaze of Petrarch who was seated at the card table. The old man tapped his nose and pointed to Robert Edward, who was speaking with May. With a tiny gesture of his hand, a slight sweep in May and Robert's direction, he inferred Crockett should go listen.

A plan presented itself to the junior solicitor as he looked from his master to Robert and May. On his approach to the sofa, he prepared his subterfuge.

Behind the seat was a small table with a collection of books he could use to feign insouciant interest. He idly picked up a volume and turned its pages whilst attempting to lean forward and listen to the conversation in front of him. The low voices, however, and Robert's erratic accent, hurt his progress. This caused him to subtly inch forward. While he thought he looked very demure, Kordelia and Brontë both marked his bizarre slouching and watched with amused, rapt attention as he leaned closer and closer to their aunt and (distant) cousin.

"But do you zink it vas intentional? Zis act of violence?" Robert Edward asked, his large nose quivering.

"Surely, even in your backwards country, a pet fish doesn't accidentally end up looking like it's been sent through a woodchipper," May grimaced.

She slumped, sinking into the couch. "But who or what is behind it is a mystery. This house has always had a tension within it. It's no secret our family has never been a cohesive unit, but it always felt as if there was something deeper and more malignant involved. I don't think this act was spirits, but you never know. You've heard the stories?"

"In my country no vun has ze fish companion, but I understand ze drama of zis. But, no," Robert said dramatically, "zere are stories of spirits in ze house?"

"It's rumored that our dear, departed patriarch, your cousin, Bixby Hawsfeffer, wasn't the kindest soul," May lowered her voice. "They say he not only tortured his uncle, who gave him this property, but there is also conjecture…" She again reduced her voice's volume. She was speaking so softly Crockett pretended to drop his book on the sofa so he could double over and lean closer. Brontë (still observing) stifled a laugh in her fist. "Well… Some believe that he murdered his first wife because she bore him a," her voice dropped again, "homosexual son."

"My stars!" Robert gasped. "Zey say homosexuals are becoming more common, but I hope to never encounter vun." He shook his head sadly. "But vut of ze cousin of Bixby Havsfeffer? Ze vun hoo vent to America?"

May spun to face Crockett. The young man had leaned so closely that his torso was laying over the couch, his head resting on a pillow. Brontë, seeing he was caught, let out a loud, amused snort.

"Could you please mind your own business?" May spit, her face flushed red. "Poor in fortune and poor in manners, a disgusting combination for a young man." She rose in a rage and stormed away from the sofa.

Robert Edward looked at Crockett. His uneven, misaligned face conveyed disgust. He then turned his attention to the fireplace. The gun had been returned to the mantle; it gleamed in the dim light.

A few moments later, Corinthiana re-entered the room. Pale and trembling, she clutched June's shoulder with her right hand as she sipped a cup of sherry with her left.

As everyone turned their attention to the old matriarch, she grew self-conscious, chugging what remained of her spirits and exhaling dramatically.

Crockett noted that sometime between the discovery of the filleted Beatrice and the present moment she found time to put on a garish, mink stole.

"Oooh deeear," she began, "it haaas beeen…" She stopped. Her lip quivered and her breaths came in grandiose, huffing gasps. A number of ululations then broke from her mouth, a bizarre war cry mixed with a seal bark.

Everyone in the room stared compassionately at their hostess, all unsure how to help the old woman in this time of intense grief. Upon her ending the warring seal noises, however, a deep, shuddering gasp led to a second, more destructive and explosive expression of grief, an octave-soaring "WHAWHAWHAWHA."

June finally put an end to it; with little gentility, she shoved her mother onto the couch. Corinthiana slumped, putting her head in her hands. Her doughy shoulders occasionally shook as she continued to emit moans and aquatic mammalian ejaculations.

"The burial will commence as soon as possible," June said. "Mummy has seen that someone or something is distressed about Daddy's death, so we must put an end to this whole affair quickly before things escalate any further."

"Hear, hear!" August shouted, his mustache jovially shaking.

"The vicar will be called on tomorrow. We will dispense with the usual formalities and have a few words said before the caskets of Beatrice and Daddy are taken to the family tomb."

"It seems simple enough," May said. "I shall be able to leave by lunch."

"There is," Corinthiana bleated from the sofa, "there is a smaaall problem."

"How small?" Robert Edward's eyes narrowed.

Corinthiana continued to make morose, audible booms, so June answered, "We don't have the key to the tomb. We can't get in."

"How did you lose it?" Brontë looked genuinely confused. "Grandfather had to have a few copies of it."

Petrarch shifted uncomfortably. "I believe one of them went down to the bottom of the river with him."

"Well, there must be another in the house!" August's mustache was the most erratic Crockett had seen since their arrival, twitching, shuddering, and bristling all at once.

Brontë thought for a moment. "Do you think it's downstairs with the family heirlooms?"

"I haaave loooked, my daaarling," Corinthiana said sadly. "But weee caaan aaalwaaays try aaagain. I think this taaask were best treeeated as a faaamily project. Perhaaaps, if weee split up, weee caaan leeeave no stone unturned, hmmm."

"I think that sounds like a wonderful plan of attack," August growled. "Kordelia and June, we can search the upstairs."

"This is nonsense," May crossed her arms in disdain. "How can a key be this important? Let's just break open the gate."

"Sister," June said, "you forget Baron Von Bunson built that tomb as if he were building the Taj Mahal. The door is solid marble. There are no windows."

"Theee Baaaron waaanted it tooo beee imposing," Corinthiana said, "like a graaand tooomb of theee Orient."

"Well, then," Brontë interjected, "first thing in the morning, let's get to work. It has to be somewhere—Petrarch and Robert, you can go check in the folly wing. Crockett and I will investigate the family vault and look amongst the boxes." She smiled at Crockett. "I think we will find it before lunch, as Aunt May said."

Crockett did his best to hide his elation at being selected by Brontë. He smiled into his closed fist, pretending he was coughing.

The group came to a firm agreement on this plan of action and disbanded. Robert Edward and May exchanged a quick glance, but no more speech passed between them. Brontë and Kordelia politely bid everyone a warm good night before heading up to their rooms. June kept Corinthiana occupied until Dexter and Martha removed the last remnants of fish guts from the main hall.

Petrarch said very little to Crockett in the journey down the rickety walkway to their rooms. There was a draft in this ramshackle part of the house which made them both shiver.

"Good night then, Petrarch," Crockett said. "It looks like we were correct about something being a bit sinister."

Petrarch appeared perturbed, an emotion the jolly gentleman rarely expressed. He paused outside of his door, his hand on the knob. "It's an interesting business about this key," he said quietly.

"You said yourself that one copy most likely went down with Bixby in the river."

"Yes, I suppose so." The old man squinted, his mind hard at work. He noted the need for a more portable thinking pipe, one which would allow for more adaptable moments of deep thought.

"In the current atmosphere," Crockett added nervously, "it's hard not to embrace that something terrible is happening around us."

The old solicitor smiled briefly. "I know my boy. It seems when I regain my balance, a clear, logical perspective on things, they go catawampus again. I find myself oscillating between asinine conspiracy theories and very mundane musings." Stroking his beard, Petrarch sighed. "Perhaps I simply need to do some more exercises—my brain is a bit addled this evening. I'll also begin thinking where an eccentric man like Bixby Hawsfeffer would hide an old key."

"I shall do the same." Crockett bowed slightly to Petrarch to say good night and walked toward his room. His hand was on the knob to his quarters when his thoughts returned to the murder of Beatrice. Brontë asking him to be her partner in the search the next morning had created a drunken fog on his brain, one which focused solely on the warm halo of their planned excursion after breakfast. "Petrarch," he said quickly, "I got distracted, but I was trying to think who did it this whole time. The blade looks like an heirloom, not a hunting weapon, but whoever wielded it would have had to find it, then use it, with some precision, to maim the fish in such a brutal manner."

"Indeed. It would have taken a steady hand." Petrarch turned to his apprentice and stroked his beard.

"But," Crockett clicked his tongue in exasperation, "Beatrice's bed is in the central sitting room. We all retired at the same time, so anyone could have slipped in and done it. Again, another tragedy, but the road does not narrow, it only grows wider."

"Well, my boy," Petrarch's eyes twinkled, "think of this with your logical, law-bent mind. Corinthiana discovered the body. I found that out from Kordelia this evening."

"But she's hardly a suspect—she wouldn't lay a hand on Beatrice."

"But what made her wake? Who had access to the weapon? And I believe this key," here he subconsciously patted his stomach, his face growing graver, "may mean more than simply a means to get into the tomb."

"You think it may be tied to a motive?"

"I don't know, my boy." The old man licked his lips. He hesitated before he continued. "I—er—" He stopped abruptly. His eyes met Crockett's. A smile returned to his face, forced but resolute. "What I do know is that while the road right now has not narrowed, we have many paths to take that may lead to resolution." Crockett felt some satisfaction in this. Petrarch added warmly, "In the daylight things won't seem so hapless as they do in this darkness."

"I certainly hope not. I hope this ends tomorrow so that we can all rest a bit easier."

"Yes, indeed." Petrarch sniffed, an indication it was time to part for the night. Crockett heard the sound of the old man's door open behind him. There was a brief pause, then he heard his master's voice, a note of humor in its tone. "Oh and Crockett, please remember to keep thinking of Miss Hawsfeffer as nothing more than a client. Electricity has yet to reach this part of the countryside, but when she spoke your name this evening, your face could have lit up half of West Hampminstershireshire had you been close to a tungsten filament."

Crockett, flushed with embarrassment, rushed into his room and closed the door.

11

The Vault

Morning brought a tentative calm to the house. Thin, gray clouds rolled in during the early morning, tinting all light an ashy gray. Few slept well, so that by nine o'clock, Martha had cleared breakfast away and all dispersed to their assigned places to look for the key.

Brontë led Crockett through the formal sitting room and into the more stylish west wing of the house. The money, which ran out while building the folly, had been abundant during this other half of the home's expansion. The long hall leading toward the addition was much more opulent. Instead of untreated wooden planks, they walked on patterned, gold-threaded carpet. Along the hall there were a number of portraits. Most of them were the family—Kordelia, Brontë, June, August. One featured both Corinthiana and Beatrice seated in the main sitting room. The artist gave Beatrice a knowing fish smile, which Crockett found very unsettling in light of the events of the previous evening.

He noted Brontë's earlier observation about her grandfather not being in many portraits held true. There was only one picture of him, very recent, which showed him with slicked-back white hair. Crockett noted something familiar in the older gentleman's visage, whether it was a trace he'd seen on Bixby's daughters or granddaughters, he was unsure.

The passage led into a great dance hall, a poor man's Versailles, with the east and west walls covered in smudged mirrors. On the north wall, a large mural paying homage to the American West was painted with great care and detail. It featured a number of cowboys rushing forward; the artist was quite talented, as it infused the ballroom with a feeling of forward momentum.

"This is…an interesting part of the house," Crockett said, admiring a particularly grotesque statue of George Washington which sat in a place of honor in the center of the dance floor.

"Grandfather always had a kind of obsession with America. We thought it may be because that's where he got his money."

"Which he got with the help of his cousin, Bixby Von Bunson."

"Very impressive." Brontë smiled. "Our family history is full of twist and turns; I'm surprised you can recall it."

"Some of it." Crockett couldn't help but blush after Brontë's praise. He was keenly aware of the luminous nature of his eyes and expression after Petrarch's comments the previous night. "It's not all me, however. Petrarch is the one who gave me a bit of a history on you all. He said Von Bunson helped your father invest in American endeavors that paid handsomely."

"Correct."

"But things apparently went sour."

Brontë nodded. "Bixby Von Bunson was involved in a western cowboy show. Dexter was his friend while he was over there. They both traveled all over the wilder parts of America, which allowed my cousin to get insights into land investments and gold mining opportunities he otherwise wouldn't have known." Brontë indicated Crockett should follow her. "He and my father made quite a lot of money, but he came to visit and…things didn't go well."

"In what way?"

"Money, the dispute over it, always causes chaos. We believe Bixby Von Bunson not only stole a large part of my grandfather's fortune, but also took what little he owed Dexter before he fled. Dexter, poor man, is an off-kilter illiterate without many prospects, so he was devastated when Von Bunson left. And, the last part of my cousin's atrocious legacy," she said scornfully, "is influencing Grandfather to buy all this crass, American memorabilia."

It was apropos that Crockett, at this exact moment, looked in the corner and saw a bizarre clock which resembled the Statue of Liberty. The face of the statue, however, had been replaced by a clock. The substitution resulted in a terrifying piece of artwork which stared menacingly from the shadows.

Brontë crossed the room and approached the mural. She stopped before the image of a proud American Indian war general, his head held high, a spear pointed forward at the coming cowboys. Brontë delicately ran her hand over the painting. She gently pushed a hidden button in the painted Indian's spear. There was an audible click, and then a panel opened, exposing a small room with a trapdoor in the floor.

"What is this?" The hair on the back of Crockett's neck prickled.

"It's our family vault. There's really not much of value, but it's where we keep anything of nostalgic importance." She noted the fearful expression on Crockett's face and laughed. "Don't worry, Mr. Cook, there are no canaries down here, and as far as most are concerned, the space is quite inhabitababble, as you might say."

Crockett's neck hair prickled again, this time, from a sensation disparate from fear. He self-consciously hid his face with his hand, the luminosity, this time, very probably able to light all of West Hampminstershireshire.

Brontë, meanwhile, went to work, deftly picking up a couple of candles and some matches placed near the trap door. She prepared a light for each of them before lifting the door and heading down into the darkness.

It wasn't as ominous as Crockett feared. The stairs were carpeted, and the walls were decorated with additional family portraits. When they had climbed down just a few yards, they entered a large cluttered room. Boxes and trunks lined the walls, but every few feet there was a statue, oversized portrait, or piece of furniture that looked rather expensive. Most everything appeared to be tainted with a kind of American extremist style—a sofa embroidered with stars and stripes, an eagle statue so real that Crockett ducked when his candlelight fell over its beak and stone eyes, and an image of Benjamin Franklin, only recognized because his name was writ along the top of the portrait—in reality, it looked like a tiny old woman holding a flag and an old bit of parchment.[23]

Crockett surreptitiously eyed the contents of some of the trunks as he passed through the room. One was full of old costumes, wigs, and dresses, the source of Dexter's different looks; he noted the head scarf and cowboy hat the groundskeeper wore upon his arrival were piled at the top of the box. He mistook a large, frizzy wig for a rat and suppressed a scream. After the earlier incident on the lawn, he had no desire for Brontë to think him afraid of both rodents and birds.

Brontë didn't notice Crockett's moment of panic; she was busy lighting additional fixtures around the room.

Along the south wall, there was a small window, a sliver cut into the stone several feet in the air. A ray of gray light fell on a portrait full of faces Crockett had not seen. It was a picture of three individuals. One was an august gentleman in a red coat with long, shining black hair; his face had been smudged with some form of ink. Next to him was a small diffident boy with a thick mop of curls, and, on his other side, a woman of ethereal beauty who appeared to be distracted, looking at the painter but also at some unseen, haunted object.

"Brontë," Crockett said. "Who are these people?"

Brontë drew closer to the portrait to gain a clearer view.

"That's my grandfather and his first wife, Lucinda. The boy is their son, Mr. Bixby Hawsfeffer, Jr.—known as Pip, who was removed from the family years ago for his activities *dans la chambre*."

"It's a shame it was ruined with that smudge," Crockett said. "The image of Lucinda is beautiful—haunting."

"I know." Brontë's voice grew melancholy. "I often wish we could have met her. Martha still talks about her to this day, how warm she was, how caring. Even Pip would be nice to know. It feels as if our family has always been so isolated here. Grandfather didn't like other people, so we've always

---

[23] This was actually the work *Ben at Tea with Flag and Parchment on 4 July*. The original portrait hangs in the Cincinnati Gallery of Fine and Less than Fine Art. It is still a top draw simply due to the gender confusion of the image. It is often referred to as The Midwest's Mona Lisa.

kept to ourselves. He especially rejected our neighbors. We'd even travel to London to visit the doctor or lawyer, as was the case with Petrarch. We just didn't lay down roots here for some reason. I think that's part of why my father resented Grandfather and this house so much."

"I'm sorry."

"No," the ironic detachment returned to Brontë's voice, "it's fine. Even having Aunt May and Robert Edward here in the house is a nice change of pace, despite their…oddities."

"Something still doesn't seem right about Robert Edward." Crockett turned away from the painting and looked at Brontë. "I'm sorry to keep mentioning it, but his face must belie some kind of evil spirit. It defies every notion of symmetry."

"I think he's just a bizarre, asymmetrical person—I mean, look at Grandfather, Grandmother, and Kordelia; we're an odd family with mixed success when it comes to physiognomy. And, as I mentioned, he arrived with a letter of introduction from my grandfather, so his appearance starts to seem very normal after looking at it." She smiled. "To be honest, the thing that makes me most uncomfortable is how quickly he and Dexter became friendly."

"I noticed they get along well."

"They do. I think it's perhaps their connection as old men who dress like they're part of a children's dramatic production."

Crockett was relieved Brontë lightened the atmosphere; the family portrait had filled him with a sense of impending dread. "The entire lot of you seems to be something from Shakespeare, Martha especially," he said.

Brontë nodded. "Poor Martha, she's always been under duress. As soon as Grandfather remarried Grandmother, she's been harassed. I told you how jealous Grandmother is."

"I'm surprised it's lasted this long, to be honest. A forty-year feud is one of epic proportions."

"I suppose Grandmother's love and, therefore, her jealous passions never extinguished. When Grandmother met Grandfather, she was very young. His money and her dreams of having a manor and an estate overwhelmed her.

She retains a belief that anyone can pull themselves up by their bootstraps and marry rich, which is, I think, why she's so unkind to you about your caste." Brontë glanced at Crockett sympathetically. "She says she fell for Grandfather's charm and looks instantly. For her it was a true, youthful passion—I suppose that kind of attraction is a force of nature."

As Brontë said these words, her eyes locked onto Crockett's. The young man felt his neck grow hot. Self-consciously, he looked downward and smoothed his trousers. Brontë started and turned her attention to an old table laid with chipped china pieces. Neither could think of any words, even trite ones, to resume the conversation.

In the prolonged silence, Crockett's mind blossomed with innumerable hopes, aspirations, and prognostications. He and Brontë could be together—despite her coming from some wealth, a landed family—they could move to London, take up a flat near Petrarch's. Petrarch had said to stay away, not to entertain even a passing fancy for Brontë, but…But.

"Do you know anything about your own family? I know you grew up on the streets, but are there any memories of your mother and father?" Brontë's voice conveyed tenderness.

Crockett spoke a bit too quickly in response, relieved the romantic spell was broken, the tension released. "No, there never was anyone," he said. "I always was in a poorhouse or children's home. When I met Petrarch, I had just been moved from a child farm into the city; I was growing older and they needed space, so they thought I may find work in a slaughterhouse or shoveling coal. I was doing my best to fit in with the new boys. They ran around and made money pickpocketing when there was no work. Used to the country life, it wasn't something I had a propensity for. I suppose I shall always retain some of the more muted, country mood of my childhood." Crockett smiled faintly at Brontë.

"As Petrarch mentioned last night, I met him one of my first days in London." Crockett suddenly realized that his Dickensian story only enlarged the social gulf between them. Rapidly, he turned the topic to his mentor. "I thought he was very interesting, Petrarch that is. He was my mark that day, so I followed him. He's very keen, so it was hard to get around to the act of thievery. And as I watched him, I admired him. He's very witty and warm with a sharp mind. I finally made my move in the public house, but he spun around before I could get close. He said, 'My dear boy, you really are a terrible pickpocket. I've been waiting for you to make your effort for some time. Why don't you come home with me for a nip of tea instead? I can at least give you a bite to eat.'

"That afternoon we had Earl Grey and biscuits and chatted. He showed me his library. I'd never seen so many books." Crockett smiled with pleasure, remembering his first time seeing the wall of gold and leather bindings. "He asked if I would like to borrow one, but I had to tell him I couldn't read." Crockett felt emotion come into his voice—in front of Brontë, he tried to push it down to keep up a reassuring, masculine presence. An expression of affection for another man was much worse than a fear of yellow birds. "He then offered to teach me—I don't think he thought I'd ever come back, but I did. I came back twice a week. His wife grew sicklier shortly after, and it forged the strong bond between us—I'd often stay late with both of them, help them with chores, meals, many of the things I'd had to do in my life on the child farm. He was very impressed with how quickly I learned. When I turned sixteen, he offered me a place as his assistant with a small stipend and a room in his home. He was the first one who ever showed me real kindness."

"That's a really lovely story." The images of Crockett's childhood formed before Brontë in a warm, nostalgic tapestry; it was a romantic mix of tragedy and compassion. "I mean it's wonderful that you two found each other in times of need. Petrarch is a great man. A sharp mind is an excellent way to describe him. He's much more intelligent and wittier than a majority of the guests we entertain here."

"Even he thinks there is something afoot with this Beatrice mess. I have to say that, while your initial thoughts about your grandfather being murdered have become less probable, the possibility that there is an interest in his fortune is becoming more believable." Crockett put his hands behind his back and looked up in contemplation. "I just can't make any sense of poor Beatrice. Why would someone do that…?"

Brontë mused on this for some time. A bird crossed in front of the small window, causing a brief shadow to flicker on the wall.

"I'm sure I don't know. Even if Grandfather wasn't killed and the trick with the séance was an inappropriate joke spearheaded by Kordelia, Beatrice's slaughter was a direct, monstrous action. It's a peculiar horror, a dead fish, but, in our family, it represents something deeply disturbing—an evisceration of a beloved family member."

Crockett began pacing in the room. "Could it have been intended to scare someone into…into what?"

"My guess," Brontë said slowly, "is that someone wanted the will read with haste. Grandmother is extremely superstitious; I mean, my goodness, she wants to entomb an empty box to appease the house spirits for Grandfather. Perhaps whoever is behind this thought it would push her into moving the proceedings along more rapidly out of fear."

"That's a very good thought…" Crockett avoided a baseball glove on the floor. "So, someone wanted to scare your grandmother. This someone needed to know how to cleanly gut a fish, find a sword, and go into the main sitting room to kill Beatrice at night."

Brontë rubbed her temples in contemplation. "Beatrice would never make a sound. The only threat of noise is making the beads around her cage jangle too loudly."

"Hmmm," Crockett shook his head. "And the evisceration took place entirely in the main hall."

"Someone may have fish remnants on their clothing, however."

"Indeed." Crockett's brow furrowed; his caterpillar eyebrows knitted together. "Perhaps I can check the laundry to see if there is anything suspicious there." He ceased his pacing and drew closer to Brontë. "Petrarch thinks that there is also something odd about the tomb key, the fact that it's missing. Do you think the will reading and the key are linked in some way?"

"I don't know how they could be." Brontë frowned. "As my grandmother said, it's been decades since the tomb was opened. Unless, perhaps, something of value was placed in there by Baron Von Bunson."

"Who was possibly killed by your grandfather."

Brontë let out an exasperated breath of air. "It's all so tangled, isn't it? I keep thinking it's someone in the house, but the past keeps coming back in these echoes."

"Like that horrifying song."

"'The Duck Man of the Old Hat'?" Brontë laughed. "Don't tell me that still has you scared."

"It's a terrifying song," Crockett said defiantly.

"Most German rhymes are. Have you ever heard 'My Mother Killed a Horse with a Snake Tooth'? That's another unsettling one."[24]

"I can't say I have." Crockett looked confusedly at Brontë.

"There's actually a German word for killing a horse with a snake tooth—*toterpferdeschlangenzahn*—which to me seems an impractical word."

"Indeed." Crockett, in the ensuing silence, counted to three softly to himself before he felt he could quickly and necessarily change the direction of the conversation. He wanted to continue discussing the mystery, as it seemed their exchange was precipitating an important discovery. "So, could we conject that your grandfather's death and the séance aside, someone killed Beatrice to precipitate the reading of the will, which may be tied to getting into the family tomb?"

"It's not a bad idea," Brontë said admiringly. "To be honest, the séance fits the motive as well, a play on the house's obsession with the occult. It's actually a marvelous idea, Mr. Cook."

Crockett turned away. Brontë saying his name with such warmth brought an embarrassingly large smile to his lips. "So now it's a matter of finding out who is interested in the will and the money." As he said this, he felt a slight pang of remorse knowing that the family had nothing…It was not his place to relay this to Brontë, but the small unspoken lie caused him discomfort.

"Which could be anyone," Brontë said defeatedly. "Everyone in the house, including me, would be interested in the money and the estate. Aunt May wouldn't inherit too much, but she would most likely get a small sum. My

---

[24] Again, Earhart mistranslated another German rhyme, which actually is called "My Aunt Murdered a Llama with a Knife-Shaped Snake."

father and mother would be freed of Hawsfeffer Manor and could return to Winterbourne House, which is in much better condition. I would most likely inherit something in the process. Perhaps Kordelia being the second-born granddaughter and Robert Edward are the only two I would put out of suspicion in terms of gaining something from the will reading."

"I suppose that makes you my prime suspect."

Brontë laughed loudly.

Crockett was lost in a blossoming affection as he watched her. Everything about the moment was as beautiful as a painting—her crinkled eyes, the paleness of her skin highlighted by the blush of red from laughter, the way her delicate hand flew to her mouth in an act of light embarrassment. This morning she had also chosen to wear trousers. They gave a faint outline to her thin hips and small waist.

Brontë looked up and caught Crockett's admiring gaze. Her face immediately turned crimson and both, again, fell into a pregnant silence.

Not wanting to live in an uncomfortable tension, Crockett spoke quickly to alter the mood, "You had mentioned you think it could be someone outside the house, a different presence than those gathered here."

Brontë shook her head. "I'm not sure. But I do know my family, and I don't think that any of them are capable of this. Robert Edward has a secure alibi—he is the only one I cannot vouch for. I was trying to think of someone else that could have been interested, but it could just be fanciful ideas. I may be as batty as the local constabulary investigating circus folk."

Crockett smiled; he did his best to avoid Brontë's gaze so as not to cause another tense moment. To avert this, he threw his glance across the room.

The sun had come out and bright rays shone through the small window high above them—one spark of light fell over a pile of objects, a bright silver sword glinting in the glow. The color in the young solicitor's face faded.

"Crockett," Brontë said quickly, "are you all right?"

But Crockett was already running across the room. The sword was in a pile of other weapons—pieces of antiquity, discarded for years in the far corner of this family vault.[25] Tentatively, he picked up one of the blades and examined it. It was as he thought. He had seen the shape, the handle, the taper of the blade before.

"What is it?" Brontë caught up to him and whispered quietly in his ear.

Crockett turned slowly; his face darkened. "Brontë, I think I know where the weapon came from that killed Beatrice."

Brontë's expression suddenly went from shock to deep thoughtfulness. She stepped away from Crockett and walked distractedly in a small circle.

"Someone took the weapon from down here," she said quietly.

"But, once again, anyone could have come down to grab it." Crockett clenched his fists in frustration.

"No," Brontë said picking up her walking pace. "Not everyone has access to this room. There is a key—I had to retrieve it from Father so that we could enter this morning."

Crockett started. "Is it usually locked?"

"Yes," she said. "My grandmother gave the key to my father yesterday. I don't know if you recall. She said she needed something from down here."

"So, we need to talk to your father..."

"*I* need to," Brontë said, ceasing her pacing. "He trusts me, but I don't think he'd speak freely if you were there. He won't mention anything unless I can bait him into incriminating himself."

Crockett's face dropped. "You don't think it was your father, do you?"

Brontë looked at Crockett with determination. "I told you, Crockett," she said swiftly, "it could be anyone."

---

[25] In the original draft, Earhart used this space to tell a prolonged story of the blade's history, including a largely fabricated story about how it was used by King Richard II to shave a fox in a bet with the Duke of Scotland. Due to the egregious amount of historical errors in the story, it was deleted for the published draft. However, the editor would like to note that the fox's name in the tale was Gibbldybibbits, which seems worth mentioning here.

12

A Prime Suspect

Crockett's mind overflowed with conflicting theories about the previous night, the séance, and the death of Beatrice as he returned to the folly wing.

The success of Brontë and his plan relied heavily on her father divulging what had happened to the key the previous night. If he was in fact guilty, that would be information that could bring things to a climax. But would Brontë be safe? He'd already taken Beatrice's life; what if it escalated further? Especially with his uncontrollable anger? And was the motive that he wanted the family fortune, which didn't exist?

Thoughts clouded his attention so deeply that he didn't notice Kordelia in the hall until he had stepped on her dainty foot. The girl squealed.

"My goodness, your head is a foot bath," she said fighting tears.

"I'm sorry?"

"It's an old Swiss saying—it loses its effectiveness translated to English, I suppose."

Crockett looked at her quizzically. "Do you….ever attempt to make a conversation that others can follow?"

"Perhaps I am leading correctly, and it is their obligation to follow better," Kordelia said. Upset about her foot, she turned and began walking away.

As her footsteps trailed away, Crockett recognized the opportunity the encounter gave him to gain more information. He spun quickly and called after the youngest Winterbourne. "What were you doing in this wing?"

"Looking!" This was all she said before coming to the end of the long hall and disappearing from view.

There was only a moment of isolation in the dark hallway before Petrarch peeped his head out of his room and beckoned for Crockett to join him.

The old man was in the midst of calisthenics, his protruding belly circled with a large sweat mark. He was breathing heavily, wiping his forehead with one of the many gloves Kordelia had left around the house.

"Did you find the key?" Petrarch asked between breaths.

"No." Crockett crossed the room and sat on the bed. He had so many things to tell the old man but no idea where to begin.

"I didn't think you would." Petrarch ceased his exercises and looked out the windows clouded with dirt. "That key is…well, there's more to it, my boy."

"More to it?" Crockett kept his gaze locked on Petrarch. "What are you talking about, Petrarch?"

Petrarch turned. "Well, I didn't think you'd find it, you see, because…I have it."

For one, infinitesimal moment, Crockett's heart stopped. An obscuring, otherworldly cloud filled the room. Reflected on its pale face he saw a second, phantom Petrarch appearing in intermittent flashes like lightning. In the first flash, the secretive old man was in the foyer, blade in hand, carving the poor corpse of Beatrice. In another, he witnessed Petrarch upstairs at the time of the séance; guided by an oral map of the house from Bixby Hawsfeffer, he found the closet, the phonograph, and set the prank of the old German rhyme into motion.

"You…?" Crockett said softly.

Petrarch shook his head. "I did hope that it would have a dramatic effect, but," he smiled wryly, "I assumed you'd give me the benefit of an explanation."

Crockett could only look at the old man pensively. In all their years together, this had been the only moment when he had felt a tremor in the trust that existed between them. "You couldn't have…"

"To make things more transparent," Petrarch interrupted him sharply, "I should say I have 'a' key."

"'A' key?"

"Passed on to me many years ago."

"When?"

Petrarch exhaled. "Lucinda gave it to me at the same time she gave me the note."

Crockett's face turned red. "Why didn't you say this when you mentioned the note?"

"A hunch," Petrarch sighed. "Crockett, I was going to tell you after we met with Corinthiana, but you gave such a quick, logical explanation about the tomb key being missing that I forgot about it."

"So, you didn't mention it to Corinthiana because…"

"It's one of the few things I remember about Lucinda's visit," Petrarch said. "That is to say, I didn't remember until all of this came up again when Bixby died. She gave me the note; she was very distracted. But then," the old man's eyes clouded, as if he was peering into the distant past, "she said, 'Petrarch, protect this. Don't give it to anyone until he's dead.'"

There was a tense silence. Crockett stroked his chin. "So, she wanted it protected from Bixby Hawsfeffer? But why?"

"I don't know." Petrarch shook his head. The old man looked tired. It was a rare occurrence for him to look his full seventy-five years.

"How very odd…" Crockett rose from the bed and paced the room. "But how could the key and her note be related? The note is…it seems to be a trite wish from a mother to son."

"Do you think it means something else?" Petrarch looked up hopefully.

"Let's look at it again," Crockett said excitedly.

Petrarch ran to his briefcase. Again, he had to dump the contents before he could find the crumpled bit of parchment. The two men placed in on the bed and read through it several times. Neither could find any secret purpose to it. Lucinda's words simply asked her son, Pip, to visit her resting place when he returned to the family home.[26]

When they finished rereading, both sat in silence. A heaviness descended on the discussion, a dark cloud of mystery. Had the death of Beatrice and the disappearance of Bixby Hawsfeffer begun all those years before? But then, what did the note mean?

Petrarch spoke first. "Let's take a step back from the current events. It may behoove us to examine the note and key at a distance."

Crockett nodded. He paced the room as Petrarch spoke.

"Before her death, Lucinda came to my office with a note for her estranged son along with the key to the family tomb." Petrarch's speech was slow, methodical. "The note is for her son, should his father die, and she was very adamant that it not be given to anyone *until* the father's death."

Crockett's frenetic pacing slowed. He took a deep breath; simply hearing Petrarch's calming voice and the facts of the case helped pin down his wild imagination.

"We know," Crockett said, "that Lucinda disappeared under mysterious circumstances."

"In the river."

"So," Crockett came to a halt. He fixed his gaze on Petrarch. "Perhaps she knew her time was coming to an end. She wanted to give her son a last message and protect it before her husband...made her disappear."

"Oh," a great, grief-filled sigh escaped Petrarch. "That is tragic. Could my friend, Bixby Hawsfeffer, truly have been that villainous?"

Crockett turned his attention to the large windows. Outside, the emerald lawn sprawled out of his line of vision. His mind clicked and turned, words

---

[26] If you have not completely given up on gathering clues in the mystery, here is the text of the original note from chapter five—*My Dearest Child, / It would appear that my fears were realized. In this event, I hope this letter finds you and that history has not made the contents less precious. / If your father is dead, you must come home. Find me where I rest and sing, like we used to, the old rhyme of "Duck Man of the Old Hat," and think of the games we played when you were young. / Although time is not kind, there is always a chance to make amends for past wrongs. I hope you will have the insights and the ability to do so for myself and your father. / Love always, Mummy*

forming into vague ideas, like a puzzle box being manipulated to find a solution. There was some fleeting idea in his head that couldn't quite be held long enough to examine.

"Petrarch," he said softly, "this exercise was very beneficial. I think we should take a more formalized approach to all of this, not just Lucinda's note. Let's review what we do know, because Brontë and I have discovered things this morning which also appear to be very important."

"My word!" Petrarch proudly smiled. Between Crockett's faint-free behavior, and his calm, logical manner in dealing with Lucinda's note, he felt his young apprentice was growing up from moment to moment.

The grief about Bixby faded quickly. He shot up into the air with a gleeful shout. "Well, my boy, let us proceed logically. I'll do jumping jacks and you state the facts!" Petrarch hopped in the air, his heavy arms flapping up and down.

Crockett steepled his fingers; he spoke authoritatively. "We know that Bixby Hawsfeffer died one week ago in the river. He drowned, despite being in good health and a decent swimmer. Brontë mentioned there were gunshots in the afternoon, but there was never any correlation between them and the death of her father."

"August shoots several times a day. A gunshot is not something odd in this house." Petrarch was already so out of breath from the effort of the jumping jacks that the words came out between gasps.

"Two weeks before his death, Bixby came to you with the will. But it wasn't the real will, the truth; it was a softened version that didn't come to the full admission that everything he had was gone."

"Huufffff," Petrarch groaned.

"Upon going home, he made a second document which revealed the truth but," Crockett suddenly grew excited, "he wanted you here!"

Petrarch gave up his exercises and sat on the bed. He smiled broadly and attempted to speak, but nothing came out. He was panting heavily; the effort of sitting erect was burdensome.

"What this means, Petrarch, my dear friend, is that you are vital to… whatever it is that's going on."

"Water...?" Petrarch mouthed.

"You think water is the key? The river? The drowning?"

"Drink," Petrarch groaned, making a grotesque face.

"Poison!" Crockett started. "Bixby was poisoned...It fits in some ways. It would explain how he wasn't able to swim to safety."

"Me!"

"Yes! Petrarch, I know. It's vital that you are here but why? Is it Lucinda's note? Or is it the key? Why would the key be so important, though? We went through that already..."

"Get. Me. Water."

Petrarch flopped back on the bed, with a final great exhalation. Crockett jumped to attention and fled from the room. He had a glass of water by his own bedside. Once procured, he returned to Petrarch's collapsed form and forced him to take a sip.

It took time for the old man to regain his bearings. After a deal of huffing, puffing, and wheezing, he was able again to sit upright and focus on the conversation at hand.

"Sorry, my dear boy. I get a little too overenergized during exercises every now and again. Jumping jacks used to be my specialty, but now..." Petrarch raised his arm and shook the loose skin on its underside. "You wouldn't believe I was the same man from all those years ago."

Crockett nodded, the pieces of the puzzle box in his head sliding into new patterns. There was a hypothesis forming in his mind, a whisper of an idea. This meeting with Petrarch, his conversation with Brontë, the sword, the paintings in the basement, the wildness of the idea of poison, all came together to form a bizarre, nebulous solution. The idea was perhaps plausible...but not worth discussion, not at this stage. If it weren't true, he'd look as if he were completely daft, creating theories from the ether. He had no desire to look like a lunatic in the eyes of either Petrarch or Brontë, his master and the woman he'd developed a warm affection for over the course of the past several days, especially since Brontë already knew he was rather skittish.

But, if what he thought were true, Brontë's mission with August would be a dead end. He suspected that August returned the family vault key to Corinthiana, who put it securely away in a place only a few would know and be able to access.

As Crockett evaluated all the clues, Petrarch eyed him interestedly.

"Are you all right, Crockett? You seem lost in thought."

Crockett jerked from his scheming reverie. "I am," he said emphatically. "I think an overactive imagination is all." He continued, "I haven't told you yet, Petrarch, but I think Brontë and I found the murder weapon—or at least its sibling."

Petrarch started. "Where? How?"

"We found a sword in the family vault that matches the weapon used against Beatrice. It was a bit of a lucky find—the sun caught the arms collection at just the right moment."

"You're sure?"

"Brontë's going to ask her father what he knows. We think he was the last one to have the key to the vault with all the weapons."

Petrarch grunted. "Another key, another turn in the labyrinth."

Doubting his own meandering theory, Crockett turned to Petrarch. "Do you think it could be August?" he asked.

"Augüst," Petrarch said distractedly. "It could be. There is motive—his belief in the family fortune. He also carried the emotional weight of being trapped in this old house with June's family for many, many years; that kind of stewing would make anyone homicidal. He could have shot Bixby Hawsfeffer in his boat and thought he'd gotten away with it. Then, of course, Corinthiana delayed everything, meaning that the money kept slipping from his grasp. If Bixby Hawsfeffer confided in him that I have a second copy of the tomb key, the killing of Beatrice could have been committed to draw that out from me and complete the burial so that he could finish the affair once and for all."

"That all makes sense. He also knew the house well enough to plan the séance scheme."

"And he's a sportsman. He'd know how to gut an animal like poor Beatrice."

The wild theory Crockett cultivated earlier, vanished in the light of this cold, hard logic. Without thinking, he chuckled to himself.

"Something funny, my boy?"

"I had an idea earlier, a fatuous one. When we lay out the facts, it seems even more so." Crockett rose from his seat next to Petrarch and paced to the window. "I think Kordelia might be infecting me with oddness."

"In this house oddness is contagion." Petrarch lifted himself up and waddled beside his young apprentice. "It seems like we have a buttoned-up idea, but I think we are merely seeing a mountain peak thrusting up from a gray mist. There are several individuals in this house who have an air of mystery about them."

"Robert Edward," Crockett said.

"May, Martha, Dexter…"

Crockett laughed humorlessly. "In that case, I'll keep entertaining my bizarre theory. With what we've seen, there may be no explanation too grandiose, too full of lunacy."

"That, my boy, is what I'm afraid of. If no key is found this afternoon, I will make it known I have a copy." Petrarch finished the rest of the glass of water in one gulp and handed it to Crockett. "I still find it a bizarre coincidence the key and the note are somehow tangentially involved in this, but, as we discussed, they could also be unrelated."

"You think revealing the key may draw the killer out? Or give us more clues?"

"I think it will provide new evidence." The old man rocked back and forth on his heels. "Find out what Brontë discovered from her father, but I also think we should start looking backward."

Crockett instinctively looked behind him.

"To the past, Crockett. To the past."

"You think the answer is there?"

"I think the beginnings of it are, if only to discover more about the money, where it came from, and where it went. Perhaps it is Au*güst*, but we have the wrong motive. Let's not rest yet. I feel the game may be just beginning."

13

Sleuthing

The key was not found.

In the afternoon, the disgruntled parties rested in the sitting room, exhausted. August had spent hours searching. When unsuccessful in his designated part of the house, he moved to others. Corinthiana made an effort at seeking out the key, but when she came across one of the many scarves she used to put around Beatrice's bowl, she was so overcome with emotion it took twenty-three handkerchiefs to dry her tears.[27]

Brontë and Crockett interacted briefly after their own adventure. It was a very short exchange, enough for Crockett to understand Brontë had not spoken to her father about the weapon.

Outside, the weather matched the tone of the house—stuffy, stagnated, still. Simply sitting on the pink couches of the great room caused rivulets of sweat to pour down Crockett's neck. June kept instructing Martha to open and close the windows, unsure whether the hot breeze from outside would cool the house or make it warmer.

In this sweaty stillness, Crockett rose from the couch with the intention to clear his head. He knew there could be no advancement in the case with

---

[27] In times of great distress, a score of handkerchiefs was considered a respectable amount to use to show one's grief. Corinthiana's twenty-three was, even for the time, a bit excessive.

everyone at rest. All parties were silent or gathering their own thoughts; no one was in the mood to speak openly about the events of the day or the past. Corinthiana was about the house, but he felt it was indecorous to speak to her about what woke her and led her to discover Beatrice. Her current emotional state was dire, a continuous string of "awrks" and tears leaked from her as she slowly paced from one end of the house to the other.

The next move in the game would come in the evening. Petrarch would divulge the truth of his key, and Brontë would have retrieved all she could from her father. That would be all that was needed—from that point, they could leap into a fresh perspective on their investigation.

Crockett was on the verge of abandoning any further contemplation of the case, but, when he rose, his eyes settled on Beatrice's opulent bed, and he remembered a piece of his discussion with Brontë—they needed to look for evidence of the killing in the laundry. Although Crockett's detective novels weren't guidebooks, they did seem to make it clear that some kind of sleuthing was always required to gather additional clues. The laundry was most likely at the back of the house, near the servants' quarters. At the very least there had to be a towel or discarded linen which held some traces of the catastrophe.

He approached Beatrice's bed and did a cursory search; nothing had been removed or sullied. Despite the fish sleeping in a bowl of water, Corinthiana had filled the gilded cage with enough amenities and comforts to rival his own sleeping arrangements. Two of Beatrice's silk pillows were thrust to the back, and it looked as though the silken sheet used to wrap her bowl was slightly mussed. The bowl itself was removed by Martha immediately after the event; it appeared nothing else had been taken. The criminal had obviously been hurried, but as was typical of cases of fishicide (Crockett assumed), there was no clear evidence of a struggle.

"Ze bed vas ruffled," Robert Edward said, seeing Crockett's interest. "But no vun could find anyzing missing!"

Crockett thanked Robert for his help and turned his attention toward the back hallway to the kitchen. He knew somewhere in the servants' quarters there was a pile of linens that was worth seeking out. Something had to

BEATRICE

carry the mark of horror that would have been left as a sign of Beatrice's demise.

Crockett avoided the general area of the kitchen after his first interaction with Martha on his way to get water. Prior to his nightmare about the carriage master and his canary, one entire dream had been about him running through a dark hallway where the only light was Martha's gleaming eye, which pursued him no matter how quickly he ran. It ended with him falling into a large pie[28] and celebrating Christmas, but, prior to the pastry, he had been quite terrified.

It was this very eye that met his gaze as he entered the kitchen. Not only the eye, but its host, Martha, covered in blood, hacking at the shank of a large animal. He'd hoped her poor eyesight would have allowed him time to quickly slip away; however, Martha focused her full attention on the young solicitor. She appeared to have a preternatural sense in the kitchen. A scream didn't wake her in the night, but Crockett's soft shoes alerted her immediately when he crossed the threshold.

"What do you want?" she asked. Her one eye narrowed; the other spun more slowly.

"I'm very sorry," Crockett said quickly, backing away. "I was trying to see if there were any traces of gore from the incident with Beatrice. We never fully investigated. Is there a collection of linens for the laundry?"

Martha shook her head. "Me, Dexter, and Awwgooost looked that night, but there was nothing out of the ordinary. It was a very clean job." Whether out of intimidation or simply poor manners, Martha absentmindedly licked some blood off of the cleaver she was using to cut up the meat.

Crockett shivered.

The look of distrust slowly ebbed from Martha's expression. She put down her blade and crossed her arms. "Clever of you to come looking," she

---

[28] Corinthiana's book *What Colour Is Your Spirit?* also had a section on dream analysis, which suggested that dreaming of pies actually belied a deep frustration with one's love life. The pie, then, could have been symbolic of Crockett's own frustration in his relationship with Brontë. The book goes on to say a pie could also mean you are adopted, your grandfather is a bricklayer, or you are simply hungry.

said. "I did laundry the day after—Sundays are always laundry days—and looked through all the rags, aprons, and linens to see if there was anything out of the ordinary."

"Did you find anything?" Crockett asked, still uneasy despite the woman's change in disposition.

She shook her head. "No, I butcher meat nearly every day. It helps align my humors and alleviate my acute female hysteria." To emphasize this, she picked up the cleaver again and slammed it into the wooden table.[29] "There was blood on a number of aprons and work clothes, nothing strange."

Crockett nodded, unsure whether he felt the old maid was less of a suspect, more of one, or simply a psychopath. "Well, thank you."

As he was about to turn away and make an escape, his eye caught Beatrice's fishbowl sitting near one of the maid's oversized blades. A rush of hope gave him goosebumps—the murderer's fingerprints could be pasted all over the clear glass.

"Martha," he said excitedly, "Can I see the bowl?"

The old woman shrugged. "Help yourself. It wasn't my favorite thing to clean. The missus wanted it spotless for Beatrice's burial in the tomb."

Crockett's face fell. "It's clean?"

"Absolutely spotless. Took me the better part of an hour."

The young man's heart sank. Should he ever be at the head of a murder investigation again, he would need to be more proactive in his evidence collection.

He was about out of the room when he heard Martha's grizzled voice call after him, "You want to take a few swings at the meat? It may make you feel better."

"No, thanks, no—I'm quite—no, thank you!" He said this staggering backward, stumbling down the back hall.

---

[29] At the urging of @badgrrlkinzay47, the editor is recommending everyone stop by "Bad Girl Meat Beats" a pop-up therapy shop in Idaho which specializes in meat-based therapies. Ms. Sprout was so inspired by this scene in the original draft of the novel that she immediately earned her counseling license through a Tibetan website so she could turn Martha's hobby into a "Cathartic Meat-Bashing Idahoian Experience."

BEATRICE

Unsettled by the events, he rushed through the sitting room to the front door. Between the eerie conversation, his failure with the fishbowl, the oppressive heat in the house, and the sight of all the slaughtered blood on Martha's clothing, Crockett's desire to flee had grown overwhelming. It was with great relief that he placed his hand on the front door and exited onto the front stoop.

Once outside, the entire length of the house between himself and the maid, he took several deep, stabilizing breaths. Although the air was startlingly warm, each inhalation proved detoxifying, bringing him clarity and pushing out his thoughts of gore, his dream of Martha, and the general, tentative fear that had swelled with each passing day in the manor. The sun on his skin also helped relieve these feelings of trepidation. After a few minutes of calming breathing, the homicidal-looking maid and her cleaver diminished from his thoughts completely. He felt more himself and could focus his attention on the house grounds.

After a few judgmental thoughts about the state of the place (a squirrel was sitting on a pile of discarded newspapers), his attention fixed on the tomb. It looked ominous in the warm, summer sunshine, a bleak, dark marble structure in the middle of an arcadian image of blue skies, white clouds, and emerald grass and leaves. The appearance of a figure near its entrance made him jump. Dexter, holding sharp pruning shears, appeared at the main entry of the melancholic eyesore. Today he was wearing what appeared to be a full suit decorated with the American stars and stripes. On his head he wore a hat which had a papier-mâché eagle perched on its tip.

Crockett felt goosepimples as he realized the groundskeeper was one of the few who had no alibi for the day of the disappearance. In his favorite detective story, *The Fantastic Death of Captain Discord*,[30] the entire murder was solved when the lead detective finally found the rutabaga farmer who

---

[30] *The Fantastic Death of Captain Discord* was never published. This line was actually a plug for Earhart's best friend's novel which they thought would be published at the same time as *Beatrice*. It is rather fitting that while most great writers of this time period referenced Dante, Homer, the Bible, or one of the English Romantic poets, Earhart chose his third-rate writer buddy.

witnessed the magician's disappearance.

Perhaps Dexter was his rutabaga farmer.

The groundskeeper saw the young man approaching and realized he would not have time to avoid the encounter. He let out a loud, obnoxious sigh and turned to face him with a look of utter disgust.

"Hello," Dexter said. Crockett had forgotten the clang of his American vowels, which he had been first introduced to during their earlier discussion over the corpse of Beatrice. Up close he now noted that, in addition to the papier-mâché bird, his hat was covered in a loose coating of downy feathers.

"Hello, Mr. Fletcher. Lovely day."

"Too hot."

"Yes—good." Crockett suddenly realized he should have planned this interview better. "Well," he tried with great difficulty to stop himself, but the only question which came to his mind followed, "Have…you ever….killed anyone?"

Dexter, in spite of himself and his annoyance with the young man, laughed loudly.

"Sorry," Crockett's face turned bright red; indeed, the power dynamic had shifted. "Mr. Fletcher, I'm trying to discover anything we missed. I'm sorry for the clumsiness, but I'll be frank—You were here the day that Master Hawsfeffer died and have access to all the house grounds and," Crockett indicated Dexter's dress, "the family vault where the costume collection is kept."

Dexter's eyes narrowed. "Is this an accusation, then?"

"No, sir. It's an open question."

Dexter shook his head. A small glimmer in his eye revealed an excitement underlying his anger. "I've been an honest, hardworking member of this house for years. Bixby Hawsfeffer took me in, even after the other Bixby—Von Bunson—abandoned me here. I did find Bixby Hawsfeffer's empty boat; Martha was with me. And I do have a key to the vault, but I only go down there for my costumes. They keep me happy, if you must know. This house has been a mess for years—everyone is always feuding. During my time here, I've seen both Lucinda and Bixby Hawsfeffer vanish. There are always thoughts of foul play because the place is a nightmare—but it's not spirits like Miss Corinthiana believes; it's plain old bad people doing bad things." He paused, his gaze locked on Crockett. "But do I think they're killing each other? No. Their rancor is petty, not homicidal." The old man crossed his arms emphatically, then spit, as if declaring this the end of his statement.

Crockett's goosepimples turned to a burning shame. "So…you don't have any idea who could have killed Beatrice?" The young lawyer's voice was an embarrassed whisper.

"As I told you that night, better that fish than one of the people."

With that, he abruptly threw his pruning shears over his shoulder and walked away.

"Thank you, Mr. Fletcher…" Crockett felt horribly embarrassed, not only in the interpersonal interaction, but, again, for his lack of composure under pressure. His fainting had ceased in moments of terror, but he was yet to gain any control over his speech. A detective who began with the question "Did you do it?" was as bad as a lawyer who covered his idiocy under words like "deblightful."

Crockett needed additional air to recuperate from the double failures of his investigations into Martha and Dexter. Perhaps he wasn't cut out to be a sleuth. There was likely nothing going on at all. His own prejudices against spinning eyes and theatrical fashion choices were clouding his understanding of what this house really was—a collection of characters, brought together by tragedies, who, despite mental imbalances, did hold some kind of affection toward each other.

Brontë also fueled his wild theories with her thoughts of murder and mayhem. It could be that the true explanation of the events in the house was simple, not linked to bizarre personal behaviors which were simply general oddities. Dexter's speech made this clear; the house was a mess. For years there had been fighting and chaos—bad people doing bad things. The death of Beatrice, then, was an extension of this, not an anomaly, but rather the natural end to years of pent-up petty frustrations and loathing. It was obnoxious but not homicidal, at least not to humans.

He felt embarrassed for the ludicrous solution he entertained earlier, one which linked the mysterious past to the nefarious present. Petrarch's earlier, rational theory and Dexter's shaming made him realize that there was no need to exert his imagination so far. If there was foul play, it was most likely a simple solution—August knew where the key was, had motive, and was probably expediting the reading of the will. He knew Corinthiana's tendency to fear the macabre; he may have been behind the playing of the nursery rhyme, too. Perhaps he even convinced Kordelia to play along with the blaming, the act of a loyal daughter. The key to the tomb and the note left by Lucinda, then, were coincidental, a forgotten part of the family. It was random happenstance Petrarch was entrusted with them all those years ago.

"Sometimes the shortest way around is the best," Crockett said to himself as he continued his walk.

His course took him toward the Tiddlymouth at the back of the house. The rush of the river calmed his nerves, helped his thoughts race less quickly and sequence more logically. As the river flowed and birds twittered, for a brief moment, the Hawsfeffer case left his focus and he reflected on the coming summer, afternoons in the park in London and long strolls along the Thames.

These thoughts imploded when Crockett arrived at the riverbank. In his musings he forgot that the river was not a topaz, sparkling vision of arcadian splendor but a hideous brown and gray snake streaked with logs and refuse from local farms. It was doubly disappointing, as the banks of the river matched this filthy, unkempt demeanor. The waving brown and green grasses were tangled and thick. They were wild and dense enough to hide the body of a full-grown man.

As his disappointment festered, he saw a figure in white on the bank, nearly hidden in the tall grasses. The ghostly individual stared into the distance, watching the clouds roll in from the west. The atmosphere of the day had entirely changed since he came outside. The wind began to moan, the first sign of another summer storm. The figure was a woman, her loose dress flitting about her in this rising zephyr. When she turned, he recognized the delicate, youthful countenance of Kordelia. Haphazardly, she lifted her arm and waved.

Crockett approached her tentatively, the youngest Winterbourne daughter, the oddest of all oddities at Hawsfeffer Manor. A smile turned up the edge of his mouth as he pondered what non sequitur would fall from her lips when they were close enough to speak. He did not have to wait long. In a few long strides, he was close enough for her golden hair to catch the wind and flap into his face.

"Hullo," she said plainly. "How was Dexter? I saw you two speaking."

Crockett's face turned red. "I think I insulted him. I insinuated he was the murderer of both your grandfather and Beatrice."

"It's not a bad guess. The local constabulary's idea of carnival folk is worse, I would say."

"I would agree." Crockett tried very hard to keep his face from scrunching due to the smell of Kordelia's halitosis. In an effort to avoid the downwind scent, he turned away and looked at the tomb in the distance. He thought back to his early morning chat with Brontë. "Do you miss him?" he asked.

"Miss who?"

"Your grandfather?" He placed his hands behind his back. "Your sister misses him. She told me the other morning."

Kordelia thought for a moment. "No," she said finally. "Brontë was his favorite—she always had more points, as you know." The young girl, in discussing the point system, remembered her breath and covered her mouth self-consciously. "He wasn't very kind—Grandfather—he never liked me much after the cat was set on fire."

"That seems unfair."

"He wasn't pleasant." She looked toward the sky; a sigh, heavy with grief, escaped her. "You know they think he killed several people."

"I heard."

"His first wife and his uncle—they say it was all over money."

"Do you believe them?"

"I tend to believe everything."

"Even the worst."

She paused and focused her full attention on Crockett. Her bright eyes twinkled. "I tend to believe the worst, then be pleasantly surprised."

"What do you think is the worst now?"

"About Beatrice?"

"Yes." Crockett tried to keep his voice from shaking. His goosepimples returned. He felt as if he was on the edge of some great mystery, some truth, about to be unleashed from the young woman beside him.

"I think it's spirits," she said softly. "Real ones—not the fake ones that burned the cat."

"Why do you say that? You don't think it's a person?"

"It could be a person acting on a spirit's power. I've been looking around the house for a better solution, but nothing has presented itself."

"You mean…a person acting on a spirit's power, like a possession?"

"Maybe not the way you think, no." She turned to the water. "The past can possess someone like a spirit, drive them to act against their natural impulses. The past doesn't die, just like ghosts don't. There's a phrase for it in the fortune teller's tongue—*Shubooie kurkbumzurburg.*"

"That's…" Crockett felt unsettled, "that's very wise."

"There's a similar concept in *The Viscount's Ram*. It's discussed during the second meat pie scene in act three."

"Is it what you think, though? It's someone from the past?"

Kordelia transformed. She was suddenly not the impish character he had been with for several days, but a real girl, tired, drained by unhappiness. "I think Grandfather was a bad man. I think he killed them both, Lucinda and our great-uncle. I think this follows. Death makes way for death." Her golden hair blew wildly in a gust of wind. She hesitated. "Can I tell you something?"

"Of course." Crockett gently stepped forward.

But it was at that moment that a shot rang out behind them. A squawk and a thud broke the moment of intimacy between them. They heard August cheer, followed by his heavy footsteps coming over the hill.

The safety of the moment was gone.

Kordelia quickly moved away from Crockett. She looked at him and smiled sheepishly. "It's not over," she said softly, then turned and ran along the riverbank.

August was soon beside him. He clicked his teeth.

"What did she say, my boy? Anything in the way of clearing up the Beatrice mess? You know she killed a cat once, burned it up in a moment of rapturous excitement."

Crockett shook his head. "She didn't say much. She's very cryptic, your daughter."

"I'd say it's a reaction to the Swiss rösti—it makes the head a little," he shook his hand by the side of his head and laughed. "We think a few more weeks in the country will get her right as rain."

A bird flew high above them. August snorted and thrust his gun up to look through the sight. A blast rang out around them.

August roared with laughter again and started singing merrily as the bird fell from the sky. He interrupted his song when he turned to Crockett, his mustache erect with joy.

"It's funny how people can get caught up when a pet dies but love sport like this. Perspective, I suppose."

He trod off toward the river.

Left alone, Crockett looked to the water. It was high up the bank, moving quickly. If Bixby had fallen into its rushing current, it would be difficult to escape, especially if there was some trouble with his heart.

A bright spot of sun rippled on the surface of the brown water, making him think of Kordelia's words about the past.

In that moment, Crockett had no confirmation whether August was a murderer, but he recognized that something in the man was indeed monstrous; he needed to be carefully watched.

14

May's Secret

Kordelia's gloomy outlook appeared to materialize and shroud the Hawsfeffer Estate in mist. Clouds kept rolling in from the west, the wind rising, a soft, intermittent drizzle falling over the countryside. It was a welcome reprieve from the intense heat of the afternoon.

Everyone was in higher spirits when Crockett went back into the house. He greeted those gathered in the sitting room, then went to his room to further contemplate the day and meditate on the afternoon's insights from Kordelia.

In her eyes (and the eyes of many), Bixby Hawsfeffer was a monster. August's role in his disappearance, even if it was cold-blooded murder against his father-in-law, could, in a sense, be justified. Even the death of poor Beatrice, when compared to the atrocities of the patriarch, seemed a parlor game.

But the truth—no matter how much it looked like August was behind the madness—was elusive until he could get Brontë to confirm her father had done it all. Part of him couldn't help but wonder if there was something more—logic led him to August, but his instinct led him to an entirely different conclusion. Despite trying to resist it, the puzzle box in his mind still shifted toward a solution, creating thousands of possibilities, the most ludicrous of them plausible when he was alone in the large house, the only sound the soft rush of wind through the cracks in the windows. Brontë's theory that there was some other mysterious person from outside the house assisting with the chaos stoked the fires of his imagination. He was rent in two, wanting to believe the logical but obsessed and inspired by the possibility of a grandiose plot of transgenerational murder.

After washing his face and putting on his last fresh shirt, Crockett knocked on Petrarch's door to seek counsel. The old man was sitting on his bed in his undershirt and trousers smoking a pipe.

"Your thinking pipe, Petrarch! This must be serious."

"It is, my dear boy! It is! The key—its revelation must be planned precisely. I'm hoping to get a response that we can use to propel our inquiries further."

As Petrarch puffed away, Crockett drifted to the wardrobe in the room and examined himself in the looking glass. He looked pale and wan. In that dim light, he could be mistaken for a ghost.

"I've been doing some sleuthing, Petrarch," he said examining his nose, which looked paler than either his forehead or chin. "This afternoon I was inspired to seek evidence and facts."

"And what did you find?"

"That I'm a terrible detective." Crockett's ears turned red. "I did have an interesting discussion with Kordelia."

"Did she tell you some nonsensical aphorism? Perhaps she saw a bear having tea party."

"She was actually very serious."

A plume of gray smoke swirled around Petrarch. "I don't quite know what to make of her. She seems overtaken by idiocy but, also, at times, as if she's the only one here who is intelligible."

"I would agree with that assessment. She said she thinks her grandfather was a killer."

"A lot of people do. We talked about that on the way here. He very well could be, which makes the case of finding who would want to kill him even more difficult."

"I think, Petrarch," Crockett said with a sigh, "that there was no murder… of a person…in this case. I think there have been a lot in this house, in general."

"If there are any more dead singing ghosts along the river, they'll need a warship to carry them all."

Crockett smiled. "Aug*oust*—"

"Au*güst*."

"Well, he interrupted my conversation with Kordelia, and I think, perhaps, it's as simple as Bixby Hawsfeffer having a heart attack in his boat and Au*güst* trying to expedite the will reading."

"So, you think he's behind the séance and the Beatrice incident? Lucinda's note and key are simply a tangent that made us worry unnecessarily?"

"I do." Crockett said resolutely. "I always jump to conclusions, get carried away, but this time, I think we have enough to believe that it's a simple solution. I had other theories…" Crockett, embarrassed, turned away from the looking glass and toward his master. "Au*güst* has motive and he had the means to do it all."

Petrarch took a long puff from his pipe. "I find it hard to believe Mr. Winterbourne has the brains for anything so complicated. His mustache knows more than he does."

Crockett was taken so off guard by the joke that he choked on his laughter. "You know," he gasped, "I think the most plausible murderer is his mustache."

"It's always who you least expect!"

The two, together, broke into a fit of uncontrolled giggles, each unable to stop as the other erupted into new fits of laughter. By the end of it, they were both on the bed, reclined backwards, Petrarch's pipe lying between them.

Crockett, finally gaining composure, said, "Au*güst* is the most logical explanation, but part of me still *wants* it to be something more…If you'll pardon a young man's musings, there is just too much absurdity in this house for the nefarious presence to be the obnoxious, loudmouthed son-in-law. I spoke with Dexter as well, and he was a staunch pragmatist—very interesting in light of his wardrobe choices. I know the gravitational pull of logic is toward a simple solution, but I feel there's something more to it all."

"So, who would you *want* to blame? If we're going to totally disregard the obvious guilt of the mustache."

Crockett, stifling a chortle, hesitated. His ludicrous theory rested on the edge of his tongue—he felt more confident in the relaxed, jocund atmosphere stating it than he had previously, but something held him back. He still wanted Petrarch to be proud of him, and he didn't want the old man to think he was batty. Just that morning, his master expressed his approval—Crockett didn't want to spoil it.

It was better to stay silent.

"All right, Crockett? You've grown quiet." Petrarch sat up. "Do you think Beatrice was involved? She faked her own death?"

Crockett didn't have time to respond as, at that moment, Brontë appeared in the doorway. Her brown hair hung loosely around her shoulders. She wore an actual dress, muslin with flower embroidered along the hem. Lace, like sea foam, splashed around her collar. Her face was flushed, the radiant bud of youth in full bloom on her white cheeks. A light emitted from her eyes which focused intensely on Crockett.

Petrarch turned idly to see what Crockett was looking on. When he realized the cause of his apprentice's excitement, he sighed. He had tried to warn the young man of the impossibility of the match, of the impropriety of amorous affection for one's clients, but they were young, and infatuation had run away with them both. He did foster some sympathy—he remembered when he fell in love with his own wife all those years before…but he didn't want Crockett's heart broken.

He rose quickly and put himself between the two youths, the only thing he could think of to stifle the electricity passing between their shared gazes.

"Miss Winterbourne!" he said quickly. "Delighted to see you. I'm sorry I'm not fully dressed." Petrarch moved as if he would put on his overshirt, but then did not follow through, instead moving back in the direction of his bed.

"That's fine, Mr. Bluster. It's always a pleasure to see you, regardless of your state of dress." She dipped her neck forward in a show of politeness. Her eyes flicked between Petrarch and Crockett, unsure of which conversational course to take.

"He knows all, Brontë," Crockett said softly. "You can feel free to speak."

A flash of relief crossed Brontë's face. She turned quickly and gently shut the door. Her skirt swished as she moved to the window, as far from prying ears as she could get.

"I spoke with him," she said quietly. "Father."

"Did he admit to having the key to the vault?" Crockett asked.

"Not in the way you would think," Brontë sighed. "I asked him directly about the key and the sword."

"What was his excuse?" Petrarch asked.

"He laughed and talked in circles. You know Father's…well, blusteriness and arrogance. He said he did have the key at one point, but he had nothing to do with Beatrice. He again opined that a cod's hardier constitution would have survived the attack."

"I think any fish would have succumbed in this particular scenario," Crockett said flatly.

"But then," Brontë's voice fell even lower, "he immediately turned my attention to everyone else—Robert Edward, Martha, Dexter, anyone who could have possibly taken part."

"Did he have reasons?" Petrarch puffed on his pipe.

Crockett tried to keep his focus, but his eyes kept listlessly traveling to Brontë's exposed collar bone.

"Nothing concrete…Robert, of course, is generally suspicious. He came into town and things became stranger and stranger. Martha and Dexter—his basis there was no stronger than pointing to a recent mystery novel he read entitled *Buttled to Death*."

"Which was about?"

"A butler who buttled someone to death. Hence, his predilection to blame the help."

"How does one buttle someone to death?" Crockett momentarily awoke from his study of Brontë's form.

"Well, the twist was the butler took his master hostage and made him buttle till he died. You know—changing lots of sheets, serving tea incessantly, and answering doors on opposite sides of the house in quick succession.

It wasn't a very complicated plot. I preferred the author's first novel *The Murderer Is the Son*."[31]

"The writer is not very creative, is he?"

"No," Brontë said, "but he does describe rhododendrons quite nicely."

"Sorry to interrupt," Petrarch said politely, "but popular literature aside, did anything actually sound like important information?"

Brontë nodded. She threw a nervous glance to the door before lowering her voice (yet again) and continuing, "The only thing that struck me as new was about," her voice shook slightly, "Aunt May."

"Aunt May…"

"Father knows what happened, you see. Why she left the convent and has been so…odd as of late."

"And?" Petrarch and Crockett asked together.

Brontë shifted nervously. "I'm sorry, it's just…It's a tawdry story."

"I assumed May wasn't what she appeared to be," Petrarch said gruffly. "The most self-righteous are often the ones who have fallen farthest."

Brontë nervously rung her hands. Her gaze drifted to the corner of the room, where a remarkably large cobweb was dancing in the breeze of the drafty window. "She was in the convent," Brontë started slowly, "but then she met someone…"

Petrarch and Crockett leaned forward.

"You see, the convent is out, away from the town. The grounds abut the land of a wealthy farmer in West Butterfieldshire-upon-Furburry. Often the novitiates wander the grounds on walks. It's actually encouraged by the higher nuns—the natural setting, the quiet, drawing people into a state to better commune with God."

"A good walk in the country does heal the soul," Petrarch said jovially.

"Well," Brontë touched her collar nervously, "it seems, she found communion, but…it was…not with anything otherworldly."

---

[31] *Buttled to Death* and *The Murderer Is the Son* are more references to Earhart's friend's works. These novels were actually published but only sold a few dozen copies, once again a bulk to Earhart's mother, Adelaide, who appeared to be a patron of woefully bad writers.

"The farmer?" Crockett blurted. This elicited loud "Shhhs!" from both Brontë and Petrarch.

"Yes!" Brontë whispered. "The farmer!"

"But what would be—"

"Who is married..." Brontë croaked. "She...she...is an adulteress."

The room fell silent. Crockett nervously eyed Petrarch. Being raised outside upper social circles, he didn't know how to react to a lady having fallen into an affair. In his life on the streets and in the country house, it was a casual occurrence to hear any number of men and women making the beast with two backs in every corner of the places he found respite, but in more polite society, it remained something he had yet to confront.

"How long has your family known?" Petrarch asked softly.

"They found out just before Grandfather died. Aunt May went to my mother and told her the whole story. But..." Brontë took a deep breath, "the interesting thing is that the farmer promised to leave his wife and marry Aunt May...if..." Here she paused. She looked between Petrarch and Crockett. Despite the seriousness of the conversation, a subtle joy, an earnestness crept into her voice. "If she could secure the debts that my grandfather owed to him."

Crockett put a hand to his forehead. "My goodness..."

"Oh dear..." Petrarch dropped his pipe to the ground.

"You saw how my grandmother acted when talking about money. You can imagine that conversation within the family. May possibly saw her only recourse was to kill my grandfather and collect her own inheritance with the hope that money would be put back into the estate to settle the debts."

Petrarch and Crockett exchanged a gaze. The family was yet to learn that they were destitute, with not a shilling to their name.

"That is a serious motive." Petrarch sat up and began to pace the room. "But would she have the resources to disrupt the séance and kill poor Beatrice?"

"I think," Crockett nervously wrung his hands, "that Au*güst* may simply be redirecting the blame."

Petrarch and Brontë both looked at him intensely.

Crockett continued, his vocal cadence growing faster. "He is the only one that makes it all match up, you see. He knew the house and how to make the phonograph go; he also knew how to gut an animal cleanly like poor Beatrice. Of course, the final nail in his coffin is him having the key and access to the family vault. Dexter also had one, but we spoke. He's fiercely loyal and has had access for ages. It—it…" Crockett stuttered at the end of the statement. It suddenly came to his mind that Brontë had not been told of Lucinda's note. He quickly pondered making it known, but before he could say anything, Brontë interjected.

"That's just it, Crockett! Father finally began talking about the key. He gave it back to Grandmother before the murder. Grandmother returned it to him to pass on to me for our search."

"Diggleshroot!"[32] Petrarch snorted. "Your grandmother had the key all evening the night of the murder?"

"She did, but…" Brontë paused here for dramatic effect, but it was too pronounced.

"Are you all right, Miss Winterbourne?" Petrarch asked.

Brontë flushed. "Yes, sorry, I was being dramatic but then forgot what I was going to say."

"Your grandmother had the key," Crockett said in hopes of assisting her memory.

"Yes! She did! And—" Having learned her lesson, she kept this pause more contracted, "Father gave it back to her in front of mother, Aunt May, Martha, and Robert; it was a very public moment."

Crockett groaned. "So…it could still be anyone. Everyone but the current occupants of this room and Kordelia saw the key change hands."

"Yes." Brontë bit her lip. "It does close a door, but perhaps there may be more likely alternatives now."

Crockett closed his eyes, deep in thought. "What if," he said very slowly,

---

[32] "Diggleshroot" was not a common exclamation at the time. In the editor's research, no words even close to this were found as Edwardian ejaculations. It is a possibility that this chapter was written while Earhart was intoxicated, as there were more grammatical errors than in other sections, and the original pages smelled like bathtub gin.

"you were right, Brontë. Maybe we need to start thinking larger than one person." He opened his eyes and looked resolutely out the dusty windows. "There are too many variables, too many pieces which would require assistance. The séance is something that couldn't have been executed by a single person."

"That is a possibility." Brontë smiled. "Aunt May and my father *both* could be suspects and in collaboration. There may simply be more than one culprit."

The three remained deep in thought for some time—Brontë pondering the likelihood of her father and aunt working in collusion, Crockett meditating on his personal, more asinine idea of the actual murderer, and Petrarch staring into space, a look of resolve creeping over his features.

After the prolonged silence, Crockett turned to Petrarch. The old man smiled dolefully at him. There was both pride and sadness in his eyes.

"My two young friends," he said warmly, "I think we perhaps…"

But before he could finish, he looked up and saw that Brontë was turned away from him. Her eyes were pools of terror, focused on the door.

Standing in the portal was the hunched form of Martha. When she saw all had turned their attention to her, she licked her lips, a menacing grimace covering her face.

"Dinner is on," she croaked. Her bulging eye spun slowly, ominously in her wrinkled visage. "Perhaps the rest of the family would like to hear your little theories."

15

A Shot in the Dark

A tense moment unfolded as Petrarch slipped on his shirt and coat. Brontë and Crockett looked anxiously at each other as Martha stared, disinterestedly, into the corner of the room. Crockett's neck prickled when her dull gaze shifted to him, the spinning eye seemingly staring through him, into his very soul.

Once Petrarch was settled, they followed Martha through the dim passage and back to the main foyer. On a few occasions, the old woman would look back, her lip curled in a sneer. Despite the foreboding nature of her countenance, Crockett was unsure whether the woman was really a malignant force or simply an oddity with a knack for making those around her feel uncomfortable. This performance was very similar to her butchering, blood-drinking behavior earlier. In truth, she had done a large number of bizarre things, but since he had been in the house, she had also been helpful, coming to Corinthiana's aid when Beatrice was killed, waking from a deep sleep and—

Crockett paused in the hall, briefly. It came back to him with a flash, the old woman's words the night of Beatrice's death—*Is it him?*[33]

---

[33] In the original manuscript, this was typed as "Is it ham?" a direct contradiction to the earlier quotation from Martha. The editor believes this chapter was written when the intoxicated Earhart's thoughts turned to food, as pig meat is never alluded to as a suspect prior to this point in the novel.

That was her primary concern upon waking. Whether from a dream or reality, the fear came to her. He was unsure, but something had shocked the old woman in the midst of danger. Something jolted her old brain into a state of panic.

Him.

But who is the "him"? Was it merely a dream, an induced panic caused by the séance, the commune with the dead, the probable pile of bodies that the house had claimed—Lucinda, Baron Von Bunson, Bixby Hawsfeffer, and now, Beatrice?

Of all the things they had seen and heard over their days in the mansion, Martha's exclamation was the one that seemed most urgent.

Who was she afraid of?

Everyone was seated when they arrived in the formal dining room. The key had not been found, and the momentum of the burial of both Beatrice and Bixby had stalled. All gathered wore looks of fright or anxiety; nervous gestures were visible down the table, from May's clutching at the black lace around her throat, to Robert Edward's twisting of his long, dark curls.

Corinthiana looked the most defeated. She was pale as new-fallen snow, her eyes red from crying. She dabbed her eyes at an even slower, more dramatic pace than usual.

Martha pulled out the seat for Brontë, before shuffling out of the room. When she was gone a heavy silence fell on all the glum party. The only sound was the ticking of the old grandfather clock in the main foyer.

Crockett's attention was drawn toward the head of the table when he heard the rustle of June's dress. She extended a pale hand and gently took her mother's wrist.

Corinthiana sighed and let her gaze slide around the table. Her indifferent stare settled on all with rising tension. Her visual assessment stopped on Crockett, a bit of flush returning to her cheeks.

"Crockett, don't yooou haaave a jaaacket for formal dining?"

Crockett embarrassingly looked down at his white shirt. The mud incident of their arrival had severely limited his wardrobe options. "I'm sorry, ma'am, my good coat was stained the morning we arrived. I don't have much else."

Corinthiana sniffed abruptly (perhaps a substitute for an oral "AWRK!") and let her gaze finish its way around the table.

When she was satisfied, she again sighed and then looked down at the charger set before her. One of her jeweled fingers began to anxiously circle the rim of her wine glass.

"I...aaam aaafraaaid tooo saaay thaaat weee aaare unaaable tooo find theee keeey," she said slowly.

"And there's no way into the tomb without it," August broke in, "other than an act of destruction."

All shifted uncomfortably.

Crockett turned to Petrarch, who was looking placidly at a tray of rolls in the center of the table.

"Grandmother, when was the last time you used the key?" Brontë asked.

Corinthiana stared into the dark for a moment before shrugging her shoulders indifferently. "I neeever did. Theee laaast time waaas when Lucindaaa died."

"All those years ago?" Petrarch asked. "No one put flowers on the tomb... or checked on the inside?"

The realization that these things should have been done swept across Corinthiana's face swiftly. Her mouth drooped slightly, and her left eyebrow twitched upward.

"No," she said matter-of-factly. "No one did those things."

"It perhaps is like in ze home country," Robert said quickly. "Ven ze people die, zey are dead. Ve don't make a party for zem anymore."

August's mustache twitched irritably. "The fact remains, death party or no, that we cannot get into the tomb to rid ourselves of the casket."

"Why does it even matter?" May barked. "There's no body! He drowned. Why did we even have the casket? Let's toss it in the river and move on with it. We should have read the will days ago."

Corinthiana's face flushed. "I will not haaave yooou speeeak of your faaather in such a waaay. Heee aaand Beeeatrice both neeed a plaaace tooo rest."

"In the play I'm reading," Kordelia said dreamily, "they burn the house down."

Something in Kordelia's tone made them all pause. Robert Edward looked at the young girl with fear. May sneered while June tapped her fingers nervously on the table.

"Darling," she finally said, her nails clicking, "this isn't one of your stories, this is a real-life..." She stopped.

"A real-life nightmare," Brontë finished for her. "Mother, the past three days have been brutal in the sheer number of catastrophes. The séance incident alone was a nasty trick, but then to have poor Beatrice..."

Corinthiana bleated at the mention of her beloved companion.

"To have poor Beatrice," Brontë continued on with more energy, "maimed, murdered, so defiled in the house...Someone at this table did it." Brontë's eyes glowed. "What I'm saying is that there is a killer in our midst, someone who's seeking some sort of compensation or revenge, and we need to get to the bottom of it."

"Darling..." June spoke so softly it was barely heard. Prior to Brontë saying it, the truth of the matter remained obscured in the secure shadow of English propriety. Now it sat fully expressed before them all.

To Crockett, it appeared no one moved. Not even a breath was taken at the mention of the accusation. The verbalization of the act as murder was uncomfortable, incredibly unpalatable, even if the victim was a dead-eyed fish.

August broke the silence. His mustache twitched and eyes glittered as he spoke.

"It wasn't me. Brontë has been on this little crusade all day—she came to me," August looked darkly at his wife, "and all but accused me of the violation of poor Beatrice."

"Father, the facts—" Brontë tried to interject but was cut off by May.

"The facts are superfluous," the disgraced nun said in her pinched voice. "No actual person was murdered. Father died in the river, a fitting end to his glib, exhausting existence. It makes sense his death would be a struggle; he made life for all those around him an equally brutal fight for survival." May's nostrils flared. Robert Edward looked nervously out of the corner of his eye, seemingly afraid the older woman would flip the table and attack them all.

"But what if he didn't drown?" asked Crockett. He looked resolutely at Brontë. "What if this is all related because someone wants the money from the estate? What if someone needs the money for some purpose?"

"And what purpose is that?" August's face was red with rage. A vein throbbed on the side of his neck. "Tell me why you thought I would make an end to the old man and go after the herring for dessert."

"A herring treacle!" Kordelia laughed heartily. "It would probably serve well with the ghost biscuits."

"Not now, Kordelia!" For the first time, Crockett noted a prominent vein in June Winterbourne's neck that matched her husband's.

"And vat vould be my reason for killing my dear cousin?" Robert Edward said in a high-pitched voice. "Hoo are ze prime suspects?"

Corinthiana picked up the charger and began to fan herself. Beads of sweat were running down her white, doughy face.

"If I may..." Petrarch stood up and laced his fingers together, placing them on his protruding belly.

All turned to the old solicitor, most with expressions of rage and disgust.

"If I may," Petrarch went on with more purpose, "I would like to state that we have only had brief conjecture about the death of Bixby Hawsfeffer. I know that despite rumors and gossip in the surrounding area, he was dearly beloved by all of you here. Augüst," he said looking directly at the Winterbourne patriarch, still the color of a plum, "he put a roof over your head and provided a warm home for your two beautiful daughters."

"Quite right," August said standing. "He was dearly beloved by me and my family."

"And May," Petrarch said turning, "despite your estrangement, you are a lady of the church. It's known you don't come here often. When could you do such a thing?"

"I hated him," May said flatly, "but I would never hurt him. Or mother's fish."

Crockett kept his eyes on May as Petrarch turned slowly to Robert Edward.

"And Robert Edward, your appearance is the most suspect. Can I ask that you speak for yourself on the question at hand?"

A collective gasp escaped from the party, as if a gas stove had just sputtered to life. Crockett's attention immediately shifted to Petrarch, who he regarded with wonder. Was the old man stating his prime suspect?

Robert Edward looked as if he expected the accusation. He stood, throwing back his black cape with a flick of his wrist.

"I see zat ze xenophobic reputation of England is correct. I shall speak my piece and clear my good name once and for all!" Dramatically his finger shot into the air. He sniffed loudly and opened his mouth in preparation for a long speech when Brontë interjected.

"It's not him," she said quickly. "Not that I care anything for my cousin, but I'm more concerned with us laboring to understand his stumbling, continental accent for the next quarter hour."

"Xenophobic!" Robert yelled again.

"Cousin Robert was here for a brief time before Grandfather died," Brontë continued, "but he went to London on business right before the disappearance and returned just after. Trust me," she said sharply, "he was the first one I suspected. Grandmother told me where he was. Mother corroborated. She was the one who rode with him to the train station."

"So!" Petrarch smiled broadly. "We have ample suspects, but no reason to doubt any of them. I think it's best to resume planning the funeral as soon as possible and put this whole mess behind us. As the only one here active in the law, I see no reason to believe anyone here is capable of the murder of Bixby Hawsfeffer or Beatrice."

With these words, the anger in the room dispelled completely. Even May's sour face showed a hint of a smile.

"Thaaat is aaall well and goood," Corinthiana said warmly, "but there is still no keeey!"

"Oh!" Petrarch smiled jovially. "But there is!" He reached into his pocket and removed a large, brass key.

Crockett's eyes flew around to all those gathered; he conducted quick studies of every individual seated around the table. He hoped someone would show some emotion, some slip in their stable constitution at this revelation.

August looked the most surprised, his heavy jowls shaking in shock—May's smile dropped, her eyes growing into wide, black pools. Robert Edward looked the least interested, his gaze following Crockett's to Corinthiana, who had leapt up (the quickest action Crockett had seen from her during their entire stay) from the table, clapping her hands. Kordelia kept her dreamy, indifferent stare, while June simply smiled, probably delighted the long burial purgatory had ended. Brontë's eyes were locked on Crockett; a deep hurt registered in them.

"You knew?" she mouthed quietly from across the table, pointing to the key.

Crockett leaned forward, ready to speak, but was interrupted by Petrarch.

"I hope you will excuse the theatrics," the old man said, "but I thought it was best to clear the air before I spoke of the find."

"Aaand where waaas it?" Corinthiana giggled happily.

"Believe it or not," Petrarch said, "this evening I returned to my files from Bixby Hawsfeffer and found this buried beneath papers. Bixby must have left a copy years ago when he came to visit."

"By George!" August's mustache shook happily. "Well, what an immense relief!"

Petrarch looked quickly at Crockett, an illegible expression on his face.

Corinthiana's look of joy faded for a moment. She nervously bit her nail. "Perhaaaps weee shooould waaait just twooo or threee more daaays beeefore theee burial."

The feeling of victory in the room immediately dissipated. All eyes flew to the matriarch.

"But vy?" Robert asked petulantly.

Everyone nodded in agreement with their cousin, perhaps the first time since his arrival that the majority feeling toward him was not one of contempt.

A tense expression crossed Corinthiana's features. It looked as if she was being torn in two, some great philosophical battle raging behind her eyes.

The moment passed like a bolt of lightning, however, and a smile returned to her face.

"No, no reeeason," she said brightly. "I just waaanted everyone tooo beee emotionaaally ready." She stood and turned toward the kitchen, her large bosom jiggling as she yelled, "Maaarthaaa! Bring out theee maaain course! Weee haaave reeeason tooo celebraaate!"

#

The plans for the entombment developed rapidly. June wasted no time in calling the vicar even before eating; although he had commitments the next morning, he agreed to meet June the following afternoon to plan the final arrangements. A lightness filled the house for the first time since Crockett and Petrarch arrived. Kordelia, May, Petrarch, and June all played whist together, while August and Robert Edward chatted near the patio discussing politics. Corinthiana sat on the main sofa; mostly she seemed happy, although a few isolated times Crockett looked over at her and noticed the same expression of pain and conflict from dinner had reappeared on her face. The expression, however, always passed quickly. Crockett assumed that it appeared whenever the old woman looked across the room and saw Beatrice's grand bed, its emptiness a reminder of the family's loss.

Immediately after the jovial affair that was dinner, Crockett pulled Petrarch aside to find out his thoughts. The old solicitor was confident in his conclusions.

"My dear boy, as I looked around the room, as I added up the facts, there was only simple addition to be done."

"But earlier we said it may have been two together."

"You did. You and Brontë were getting quite carried away, but you heard me reason it through in the room. Robert Edward is the most suspicious, and he has a very secure alibi. May is spiteful, but who would work with her? She has no allies here. And, as I mentioned before, *Augüst* is a bit too dense to plan something on his own."

"You can't give up!"

Petrarch gently reached out and gripped Crockett's shoulder. The young man's head had fallen in frustration, but his old master lifted his chin with his finger and looked into his multi-colored eyes.

"I love your tenacity, Crockett, but we've both let our imaginations get the better of us. Brontë seduced us both into a game of chasing a phantom murderer. To be sure, she was aided by a number of artifacts—Lucinda's note, the tomb key, the disappearance of Bixby Hawsfeffer, and, of course, the death of little Beatrice." Petrarch sighed. He turned away and looked out the front windows of the house into the twilight. "I apologize for fueling your fire, my boy, with our clandestine conference and my own musings on some secret history. When you assess the facts, there is only a mundane puzzle which hinges on the family fortune. Someone wants money and is playing on Corinthiana's love of the spiritual world to scare her into ending this affair."

"But…Beatrice…" Crockett felt betrayed. He knew in his heart that Petrarch was most likely correct, but…Brontë had lit his soul with a wonderful fantasy, part of which was solving this mystery and taking her as his wife. It was asinine, impossible, but in the moments before dinner, it seemed to Crockett the only way the mad journey at Hawsfeffer Manor could end.

The young man shook his head sadly—he made one last attempt to convince his master that they should continue forward. "Don't you want a resolution, Petrarch? Can you rest not knowing what happened?"

Petrarch's eyebrows knitted together. A note of melancholy came into his voice. "Crockett, I have seen a great deal in my years as a solicitor, and I can say that sometimes it's best to let sleeping dogs lie."

"You think…"

"I think that someone wanted to expedite the end of this, and most of those reasons are actually quite logical. Many have bills to pay—May is in love. There is no reason to think of this as a murder of Master Hawsfeffer; it seems to me that it was simply a fortunate event for members of a family who are all in financial troubles. Even if there is no money, they all fanatically believe in it."

Crockett was crestfallen. "But…"

"And Lucinda's note and key were simply a mother's last attempt to reconcile with her son. I'm sorry to disappoint you, my boy." Petrarch turned from the window and gently patted Crockett's shoulder. "I did do some of my own investigating. I asked Corinthiana what woke her up the night of Beatrice's murder, and she said she wasn't sure. She thought she may have heard something and that pulled her out of bed—she believed it to be a fish-mother's intuition."

"Oh, Petrarch…" Crockett felt a sad resolve creep over him, a resignation that the truth could never be known. The fantasy of his and Brontë's triumph over the Ghost of Hawsfeffer Manor faded into a dense fog. "Perhaps some mysteries simply aren't meant to be solved. It doesn't help that neither you nor I are detectives. I can't even conduct an interview without bleating an accusation." Crockett winced remembering his conversation with Dexter.

"I agree, Crockett." Petrarch gently gripped his apprentice's arm, "I think it's best for us to leave this place. The atmosphere…and," he looked knowingly through the doorway at Brontë who sat in his eyeline in the sitting room, "the company are quite going to your head."

Crockett felt his face grow hot. "I didn't…I'm sorry."

"There is no need for an apology, my dear boy. Warm affection can make us all follow pursuits to ill ends. You learned that lesson the day you told Mrs. Brettwick I was dead to avoid disappointing her about her will."

Crockett feigned a smile, but as he watched Petrarch enter the sitting room, he felt his chest ache. He could not argue with the logic, but it did not make the moment any less painful. Why did the location, the place, the amount of money held at the state of one's birth dictate where a heart could find connection?

These thoughts distracted the young man as the evening progressed. He tried to maintain an interest in the conversations of those around him, but he had descended into a state of melancholy. Only Brontë shared his mirthless attitude. She sat quietly at the side of the room immersed in a book. Crockett tried to speak to her, but he was met with iciness.

"How do you feel? I think for now the matter is all buttoned up," he said sadly.

"Is it?" She answered, her eyes never leaving the page in her book.

"Well, there is a resolution."

"For some."

He spent the rest of the evening watching the card game and occasionally bending an ear to the ongoing discussion about the German navy between August and Robert Edward. When Petrarch grew tired of the card game, he let Crockett sit in for several hands as he reclined on the sofa and started to gently snore.

Near eleven, the entire party had grown sleepy, the events of the past several days leaving them all exhausted. After everyone retired, Crockett turned his attention to his sleeping master.

"I supposed I should help you to bed, Petrarch."

But just as he moved forward, his hand in position to shake Petrarch awake, he felt a pair of eyes on him. Nervously, he looked up and saw Brontë staring at him from the threshold of the sitting room.

She crept forward softly, keeping her voice low.

"I can't believe you'd keep the key a secret," she said violently, her soft tones a flurry of hisses.

Crockett's voice shook. "I'm so sorry—Petrarch and I didn't know that it mattered; I didn't want to draw your attention to it for no reason. And, for what it's worth, I was going to tell you in the room, but Martha interrupted us."

Brontë's gaze softened. "You were?"

"I was." Crockett's heart thudded in his chest.

"Crockett," she said sadly, "it's not the fact that you kept the key secret from me; it's that I felt betrayed when you turned with them. You seemed always in the same frame of mind with me, secure in the belief that something macabre happened in this house." She breathed in deeply. "I…do you remember the morning when we met on the lawn, and I told you that no one is truly honest in this house?"

Crockett nodded. He longed to reach out, pull Brontë into a warm embrace.

"I felt that…I'm sorry if it's maudlin…" Brontë looked the most uncertain Crockett had seen her. She was shaking, agitated. "I just thought you did tell the truth. I trusted you in a way…but then, tonight…" She exhaled dramatically. "It was as if I lost it all. You turned to the easy solution with everyone else."

"Brontë…" Crockett felt overwhelmed. Although he had been won over by Petrarch's logic earlier, he now felt as if his only recourse, the only act fate drove him toward, was to follow Brontë to the very ends of the earth, regardless of logic, evidence, or propriety. He wanted to speak more, but words would not come easily, his tongue was leaden with emotion.

Brontë shook her head, tears in her eyes. "Everyone is so happy now, returned to a pre-death bliss that never existed. Even Kordelia…" She took a deep breath. "You don't know this house, the oppression of it. People talk about the ghosts outside on the river, but they don't talk of those inside." Brontë stopped. Her lips ceased moving, formed a thin, harsh line. She took a deep breath, the emotion slowly draining from her face. "It's been lonely," she said finally, resolutely. "But less so with you here."

Crockett's face flushed. He hoped that the earlier luminosity of his expression had dimmed and this show of emotion wasn't visible. He failed to speak; he was overwhelmed by the many things transpiring in this quiet moment—Brontë's soft tones, her moment of vulnerability, her recollection of their first moment alone together on the lawn. More than anything, however, was that the connection he felt was true: the feeling of being understood. All his years on the streets, then in Petrarch's carriage house, he had never felt something so vulnerable, like a thread, a pulsing wire attached between himself and another person. With Petrarch there was a paternal bond which had formed into an emotional fondness, but with Brontë…It was a current of passion which his guarded heart had never had the urge to emit. Looking into her eyes in that moment, he felt a rush of emotion which he'd only ever read about in poetry, a vulnerability and brokenness he now consciously understood as love.

"I," he said slowly, his tongue thick, "I feel the same."

A silence unfolded, tender and full. They looked into each other's eyes, unspoken emotions, an effusive tenderness, passing between them.

In the heat of the emotion Crockett's tongue loosened itself. His full, insane theory poured out. "I don't want to admit that it's over, either," he said hurriedly, "that there is a simple explanation for it. Truthfully," his face flushed yet again, "I…I actually had thought the murderer may be Bixby Hawsfeffer."

There was a brief moment of silence, Brontë's eyes sparkling with tears, but then her face broke into a wide smile. She laughed into her hand. As she giggled, Crockett heard, what sounded like footsteps behind him.

"I'm so sorry," Brontë said trying to recover her composure. "It's just—it's a bit, you know…You think the murderer was the murdered?" she asked.

"No, no!" Crockett grew anxious. "I thought it was his son, Bixby Hawsfeffer, Jr.—Pip—returned. Somehow…from Paris…"

Brontë smiled, her whole face shining. "So, you haven't given up on the truth, however ludicrous it may be."

"I haven't," he said resolutely. "Petrarch wants to, but I don't. I don't want to lose it."

Brontë cocked her head slightly. "Lose what?"

The young solicitor, heart pounding, was no longer using his reason. His tendency to make confused, rash decisions had been enhanced by a multiple of thousands in the presence of Brontë. With her so close, their affections spoken out loud, he was losing his senses.

"It, I, well, you know, the truth," he said stiltedly. He tried his best to calm himself, to try to subdue the tenderness he felt. "I don't…want to lose the truth of us. Of us between us. The truth of which us is a part in which the mystery is us."

Brontë nodded. She looked as if she would speak but halted. Neither of them had an idea how to carry forward; in truth, they both wanted to luxuriate in the moment, live in it for a long while, trying to understand the importance of it. No words could bear the weight of what their emotions felt. It seemed meaningless to speak.

Crockett finally spoke. His words were tentative, almost a whisper; it was as if he believed his raised voice would shatter the moment like glass. "I just don't want it to be over," he said.

Brontë took a deep breath. A full spectrum of feeling crossed her facial features in the next moment. It started with a flush of embarrassment, turned to a slight frown, but then burst into an enthusiastic grin. "Yes!" she said quickly. In a rush of emotion, she gripped Crockett's hands. "We don't give up. Tomorrow we take our last chance to find out what is really going on. We interrogate everyone, and we move toward a *real* resolution. Emotions will be high; everyone likes to pretend that they're glad Grandfather is gone, but there will be sadness, and people will start to talk. It may be luck that Petrarch produced the key and put us into the final stages. We have little time before the funeral, but we have to use it. We'll get into some deblightful troububble."[34]

"Yes," Crockett said breathlessly.

Brontë held Crockett's gaze. They both nodded enthusiastically, dramatically for some time. It was the clock chiming which tore them from their reverie, both parties jerking away as if from a dream. Brontë realized she had been holding Crockett's hands and dropped them quickly. She felt embarrassed and stepped away from him.

She bowed, slightly curtseying. "Yes," she said nervously. "Yes, then until tomorrow." A pink hue rose in her cheeks as she again stepped away from Crockett and crossed into the foyer.

Watching her leave, rather than ebb, his emotions rose higher. His whole being set alight, overcome by the new feeling of love.

Brontë experienced the same current of affection as she moved away from the young solicitor, one that she had not felt before. She grew giddy crossing the cavernous entry, but as she took her first step onto the foyer stairs, she paused; a shiver rushed down her spine.

She felt a pair of eyes watching her, some malicious presence awaiting her in the dark.

---

[34] The editor will remind the reader, at this point, that he is not that bad of an editor. This misspelling alludes back to Crockett's mistake with Mrs. Brettwick when he referred to Petrarch being dead.

Her giddiness faded. She turned, frightened, to assess the shadows behind her. But, when her eyes turned to the mysterious presence, she saw only Crockett's gleaming smile. His eyes also sparkled like diamonds in the dim light. She waved upon catching his gaze; she couldn't stop herself from giggling as she hurried up the stair.

When she was gone, Crockett sighed. The road ahead was obscured in shadow, but his heart was light. He and Brontë created a way forward together. His body felt weightless as he helped Petrarch back to his room. The old man mumbled quietly as they passed into the east wing of the house.

#

Crockett had long put Petrarch to bed when the shot rang out. It was a single, loud blast, then the sound of shattered glass followed by a heavy thud. There was a brief silence before the rush of thundering footsteps echoed from all corners of the house; the roused family sprinted to find the source of the explosion.

They found Crockett in the room holding his master. The old man's face was a stark white; his mouth hung open, exposing the deep black of his gaping maw. Everything in the room was in disarray—the drawers of the secretary pulled out, a table flipped over, and the old solicitor's bag ripped of its contents. The weapon, the gun which had hung over the fireplace, was left at the room's threshold upon the shooter's exit.

No one spoke as they assessed the scene of violence. Tears fell down Crockett's face. He held Petrarch and stroked his white beard.

Kordelia found her own glove next to the gun. As she held it up in the dim light, it felt as if it was imbued with some dark force, a ghoulish relic from beyond the grave.

16

Detective Lucian Lucretian Pimento

Even with the history of murders, eviscerations, entrapments, and drownings, the fear of Petrarch's demise filled the house with a different kind of tense, raw emotion. The scene resembled that of a pietà, only in lieu of a beatific Mary and a sinewy Christ, at the center of this tableau was a gaunt, variegated-eyed Crockett holding the rotund Petrarch. The supporting cast flanked him in various stages of grief, shock, or (for Kordelia, holding her glove) a kind of alarmed sleepiness.

It was Robert Edward who broke the ominous silence. He noted, in all the chaos, that one of the telltale signs of death was absent.

"Zere's no blood," he said, the beginning of a smile creeping over his face.

"Perhaps he was too old to have any," said Kordelia quietly.

"It's not the blood," Crockett said. "His…heart…I think the shock…"

But as if on cue, Petrarch pulled in a deep breath of air. The sudden movement caused Crockett to jump, throwing the old man, his head colliding with the side of his bed.

Everyone gathered gasped. The sound of his head hitting the wooden bed legs cracked nearly as loud as the gun.

Crockett flailed wildly, leaning over the old man and shaking him.

"Petrarch! Oh, no…Oh, Petrarch!"

"My necessitous friend!" August shuffled forward. "Let me try. My great-grandfather was a physician. Or knew a physician. Either way, I should be able to help."

Crockett stepped aside so August could lean over the body. He gently caressed his face and called Petrarch's name softly.

"Petrarch? Petrarch, old boy, are you all right?" He gave the passed-out man a moment to respond, before urgently raising his arm and slapping him so fiercely across the cheek that Corinthiana screamed.

"AWWWRRRRKKKKKK!!"

Brontë shoved him off and fell over Petrarch like a mother hen on her endangered chick. Her eyes were wild as she glanced between Crockett and her father. "What is wrong with you both? Let him have some air!" She turned to Martha who was standing just out of sight, concealed in a shadow thrown by the lamplight. "Martha, can you get some water, please? Robert," she turned to her cousin, "help me lift him onto the bed."

The two did their best to lift Petrarch's girth upward, but, at the last moment, failed miserably, his circular body crashing downward, a second great crack of his head on the bed frame resounding throughout the quiet room.

"Perhaps," Kordelia said dreamily, "we leave him as he is. If we help him too much more even the Danube Mob won't be able to set him right."

They compromised by taking the heavy blanket from the bed and placing it over the solicitor. Brontë took a pillow and laid it gently under his head. At this point, a large bump was forming from the first crack, accompanied by a deep purple bruise near his eye where Brontë and Robert had dropped him on their second attempt at aid.

Silence followed as they stared down at him, unsure whether he was dead. They partly wondered if they could all be guilty of murder for the many bumps and bruises they collectively inflicted.

A howling wind disrupted the quiet. August turned his attention to the shattered glass where the bullet had exited the window. The hole was high up in the window, smashing the windowpane nearly eight feet off the floor.

"An odd shot," he said softly. "It looks as though they weren't shooting to kill."

"Or," said Kordelia, "perhaps inexperienced in the arts of riflery."

"Sister," Brontë's voice was filled with rage. She spoke with her tongue in the back of her throat. "What was your glove doing in this room so near the weapon?"

"Other sister," Kordelia spoke quickly, "I've been losing them everywhere. They slip off so suddenly. At school one must always be wearing gloves, or you can be taken to the headmistresses for The Grating. I suppose I keep carrying them and dropping them out of habit."

"What is 'The Grating?'" This question was posed by a chorus of voices, all interested, yet also fearful, of the response.

"Well," Kordelia began, "the headmistress raids your cheese cupboard and takes your supreme cheese, which she grates vigorously in front of you as punishment."

"Supreme cheese?" June awkwardly combed her hair with her fingers; she gazed on her youngest daughter in confusion.

"It is a Sviss tradition," Robert said. "All Sviss have zer favorite cheese—ze supreme cheese."

Crockett coughed loudly. He hoped this would refocus attention on the incapacitated Petrarch.

"Well, supreme cheese or no," Kordelia went on, "I didn't shoot Petrarch. I can barely lift the weapon." She motioned to the gun lying at the door to the room.

"Vy vould zey try to kill him? He is a harmless old man," Robert looked, Crockett thought, the most concerned he'd seen him since he'd arrived at Hawsfeffer Manor.

"Theeey were loooking for this." Corinthiana held out the tomb key. It shone a dull gold in the dark.

Everyone subtly scanned the expressions of the others.

"That's why everything is turned out," August said. "They thought he'd hidden it away."

"Who knew you had the key?" Crockett asked.

"No one," Corinthiana said fluffing her white hair. "Heee gaaave it tooo meee in secret."

"So, it could be any of us," Brontë's voice simmered with anger, "just like with everything in this *silly* house."

June gasped. "My dear, we are all frustrated with this bizarre string of sadnesses, but that is no reason to use such foul language."

"Apologies, Mother, but the web only grows more tangled. I thought something happened to Grandfather but then Beatrice and now Petrarch! I thought…" In frustration she raised her hand to her forehead. "I thought we were getting closer to the end of it." Earnestly she threw a glance at Crockett. The earlier jolt of affection still existed between them, but it was dimmed, less powerful under the duress of Petrarch's injuries.

"Well, murder or no," June stood tall, "we must act as ladies. We should also get this glass cleaned up and call a doctor." She turned to her husband. "Where is Dexter? Didn't he hear any of this? We could have woken the dead."

"I haven't seen him since he cleaned up the remains of Beatrice," August said.

Martha stomped forward and handed over a sheet of paper to Corinthiana. "Found in the pantry this evening before I went to bed."

Corinthiana looked around nervously. "Theee lights aaare raaather low. Caaan aaanyone reeead in this daaark?"

Brontë grabbed the note from her grandmother and read slowly.

"Deer Peeples of the howse. I don' like the corrant climatt and will excoose meeself from the danjer. Tis bin an intertanen fyoo decates wit you all. Cordelilly, Dexter."

"Really not bad for someone who is borderline illiterate," June said.

"He did seem very perturbed and upset when I spoke to him yesterday," Crockett added.

The discussion of Dexter's abrupt exit from his service was interrupted by a loud banging coming from the front entry hall. Corinthiana grasped at her neckline, searching for an absent, opulent necklace, as she looked around in panic.

"Whooo?" she asked staring into the dark hallway.

August, Robert, and Crockett fled the room toward the main foyer. Upon entering the main hall, they were met with a menacing sight. Three men were gathered. Two of them were of an ordinary sort—one had a thick mustache and wore a policeman's uniform; the other was dressed in a brown suit, thick scarf, and bowler. The man in the bowler looked as shaken by their arrival as the men of the house. Although his hat was pulled low over his eyes, Crockett felt he looked familiar.

The third man stood in the center of the group, his bald head shining. He was far from ordinary, one of the most bizarre-looking men Crockett had ever seen. He wore a red jacket lined with shining gold material. A large feather jutting from the lapel pocket added an overenthusiastic exclamation point to his whole appearance. On his nose were a pair of small, pince-nez which twinkled in the light of the lamps. Despite having no hair on his head, two large sideburns decorated the sides of his face. His nose twitched as he assessed the three men before him.

"Hullo," he said shortly. "My name is Detective Lucian Lucretian Pimento." His voice was as crisp as his oxford shirt, more polished than his brown shoes. "You may simply refer to me as Pimento."

"Ah! It vas very good you could come so qvickly!" Robert Edward looked with relief at August and Crockett. "I called him as soon as I heard ze gun!"

"How did you know who to call, old man?" August's mustached twitched suspiciously.

"Vell," Robert said, "zings haven't been....Hoe do you say...non-murderous here? I asked Corinziana for ze contact of ze local police."

"Oh, no," August shook his head. "I think I'd trust the local milkmaids to solve a crime before these incompetent gentlemen. We'll be looking for squirrels who can shoot guns as part of the investigation."

"Do you know any?" The man in the police uniform pulled out his notebook and began scribbling frantically.

"No, old chap." August, for the first time since Crockett met him, looked thoroughly defeated.

"It alarms me that you have so little respect for the local constabulary, sir." Detective Pimento looked disgustedly at August.

"Master Pigmanto, was it? You all haven't really solved anything since the reign of Victoria, so you'll excuse me if I have my reservations."

"Well, we shall take this opportunity to prove ourselves." Pimento turned very sharply to the man in the scarf and bowler. "Which reminds me, Doctor, please go see the victim. We have much to do."

The old man nodded. He turned to Crockett, who led him out of the foyer and into the bedroom. As they marched away, Crockett furtively tried to steal glances at the bowler-man's face, trying to place him in his memory.

In the foyer, Detective Pimento remained motionless staring skeptically at August and Robert. "And who are you gentleman?" he asked.

"I am Au*güst* Winterbourne." August did not extend his hand but looked with contempt at the detective.

"August, a pleasure."

"No, it's Au*güst*." August pronounced his name so precisely spittle flew onto Pimento's red jacket.

The detective wiped the saliva from his lapel. "Mr. Winterbourne then," he said quickly. "And you, my foreign friend?"

"Robert Edvard Harrington, at your service." Robert bowed dramatically.

Pimento's nose twitched. "Indeed. What am I to expect when I see the crime scene?"

"Already having us do your work then?" August crossed his arms over his chest triumphantly.

The detective glared. "Perhaps you can be of more assistance, Mr. Harrington."

"Somevun tried to kill ze old solicitor," Robert said nervously. "But he vas a bad shot and ve vere afraid he died of a heart explosion."

"But he woke up," August said, his tone bored. "So, perhaps, it's best if you went away and left us."

Pimento's eyes flicked between the two men. "Why was I called, if there is no murder proper?"

"Vell, ve zink zat zere is something afoot."

August's mustache shimmied as he leaned in close to Robert. "Let's keep this all in the family," he said quietly. "There's no need to include anyone else."

"Mr. Winterbourne," Detective Pimento's voice grew grave, "I'm not here to squabble; I'm here to investigate an evil incident. I have no desire to exchange barbs with you throughout the night. If the situation is as you say, then I will happily go on my way."

August's mustache shook happily.

"*But*, before I leave for the evening, I will need to see the solicitor, and I will also need to know why our dear, foreign friend," he said motioning to Robert, "is so upset."

August, for the first time, lost some of his resolve. The truth was quite complicated, and, had the police not proven to be incompetent for decades, would have been included from the first.

He looked at Robert sheepishly. Neither man spoke.

Detective Pimento shook his head in annoyance. "Out with it, please. I do not do well with those who waste my time."

August sniffed haughtily and began to speak slowly—although, he was an expert at feigning confidence, he had no idea how to describe the present situation in which his family found themselves. "About one week ago, the patriarch of the family died by drowning," he said, a note of uncertainty in his voice.

"Where?" asked Pimento.

"In the river which runs along the back of the estate."

Pimento flicked open a notebook, his eyes holding the gaze of August. While keeping eye contact, he began to scribble in his notebook. "And?"

"And we all gathered at the house for the burial, of course, or rather… entombment, to mark his passing since there is no body." As Pimento seemed to swell and gain authority, August diminished, growing almost deferential. In just a few, brief moments, the detective had undermined August's abundant ego and made him a simpering puppy.

"No body?" Pimento let out a large breath from his nose. "Interesting."

"As others arrived, things have grown odder with each passing day. Corinthiana, his wife and my mother-in-law, wouldn't read the will, you see. Then, May and Robert Edward arrived late. The fish was murdered."

"The fish?" Pimento stopped writing; his penetrating gaze bored even more intensely into August. "A fish was murdered?"

"Beatrice, y-y-y-yes," August stuttered. "She was eviscerated and hung by the door."

"No accident then? This fish…was…why did its death matter?"

"She was our matriarch's pet. She's from the country, you know. She grew up with pet trout." For the first time the absurdity of Corinthiana's fish companion hit August with full force. He took a moment to regain his composure and continued. "Someone disemboweled Beatrice using a sword."

Pimento's hand resumed writing, racing across the page. "You know it was a sword?"

"Yes, the weapon came from the basement. My daughter discovered it."

Pimento's eyebrows raised as he continued writing. "Please continue."

"Then tonight it was discovered we had a copy of the key for the tomb to complete the entombment and carry on with the funeral."

"There was no key before?" Pimento asked coldly.

"No."

"So, the delay in the will reading wasn't a delay so much as the entombment itself was delayed due to no key?"

"Perhaps, yes. Corinthiana wanted to do the will reading and the entombment concurrently."

"I see." Pimento took a break from writing and daintily tapped his chin with his pen. "And that brings us to the present scene?"

"Yes." August grew more and more nervous. He spoke quickly, fat droplets of sweat running down his forehead. "It appears someone thought Petrarch, our solicitor, had the key in his room, so they fired the gun and searched the premises."

With a flick of his wrist, Pimento shut his notebook. In a few quick, gliding steps he made his way toward the hallway which he'd seen Crockett and the doctor exit into. The man in the police uniform followed quickly.

"So!" August called out anxiously behind him. "You think it's all a family squabble? No cause for alarm?"

Pimento stopped only for a moment. He turned his head, the feather in his jacket shaking with the sudden shift in momentum.

"Now you are asking for the advice of an incompetent detective, Mr. Winterbourne?" The detective's mouth tightened, creating a harsh gash of a smile on his face. "My intuition says something ominous is hidden here. Murder can have many faces and, in this house," he said softly, "I can see its eyes shining in the dark."

17

Tick Tock

Detective Pimento quickly dispelled any inhibitions the family had regarding the intelligence of the local police. Deftly, he entered Petrarch's bedroom, launching direct, penetrating questions at all those gathered. His eyes flitted surreptitiously between the entire cast of characters; a few times he smiled knowingly to himself as he scribbled in his notebook.

During the interrogatory assault from the detective, the doctor inspected Petrarch and confirmed that the old man had no permanent damage, and that he was, in fact, still breathing.[35] His one contribution was taking a bottle of unmarked pills from his bag and advising Corinthiana to "administer 'ery hour er day, whichever camed first." He then presented the widow with a potato with a wink. This confused everyone greatly, however Pimento assured them all that keeping a ripe potato in the room with a sick person was a Welsh tradition going back to the twelfth century.

Within three-quarters of an hour of the detective's arrival, the family was moving back to bed, Petrarch was snoring peacefully, and the whole incident faded like a faint cloud of smoke.

---

[35] Earhart initially inserted a long, slightly humorous incident with leeches in this scene, but it was withdrawn due to its scientific inaccuracy. Additionally, Mr. Kentworth seemed to think leeches were actually caterpillars as he kept describing the creatures as "long and furry, always with their eyes to their future as decorative ornaments in vegetable gardens."

As the sun began to creep up the horizon, Detective Pimento dismissed his policeman companion (who still seemed very stuck on the squirrel with a gun theory) and the doctor and convinced August (now defending the reputation of the local constabulary) it was imperative he stay through the morning to have more questions answered.

He was shown into quarters on the west side of the house. These chambers were not commonly used, but Martha kept them well enough to allow him to rest in a comfortable bed with clean linens. The murals painted on the walls and ceiling portrayed a brutal, bloody triumph of Americans over the French. Although extremely horrifying, Detective Pimento did not see the extremity of the gore painted above him until the sun reached its full morning strength.

Crockett slept a few, scant hours. When he awoke, he found Petrarch was still snoring loudly, however the rest of the house was awake and alert. Corinthiana had been accosted by Detective Pimento in her night clothes directly upon waking. The woman was so surprised that her vowels were contracted by nearly seventy-three percent,[36] and she had no time to put on a single jewel, bauble, or trinket. She was guided to a small interview station the detective curated in the office on the second floor, the same room of the séance only a few days earlier.

When Crockett arrived at breakfast, he found that most of the family had already been questioned by the side-burned inspector. Taking his seat at the table, he smiled shyly at Brontë. Despite the worry in her eyes, this token of friendship from Crockett made her spirits lift. She waved at the young solicitor, suppressing an inclination to giggle.

"He's a rather direct fellow," August said sipping tea. "I certainly trust him. He's not at all like those policemen who came out for Bixby's death. He came right out and asked me if I had anything to do with the shooting or murder."

"That seems so uncouth," June shook her head. "Detectives are meant to talk around the subject, and then, of course, surprise you only at the end

---

[36] The editor has no insight into the research methodology which generated this data.

with their accusations, not make them straight away."

"The gentleman is gifted at his work, my dear June" August added. "He felt so ordinary, so normal, almost familiar, as if we'd spoken many times before."

"Now that you mention it, yes. Despite his uncouthness, he was a very friendly, quotidian sort of chap," June said. "He was much more intimidating last night."

"Did he accuse you, Mummy?" Kordelia asked.

"No, not directly, but he did, of course, bring up all the savage things that have been going on…Poor Beatrice. At least Petrarch survived, you know."

"Did he accuse you, Kordelia?" Brontë was pacing the room having already completed her interview and breakfast.

"I don't know," Kordelia said dreamily. "He didn't not accuse me, but I'm unsure if the lack of direct accusation was fully accusatory."

"I zink he vas out of ze line! How dare he come into zis house and accuse me! I am ze vun so curious about ze dying of poor Beatrice!" Robert Edward was waving his arms maniacally, his cape swirling as he gesticulated.

May entered the room at that moment. Her eyes were red and puffy; she couldn't stop wringing her thin hands.

"Is it you Aunt May?" Kordelia asked nonchalantly. "Are you the one leaving my gloves around and slicing up the pets?"

May flinched. "That's not funny, Kordelia. You should have better manners than that. You're a young woman for goodness' sake."

"Please leave the disciplining of my children to me, May." June's eyes narrowed as she assessed her younger sister. "We don't want them picking up your 'manners' of taking what's not yours."

A blast of air issued from May's nostrils as she leaned over the table. Her hands turned white gripping the edge. It looked as if hot flames would flow from her mouth, but just as she prepared to speak, her teeth bared savagely, Corinthiana entered with a great sigh.

The old woman's pace was even more theatrical and sluggish this particular morning. Crockett counted ten seconds before she successfully took three steps.

Distress over their mother averted June and May's impending argument. May reached out and took Corinthiana's arm.

"Mother, are you all right?" she asked.

"Oooh," Corinthiana bawled. "Hiiighs and looows. Hiiighs and looows!" The elderly woman shuffled forward. May kept hold of her, assisting her to the head of the table. "I just waaant tooo laaay poor Beeeatrice and Bixby tooo rest. Whaaat dooo weee neeed this odd inspector for?"

"Due diligence, Grandmother," Brontë said urgently. "The other things were peculiar, but the gunshot and the attempted murder of Petrarch tip the scales to a new kind of malice."

"Malice. That is a wonderful word for it, darling," June beamed.

"It is," Kordelia said. "More points for Brontë. I would have said something like…misconfusion."

"Pooor young maaan," Corinthiana called out looking down the table. "Aaare yooou aaall right? Yooou seeem distressed."

Crockett's lack of rest was writ on his features. A gnawing fear about Petrarch and a deeply personal rebuke of himself and his own actions showed up in deep shadows under his eyes and a waxen complexion. He thought he was in better control of his own reactions and emotions, but last night proved to be a regression on all the fronts in which he believed he had advanced. He'd lost control of his amorous feelings for Brontë and reacted poorly to Petrarch's suggestions the investigation be closed. In the dawn light, this emotional turmoil manifested itself in his pale and exhausted countenance. His thin fingers rubbed his different-colored eyes.

"It was a bad night. I was lucky to get any sleep."

Brontë smiled at him. "I think we all slept with a bit of caution."

June gazed between her daughter and Crockett, a sudden understanding coming to her. In one warm gaze between the young people, she ascertained all which had previously been invisible to her about their growing affection. Her hand immediately went to cover her heart.

"Brontë," she said, her voice raspy with effort, "perhaps you should come with me to see the vicar and finalize arrangements for the entombment this afternoon."

"Are plans still moving forward?" May was so elated her mask-like face broke into a (relatively) broad smile. "I thought with the recent events we'd be postponed yet again."

"Burying father—or his casket—and Beatrice won't stop the investigation, May. Things will proceed as planned," June said curtly.

All gathered breathed a collective sigh of relief, except for Brontë, who looked at her mother as if she had just voiced how much she admired the German Kaiser.

"Mother, I'm fine here," she said. "Kordelia can go with you to the village."

"No!" June responded so dramatically that everyone in the room looked toward the eldest Hawsfeffer daughter. To recover, she cleared her throat with several, very unladylike coughs and feigned a smile. Without thinking, she reached out and grabbed her mother's teacup, taking a long draught.

"My deeear," Corinthiana said, "thaaat is my teeea."

Ignoring her, June plastered on a cloying smile; however, her eyes belied a deep fear. "Brontë, come with Mummy! It will be nice to get air, and we'll be out of Pugmanto's way."

"His name is Detective Pimento, Mother," Brontë said looking at June questioningly. "Anyone else can go—I feel like I'd be happier here rather than making the long journey into town. I'd rather not put on formal clothes."

"Darling," June's voice grew frantic, "you're coming with me. Get ready. I'd feel safer if you were by my side. I worry about you, darling!"

"Do you worry about me?" Kordelia asked nonchalantly.

June nodded disinterestedly in the direction of her other daughter.

Brontë looked at her grandmother who was busily cleaning off the rim of her teacup where June had placed her lips. Uncertainly, she left the room after a nod of acquiescence to her mother.

Martha shuffled in immediately after Brontë's departure, her eye spinning more quickly than usual.

"You!" she said gruffly pointing to Crockett. "The detective wants to see you."

#

June was correct. The menacing, no-nonsense detective of the previous night was gone. In his wake was a pleasant, almost jolly individual wearing a broad smile. Crockett took him in again, the same red jacket, the same unkempt sideburns and spectacles. The familiarity described by August and his wife was perhaps more in relationship to the blandness of Detective Lucian Lucretian Pimento's presence rather than any sort of casual, welcoming air he exuded. It was odd that the previous night he had been a dramatic, vengeful force, but in the morning light, he appeared diminished, innocuous in the rays of the sun.

"Crockett!" he called as the young man entered the room. "Please, come in. Excuse the formalities of this, but it's part of the job."

Slowly, Crockett crossed the room and took a seat in the leather armchair that faced the detective. For a long moment neither man said anything. Detective Pimento's eyes glittered with a knowing, incomprehensible sheen. Crockett eventually shifted in his chair, feeling he was being looked through rather than at.

"How are you, my boy?" The detective leaned back; the feather in his lapel shook.

"I'm well enough," Crockett said. "I didn't get much sleep."

"No one did. It was quite the evening." A wry smile turned up the edges of the detective's mouth. "It sounds like it's been the general way of things since you've arrived at Hawsfeffer Manor."

Crockett sighed. "It has been...for lack of a better word, chaotic. Beatrice...Poor Petrarch..."

"Your dear master..." Detective Pimento tsked compassionately. "What a sad event."

"Unbelievably so," Crockett felt his eyes grow damp. "I thought I lost him..."

"He means a great deal to you?"

"I would say he's like a father to me." Crockett quickly wiped his eyes. Self-consciously he cleared his throat. "He took me off the street. Without him, who knows where I'd be."

"What a wonderful story."

"For me, I suppose."

The two men again settled into a pregnant silence. Pimento leaned forward; Crockett noticed his breath smelled like an oven full of coffee beans.

"What else should I know about you, Mr. Cook? Do you have any secrets that would bear on the case?"

"No, sir," Crockett's neck grew warm. "Nothing that explains the events that have transpired in this house."

"But secrets that explain other things?"

Crockett's ears turned a bright red.

Pimento laughed heartily, his head falling backward. "My dear, boy! There is nothing to fear! I only need to hear the facts. If you're not guilty then there is no cause for the flush on your cheeks."

"I'm sorry, Detective." Crockett wiped his brow with the back of his hand. "I'm a little unsettled. Things have been so muddled here. Since Petrarch and I arrived, we have seen many oddities."

"Oddities?" Pimento savored the sound of the word. His tongue flicked out and flashed across his lips. "And what do you think of these oddities, Mr. Cook?"

"I don't know."

"Take this room, then," the detective said. "We'll go piece by piece through it."

"Why this room?" Crockett's caterpillar eyebrows knitted together.

"The room with ghosts—the haunted room."

Crockett, without thinking, chuckled to himself. The séance seemed a dim memory, a bad joke. "It is," he said. "That was a very interesting morning."

"I'm sure. Do you have any thoughts on who played the little trick?" Detective Pimento stared intensely at Crockett.

"To be honest," Crockett said, delighted the conversation had become more natural, "Brontë and I have been attempting some detective work on our own. We think it's unrelated to the other crimes—the other situations—I guess is more correct to say."

"Really?" Detective Pimento leaned forward. His eyes twinkled, almost merrily, in the warm, golden sunlight. "Unrelated?"

"I believe it was Kordelia," Crockett said. "She was the one who led the séance. Her gloves were found near the phonograph. She's very strange, I think harmless, but it seems the type of joke she would play." Crockett tapped his fingers on the desk. "I do think, however, that there was someone assisting her. I don't think one could execute that kind of trick on their own."

Detective Pimento's smile grew wider. "An admirable theory. One similar to my own. Do you have any idea of the accomplice?"

Crockett sat back in his chair. While he assumed the phonograph trick was a result of Kordelia and perhaps her father looking to expedite the will reading, he still harbored his other theory about who truly murdered Bixby Hawsfeffer. "I'm not sure, maybe Augüst—but, as I said, I think it was done in fun. I don't know if it matters."

"My dear boy," Pimento rose. "Everything in this kind of case matters."

Crockett watched the detective move to the window, the same window the bird had crashed into during the commune with the dead.

"Mr. Cook, do you mind if I ask you something? We can put aside the phonograph accomplice for now."

The young man grew nervous. "Yes…of course, you may ask me anything."

"Good." Pimento put his hands behind his back and stared upon the house grounds. "You see, I've already eliminated you as a suspect. You don't know the house, and you couldn't have found the key to get to the sword that killed the herring."

"Beatrice…"

"So, I trust you." Pimento turned dramatically. "Would you mind if I expressed my own opinion of the events to you? Perhaps you could provide additional context or insights."

Crockett nodded apprehensively.

Pimento did not notice the reservation in Crockett's expression. The detective sniffed assuredly and turned back to the window. "Good, my boy. You see I need to know everything. This case, I believe, is not one that is dangerous, but one that stems from what is being unsaid, what is being kept secret. In West Hampminstershireshire we don't get many murders …or attempted murders. To be honest, it's your opinion that is of the most vital importance to me. You come from the outside. You can see the relationships of these people better than most, better than they, probably better than I. You have been here, in the thick of it, heard them talk, heard them plot, heard them complain. I need you to be absolutely honest, overflowing with veracity. You," the old detective turned and began to walk toward Crockett, "you are the key to this, my dear boy. Petrarch is incapacitated and I need you to be my eyes and ears."

Crockett looked deeply into the detective's eyes. He felt both seen and, yet, looked over, as if he were standing in front of the star actor the audience desperately wanted to view. But, as Crockett hesitated, Detective Pimento extended his hand and gently put it on Crockett's shoulder.

"I think we can take care of this case together," he said.

A shock went through the young man, a jolt of profound feeling. The conspiratorial nature, the warmth, the fatherly touch overwhelmed the solicitor's young assistant. With Petrarch injured, Crockett needed a new, avuncular confidant to share his secret, and something in the assured touch of Pimento struck an emotional chord deep inside him. The mistrust he felt moments before, loosened. Pimento, whether through detectivian[37] wisdom or emotional warmth, had created a bond. Without thought or compunction, Crockett spoke.

"Bixby," he said quickly.

Detective Pimento's eyebrows rose. His mouth punched out like that of a fish, a haunting resemblance to the deceased Beatrice.

"Actually, Pip Hawsfeffer, otherwise known as Bixby, Jr." Crockett went on breathlessly, "I think it's Bixby's son who is behind everything. He's back and he's interfering with matters to take what he thinks is owed him and avenge his mother's death. I think Kordelia's phonograph trick was merely an amusement, but Pip killed his father and then killed Beatrice to

---

[37] While this isn't technically a word, the spirit of the word and its usage here seem justified. Apologies to the editor's sixth-grade English teacher, Mrs. Stubbs.

get revenge on his family and…attain something…That's what I'm unsure about."

Detective Pimento's face shifted from the surprised fish expression, to one of deep confusion. Slowly, he moved around the desk to his seat.

"The homosexual?" he asked. "The one in Paris?"

"Yes. Have you heard about the note? I think it's vital to the case, but I don't know what it means."

"I have not," he said drily, his body slowly lowering into the leather chair. Crockett noted that he appeared to want to say more, but, for some reason, it was withheld.

When the detective did not speak, Crockett continued, "Corinthiana most likely didn't mention it because it doesn't link to anything. But what if it did?"

"What is in the note?" Pimento nervously played with his lapel. "Who wrote it? Who was it to?"

"It was from Bixby's first wife, Lucinda." Crockett paused, unsure whether the detective was humoring him or believed in some part of his fantastic theory. "It was addressed to Petrarch to be opened at the time of Bixby, Sr.'s death. It included the key to the tomb. *That's* why Petrarch had it—he didn't really discover it in his papers."

"Yes?" Pimento's eyes lost their merriment; in its place an intense thoughtfulness flooded in.

"Lucinda wrote a note shortly before she disappeared. It seems benign, but it could mean something very important. It simply asks Pip to visit his mother's tomb, but…well, perhaps it was a code of some kind."

Pimento was still off-kilter. His words came slowly, laboriously. "What do you know about Lucinda?"

"Nothing of importance." Crockett leaned back in the chair. A deep sense of relief accompanied his confession. Even Brontë laughed at his theory, but Pimento seemed, at the very least, interested. "I know she was Bixby Hawsfeffer, Sr.'s first wife and that she disappeared many years ago. There is suspected foul play."

"Do you think they're linked then?" Pimento asked. "Do you think that her death all those years ago and the current..." he hesitated briefly, "...troubling incidents are linked across time?"

"That I don't know," Crockett said. "I just have a feeling that, not only is Bixby the younger involved, but someone in the house is assisting him." Crockett hoped that this would jar the detective—make him gasp in appreciation—but he only looked more troubled. Crockett continued, "The people in this house are eccentric; they all have motive. It's not a far reach to suspect that we all could be guilty. We should be looking at everyone, even Petrarch, Martha, and Dexter."

Detective Pimento came to rapt attention. Crockett looked at him uncertainly. "Yes, Detective?"

"Sorry...Dexter..." he said slowly.

"Yes, the groundskeeper," Crockett continued. "He ran off. I spoke with him, and I can say I think he's the least likely to be involved in any of this."

Detective Pimento turned his gaze out the window. "It's an interesting assortment of characters," he said thoughtfully. "We need to get them all organized, but our time is short."

"Short?" Crockett felt an impending sense of dread.

"My boy," Pimento turned his head toward him ominously, "there has been an attempted murder, and the killer and the victim are still undiscovered. It's only a matter of time before there is another strike made against the old man. My guess is that the solicitor knows who did it, and the perpetrator is moving about the house in abject fear of him awaking and confessing. We stand on the edge of a knife." Pimento laced his fingers and placed them behind his head. "Our time is running out, like sands in an hourglass or the winding down of a grandfather clock. Tick tock," he said emotionlessly. "Tick tock."

18

Portraits of Death

C rockett felt the same dread of the night before creep over him. The feelings of guilt and panic slithered over his skull and rippled across his skin in the form of goosepimples.

Pimento drummed his fingers on the large desk.

"Crockett," the detective said heavily, "I mentioned that I needed you to be my eyes and ears, and that is the truth. If not to support me, can you please assist in the case to help your dear Petrarch?"

Crockett felt his heart clench. He nodded emphatically.

"Most excellent!" Pimento's feather shook. "Now, you know this house and those in it better than I. Is there," the older gentleman raised his eyebrow slightly, "someone with whom you share confidences? Is there a person who could give you information that I may not get from my general interviews?"

Brontë. Crockett saw her surly face the night before when she had felt betrayed by him. Was this also a betrayal? Did he break her trust by confiding their thoughts and secret musings to the detective?

Detective Pimento eyed him warily. "My dear boy, time is of the essence. I need your confidences and your assistance to move toward a resolution as quickly as possible. Is there someone who can give you more information on Lucinda Hawsfeffer?"

"Yes." Crockett nervously wrung his hands. "I can ask someone. The last time I attempted an interrogation it was unsuccessful…but as it says in

The Fantastic Death of Captain Discord, 'experience is the key to sleuthing mastery.'"

"Indeed." Pimento said. "I never consider any solution to a case too odd and your Bixby Jr./Pip theory is so ingeniously off-beat that it could be correct." The detective's short figure rose from the desk. He began to pace slowly around the room. "I want you to find out as much as you can about Pip and Lucinda. Try to find a tie between the past and present that binds the disappearances *then* with the happenings *now*. I shall do my standard review of the remaining leads—go to the basement and assess the rapiers, scour the river where Bixby, Sr. disappeared, and examine the rest of the rooms of the house. We will convene near teatime and see if there is anything new in terms of evidence." Pimento ceased pacing and stood erect. The businesslike detective of the previous evening and the merry, elder man of the morning merged into one. "You know, Mr. Cook," he said, amusement in his voice, "you may make a good detective someday."

Crockett smiled, imagining himself as Captain Discord, triumphantly rooting out the Hawsfeffer's rutabaga farmer.

#

By the time Crockett left the study, Brontë and her mother had gone to see the vicar. Kordelia confirmed that they would return "soon or not so very not soon in the mash,"[38] which left Crockett feeling morose as he walked idly back to his room in the late morning.

Petrarch was still snoring contentedly in his chamber, asleep from the concoction of medicines and concussions the previous night had blessed him with. Crockett felt relief sitting next to the old man, seeing a small smile stretched across his old face. His steady workout regimen had left him strong enough to survive the shock. For that, Crockett was extremely grateful.

---

[38] This is a play on the old Scottish saying, "We shall see ye whither be yesterday, today, tomorrow, or evemorrow 'til the morning mash."

As Crockett sat by the old man's bedside, his thoughts strayed to the week's chaos. He needed to follow his instinct. He ruled out whether the séance was related—it was simply a red herring[39]—the violence against Beatrice, however, bore some grave importance. He was sure of it. Additionally, the aggression against Petrarch yielded no clearer vision of the answer either. Crockett had been sure in that chaos someone would have been more apprehensive, more apparently nefarious, in the heat of that disastrous event, but everyone had been helpful, shocked, and disgusted. But he had also been shocked—perhaps he had not observed things correctly.

Sighing, he reached out and grabbed Petrarch's hand. "I'm sorry, old man," he whispered. "I still am so inexperienced, so wildly unpredictable in moments of crisis. This whole thing has gotten out of hand. I thought…you know, when Brontë told me she didn't think it was over, I believed her. I couldn't have foreseen this, though."

Crockett gently pressed Petrarch's hand to his forehead.

He needed to think.

The murderer, in his mind, was the youngest Bixby, Pip. That was the strongest link to Lucinda's note—he, perhaps, saw it, or got wind of the truth of what happened to his mother, and was seeking vengeance. But in order to execute a plan of this complexity, he would need help from inside the manor. Crockett knew if he could simply find the accomplice, he'd find Bixby. Someone had to have retrieved Corinthiana's key to the family vault and taken the rapier used to kill Beatrice. The killer knew how to carve a fish, so they must have some kind of background in food preparation or fishing for sport, which could lead to Martha or any of the men in the house. Corinthiana discovered her pet, seemingly without guidance, so that added no clarity to the events. If he narrowed the list of suspects down, the most likely to be assisting in the malevolence would be Martha, August, May, or, even, Kordelia—they all had motive and ability to execute a strategy of this scale. Robert had a clear alibi and reason for being there, Dexter loved

---

[39] The editor acknowledges the complicated humor around a red herring in a book about a murdered herring.

Bixby Hawsfeffer and was now gone, June had shown no proclivity in any direction (however, her vein bulging at breakfast raised some questions), Corinthiana was too bumbling and emotional to do much more than her hair in the morning, Petrarch was the opposite of murderous…and Brontë… it simply couldn't be her.

In fact, he needed her to come back—they could review their notes of the events together.

Brontë…Crockett sighed.

Did she trust him? Could there be something there? Or was it all a part of his overactive imagination? The intensity of their affection reached a fever pitch the previous night, but that may have simply been the nature of the exchange and their trust which had fused quickly under the influence of the week's trauma. Was his idea of Pip coming back from the past just as fantastical as a romance with the eldest Winterbourne daughter?

A quiet knock disturbed his reverie.

Crockett turned and saw Kordelia staring at him from the shadow of the hallway.

"Hullo," she said sweetly.

"Hullo. You may come in, Kordelia."

The young woman glided to the bed. Her wide eyes looked at Petrarch with a deep empathy. "I came to be sure he's all right."

"It sounds like he will be fine. He's been sleeping a long while."

"Not from the concussion," she said. "There are bats in this room. They sometimes defecate on the bed. I didn't want him to be used as a toilet."

Crockett sighed.

Kordelia gently ran her finger over the bed cover. She breathed in sharply.

"Are you all right?" Crocket asked.

Nervously, the young woman looked at Crockett. "I heard you," she said softly. "With the detective. I used the same vent that was used to pipe in the music from the phonograph."

Crockett frowned. "Oh?"

"It's a wonderful theory. It gets around all the characters in the house. It's someone outside it. Bixby from the past." Kordelia drew closer to Crockett, her voice lowering. "It's very like *Mère, Bélier, Mort, Chapeau*. In the play the viscount's ram is the one poisoning the well by defecating in it. It's revealed in the fourth meat pie scene."

"I feel this conversation has discussed defecation with alarming frequency," Crockett said.

"It's the one you don't suspect. It's like the play or a book." Kordelia leaned in conspiratorially, her voice becoming a whisper. "There are only a few people who can link the past to the present. You should talk to them." She hesitated and then, in a barely audible tone, she quoted the same passage from the day they met on the river. "The past doesn't die, just like ghosts don't."

Crockett turned toward her, but the girl had moved away. She was skipping from the room.

"Martha," she called back in a sing-song voice, "is cleaning up the detective's room."

He would at least be able to ask the old maid some questions that focused his theory and could eliminate or aggrandize Pip's status as a suspect. The first time he'd encountered her cleaving meat, it hadn't yielded results, but time was running out, and perhaps after that first exchange, she would trust him and recognize a rapport between them. As Kordelia's footsteps died away, Crockett took a deep breath and squeezed Petrarch's hand. "There are worse ideas," he said quickly and rushed after the youngest Winterbourne daughter.

#

Kordelia disappeared, so that when Crockett found himself in the west wing, he was alone in his quest to face Martha. Tentatively, he knocked on the open door to the detective's room, which she was still cleaning. He waited patiently for the old woman to call him in. She ignored the sound, however, and continued sweeping, her shuffling gate the only sound in the room. Crockett was unsure if it was his imagination, or if the maid's roving eye was fixed on him, but it made him feel unsettled.

He attempted two more knocks, to no avail, before stepping into the room.

"Pardon," he said, his throat congested due to nerves. "Excuse—pardon? Ma'am?"

Martha stopped for an instant before resuming sweeping.

It was clear she saw no rapport between them.

Crockett cleared his throat and debated his next course of action. At the very least, he knew he had to refrain from directly accusing Martha of the murder. As he pondered the most useful questions to ask, he looked up and discovered the macabre mural painted on the ceiling. It was a dramatic scene of the French and Indian War in America. The picture was painted with intricate detail, the blood a dark, rich red. In the center of the portrait was a proud American warrior on a large, white horse, his eyes breaking the mystique of the painting, looking straight out of the artwork and at the viewer. Crockett had never seen anything like it before; he shivered slightly in spite of the warmth of the day. Something about the face appeared familiar, but the young man couldn't quite place the visage in his memory.

"Master Bixby Von Bunson," Martha croaked, never interrupting her sweeping.

Crockett looked to her, trying to catch her eye. He pasted a smile on his face in an attempt to disarm the old woman. "I'm sorry," he said moving closer to her. "Bixby Von Bunson?"

"Yes," she said shortly. "He had all these painted before he disappeared. He painted himself into the pictures."

"And Bixby Hawsfeffer allowed that? He supported his cousin painting himself into the images in his house?"

"They were very friendly before they weren't," she said coldly. "When Von Bunson went to America he made them both a large sum of money. Dexter is painted in them, too. They came over from America together. He and Bixby Von Bunson were very close friends…then things fell apart."

Crockett stared at the old woman. It was as if she was saying something important and, yet, as if she wasn't saying anything at all. Most of this was information Brontë shared with him during their adventure in the family vault. The number of Bixbys and betrayals in the family was certainly a point of interest, if nothing else.

"If you go into the study upstairs, the painting over the fireplace is the same, just them in different dress. More English." She paused here, and for the first time looked directly at Crockett.

A tense moment unfolded between the two individuals. The single eye rolled slowly in its socket.

Crockett cleared his throat. "Why did Von Bunson leave?"

"Money," the old woman said. "He wanted the house back, but it was legally Hawsfeffer's, you see. The two men couldn't agree on what to do, so he went back to America."

"And he's never been back?"

"Never. There's been no word of him for decades." She again looked as if she wanted to add something more. Hesitantly she spoke, "Miss Corinthiana had me deliver a secret letter after the master died."

Crockett took a step closer. His heart thudded in his chest. "Do you know what was in the note?"

"I promised the lady I wouldn't look. Martha keeps her promises."

"But you think that it was addressed to Bixby Von Bunson?"

Martha looked around anxiously. "I have no firm idea, but it was my guess. Even if it was, with his habits of traveling with the Wild West show, it would never get to him. She was wasting her time."

"Is that…" Crockett's memory flashed to the night of Beatrice's death. "Is that who you referred to when we woke you? When you said, 'Is it him?'"

Martha appeared surprised. "I said that?"

"Yes, when we woke you."

The expression of surprise flickered then faded. "I suppose it could be anyone. There's lots of *hims* in the house." She cleared her throat, a large amount of phlegm gurgling in her windpipe. With a loud "pfft!" she spit it into her apron.

Crockett did his best to hide his revulsion. "Ummm…But do you know why she would have written to Bixby Von Bunson when she heard about Bixby Hawsfeffer's death?"

"No," she said abruptly, wiping her mouth with the back of her hand.

"Me and the lady don't particularly get along. We've grown closer out of necessity since the death of Master Hawsfeffer, but it's not warmth that brought me into her confidences."

"I see."

Martha shuffled toward the door, dragging the broom as she went. "I'm glad you're still looking" she said. "I hope you find something. You and Brontë are sniffing around…you're brave for doing so. They say Hawsfeffer Manor swallows its secrets. It swallowed Old Baron Von Bunson. It ate Lucinda, and now," abruptly she stopped her steady shuffle, "it has taken Beatrice and has its eyes on Petrarch."

She resumed her movement again, trailing past Crockett. He could smell the odor of soap and dust on her clothing. Although not a warm woman, Crockett felt some sort of genuine kindness in her words, in her wish for Brontë and him to find something. Unlike after their meat cleaving exchange, he now at least felt he could trust her. There was also something disarming about seeing her alone in that large room. The frightening image of her greeting him at the front door upon his arrival was less ominous now that he saw her attending to her regular duties.

"Martha," Crockett spoke softly, "I was speaking to the detective this morning and he asked if I could find out more about Lucinda Hawsfeffer."

"Lucinda?" The old woman appeared genuinely startled.

"Yes, you see we both have an idea that perhaps the events of this week are tied to the past in some way. Lucinda's name came up in our conversation, but we don't know anything about her."

Martha turned fully toward Crockett. A smile appeared on her wrinkled face. "The past?" Her eyes clouded with a maternal glow. "Well, Lucinda was a beautiful woman, inside and out. If you believe what they say happened to her, then you know that it was the worst tragedy to happen in this house. The day I watched her put into the big tomb…It was a dark one."

"Was it true?" Crockett took a step closer. "What happened to her…?"

Martha's smile faded. She shook her head. "As I said, the house swallows its secrets. I do know that the day she died was one of the saddest I've seen while serving this household." Her eyes moistened, but she had turned away from Crockett before he could see if there were proper tears. "If you're nosing about the past," she said softly as she moved out of the room, "I'd say you should look at the paintings. You can take the back stair through the ballroom if you want to go up and look at the one hanging in the study; it is a servant stair normally, only used by me and Dexter, but it's useful for a number of things."

Crockett barely heard her, he was too focused on his final question, the one that burned inside him. His voice cracked. He finally asked, "In terms of the past, can you say whether Bixby Hawsfeffer, Jr., Mr. Pip, has ever been back? Could he have caused this chaos to seek revenge and take back his fortune?" He held his breath in anticipation of the response.

Martha's shuffling slowed, minutely. "That is a boy I haven't seen in quite a long time," she said turning out of the room, "a very, very long time. In this house he is as dead as Lucinda and Beatrice put together."

Crockett shook his head as the old woman turned the corner. The sound of her hobbling gait faded as she passed down the corridor.

He quickly analyzed the interview—a second note, Lucinda's death, and the complete disregard of his inquiry into Pip.

Deep in thought, his eyes lifted to the ceiling. He assessed the painting. The figure of the rider on the white horse looked triumphantly down at him. Even six feet above him, his blue eyes sparkled. The visage was striking—it made him think of the painting in the basement; it was tragic the face of the young Bixby Hawsfeffer was rubbed out, ruining it.

Crockett sighed. He looked into an American soldier's eyes, then turned his attention to the carnage of the corpses littered throughout the rest of the mural.

"So much senseless violence," he said to no one.

A dust mote floated through his line of sight and drifted across the room. Resignedly, he put his hands into his trouser pockets and walked into the hall. It was his dearest hope that Detective Pimento had come to some other conclusion, less fantastic, more practical. In his heart, however, was the nagging feeling that Martha may have been right. The house would simply swallow this secret as it had all the others. His fear was that, in the chaos, it may swallow them all.

19

Toward the Climax

Pimento and Crockett gathered back in the study after their separate investigations. Crockett felt melancholy, his conversation with Martha leading to nothing substantial (although he felt pride in getting any answers at all). He divulged the full details of their exchange in a plodding, defeated manner as Pimento smiled at intermittent points in his narrative.

"I hope your investigation yielded something more useful." Crockett felt a pang of hope looking into Pimento's eyes. They were bright and smiling, his glasses giving off glints of sparkling light.

"Well, my dear boy, I think you will be very happy with what I found." The detective leaned toward Crockett conspiratorially. "You see Corinthiana told me the truth about that secret letter Martha spoke of. The contents will lift your spirits."

"The letter from Corinthiana to Bixby Von Bunson?"

"Oh, ho!" Pimento steepled his fingers together. "But was it to Master Von Bunson?"

"I don't know!"

"Well, I have been in conversation with Corinthiana."

"Yes!" Crockett leaned forward.

"And she told me what was in the letter."

"Yes!"

"She said it was sent under the cover of night because…it, perhaps, could be viewed as scandalous."

"Yes!"

"So, she confided it to Martha in the dead of night."

"Y—es." Crockett was quickly losing his enthusiasm.

"Well, my boy, the letter, the letter of which Martha has spoken to you, of which I have spoken to Corinthiana, which was directed at a heretofore unknown party which I will reveal in this next moment…" Pimento paused here looking intently at Crockett.

Crockett looked back at him, perceptibly extending his neck forward to imply he was ready to hear the reveal of the mysterious addressee. The two men remained locked in an uncomfortable silence, each waiting for the other to advance. During this odd standoff, Crockett noticed the detective's sideburns looked wilder than they had previously, uneven on his round face.

Finally, Crockett softly said, "Yes?"

"The letter—it was, definitely, spoken from Corinthiana's mouth directly—was addressed to none other than the estranged, distant—"

Pimento went on for some time, stringing together a litany of adjectives and descriptions, all providing a robust portrait of the mysterious letter recipient. At a certain point, Crockett lost all interest, his thoughts turning to the bird who had unceremoniously died during the séance, then, in turn, to the ghost biscuits which he had never had the opportunity to try.

"And what do you think of that!" Pimento leaned back in his chair triumphantly.

Crockett, coming back to the conversation, nodded and said, "Yes?"

"Mr. Cook! It ties back to your theory! The letter was intended for Pip Hawsfeffer!"

"My stars!" Crockett put his hands to his forehead. "So Corinthiana alerted him to his father's death!"

"Indeed." Pimento played with the feather in his lapel. "It appears he had nothing to do with the death of Bixby Hawsfeffer, Sr., but he may fit somewhere in this web."

"So, I may be right!" Crockett's face glowed with pride. "After the sore

TOWARD THE CLIMAX

defeat in his conversation with Martha, he felt they were at the turn of the tide.

"My brain is still parsing all this new information," Pimento said energetically, "but I think we should review the current facts of the case as we prepare for the evening. I feel," the detective adjusted his glasses, "that we are heading toward the climax."

Crockett nodded. His heart pounded in his chest.

Pimento cleared his throat and commenced. "Our current suspects are Corinthiana Hawsfeffer, her daughters, June and May, Robert Edward Harrington, Pip Hawsfeffer," here he winked at Crockett with warmth before continuing, "June's husband, August—"

"Augüst," Crockett said out of habit.

"Awgoost, yes, his and June's daughters, Kordelia and Brontë, the groundskeeper, Dexter, who has left us, Martha the maid of many years, and, of course, to be completely fair, yourself and your master, Petrarch Bluster."

"It's a rather long list."

"But it grows much shorter when we review motive."

Crockett's eyebrows went up in shock. "Detective! You found motive? Brontë and I have been confounded all week. Even if my theory is correct, why is Pip involved? Does the note to Lucinda reveal some hidden fortune, or is Pip being contacted simply a coincidence? Did someone actually kill Bixby Hawsfeffer? Did someone want to expedite the reading of the will? Is there some treasure buried in the tomb of some importance…? The séance incident seemed a trick to scare people but—why? I'd thought it was Kordelia, but there are beginning to be too many coincidences—the Lucinda letter, the Pip letter, the séance…And, likewise, the death of Beatrice seems to be some sort of warning, but, for what?"

Crockett paused, exasperated, lost, and hopeless in his own thoughts. Detective Pimento eyed him shrewdly.

"And there is," the detective said, "the attempt on Mr. Bluster's life. Allegedly, it was someone searching for the tomb key."

"Oh, yes, that, too," Crockett said. He sounded as if he was speaking from far off. "So, you think someone wants inside the tomb, then?"

Detective Pimento sniffed. "Do you?"

"I don't know what anyone wants. I told you, we've been absolutely confounded."

"But what have you found? Talk me through your theorizing." Detective Pimento leaned forward slightly, his lips pursed.

"Well, I thought it was Augüst at first, before my theory with the younger Bixby Hawsfeffer. You see Mr. Winterbourne has been stuck in this house for years, an emasculating situation, always at the hands of his father-in-law. I thought he wanted the money, so he was the one who killed the patriarch and then, perhaps, revising my previous theory, he was the one who tricked the family with the séance and then killed Beatrice to precipitate the will reading."

"But you no longer think that?"

"No, Augüst didn't have the key to get the rapier. He flatly denied everything."

"But let's return to your idea of *two* people working in collusion. Augüst didn't have to have the key"

"Perhaps," Crockett looked into the detective's eyes. "That's what lead me to the Pip Hawsfeffer theory—I thought someone outside the house was running the affair. It could be someone who knew it well, or, at the very least, knew the people within it. They were pulling the strings while someone else took action in the house."

"What if," Detective Pimento's smile grew immense, "it could be our dear Aunt May's lover?" He stared intensely at Crockett.

"I hadn't…thought of that." A smile crept over Crockett's face but quickly faded. "My goodness, this is getting far too complicated."

"But hear me out, my boy. You see, May would have wanted her father dead. With him out of the picture, there would be debts repaid that would return to her farmer beau's hands. When I spoke to her about this affair this morning, she burst into tears. It's a very emotional situation."

"It's a very interesting theory. It could make it fit together," Crockett added. "The farmer would have the skills to dismember Beatrice while May was safely in bed. And...er...I suppose he could get the gun and go after Petrarch." The young man sat back in his chair and breathed deeply. It could make sense. But the solutions to the mystery seemed only to be getting more nebulous rather than taking on a clearer shape.

"I still don't understand the attack on Petrarch," Detective Pimento said, never keeping his eyes off Crockett. "That is the one thing that doesn't fit my May theory. Why would she go after the old man?"

"Unless there is something in the tomb..." Crockett mused.

"Corinthiana says it hasn't been opened since the death of Lucinda a very long time ago."

Detective Pimento rose. Slowly, he began to pace the room. His steps were labored, theatrical as he crossed toward the door. His feet lightly brushed the carpet, a soft whisper of tensing fibers meeting each footfall.

"Maybe someone *thinks* there is something in the tomb. There could be some kind of family rumor that Lucinda had a large diamond or some expensive jewelry." Crockett turned toward Pimento.

"They would have told us this before," Pimento said. "Augüst would have boasted about it at some point." Pimento shook his head emphatically. "No, I don't think there is anything in the tomb. I think the attack on Petrarch was out of revenge, an unplanned junket in our little journey."

"Revenge?" Crockett looked shocked. "Why?"

"Perhaps Petrarch knew something—or someone. Did he confide in you, Crockett?"

"He did," Crockett said. "He told me everything."

"Perhaps he also had secrets."

Crockett hesitated. Pimento could see the wheels of the young man's brain working with difficulty. Outside, rain began to pelt the windows, another summer storm announcing its arrival.[40]

---

[40] It has occurred to the editor that there are a great number of storms at convenient, atmospheric times in the novel; however, due to sheer laziness, the editor has left them all in. It was far too much work to dig through the text and make sure weather lined up with the appearance of mud, rain on windows, clouds, etc. The reader will simply have to deal with it. Since we're almost to the end, the editor has faith we can get through this together.

As if on cue, the door to the study was thrown open and Petrarch himself entered. Despite a dressing around his head, the old man looked the picture of health. His round cheeks were red, his eyes twinkled merrily.

"Hullo," he said warmly. "How are things coming along?"

"Petrarch!" Crockett rose and ran toward his master. He gripped the old man's hand with tenderness. Tears formed on the edges of his multi-colored eyes. "I thought I lost you last night—I thought…"

"Dear boy!" Petrarch gently pushed Crockett away. "I'm quite fine. I have an overwhelming headache, but other than that, I feel in the prime of my life."

"So, you can tell us what happened?" Pimento asked.

"What did happen? And who are you?" Petrarch's eyes narrowed.

"I'm Detective Lucian Lucretian Pimento. I was called here last night."

"Why would you come last night?" Petrarch suddenly looked very alarmed. "We played cards and went to bed. Now I'm up for breakfast."

Pimento and Crockett exchanged glances.

"Petrarch…" Crockett spoke slowly, "you don't remember last night?"

"I do remember whist. Kordelia cheats, if you ask me, no way she would take me in a straight game. I was best at my gentleman's club for three years running."

"Someone tried to kill you, Mr. Bluster." Pimento crossed his arms over his chest. "You could still be in danger."

Petrarch began spluttering oddly. His lips flapped open and shut but no words formed, only bizarre "pffts" and "pffatzzzs" escaped his mouth.

"Petrarch, someone shot at you last night," Crockett spoke softly. "We found you passed out on the floor—and then," Crockett's cheeks flushed, "then, you, bumped your head on the bed trying to get up."

"Someone tried to kill me?" Petrarch said slowly. "I was attempted murdered?"

"I would say murder was attempted on you, but yes," Pimento said.

"Well, by Jove, that does complicate things." The old man began to pace the room quickly. It was only then that Crockett noticed he had not put on pants, or rather, he had wrapped the pants around his waist as if they were a belt.

"Petrarch, perhaps we should get you to back to bed. I think the shock of last night hasn't completely worn off." Crockett attempted to catch the solicitor, but he was running in a circle erratically like a chicken.

"You don't have your pants on, sir," Pimento said, the harsh tones used upon his arrival returning to his voice. "You shouldn't be up here."

"But, you know, I thought I had it figured out! The whole sequence of events. I thought it was August –"

"Augüst," Pimento and Crockett said together.

"But it wasn't malevolent, you see, it was simply to keep things moving. He was tired of the old man stealing attention, even in death. Aug—well, you know how to pronounce it—he wanted his money and to be done. He told me he had a plan to move the family to his family's home in West Cheshiret onwildonshireshed. Crockett," the old man ceased running around for a brief moment, "that is why I told you to forget it all and go along with the entombment. It wasn't a malevolent murder, simply some parlor tricks used as a means to an end."

As Petrarch reflected on this, the party grew. Brontë and her mother entered the room. Brontë threw a glance at Petrarch and then at Crockett. She mouthed words to him that Crockett could not understand.

"Petrarch!" June began to awkwardly chase the old man, who had resumed his chicken run at an increased rate. "We need—we need to get you back to bed!"

"No, but, I'm thinking," Petrarch said. "Fetch me my pipe!"

Crockett and June ended their pursuit and stood to the side of the room as Petrarch spoke quickly and intermittently.

"You see, I thought, well, I had been speaking with everyone and I was going, Crockett, my boy, I was going to tell you it was all solved and put to bed, so to speak. Robert Edward is a creepy bugger, but not into murdering—also can't hold a knife—I tested that at dinner. I was running my own investigation, better than this strange gentleman, if you ask me."

It continued in that way for quite some time before Brontë delicately stepped forward and gently gripped the old man's arms.

"Dear Petrarch, I think you may be a bit scrambled still from the events of last night."

"The whist! Yes, your pet alligator cheats at that game, if you ask me."

"Alligator?" Brontë looked distressed.

"I think we better get Master Bluster back to bed," June said quickly, coming up behind Petrarch and gently shoving him toward the door. "He's been through a lot over the past twenty-four hours."

"Diggleshroot! The fish!" Petrarch tried to push away from June and Brontë and run toward the desk. "The herring, I think, wanted the money. That's why she was killed by the maid. Maids can't be replaced by fish, you see. No opposable thumbs!"

Brontë and June kept their grip and shuffled Petrarch toward the door. The last words Crockett and Pimento heard him utter before disappearing into the hallway were, "The key maybe did it! Killed the fish and the bird!"

Muffled yells were heard down the hall as he was carried back toward his bedroom. Pimento's mouth twisted upward into a slight smile.

"It seems our chief witness isn't in the right mind to give testimony," he said.

Crockett shook his head. "Oh, dear. I hope he can recover. The poor old man didn't deserve any of this. It was all my fault."

"Was it?" Pimento's eyes again took on their cold, direct stare. "Your fault, in what regard?"

Crockett's brow grew damp with sweat. "I mean, not in…I just mean to say his head. I dropped his head."

An uncomfortable moment unfolded between the two men. Crockett suddenly felt seen in a way that shook him. It was the same sense of existing he'd felt on the streets when rich men and women would see him running in rags. It was the feeling he'd had every day before he met Petrarch.

Pimento's eyes narrowed and widened in a tense, staccato succession. He sniffed loudly.

"Don't blame yourself, Crockett," he said, an edge on his voice. "You can't blame yourself for an accident like that." The word accident sounded calculated, too pronounced and precise.

TOWARD THE CLIMAX

Crockett's heart raced.

"I'm going to go downstairs and ask a few final questions to May and Robert Edward. I'll see you in the sitting room before dinner?" Although posed as a question, Crockett felt threatened.

"Yes," he said quietly. "I'll be down soon."

"Good."

Pimento abruptly bowed. When he stood erect, a smile was on his face, but it wasn't the same, warm smile he'd worn that morning when he'd made Crockett feel so comforted. This smile was one of hidden disdain.

The door closed softly behind him. Crockett leaned over and braced his elbows on his thighs. He took several deep, exaggerated breaths.

Maybe Pimento knew...He could think he knew but not know what Crockett knew, which was the full truth.

Crockett paced toward the desk. Sitting in the center was Pimento's detective notebook, the same one he had written so deliberately in during the morning. Crockett looked toward the door to be sure no one was coming and then flipped open the pages.

It was not what he had expected.

There were no words, only small, erratic scribbles. Page after page was covered in the marks with no meaning. Crockett flipped more quickly through the book, thinking at some point he'd find words, real words with names, motives, dates, and times.

But there were none.

His breath grew ragged. He looked up and then he saw it—It was the painting Martha mentioned earlier that afternoon. A roll of thunder blasted near the house, shaking the windows. Lightning ripped across the sky and illuminated the portrait.

The portrait was of a man in a similar triumphant pose as the general in the mural downstairs. Crockett's gaze wasn't fixed on him, however, but on a background figure, an assistant, or friend, who was standing behind the painting's main subject. The man was bald, wearing glasses.

"Ghosts..." he said softly to himself.

Crockett slammed the notebook shut and stumbled toward the door. It was at that moment he reappraised something Martha had said.

You can take the back stair through the ballroom...

The puzzle box in his brain clicked, the final solution presenting itself. The clues of the case aligned with startling clarity—Lucinda's note, the key, the paintings, the rapier, Beatrice, the secret note, and murder. There was just one more thing he needed to see again—it was imperative he find Corinthiana or August.

He needed to get back into the vault.

20

Bixby Ex Machina

Thunder rumbled and rain pelted the windows of the house. Brontë only saw Crockett for an infinitesimal moment. He ran through the main sitting room toward the west wing. His long legs fumbled with reckless speed. She had risen to follow him, but the detective asked her a question, which forced her to stay in her spot. As Pimento spoke, she kept looking toward the hallway into which Crockett had disappeared.

"So, it's all settled then?" Pimento asked.

"Sorry?" Brontë's eyes remained fixed on the empty hallway.

"Your grandfather's funerary plans. Everything is arranged?"

"Yes." Brontë's eyes flicked back to the detective. "We met the vicar and discussed the ceremony. It will be a short, quiet affair."

"You were gone an awfully long time." Pimento's eyebrow quivered upward.

Brontë suddenly felt very nervous. Her gaze settled on the detective with renewed focus.

"Mother wanted flowers, so we stopped by a florist as well. We also checked in at the grocery and ordered some additional meat from the butcher for the meal tomorrow."

"Crockett seemed to miss you."

Brontë averted her gaze. As she tried to keep her voice calm and casual, it only betrayed her, lilting upward. "He's charming. We've had good conversations this past week." She felt her cheeks grow hot.

"I see. Can you speak to his character?" Pimento asked, an edge to his voice.

"Character?" Brontë searched the detective's face. "He's a wonderful man. He's been very helpful throughout this whole affair." The part of her personality that was her father's flared up as her eyes narrowed and a small vein appeared on her neck. "It is *your* character I would bring into question, Detective. Crockett has been a delight; at times I feel he is the only one who is trying to understand the severity of the situation."

"I see." Pimento politely bowed. "I can surmise you won't be able give the clearest perspective on our handsome, young assistant to the solicitor."

Brontë bit her tongue. She was moments from letting something slip, much more cutting than the "silly" her mother reprimanded her for earlier.

It was May who interjected, putting a stop to the vitriol waiting to pour from her niece.

"I would not say handsome, unless you're attracted to equine features," she said sniffing. "And, yes, he is benign. Although of a poorer caste with disgusting manners, he could hardly have reason to harm anyone in this house. He also lacks the knowledge to execute many of the grislier crimes enacted this week."

Brontë remained silent, grateful her aunt had stopped her from speaking, but holding a new, burgeoning rage directed at the older woman.

Detective Pimento, Brontë, and May remained silent, an oppressive quiet hanging between them when August approached.

"I suppose we're all ready for supper, yes?' He looked around at those gathered and cleared his throat. As his gaze drifted from Pimento's scornful glance to Brontë and May's darkened visages, he clicked his tongue nervously. "I see I've walked into a charged conversation."

Detective Pimento's mouth twitched. "We were just discussing young Crockett."

"Ah! As indigent as he is, not a bad fellow. He has no sense of humor, but you know that's getting harder and harder to find with this younger generation. He just rushed off after begging me for the vault key. He was in an awful hurry about it."

Pimento threw a knowing glance at Brontë. "How interesting. He seems oddly enticed to the place with so many family heirlooms."

"Why don't you come out with your accusations, Detective?" Brontë's eyes flashed. "I think it's quite obvious you have an idea that Crockett, a stranger, new to this house, unrelated to the family, is somehow fatally wound into this tragedy unfolding around us."

"You err only when you say 'unrelated.' It seems he's found very close connection with you, Miss Winterbourne."

August's mustache jumped. "Now, now, my good fellow, I will not have you making incriminating statements about my daughter."

"I'm just stating observations, points of interest." The detective was enjoying himself, his eyes sparkling.

The vein on August's neck bulged. "This is most definitely not a matter to be taken lightly, sir! If you ask me, you're lucky I haven't laid my good wingtips on your buttocks in the general direction of the front door."

June and Corinthiana, hearing the raised voices, rushed into the room. Kordelia, who had been present for the entire discussion, lifted herself higher on the couch to get a better look at the feud.

"You're getting awfully heated over a few throwaway remarks, dear boy," Pimento said. "A detective must look at every possible outcome."

"Well," August growled, "when your outcomes are coming out without coming of evidence, you can count me out!"

The gathered party took a moment to parse the meaning of August's statement. Robert Edward entered the room during this scene of confusion, his cape billowing behind him.

"Vat is going on?" he asked. "Augüst, I can hear you from ze dining room."

"We were just politely discussing the facts of the case," Pimento said calmly. "And I can say that after much deliberation and many interviews, I have a very good idea of who is to blame."

A collective gasp came from the family. Pimento took a moment to admire his effect on the crowd.

"There were several interesting theories put before me. May," he motioned toward the woman in black, "suggested Robert Edward, of all people. Her evidence based solely on xenophobia, if I may take a reductive view…"

"Well, most of us do fear xylophones," Kordelia said from the couch. "They can be as terrifying as out-of-tune harpsichords if you play the wrong scales."

Pimento sniffed slightly but ignored the young girl's assertion. "Brontë," he continued quickly taking a step behind the youngest Winterbourne daughter, "suggested that it was her own father."

Brontë blushed.

August's face grew red; he started to scream. "I told you! These ungrateful daughters make you want to BRAIN them after they BETRAY you!"

Pimento's face expressed annoyance. He shushed August and continued speaking, "But to me the most interesting of all the theories, the most fantastic and magical, was from our dear Crockett. He wanted to drive my attention, not just away from the present, to a far and uncertain past, but to a different continent. His theory," Pimento again smiled to himself, relishing his moment, "was that the murderer was none other than the estranged—"

It was at that moment that a vehement pounding came from the main hall. All gathered, even Pimento, let out an exasperated breath of air, Corinthiana a staccato "Awrk."

"Is anyone expecting company?" June asked nervously.

Her question was met by no responses, only more vehement pounding from the front door. Time stopped for the confused crowd; everyone took turns looking to others for an explanation of the evening visitor. Something in Pimento's speech caused all of them to look at the darkest, worst-case scenario. In those moments, the possibility that it was simply the doctor checking on Petrarch eluded them. They were all sure it could only be some avenging angel. Had the door been thrown open and the devil himself been present on the doorstep, the clan would not have been fully surprised. In those frozen seconds, any possibility was probable.

The door thundered again, this time interrupted by Martha, who greeted their visitor. Everyone in the sitting room, Pimento included, listened to every voice, footstep, and creak of the front door with trepidation.

"Hello," they heard the old maid say tersely. "I'll announce you."

The old woman and her roving eye appeared in the door of the main sitting room. She licked her lips, and, with no surprise in her gravelly voice, spoke.

"Bixby Hawsfeffer, Jr.—Mr. Pip—is here from France, I suppose."

She shuffled off and, in her place, Bixby "Pip" Hawsfeffer, Jr. entered the main sitting room.

Had a flamingo wearing Britain's crown jewels entered the room, it would have been no more opulent and ostentatious than Pip himself. The middle-aged gentleman was dressed in a suit of bright pink, a powdered wig set on his head. A dusting of white makeup covered his face, while his lips shone a startling red in the light of the lamps. His clothes had been dampened by the rain, but this seemed not to bother him in the least.

"*Bonjour,*" he said grandiosely. "*Je suis* the son of Bixby Hawsfeffer, returned from his time abroad, called forth..." He paused here for no particular reason that anyone could assess. Corinthiana was about to speak, when he loudly continued, "Called forth at the hand of his stepmother, Mrs. Corinthiana Hawsfeffer, via an epistle, to pay tribute to my fallen father, despite a loathing in his life of my personal, *homme*-centric, choices."

Unsure whether he was finished, the rest of the crowd mumbled an uneven number of *Hello, Pleasure,* and *How do you do*'s.

Martha returned to the sitting room with a cup of tea and shoved it into the visitor's hands. No one else knew what to do.

"*Oui,*" he responded to no question in particular, "it is painful for me to return to this house, knowing that I am estranged, *la éloignée,* and under the realization that I shall never make amends or say words of warmth to my father, but I have chosen to come on my own free will to pay my respects to him, braving the sodomy laws of fair Britannia. Even if we did not agree in life, in death," here he paused again for dramatic effect, "in death we perhaps shall be reunioned under the love of grace and forgiveness."

"I—" Corinthiana started to speak, but Pip dramatically threw up his index finger to silence his stepmother; for the first time in her long life, the Hawsfeffer matriarch was being out-drama'd. The rest of the Winterbournes and Hawsfeffers waited with breathless anticipation, expecting more of the explanation for their estranged half-sibling/half-uncle's appearance at this hour.

Pip relished the attention. Although his nose was raised skyward, he looked down intermittently to make sure he had everyone's attention. "My fondest memories," he started again, lowering his voice to add emphasis, "are, of course, of my mother singing to me as I fell asleep. Every night she would sing the old song of 'Duck Man of the Old Hat.' As she warbled of the figure's torture and kidnapping propensities, I would smile, and my mother would ask me to search under her own hat for notes of love and affirmation. It was this, of course, that led my father to burn her hats after I had left for France, consumed with the idea that hats, specifically notes in hats, were the root cause of *mon homosexualité*."

Robert Edward, who had been wearing a top hat, felt it self-consciously.

Pip cleared his throat in a loud, grandiose manner. His eyes, previously directed skyward out of pomposity, drifted downward. As he took in the gathered party, his blue eyes flitted between faces without much interest. "Memories," he continued, his eyes on May, "of course, the best of times, seeping through my mind's eye like a warm soup served in the Champs-Élysées. It was this balm that drew me here. I was shocked to receive such a letter, *le silence* from my home resounding over the past decades. But as I opened the note and thought about my mother, this house, my father, I knew I must come home, if only to lay to rest the pain and loathing I have had for it over the decades. The rancor has grown out of a salted earth, with it the roses of my mother's love, twined in brambles of my father's judgments, rippled through with wildflowers that represent friendships, also birds are on the tree, which have symbols I have yet to give them."

"I'm sorry..." Kordelia rose from the couch and approached her uncle. "That line seems very familiar, '...seeping through my mind's eye like a warm soup...' Uncle, have you read *Mère, Bélier, Mort, Chapeau?*"

As she drew closer to Pip, the elder gentleman's nostrils flared. "My dear... Is that your breath?"

Kordelia nodded. "Halitosis—it loses me quite a few points."

Pip nodded, feigning understanding. With renewed vigor, he resumed speaking, taking a step back and raising his arms theatrically. This caused him, inadvertently, to throw the teacup Martha had given him, against the wall. "It's out then, strange *fille éthérée avec mauvaise haleine!*" he exclaimed. He moved his hand to his forehead for additional dramatic effect. "Yes, I am the famous author who penned that work under my French *nom de plume*, Jacques Eiffel-Montmartre. It was I who insisted on four crepe scenes instead of three. Let this be a lesson to all who are told that you have too many crepe scenes—there are never too many! I do hope you read the original and not the German-language version, which has the ridiculously adapted ending with the Mob. Anyway, you must always believe in your crepe scenes and not mobs. Believe in your dreams. You must strive like the falcon over the winds of the Irish coast and believe. Believe in yourself as if you are the only one who can say what you indeed speak that which you mean."

This phrasing caused confusion (for everyone but August, who appeared to appreciate Pip's tendency to string together nonsensical chains of words); however, Pip did not notice the questioning looks of his audience as he drove to the conclusion of his speech.

"We are family here. I have come hundreds of miles to say *au revoir*, and so, I hope that you too, can also, herewith, meet me where I stand as the man who is who he was. Let us forget our past and meet on a common ground, littered with the rhododendrons of our own forgivenesses."

He stopped and bowed slightly. For a moment there was only a confused silence, disrupted by Kordelia, who began clapping enthusiastically. The hall rang with the sound of her applause and little else, until after a full minute, she became self-conscious and stopped. Corinthiana shuffled forward in her usual, slow dramatic gait, looking back uncertainly at the rest of the family. She had hoped someone else would offer an olive branch, but the sheer number of themes in Pip's arrival speech rendered most of the party dumbfounded. Since she had written the letter that invited the sodomite, she took the responsibility and offered a greeting.

"Well," she said slowly, "it is very nice yooou were aaable tooo come. In truuuth, I waaas reticent tooo beeegin theee funeraaary events without yooou." The old woman stiffly reached out and patted Pip's shoulder. "Maaarthaaa, caaan yooou taaake his coat, pleeease?"

Martha stomped back into the room and took his bright pink coat. Pip, once rid of his garish outerwear, adjusted his wig and assessed the room once again with a mixture of disdain and indifference.

Thunder rattled the windows, punctuating the emergence of Crockett, who had been hiding in the shadows. He marched into the room, his arms full. In one hand he held a rapier from the basement; in the other arm, he carried what appeared to be a pile of old clothes. Confidently, he threw the objects down as he took his place in the center of the room.

The appearance of the young man caused a ripple of anxiety, mostly due to his feral demeanor. His eyes were wild, his breath coming in quick, manic spurts. Everyone in the room felt ill at ease, including Brontë, who wanted to approach her dear friend but was also uncomfortable due to his rabid state.

"I know…" he panted. "I know who it is! In Pip's speech…It's the clue about Lucinda's note. Her…"

"Pip." Detective Pimento interrupted him loudly. He marched authoritatively into the center of the gathered party, taking his place next to Crockett. His eyes twinkled, almost as manically as the young man's. "We know, Crockett. You think that somehow the man who came thousands of miles and only just arrived is responsible for a string of mayhem and death that spans back weeks—a poor theory."

"I don't think—"

"You don't," Pimento's teeth bared into a grimace. "Your thoughts don't come intelligently or clearly, I would say. Do you have something else to add to the conversation? Do you perhaps think the one responsible for the crimes is a pigeon? Maybe a fox who looked especially guilty in the garden. I hear the local constabulary is still following that lead on the squirrel with a gun. Perhaps you can join them."

Now it was Crockett's turn to grow fierce. "You would belittle me—"

"Belittle? I wouldn't say it's belittling to call someone a charlatan when they act charlatanesque."

Pip was impressed by the usage of the word "charlatanesque" and wrote it in a notebook which had been concealed in his pocket.

Pimento turned and looked at Crockett directly. He tilted his head down so that he gazed directly at the young man over his spectacles. "I have watched you, Crockett. I pulled you close, and I let you work it out yourself. What an interesting exercise it was for me."

Crockett's gaze flew around the room searching for Brontë. He found her, standing uncertainly behind her father. "Brontë!" His voice softened. "Brontë, I know who it is. It's crazy the real killer—well, it's—"

"Crazy?" Pimento said quickly. "I should say so."

"Don't call me crazy!" Crockett glared at the detective. His voice took on a hard edge. Despite the severity of the situation, Brontë found Crockett's ferocity titillating.

"You're right," Pimento said quietly. He turned away from Crockett and moved forward, placing his hands behind his back. "Perhaps I should call you what you are." He looked back at Crockett, his gaze vicious. Crockett's grimace faded as he realized the detective's move in the elaborate game of chess. Pimento turned back toward the family, a satisfied grin on his face. With a joyful glint in his eye, he pronounced his accusation, "Murderer."

21

Pimento, Triumphant

Lightning ripped through the sky illuminating the room in a white glow. A gasp as loud and pronounced as had ever been heard in Hawsfeffer Manor erupted from the family. In a moment, there was a flurry of bodies, and Crockett found himself bound and gagged on the floor of the sitting room. Robert Edward and August took the initiative; they held the young man down as Pimento paced triumphantly about the room.

Brontë's eyes filled with tears. She looked anxiously at Crockett, who writhed on the floor trying to loosen his bonds. He yelled loudly, but it was muted by the (rather fetid) sock of Robert Edward, which had been put in his mouth to gag him.

"Surprised, my dear?" Pimento looked into Brontë's eyes. "You shouldn't trust a man from the streets. The lower classes are predictably disgusting. I knew from the moment I saw him he was dubious. But it was just a matter of good detective work to earn his trust and get him to incriminate himself." Pimento turned to Crockett and smiled malevolently. "Good boy, Crockett. You did just what we expected."

Crockett was nearly foaming at the mouth. He convulsed and twisted to try and break free from his binds.

"But…how?" Brontë shivered. "How could he…?"

"My dear," Pimento gently took Brontë's hand, "he's a con man. My theory is he has been stealing from the old solicitor for years, just awaiting the proper time to show his real teeth."

"But what's his motive?" May asked. Even she—who normally enjoyed a grand scene of fire-and-brimstone vengeance, especially against the poor—was flabbergasted. She flicked her eyes between family members for some aid in understanding.

"Where should I start?" Pimento approached the fireplace. Once he arrived at its marble depths, he turned dramatically. "He arrived with Petrarch and knew the whole history of the family. He's a smart boy and recognized that, not only did the family have a plethora of characters, but the Winterbournes also had two eligible daughters."

Crockett screamed through the gag.

"Shhh, dear boy! You're afraid of it getting out? Well, it's too late." Pimento put his hands in his trouser pockets and stepped toward Crockett. He kicked the young man sharply. "Upon arriving, our young, astute observer took an assessment of the house. It can be assumed he brought with him the record of the nursery rhyme having known that it was a cause for alarm in the neighborhood and would play into the local myth that the song belonged to the ghosts of the house. He set it up, a clever manipulation of the phonograph. It was created with some string and a handmade timer which delayed the contraption from playing until midway through the séance. The idea was to trick the family and," here Pimento looked at Brontë, "draw one of the young women into his trust."

"I don't believe you." Brontë's lip trembled.

Pimento's smile only grew broader as he continued. "Beatrice's death was configured with the help of the absent groundskeeper. No doubt our dear Crockett has promised him a cut of the fortune when it is secured. I bet our Mr. Dexter Fletcher stayed very close to the house. If we listen, I would not be surprised if we could hear him breathe."

At this moment, Crockett shook harder than he had previously. With all his fury, he kicked at the bonds and tried to throw Robert away from him. Both Robert and August needed all their strength to pull him back down to the ground. August gave him a mighty blow to the stomach that quieted his screams.

"Didn't like that, did you, Crockett? The truth hurts, I suppose." Pimento's gaze floated over the crowd. Everyone was riveted except for Pip, who was straightening his waistcoat in the reflection of a brass urn. "The real violation, I suppose, was him turning the gun on his own master, our dear, dear Petrarch."

Pimento leaned over Crockett and smiled. It was a hideous expression of joy. Tears fell from Crockett's eyes; he shook his head vehemently.

"You deny it, Crockett?" The detective looked toward Brontë. Tears also streamed down the young woman's face. "Miss Winterbourne, why don't you ask him?"

Brontë put a hand to her mouth. She looked frantically at her mother, who turned away. Pimento had his hand on the sock, ready to release it so Crockett could speak.

"Ask him, Miss Winterbourne." Pimento's eyes were wild with giddiness.

Brontë said nothing. She looked anxiously at her father and sister, who both avoided her gaze by looking out the window. Her mouth opened several times, but no sound came out. She placed her hands over face, her body wracked by a violent sob.

Pip, his waistcoat straightened, sighed and marched forward. He had been growing bored with the whole affair; the day had been long, full of travel, and he was very much looking forward to dinner. "Well, let's move on with it then," he said casually. He folded a handkerchief around his hand, to keep from having to touch the sock. He leaned in close to Crockett. "Poor man with weird eyes, but a rather nice physiognomy, did you shoot the old man—Petridge was it?—to whom they are referring?"

Pimento, slightly disappointed that the middle-aged dandy dimmed the dramatic effect of the confrontation between lovers, motioned for him to release the gag. The youngest Bixby gingerly reached in and removed the sock from Crockett's mouth.

A flurry of protestations escaped the young man as soon as his tongue was free. "Brontë, he's lying. It's not me! What do I have to gain? There's no money! There's none!"

Corinthiana covered her eyes. May nervously assessed her shoes. Even August looked slightly embarrassed, his mustache lifting apprehensively.

"There's nothing to gain…There's no motive! I know who it is, it's—"

Pimento motioned for Pip to replace the sock, which he did, rather awkwardly—at first stuffing it in too gingerly but then a bit too roughly. When it was fully inserted, he gently patted Crockett's head then turned his attention to Beatrice's bed; its garishness escaped his appreciation when he first entered the room.

The detective sighed and began to pace. "You aren't answering the question, Mr. Cook," he said. Abruptly he spun and kicked Crockett, this time much harder. Crockett groaned.

"Crockett…" Hope sparked in Brontë's eyes. She drew forward. "Did you do it? I know you wouldn't hurt Petrarch; just tell us you didn't."

Pimento stepped toward Crockett and knelt down. He lifted the gag. Crockett looked at Brontë with clear, sad eyes. "Brontë…Brontë…the gun, the shot—that was it. And it was for you. I did it for you, because you said it wasn't over. You know how I panic—I goat freeze, I…get in trouboule with it. It was rash and stupid…But the rest—"

Pimento laughed loudly and replaced the gag. Brontë's breath left her. She fell to her knees.

"Guilty. Guilty as the day is long. Guilty as the stars in the sky!" Pimento waved his hands through the air dramatically.

"That's rather poetic," Pip said turning his attention away from Beatrice's bed and taking his notebook back out. "I may steal that."

Crockett tried to keep Brontë's gaze. He futilely attempted to explain the rest of his story through the course fabric of Robert's sock.[41]

Pimento stood erect, a look of pure delight on his face.

"I think the best action would be to take our fish-murdering fiend into

---

[41] It should be noted the sock is getting an odd amount attention at this point in the novel. In the original draft, Earhart had put much more effort into its description. One of Earhart's oddities, in addition to drinking and second-rate novel writing, was collecting socks from varying regions of the world, not only to wear, but at the end of their usefulness, to turn them into delightful puppets.

the family vault and lock him there until the appropriate authorities can arrive. Madame Hawsfeffer?"

Corinthiana peeked through her fingers and looked at Detective Pimento. "I suppose…I meeean…Yes?"

Pimento motioned for Crockett to be moved. "Could you please phone the police, Mr. Harrington? Let them know the Mystery of Hawsfeffer Manor has been solved."

It was at this moment that Petrarch entered the room. His eyes were still wild; he remained robed in his sleeping gown.

"Hello," he said casually. His eyes scanned the room lackadaisically until he saw Crockett, bound and gagged, being dragged toward the west wing. Upon this sight, he sputtered like a broken American motorcar. "Pffft—Pffft! My goodness! Crockett? What is this?!"

"He's killed the herring and tried to marry my sister to get the family money," Kordelia said quickly. "All very standard fare, I suppose…for a murder mystery."

Petrarch's jaw nearly fell to the floor. "But, why?" He searched the faces of all those present. He jumped when he saw Pip in his pink trousers. "Who are you?" he asked, momentarily forgetting his assistant was being accused of murder.

"I, my dear, portly friend, am Bixby Hawsfeffer, the younger—known colloquially as Pip—son of the admirable, but bigoted—"

"That's dead Bixby's son," May finished quickly. Then, quietly, she leaned toward Petrarch and continued, "He'll monologue all day, if you let him."

"Yes…of course. Could…?" Petrarch began spinning in circles hoping someone he made eye contact with would tell him more.

No one, however, knew exactly what to say.

"Well, this has been an interesting evening, to be sure." Pip politely bowed to the gathered crowd. "I must get some food and away to bed. It's been a very long day, and I feel like I need a good rest before the funerary services begin. I've prepared a light speech for the occasion. My dear stepmother has agreed to give me an hour, perhaps hour and one-quarter, for a few brief thoughts on the subject of my father and, of course, the very fragility of existence—"

Martha, for which everyone was infinitely grateful, interrupted him to push him back into the foyer and toward the hall to the east wing.

"You're staying over here," she said angrily, shoving him forward. "I'll get your things and have them delivered."

"Oh, yes, of course, the guest wing, how lovely and delightful. I do hope there are enough mirrors, you see I require quite a bit of preening upon waking and in the middle..." Pip continued talking as he disappeared from view.

When he was gone, Detective Pimento placed his hands behind his back and rocked on his heels.

"Another victory for Pimento," he said proudly. "No one escapes his keen eye."

The rest of the family shifted uncomfortably. Even the aloof Kordelia looked as if a question was hanging on her tongue, moments from being launched in the detective's general direction.

"Excuse me," Petrarch said, absently rubbing his stomach, "but what is going on? I evidently was concussed and put back to bed. I think I've put the general timeline together now, but can anyone tell me why poor Crockett is being dragged away bound and gagged?"

"Well," June pulled a strand of hair away from her face, "you see, it, well, it appears that...I suppose the truth of the matter is..."

August took up the argument with equal confusion, "I think my wife is trying to say that what Pimento has done is unmask the...very surprising... the person who he believes is at the root of all the shenanigans...you know Beatrice, the phonograph...and such..."

"I," Pimento interjected joyfully, "have found our killer. It was Crockett. That is the end of our mystery. The end. It is over. Everyone go on to supper because I have solved it."

"But why would Crockett do such a thing? He doesn't have a motive, for... well, any of it." Petrarch began to scratch his belly more fitfully.

Brontë's eyes briefly lit up again, but the spark quickly faded. "Petrarch," she said, "I didn't believe it either, but," a silver tear loosed itself from her eye, "he admitted to trying to shoot you."

"Shoot me?!" Petrarch yelled. "He would never!" Petrarch thought briefly of the young man, his freezing, his general panic under stress. He sighed. "I suppose he has been under a bit of duress."

"My dear, Petrarch," June said softly, "he did confess it. We don't know… why…exactly…but he said…it."

"It was admitted by him," Pimento said harshly. "You can't trust anything about him. His variegated eyes, ha! The very mark of a traitor!"

Petrarch shook his head emphatically. "Even so! The shot was a terrible one, and Crockett couldn't have done the rest! I simply don't believe it!"

"Belief," Kordelia said softly, "is like the foam on the sea, a passing dream of tuna fish."

"Darling," June said wringing her hands, "having heard of the authorship of that play, I'd much rather you start quoting Shakespeare, or even Ben Jonson, if you must go with second-rates."

When Martha returned from settling in Pip and bringing him a tray of ghost biscuits to calm his appetite, she directed the family to the dining room for supper. Few felt inclined to eat. Corinthiana immediately returned to her chambers, surprised that, knowing the name of Beatrice's killer, she was no less uneasy than before Pimento made his revelation.

Kordelia and Brontë came to a truce in their embattled sisterhood and held hands as they walked outside to take a turn in the garden. For the first time since he had met them, Petrarch saw an affection between the two girls, the game of points and comparisons set aside. Their very roles appeared to have exchanged as Kordelia led Brontë, the elder sister laying her head on the younger's shoulder.

June and August stayed in the sitting room. June appeared to be in shock. Even August, his face usually a shade of red from some unnecessary rage, was pale and thoughtful, his attention focused on his wife.

Petrarch, May, and Robert Edward (once returned from incarcerating Crockett) did sit down to Martha's meal, but it was a joyless affair. May and Petrarch mindlessly shoveled food into their mouths as Robert Edward spoke on the general untrustworthiness of the poor.

"It is ze international truz," he said sadly. "Vun cannot trust ze people vizout ze money. Zey are alvays murdering or looting. Ve should have known as soon as Crockett vas born in his poorness."

Outside the storm had lifted, and a handful of sparse stars peeked through the thinning clouds. Far in the west, a thin line of red sky marked the sunset. A few birds were singing happily in the trees, their song an odd juxtaposition to the confusion and suffering which weighed on Brontë's heart.

The two sisters strolled beyond the house, toward the river. Although the track was thick with mud, neither of them paid attention to the dirt splattering on their shoes. Kordelia was occupied with the look of distress on her sister's face, the sister who she had always believed could not be broken by anything or anyone. For years, as she went in and out of boarding schools and (unfortunately) burned cats, it was Brontë who remained a pillar of constancy in their home, the one beacon of stability around which the chaos of her mother, father, and grandparents turned. She wracked her mind for something to say, some brief, warm emollient, which could bring a smile to Brontë's lips. Somehow, even the words of a play were inconsequential in the intensity of the moment (even if they were writ by their estranged half-uncle).

Brontë was preoccupied with the (supposed) betrayal of Crockett. It was unbelievable that she had not seen, not noticed, not conceived that he was capable of such acts. Perhaps everyone, at their core, could do the most despicable thing when the right circumstances presented themselves. She would resign herself to the truth of Crockett's duplicity, but just as she came to the brink of acceptance, she would remember his eyes, the way he had looked at her the first time they met, the morning in the garden, during their adventure in the vault, and the night before the incident with Petrarch. She had seen goodness; she had seen (dare she think it?) love in those green and blue orbs.

Her thoughts swirled in this loop, denial and acceptance, as she and Kordelia strolled, arm-in-arm, farther away from the house.

It was Kordelia who eventually broke the silence, finally deciding on something which she thought could be consoling.

"I know I can come off as a bit crazy," she said, "but I crazily think Crockett is blameless."

Brontë lifted her head from her sister's shoulder.

"You see," continued Kordelia, "we spoke once, out here, and I think he really wanted to figure out what was happening. I told him then that I always believed the worst in everything to be surprised by the better. But," Kordelia squeezed her sister's hand, "I don't think there was the worst in Crockett. I think he was always better."

Brontë now turned toward her sister and smiled. "I appreciate that, Kordelia. Thank you. I also feel like I knew him very well, and he's not capable of any of this. Even if he did, in a confused fit, shoot a bullet in Petrarch's room, he wouldn't harm Beatrice, and I refuse to believe he had any interest in marrying me for money."

Kordelia sighed. "It seems to be another twist in this strange labyrinth." The girls stopped walking. Brontë looked toward the sky. Kordelia crossed her arms and turned to the house. "You know," she said quietly, "when I was with Crockett, I told him my fear about this whole situation."

"And what's that?" Brontë asked.

"That it's a spirit from the past." Her voice lost its warmth; both women shivered. "That it's still not over."

22

Brontë at the Brink

When Kordelia and Brontë returned to the house, they were met with the news that Pip Hawsfeffer had been pushed from the window of the folly. In the grand scheme of all concerns at the Hawsfeffer household, all believed it ranked far below the death of Beatrice and just under the importance of Corinthiana's pre-bed sherry ritual.

"He was a sodomite and, therefore, a criminal," Pimento said stroking his chin, "so, in terms of general death gravitas, I'd say we enjoy this evening's triumph before circling back in the morning."

"He was also a bore," June Hawsfeffer added. "I really think we'd be hard-pressed to find someone without a motive to kill him, even with Crockett locked away, it could have been any of us."

"He's also not dead." Martha is the one who made this general observation as she and August dragged his body into the main foyer. "Maybe a few broken bones."

"Egghhh," Pip mumbled.

"Thaaat is very goood news," Corinthiana said warmly, pouring a glass of sherry.

In the end, Pip was moved to the sofa in the sitting room and the doctor was called to check on his injuries. The general air of confusion and distrust carried on, although, distracted by the wounded Pip, Corinthiana and June worked with alacrity to make sure the maimed guest was attended to.

Most of the house retreated to their own quarters, fed up with the tension and chaos of the evening. No one quite knew what to do with the revelation that Crockett was a pet killer and had intentions of marrying Brontë for the family fortune, but it did provide a solution, even if improbable, which explained the odd series of events.

June and Corinthiana did not take long to latch onto the alternative history which this solution presented.

"He was a bit furtive," June said adjusting Pip's feet on the sofa. "I suppose I thought it was a social backwardness due to his state of poverty, but it may have been a general air of malfeasance."

"I think yooou haaave it there, my deeear. I noticed his spirit waaas theee color of baaat droppings. His penury is tooo blaaame; remember theee night heee didn't wear a formal dining jaaacket? One maaay remooove theee raaat from theee raaat house, but one maaay never uncheeese the raaat."[42]

Brontë said nothing as Crockett was rewritten a villain. She merely helped wait on her half-uncle and pondered over the events of the evening. After her discussion with Kordelia and further meditations on the subject, she was sure of his innocence. The Petrarch plot was idiotic, but he had done it to assist her—to get to some truth that he thought only an attempted murder would push them toward. She was certain that Petrarch would agree with her; he would not betray his apprentice over an ill-planned scheme. Crockett made mistakes, but he was not the shadowy figure causing the true chaos in the house.

"He couldn't be!" she told herself as she watched Pip's labored breathing. "Crockett, even with his brains, couldn't have hatched the plan with such efficiency in only a few days. How did he get the vault key? He couldn't have emotionally manipulated me to that degree."

Corinthiana and June retired to their chambers. Robert Edward remained awake but said little, pacing slowly through the main room and occasionally

---

[42] In the editor's research this saying was never used by anyone at any point in time, although a white hip hop group out of South Dakota did release an EP *Uncheeze the Rat* in 1997.

heading toward the west wing to walk the long gallery and look at the portraits.

June had encouraged Brontë to go to bed, but she insisted on waiting up for the doctor and making sure Pip was attended to.

The doctor arrived; to Brontë's surprise, it was a different doctor from the one that appeared the previous evening to aid Petrarch.

"Hullo," he said curtly. This gentleman was rotund and confident. His bald head shone in the glow of his lamp. "Where is the wounded fop?"

"I'm sorry," Brontë said, "but, where is the other doctor?"

"Other doctor?" The little man shook his head. "I am the only doctor in this part of Hampminstershireshire, my young lady."

"But the other gentleman from last night…"

"Well, I can guarantee it certainly wasn't a doctor if it wasn't me." He sniffed at this and pushed past Brontë into the main foyer. "Now, where is the wounded gentleman?"

Brontë showed the new doctor to Pip and made sure he had all he needed before silently stalking off toward the east wing.

To her relief, a light was on under Petrarch's door. She knocked softly and waited for his response.

"Yes?" the old man grunted. "Please, no disturbances just now."

"Petrarch?" Brontë said as sweetly as she could muster. "Could I please come in?"

"Ah! Brontë! Yes, please, my dear. I was assuming it was your father or Robert Edward with news of another murder, and I can't really process another death at the present."

Petrarch opened the door quickly, then resumed, what Brontë guessed to be, part of his vigorous exercise routine. In this particular motion he sat on the bed, laid back, then lifted halfway up, a grunt escaping as he did so.

"Petrarch, I don't think it's Crockett," she said, shooting straight to the heart of the matter.

Between grunts, Petrarch responded, "Of course it's not, my dear. I'm now trying to figure out exactly who it could be. He very well could have shot me—he's linguistically killed me for clients before. For a woman not nearly as beautiful as you." Brontë flinched slightly with embarrassment as this was said, but Petrarch gave her a friendly wink. "Either way, he's not behind the Beatrice nonsense. He makes mistakes but never with a nefarious purpose." He paused here in his exercises, worn out, and laid back on the bed. "You know that before I was shot, I was ready to put it all to bed with the *August* theory, but now we simply cannot. We have to clear Crockett's good name. But the path to the correct person is riddled with so much confusing information; I'm beginning to think it could be everyone—you know, in some way, perhaps everyone did contribute to the deaths."

"Well, I didn't…"

"Perhaps your father and mother, then? They have motive. Your Aunt May does. Robert Edward doesn't, but he's shifty and from the continent, so it wouldn't surprise me, of course…"

Brontë bit her lip. "Petrarch, the doctor is different."

"I'm sorry?"

"The doctor from last night isn't the doctor that arrived tonight."

Petrarch lifted himself up again but remained seated. "Well, that is odd in such a small hamlet. There wouldn't be two doctors."

"So, the one who came with Detective Pimento wasn't a doctor." A small, triumphant feeling leapt up in Brontë's breast. She moved to the splintered window, a breeze blowing through the bullet hole. "Why would Pimento bring another doctor…?"

"Perhaps it was a favor to someone he knew. The doctor may have been preoccupied…"

"What if it is Pimento?" Brontë asked quickly. "He's behind it. He brought those people—they weren't real people but a fake doctor and a fake policeman."

Petrarch's eyes softened. "Brontë, that makes less sense than the explanation that it was our dear Crockett. I think, perhaps, your imagination is running away with you."

"But Petrarch, couldn't Pimento…couldn't he be connected somehow?"

"In what way?"

"Well, it seems like it has to be two people. There was never anyone conspicuously gone when the odd events occurred. Perhaps Pimento isn't Pimento at all!"

"Pimento not Pimento…" Petrarch stroked his beard.

"We can't trust him." Brontë walked rapidly toward the door. "We have to get Crockett out of the vault. He can help me put all the pieces into place."

"Darling," Petrarch rose and moved to Brontë. Gently he took her hand. "I think we should go to Pimento and ask about the doctor. There will be an explanation. Don't let the chaos of this week make your judgment chaotic. We saw what it did to poor Crockett."

Brontë looked at Petrarch as if he wasn't there at all. "I see," she said softly. "Perhaps…"

Before the old man could say another word, she grabbed her light from his nightstand and left the room. Her pace quickened as she moved down the hallway toward the foyer.

Her mind raced with images of Crockett—his stares, his stuttering words, his tall, gaunt frame, the warmth of his smile, the adorable way he screamed when he thought she was a large canary.

"It can't be him," she said to herself. "It can't be, but it could be the detective…"

She suddenly remembered Crockett held down on the floor, his eyes panicked. The screams that came from behind the gag were visceral; even the memory pained her.

Pausing on the stairs, she debated her next course of action. Should she go to Pimento? But certainly a villain puppeteering the chaos of their house wouldn't tell the truth. There were so many convenient facts he manufactured in the accusation of Crockett, could she really trust what he said? But where else could she go? Even if she freed Crockett, would there be anything they could do together?

Her train of thought was derailed by a noise from above her. It sounded as if someone was moving in the hall atop the stairs. Her heart pounded in her chest. She lifted her eyes and scanned the darkness. Raising her lamp, skeletal shadows leapt up, dim light threading through the spindles of the banister.

She turned to the main sitting room, but the doctor was visible there. He was accounted for, still attending to Bixby.

"Hello..." her voice failed her, calling upward. The word came out as a rasp, a nervous, shaking utterance.

Closing her eyes, she thought again. *What is there to do?*

Then the image came to her. It was the same scene of Crockett shaking on the floor, bound and gagged. In this instance, however, the words he screamed came back to her.

"I know who it is, it's—"

"Crockett knows...," she said in a whisper. "He knows."

Her feet pounded up the stairs. The terror of the earlier sound left her mind; her resolve was bent solely on getting to Crockett. Rapidly, she moved down the hall, stopping outside her father and mother's door. Without a knock, she pushed open the chamber.

All was dark except for the slice of light falling from her lamp. In the corner a clock ticked sadly. She raced toward her father's bedside. He was fast asleep, snoring loudly.

"Father," she said, her voice harsh. "Father, wake up." She set down her lamp on the bedside table and shook him.

August moved slightly but did not awake. June mumbled something incomprehensible about her corset but did not stir.

"Father," she called more loudly. "Father, wake up!"

August smacked his gums; his eyes slowly opened.

Brontë nearly fell off the bed when she heard the shrill, screeching noise that came from her father. It was an instinctive thought which made her reach out and place her hands over his mouth, muting the girlish shriek.

"Father..." she said quietly. "Is...that really your scream?"

Her mother, remarkably, simply rolled over and began to snore. In the hallway, she thought she heard the sound of quick, panicked steps.

August didn't answer. His screams had ceased, but his breath came in short, erratic bursts. After several even breaths, Brontë gently lifted her hand.

"Father," she said. "I need you to regain your composure."

He began to calm down, however his eyes retained their wild, pained expression.

Brontë gently stroked his arm, keeping calming eye contact. Her father finally opened his mouth, uncertainly. He threw a cursory glance at his sleeping wife.

"That wasn't me," he said quickly. "I think your mother sleep-screamed. My own panic sounds are very guttural, masculine, like a kettledrum."

Brontë pinched her nose in exasperation.

"But…but…why are you here, anyway? Is something wrong?" he asked.

"Father, I need the key to the vault. I need to talk to Crockett."

August blanched. "Darling, no. He's a pet killer!"

"I don't think he is." Brontë gripped her father's arm and looked deeply into his eyes. "I think our detective isn't who he claims to be and has made false accusations."

"I can't." August shook his head. "I can't let you go down there! On the chance that he did what Pimento said he did to Beatrice…I couldn't let myself, with a clear conscience…"

"I need to speak with him." Brontë's voice grew louder, harsher. "I need the key. Come with me if you don't want me to go alone."

"Darling, I…I can't let you…"

Brontë rose and looked around the room. In the corner was her mother's secretary, a bundle of unopened letters spilling across its wooden surface. She looked between it and her father. Again, her imagination went to Crockett, the poor boy laying on the ground, gagged, kicked.

It was perhaps the fact that it was the witching hour that Brontë took the course she did, or maybe the influence of Crockett's erratic, poor decision-making. Regardless, with night at its deepest and the moon shining dolefully on the house, the darkest idea, the most insane conclusion, was what came to her mind first. Crockett would, perhaps, die in the vault, his screams unheard. Having killed Beatrice and set into motion the nightmare of the previous week, who is to say what the killer may already be doing to him, alone in a dark, shadowy corner?

Her steps took her across the room. Grabbing her mother's letter opener, a long, sharp, steel blade, she turned and crossed the room to her father. With no intent to harm, she raised it high into the air, it's shining tip aimed at his heart.

"Father," she said sullenly, "the key, please. This must end tonight."

23

Crockett's Confession

Her father again screamed, this time waking her mother. The chaos of the scene, from an outside perspective, may have been humorous—the young woman in trousers raising a letter opener over her father who was shrieking like a woman, her mother, still overfilled with sleep, yelling "My god, don't tighten it further, I may crumble!" (speaking of the corset of her previous dream). To Brontë, however, it was not humorous but another obnoxious hindrance in her getting the key and saving Crockett. The conclusion of this task, in her imagination, would lead to the two of them, arm-in-arm, solving the mystery and restoring peace and order to the house.

But before this happy ending could be writ, she had to, again, cover her father's mouth, this time whilst pointing the letter opener's blade at her mother.

"Mother, no time to explain, but I need you to help me get the key from father for the vault."

June's mouth opened slightly.

"I know. But I don't think Crockett is the killer. I think it's the detective and I need to save Crockett in order to save our family."

To Brontë's surprise, June merely shook her head condescendingly. "Brontë, my sweet, that is a ridiculous conclusion to come to. Were this a mystery novel I would shame the writer who'd pen such a ludicrous ending.

It has to be Crockett! He's an excellent suspect and impoverished. That makes much more sense for a killer."

Brontë in exasperation lifted her hand from her father's mouth and, at the same time, took a long slash to his arm with the letter opener.

"Ow!" August quailed in his high-pitched caterwaul. "Brontë, that hurt!"

"Give me the key!"

August looked to June, who, rolling her eyes and shrugging, said without compunction, "Give it to her, Augüst. Let her play the fool."

With the key in hand, Brontë ran from the room with her lamp. The doctor attempted to hinder her flight in the main living room, but she did not pause for an update on the condition of Pip.

Storming toward the west wing, she was breathless by the time she reached the mural which concealed the vault. Quickly, she clicked the button to reveal the trap door. Fumbling with the key, she opened it and descended into the darkness.

Her heart pounded as she drew nearer to Crockett. Each step was one closer to his earnest gaze, his quiet laugh, his disarming smile.

When she came into the open vault, she found him, frantically pulling at a rope that bound him to a rather dusty suit of armor. He had been feverishly jerking at it, trying to make his way to the stairs.

Brontë melted when he looked up and caught her gaze, a broad, beautiful smile growing on his pale face.

"Brontë!" he said, the word like a flower blooming.

"Crockett…"

The two met, unsure how to properly greet each other. There had been previous tension of an amorous inclination, but there had also been the rumor of Crockett's betrayal. Now Brontë stood, remembering the moment of his confession to shooting Petrarch, but also staring into his eyes, the eyes that were the only respite and refuge from the maelstrom of fear and death that surrounded them for the past several days.

Crockett reached out, his hands bound. When Brontë hesitated, refusing to take his hands, he awkwardly raised them and saluted.

"I believe you, but I also…" Brontë said. "Can you explain it all?"

"I did shoot at Petrarch," Crockett said quickly.

"Petrarch and I thought that was the case. Can I ask what course your logic took to that conclusion?"

Crockett shook his head with shame. "It was stupid, an almost fatal mistake. I get so muddled in high stakes situations; I—it was, you…" The young man looked boyish, his thick eyebrows raised. He clasped his hands together in a penitent pose. "I did it for you."

Brontë felt her cheeks flush. She couldn't help but feel flattered. "Why?" she asked softly.

"You weren't ready to give up, even when everyone else was. You knew something else nefarious was going on in the house. When you came to me last night, you…" He stopped here. His cheeks became so luminous as to almost glow in the darkness of the vault. "I've never really felt the way…" He paused again. His mouth opened, then closed. With a staccato cough, he cleared his throat. "I knew I had to help you. I knew, in that moment, that what you believed, I would believe, and that to set you free from the pain and panic of this house was a sworn duty, a quest."

Brontë's heart fluttered. All need for a proper explanation faded, but Crockett forged on.

"So, I took the gun, shot at Petrarch, and pretended to raid his room to precipitate the end, you see. I thought that if I could get everyone in the room and suggest that someone stole the key, then the guilty party would incriminate himself. But…" Crockett shook his head. "But I didn't think that Petrarch would become so stunned! You should have seen him on the way here—his exercises—I didn't think a noise would shake him so profoundly." The young man's head dropped onto his chest. Tears formed at the corners of his eyes. "I thought he was dead, Brontë…The man who has treated me like a father, who took me off the streets! It all went sideways…"

"I would say sideways is the direction of this whole tale of Beatrice's murder. Nothing has made sense from the moment everyone arrived in the house."

"So sideways to be almost inverted!" Crockett sighed. "I didn't pay any attention to everyone when they arrived in the room. I didn't…do anything, so it was all for nothing—the fake shot, the chaos and panic—then we almost killed Petrarch again."

"Twice," Brontë added.

"Twice, yes, but nothing was clear. None of it made any more sense until the next day when I…"

Crockett lifted his eyes to the exit of the vault. His face contorted into one of terror.

"Where is he?" he asked.

"Who?" Brontë took a step back.

"It's the note—the portraits!—that was your clue. It's very much Dexter but not Dexter, it's who he…Oh, dear, no one is who they say they are." Crockett shut his eyes and slowed his breathing. When he opened his eyes, he was calmer, more collected. "It's too complicated. Cut my bonds, Brontë. I have to run after him. He could already have it."

"Have what?" Brontë's eyes sparkled; pride filled her voice. "You know! It's Dexter but not Dexter. Is that who it is? You know!" She suddenly remembered the soft footsteps as she pondered her course of action on the stairs. "It's someone in the house!"

"It is. And I do know, but we've already wasted too much time. I have to get to the tomb before it's destroyed."

Brontë hesitated only for a moment. Crockett's eyes were so earnest, so intense, that she couldn't deny him. She trusted him fully.

In the corner of the room, she found one of the rapiers from the collection of blades that was used against Beatrice and approached Crockett. With one swift slash, his bonds fell, and the young man was freed. He flexed his wrists and turned to the stairs of the vault.

The puzzle box in his mind was opened. Adrenaline flooded his veins, surged through his heart. The conclusion of his future action remained shrouded in mystery—when he confronted the killer there could be any number of outcomes. His life was on the edge of a knife. In his present pursuit he could emerge as the conquering hero or vanish into darkness, another victim of this Hawsfeffer ghost.

It was with this fear of death in mind, his pulse racing, that Crockett turned to Brontë and stepped toward her. Rather than in fear or chaos, his frantic emotions aligned, in this moment, in a surge of courageous, amorous passion. Brontë shook with joy as he pressed in closer; she could almost feel the heat of his affection, the adrenaline and uncertainty that raged through his body. They paused, a short distance from each other. Then Crockett pressed his lips to hers. It was the first kiss for either of them, a heated, uncertain mashing of lips.

When he pulled away, they both looked stunned.

"Crockett..." Brontë whispered.

"Wake the house," Crockett said, a smile turning up the edges of his lips despite the uncertainty of the coming hour. "I'm going to try to stop him, but I need you to be ready. Get your father, his gun, and run to the tomb as soon as you can."

This time it was Brontë who pulled him close. She kissed him—an electric current fused them once more for the length of a heartbeat.

"Who is it?" she asked quickly as their bodies parted. "I'll need to tell Father."

But Crockett was already running to the stairs. He called back a name that only raised more questions than it answered.

"Bixby..." she said to herself as Crockett's footsteps disappeared. "I suppose it could be...but which?"

24

A Murderer's Monologue

Crockett hurtled toward the family tomb like a bolt of lightning. He stopped only for a few moments when Pip yelled for his attention as he charged through the main sitting room.

"Are you all right?" Crockett asked.

"Yes, my murderous friend, I just needed a little attention. *Le médecin* has gone, and I could use fresh water, if you please. I also saw the man who pushed me from the window; without a doubt it is—"

"Oh, I know who it is," Crockett said quickly. "Terribly sorry, but I need to go stop him from destroying a very valuable family secret."

"Ah!" Pip nodded. "In that case, you can bring the water on your way back. *Bonne chance, monsieur!*"

Crockett gently patted Pip's head unsure of what else to do. As he raced out of the house, he marked that, for having been thrown from the second story window, Pip appeared in full health. He assumed the flexibility required for the sodomite's lifestyle rendered him limber enough to withstand the drop, much in the same way that Petrarch's rigorous exercises allowed him to survive the shooting and subsequent head injuries.

Tearing out the front door, Crockett fled the house and entered the dark of the yard. The night was silent except for the crunch of his shoes on the sparse gravel of the walkway. A point of dull illumination filled the light of the family tomb only yards away. It was in this moment that Crockett finally felt fear—the buoyancy of Brontë's kiss faded when his thoughts turned fully to the impending encounter with the man who orchestrated not one, or even two, but three murders (perhaps three and a half to four depending on how one counted attempted murders and faked deaths).

The one hope Crockett clung to was that the murderer did not anticipate him coming. Even with the aid of the fraudulent detective, he could not have foreseen Crockett discovering the game moments before being bound and carried away to the vault. And he wouldn't have counted on Brontë's freeing Crockett for a final confrontation.

With renewed courage, Crockett increased his pace up the large hill and toward the tomb. He was about to enter the dark mouth of the marble structure when the murderer emerged.

He still wore his costume, the long black cape, tonight with a luminous green lining around the inside of the collar. A snide smile was on his face, one hand holding a lamp, the other a revolver, pointed at Crockett's chest. It suddenly occurred to the young man that the incredible ugliness of the face before him was not due to a central European genetic deficiency but rather to poorly done stage makeup. Both his nose and eyebrows were false and attached with cheap wax.

There was little time to dwell on the old man's ruinous face, as Crockett only had eyes on the small bit of parchment in his grasp. A surge of joy shot through his heart when he saw it, the thing at the center of it all—Lucinda's last note. It rested, unopened, in the same hand in which the traitor held the gun. After so much blood and terror, it appeared to be an afterthought, a forgotten piece of rubbish.

"Hello, Crockett," he said, his voice soft as an adder slithering. He gleefully dropped the malformed and problematic continental accent of his alter ego, Robert Edward Harrington.

"Bixby," Crockett said harshly.

"Ah, dear boy, but which?" The old deceiver's teeth gleamed in the dark.

Crockett proudly recounted the solution to the mystery he chased the previous week, "Bixby Von Bunson, fallen heir to Baron Von Bunson, American turncoat and traitor, murderer of Bixby Hawsfeffer, Lucinda

Hawsfeffer, and Beatrice."

The villain Bixby laughed quietly, a hissing like gas leaking from a pipe. "Well done, my boy. Petrarch was correct about you. He raved when we met just a few weeks ago. *Prodigy*, I believe, is the word he used." His soft laugh transformed into a witch-like cackle. *"Despite his very austere upbringing…*I believe that's the euphemism he used for your lack of class and education." Bixby lowered the revolver and stroked the barrel. "I thought you may get at the Dexter bit, but I didn't think you'd follow the threads all the way back to me."

Crockett's caterpillar eyebrows furrowed. "Martha pointed me to the portraits."

"Ah!" Bixby clicked his tongue. "Old Martha. She was very loyal for a long time. Even after we killed her dear Lucinda. We'd have killed her then if Dexter hadn't held a consuming love for her. He never did win her heart, but he took her eye. I suppose all love turns sour when it's not nurtured correctly."

Crockett shivered.

"Oh, dear boy! The world is a harsh place!" Bixby was enjoying himself thoroughly; his theatrical narcissism being fed after years in the darkness, a literal lifetime of secrets. "I learned that during my time in America. It's a hard lesson to learn, but once it is imprinted on you, it makes things easier—well, it makes it easier to take what you want, I should say." The older man smiled, his teeth cutting an ominous crescent in the shadows.

Crockett's body shook with fear and loathing. "That's what made it easy to kill them…All of them…" Far from goat-fainting, he desired to leap forward, to have his hands find the old man's throat and squeeze. The gun, however, kept him at bay. While Bixby still held it in his grip, Crockett had no chance to play a hero.

"Money actually made it easy to kill them," Bixby said. "My dear cousin, Bixby Hawsfeffer, took my inheritance, so I took it all back. Imagine! You return home from the wilds of America, hoping to be embraced as a prodigal son, and you discover that your cousin has killed your father, soaked up all your inheritance, and picked offensive draperies to hang in your family's sitting room. It's more than one man can bear."

Crockett, for the first time, was surprised by the old man's revelations. "Bixby Hawsfeffer killed your father?" He was impressed by the Von Bunson-Hawsfeffer families' propensity for murder.[43]

"Yes," Bixby said, "that's not why I killed Bixby Hawsfeffer, though. I never really liked my father, so I considered it a favor."

Even for a murderer, Crockett was shocked by the depths of Bixby Von Bunson's villainy. "So...you killed him and Lucinda to get the money back?"

"Well, it wasn't enough to kill him. Killing still leaves a dead person as a remembrance; I wanted to erase him completely."

Crockett swallowed. Very faintly he thought he heard the sound of a commotion coming from the house. His heart leapt upward at the hope that someone may be coming out to find him. It was a small thread to cling to as he stared into the eyes of the maniacal Von Bunson.

"So, I took my cousin's place." Bixby's eyes narrowed, a look of pure, evil glee writ on his features. "We killed Lucinda, which was *very* dramatic. She nearly got away with her little plan with that adorable note Petrarch was so kind to bring with him."

"That..." Crockett said coming to a realization, "is what started all this."

"Correct!" Bixby spun the revolver on his finger. "Another top mark for Crockett! I went to Petrarch to update my will—I'd been a bit of a spendthrift, as you know—and it was then that I found out about Lucinda's little epistle. He left it in my file, you see. I came across it by a stroke of good fortune. It included the instructions, but Petrarch had the key, and I couldn't ask after it." Bixby chuckled. "I would never have believed that all those years ago she knew Dexter and I were up to something."

"So, she went to Petrarch to deliver the note. Oh..." Crockett looked to the nefarious Bixby in understanding. The elder gentleman watched him put the rest of the pieces together. "You saw that she directed it to be released

---

[43] The penchant continued on for several generations. @badgrrlKinzay47, in addition to hoping this novel brings her some money, is also in talks with a TV network for a reality show called *The Aquatic Murder Kids* about "the descendants of homicidal families looking for love, friendship, and drama...on a boat."

only upon Bixby Hawsfeffer's death. She thought that would mean you had taken the fortune, and you knew her inclusion of the tomb key intimated something was hidden there."

"She didn't think I'd make him disappear completely and assume his identity." Bixby again cackled with glee. "With the shock of the revelation of the letter, I knew I had to put a plan into action. I forgot about updating my will, which is why I had to use the services of the second solicitor in secret so that I could still get Petrarch here with the tomb key."

Another sound, this one much more pronounced, came from the house. Crockett turned hopefully toward the mansion. Von Bunson grew nervous. His gregarious mood ebbed.

"We're waiting for one more," he said looking toward the house. "If he doesn't hurry, I may have to dispatch you myself."

Sweat trickled down the young man's brow. Had the stakes been lower, he may have returned to his old reactions of cowardice, but something about his confrontation with the fake Pimento earlier, his piecing together of the mystery, and the kiss with Brontë imbued him with new courage, a heat to his blood which had never been there before.

He stood taller, his hands raised in surrender. He attempted to play to Von Bunson's ego. "Before you end it, though, I must know how it all played out—the present bit with Dexter, the family, and Beatrice."

Von Bunson flushed with pride. "So, you didn't piece it *all* together, then?"

"Most of it." Crockett tried to speak slowly, giving time to whatever entity was making the noises in the house to reach him. "As I said, Martha mentioned the paintings. I knew there was familiarity to Pimento, but I couldn't place it. Then I saw both the murals in the west wing and the portrait of you and him above the fireplace. That's when I realized that it was both of you, together. It all came tumbling into place then—I understood that's why the portrait of the real Bixby Hawsfeffer and Lucinda had been marred in the basement."

"Ah! Yes." Bixby nodded. "I'd forgotten that portrait. Again, Dexter's affection for Martha gave another clue. Martha asked that it be kept as the sole remembrance of her friend, Lucinda."

"But that's why you didn't want to be painted until you were older, 'gray haired,' as you told Brontë." Crockett furtively stole a glance at the house—the noises had faded. "You kept the original portraits—you disguised as a war general and hero in the west wing murals—as a trophy to your old self. Even though you got rid of Hawsfeffer, you wanted them up. You took a chance no one would recognize you in them."

Bixby Von Bunson was silent. His glittering eyes stared at Crockett; to the young solicitor's surprise, the look was not one of contempt or loathing but a certain fondness.

"You know, Crockett," the old man said, "you and I aren't terribly different. I'm better in every way, of course—richer, more handsome, cleverer—but there is a charming similarity. You are shockingly intelligent. You pieced so much of it together. I'd like to think in the same way I would have."

"I'm nothing like you." The hair on Crockett's neck stood up.

"Aren't you, though?" Bixby took a step forward, his eyes locked on the solicitor's assistant. "We both hoped to ascend from what we were. You were on the streets, shoved into Petrarch's closet to learn law; I was moving out of my strangling British background to reinvent myself in the wilds of America. But, neither of us could find acceptance, could we?"

"That's why you came back from America?" Crockett felt a slight pang of empathy. Despite Bixby's tendency toward homicide, some raw emotion was creeping into the old man's voice. Crockett let himself think of a younger Von Bunson, abandoned, alone in the vast wasteland of America. "You couldn't find acceptance…"

"I couldn't find it anywhere." Bixby lowered the gun. Crockett's shoulders, which had been full of tension, relaxed slightly. "When I was young my father didn't like my flair for the dramatic—magic, smoke, mirrors, that kind of thing. We didn't get on well. So," Bixby crossed his arms and began pacing, "I went to America to find a new beginning. And the people there loved it."

Von Bunson appeared to swell with authority. He was on stage, recounting his storied past; Crockett was now a member of an abstract audience. His gesticulations grew more dramatic, his voice louder. "The Americans loved the deception, the art of illusion. P.T. Barnum made freaks into stars. Drama, intrigue, magic…I met Dexter when I joined the little traveling show, and we tried our hand at it. We had quite a measure of success."

The noises in the house ceased all together. A fear grew in Crockett that he would not be saved, that the heroic conclusion he envisioned when he had seen Brontë descending the stairs to his prison could fade to darkness.

But Bixby had lost his sense of urgency. The old man, awash in a wave of memory, continued his tale. "Dexter and I wanted to be the next Barnum and Bailey with a traveling Wild West show, but things didn't turn out. When we went out on our own, we took a third partner, but he wasn't willing to play nice."

"Not nice at all!"

Crockett leapt high into the air. A similar shriek to the one which escaped him during his early morning chat with Brontë erupted as he lifted off the ground. It wasn't a canary that inspired a fear in this instance; although, it did have some avian qualities. Pimento, his large feather shaking, appeared from the shadows. He held a second gun pointed at Crockett's back.

"Shhh!" Bixby ran forward and put a hand on Crockett's mouth.

Pimento laughed. "You were coming to my favorite part of the story, Bixby! And don't worry about the boy's shriek." Pimento motioned for Bixby to let Crockett go. "I've convinced the house that I'm coming out to stop him from… something…something about the river, I think I said." Pimento shrugged. "I'll be honest, it wasn't very clever. I am running out of lies to tell."

Bixby relaxed. "The boy knows. Well, he knows most of it."

"Does he know who I am?" Pimento wiggled his eyebrows.

Crockett looked at the fake detective darkly. "Dexter," he said.

"Well done!" Dexter said. Both he and Bixby clapped.

"Would you like to tell the rest of our story, Dexter?" Bixby asked. "You can add some panache!"

"Oh," Dexter straightened his jacket. "Let's just say that I practiced what I did to Beatrice on our third partner. When he wouldn't give us a fair shake, I gave him a fair taste of a blade."

Bixby laughed so loudly Crockett jumped. "Oh, clever! 'Shake' and 'taste'—slant rhyme, delightful!"

"Thank you!" Dexter smiled. "Anyway, it was murder but nothing personal."

"We English try to keep murders dispassionate. I tried to teach that to Dexter—he took to it, even if he is a dense American."

"Well!" Dexter wagged his finger. "You killing Bixby Hawsfeffer and assuming his identity was rather personal. I'd say *you* are the bad Brit."

"We all get carried away! You took the Beatrice disembowelment a few steps too far, if I may say!"

Crockett cleared his throat to interrupt the two old men. He found their banter annoying, especially in light of his diminished hopes of help arriving.

"Where's Brontë?" he asked. Hoping that if he was going to die by the hand of these two blowhards, she, at least, would be safe.

"Oh! Your dear little friend!" Dexter looked toward the mansion. "She's being held in her room. It didn't take much for me to convince the rest of them that she was hysterical. I simply reminded them all that she was, in fact, a woman, and they quite agreed with me. I convinced them you used her to escape, and I was coming to save the day." Dexter tsked and shook his head at the young solicitor. "You should have told them it was Robert, Crockett, for as smart a boy as you've been, no one has even asked where the estranged continental cousin is tonight."

Both Dexter and Bixby found this painfully amusing. Crockett's scalp grew hot with embarrassment.

"Well, then let's get to the conclusion, shall we." Bixby pointed his gun at Crockett with renewed vigor. "We'll give you the close of the drama then dispatch you. I feel you should know the full story before passing on. It gives the narrative arc a nice, tight ending."

Crockett's heart thudded against his chest. With Brontë subdued and the family holding her hostage, there was no one to save him. The only saving grace was the duo's own delight in their cleverness; with Dexter present, Bixby was even more willing to wallow in his triumph. If he could keep convincing them to talk, perhaps he could buy time…

"The murder of our partner precipitated a return to England," Bixby resumed. "I knew we still had opportunity back home. My parents were wealthy, and I promised Dexter he could have his fair share."

"Plus he promised me the time," Dexter added, "to work more on my art."

"But when I returned home..." Bixby groaned. He raised the revolver to his forehead and struck a tortured pose as if on stage.

"It was very dramatic." Dexter shook his head. "Bixby was very upset."

"My cousin had taken it all! So, I had to erase him. We planned and schemed for quite some time. First, dispatching Lucinda in the river. We made it look like an accident, then—"

"Oh, that was a clever bit!" Dexter looked skyward with fond remembrance. "We played it all perfectly! Once she was gone, Bixby Hawsfeffer went into grieving."

"We used the time to dismiss the servants."

"Except for Martha..." Dexter said. "I never could let her go, even though she never wanted me..."

Von Bunson rolled his eyes; he was quite fed up with the unrequited love of Martha and Dexter. "Anyway, once the house was clear, we poisoned my cousin and...well, that was that! I used some slight costuming and took his place. It erased him completely and avoided any legal complications."

"Does Corinthiana know...?" Crockett asked.

"She doesn't." Bixby shook his head. "She was very beautiful, an empty-headed farm girl. Not only would she be a delightful wife, but she also would spread rumors of our whirlwind romance. Locals would be led to assume our relationship was the reason Lucinda disappeared."

"But Lucinda left the note." Crockett looked to the piece of parchment in Bixby's hand. It rippled slightly in the warm, summer breeze. "She left the note with Petrarch which would guide her son to the tomb. That second epistle," he motioned to the letter in Von Bunson's hand, "explained what happened to his father. It was the game from his childhood that was the hint."

"Yes! It was very clever of her," Dexter said. "I knew it had to mean something, which is why I had to get Martha to explain it me—the hat game and all that. The note was concealed under her stone Tudor beret on her sarcophagus."

"What does it say?" Crockett leaned forward.

"In no uncertain terms it discusses her fear of a plot between me and Dexter which put her and Bixby Hawsfeffer in mortal danger. It alludes to the reasons for the murder, but it is not entirely factual. However, if it were discovered, my claim to the house would be removed, as would that of my wife and daughters."

"But there's nothing left…" Crockett said. "You're all in terrible debt."

"They can sell the house!" A terrifying resolve crossed Bixby's face. "I will not have my wife, children, and granddaughters shamed into non-existence." His nostrils flared. "This," he said shaking the note, "will be destroyed and then we will all move forward, forgetting this whole messy business forever!"

This moment of outrage brought Bixby to his senses. The imminent discovery of both him and Dexter-Pimento on the grounds made the matter at hand more urgent. He, again, aimed his gun at Crockett and narrowed his gaze.

"But!" Crockett shouted. He still had a large number of questions. The events around the mysteries at Hawsfeffer were unnecessarily complicated.[44] "When did you decide to fake your own death?" The question came out more pleadingly than Crockett would have liked, but he pressed on, "Was it simply to get the tomb key?"

To Crockett's great relief a smile returned to the old man's lips. "Dexter, how could we forget that piece?!"

"It is very important in terms of fleshing out the plot." The fraudulent detective was looking at his shoes, perturbed at the mud which collected on them in his excursion on the grounds.

"I'd looked for a copy of the tomb key a long time ago. It was for a very unromantic, non-murderous reason; I simply thought it may be a good idea to clean the thing—all the dead bodies, you know. I raided the house and

---

[44] The editor would agree with Crockett's sentiment in this moment; it was, as Petrarch may say, "a true dillyfog" putting it all together.

found nothing. I asked everyone if they knew where to find it. It seems there were only two: one buried with Bixby and the other given to Petrarch by Lucinda.

"Well, it may have been a bit of a panic response, but when the Lucinda note was revealed to me, I knew I had to act quickly to get Petrarch's copy."

Somewhere in the distance, Crockett heard more sounds. Hope swelled in his heart.

"I was the one who suggested the fake death," Dexter added. "We are both getting old, so we thought it wouldn't matter much anyway. We threw the plot together quickly so we could get Petrarch to the house with the key."

"You couldn't simply ask him for his copy?" Crockett asked.

"It was legally impossible. Lucinda willed it to never be passed on until the death of myself."

"The whole thing was very irksome," Dexter added.

"Faking my death to get the key was simple in execution," Bixby continued. "I yelled and disappeared into some brush, and Dexter ran to the house to get a witness. The most complicated parts were creating the second, real will in secret while making sure Petrarch would come to the house for the reading. The other niggling item was building out the Robert Edward plot in advance to make sure alibis were covered and I could be present at the will reading." Bixby laughed to himself. "That required me to go to London as Bixby, return as Robert, only to leave as Robert and return as Bixby to die as Bixby then return as Robert."

Crockett, in spite of himself, grew impressed with the complex nature of the plot. "So, you drew out the plan, prepared the fake correspondence between Robert Edward and Bixby, then staged a trip to London in which you would change into Robert Edward and visit the house."

"Correct—it was very, very lucky Dexter and I kept all of our old costuming from America. We had a number of rather fun disguises to use." Crockett wondered if 'lucky' was the operative word to describe the poor makeup and sad costuming of the two men before him.

"I'd also like to thank you, personally, Crockett," Dexter bowed courteously. "I'd written that elaborate speech to give to the family, but no one was very interested in my part in all this. If you hadn't gone nosing about with your investigation, I wouldn't have gotten to give it to anyone."

The noises from the house became more frequent. Bixby and Dexter turned their attention to the large, white façade with fear in their eyes.

Crockett threw in another question to redirect their attention back to their own vanity. "What now, then? Once you kill me, what happens? Bixby, you can't go back to your family. You're technically dead, and your alter ego, Robert, belongs back on the continent."

"It's true, but I can visit as the dear, old cousin. Dexter and I can make our way to Belgium and resume our old tricks. They love magic, and the waffles are to die for. We could even write a wonderful stage drama about a thieving solicitor's assistant."

"I've waited years to get back to performing," Dexter said. "You probably noticed I've been keeping in practice. People thought I was crazy, but it was really my art."

"A common mistake for many a thespian, I'm sure," Crockett muttered.

"But, enough," Bixby threw back his cape. "I'm glad you finally had interest in the plot, Crockett, but now we must bid you *adieu*. Dexter, you may do the honors."

Crockett felt the barrel of the revolver press against his skull. With death before him, all his emotions merged in that moment—it was a nexus of every feeling he'd ever experienced. He took a deep breath; his eyes watered with nascent tears. Perhaps there would be no god from a machine to save him (or even Kordelia's Danube Mob). His life would simply vanish under a cloud of smoke in the darkness of this family estate. In the wake of the violence, he would have only a ruined reputation, a grieving Petrarch, and… Brontë.

His throat seized. The convergence of all feeling evaporated, leaving only one emotion.

"Please, just one thing," Crockett said, his voice breaking. "Tell Brontë that I did have the fondest affection for her." He paused, a tear sliding down his cheek. "I very much loved her."

"How very nice." Bixby sneered. "I can assure you, you would have never had my permission to marry her. A second-rate solicitor does not belong in the same parlor as my granddaughter. It's a shame the current circumstances brought you into such close proximity." Bixby looked at Crockett with a glint of amusement. "Somehow this sad confession of love makes this all the more enjoyable. Dexter," Bixby took a small bow, "you may end it."

Crockett felt the cold gun push forcefully into his skull. Tears ran down his face without restraint. There was some sense of sadness, but, deep inside, he felt a flowering of acceptance. As he closed his eyes and awaited the carnage, he allowed himself to imagine Brontë's smiling face, haloed in warm, June light. The memory of her kiss rushed through him, turned his fear to joy. Brontë smiled in Crockett's imagination. She opened her mouth.

But no human sound came from her, no voice. It was the violent blast of a gun.

25

The Battle of the Tiddlymouth

Crockett opened his eyes expecting to see Jesus, or another man of Anglo-Saxon heritage,[45] robed in white, welcoming him to the afterlife. Instead, he was met with the same darkness of the grounds and the shocked expression of Bixby Von Bunson staring into blackness. Although the sound of the gun faded, the night was far from quiet. Screams were erupting from behind him. He turned to see Dexter Fletcher writhing in agony, a deluge of blood, black in the night, pouring down his leg.

"My god! My god!" Dexter rolled on the ground, clutching himself.

A quick glance up brought Crockett's eyes to the figure who saved him; Martha stood with the gun from the sitting room held in her grasp.

"The secrets end here, Master Von Bunson," she said. Her eye spun in earnestness. "Let the boy go."

Bixby's face lost its look of shock. His eyes burned, his expression one of pure malice. He turned his gun on the old housekeeper.

"You…How dare you interfere!"

It was at that moment Crockett acted. Lunging forward, he toppled Bixby. The two men fell, a mess of limbs. While Bixby clawed and groped, Crockett strove to get Lucinda's confession. It was this choice that led him to gain

---

[45] It is unclear if Earhart knew Christ was both Jewish and from the Middle East.

possession of the paper but Bixby to reclaim his weapon.

Crockett stood, his hands up, the paper held tightly in his grasp. Bixby, gnashing his teeth, pointed the gun directly at him.

"Bixby!" Martha yelled from the darkness.

In a flash, Bixby spun and sent bullets flying toward Martha. His first two shots missed, but the third found its target. The maid crumpled, the projectile hitting her shoulder. Crockett took the moment of confusion to run, as fast as he could, into the darkness.

It was only a few strides into his escape that he doubted his decision. He remembered little of the grounds. The only time he walked past the gardens he was preoccupied with thought. The lights in the house were dim, as was the bleak glow coming from the mouth of the family tomb. He scrambled over the rocky pathway, tripping over brambles and branches. Luckily, he could hear the rush of the Tiddlymouth and direct his course toward its general direction.

"Blast Dexter and his terrible groundskeeping," he said quietly to himself tripping over a large root that crossed the path. "At least his employment is now explained."

While Crockett should have been terrified, the chaos of the night rendered him only with thoughts of moving forward, of survival, and of protecting Lucinda's note, the only thing that would give the insanity of the week some measure of reason. The desire to save Lucinda's epistle, mixed with focusing on the uncertainty of his trail through the garden, made the idea of a rabid, armed Bixby Von Bunson pursuing him in the dark an ancillary threat.

But Bixby was coming. The older gentleman, well versed in the layout of the grounds, picked up speed. He could be heard tramping through the garden's overgrowth, his pace quickening. Crockett's only advantages were his youth and a few moments of lead time.

His heart raced as he rambled over the unruly route forward. In his rush to escape, he tumbled, lurching forward and sliding through the thick mud to a spot near the riverbank. The water rushed by, the ominous (and atmospheric) rains of the previous few days making the current a treacherous, roaring presence in the dark.

THE BATTLE OF THE TIDDLYMOUTH

Even in the chaos of his pursuit, Crockett had to sigh, realizing that his only pair of unmuddied trousers was now unsalvageable.

Bixby heard the cacophony of Crockett's fall into the weeds, but the darkness of the night hindered him from seeing the location of his landing. The grasses along the bank were high enough to shield the young man from view. In reality, the men were a few yards away from each other, but nature and night kept them hidden, two men on the opposite ends of a great void.

In most detective novels,[46] Bixby would have fired shots into the weeds, scaring Crockett like a bird from the brush, but the old man's poor shot left him with only three more bullets—all of which he knew would be needed to finish Crockett once and for all.

Breathing heavily, Von Bunson gathered his thoughts, pondering how to trap the solicitor's assistant. Not a physical match for him and uncertain of his own ability to fire a gun accurately, he knew he had to rely on the only skills left to him in the night. They were his greatest gifts, but ones which had to be used with precision to end his crusade successfully—persuasion, deception, and theatricality.

"Crockett, dear boy, come out," he said, infusing an avuncular charm to his voice. "The game's run afoul, and there's no need to hide. You've won. You solved it all."

Crockett said nothing. He, too, had his brain working in a frenzied state to counter the scheme he knew Bixby was plotting at that very moment. As he sat in contemplation, Bixby's only answer was the whisper of grasses and the rush of the river's current.

"Quiet, I see." Bixby's teeth ground together. "Clever, also." The old man's mind raced. "Dexter and I thought we had everything buttoned up before you interfered. Everyone had decided to move forward with the burial, the tomb would have been opened, and we would have snuck away with the note."

---

[46] In Earhart's notes, he very dramatically stated that this book was "not one of those usual, awful detective stories." It was, perhaps, in one of his drunken fits (there was sherry spilled on the pages of this particular passage in his diary) that he referred to the book as a "Mysteridramaganza," some sort of portmanteau of mystery, drama, and extravaganza.

He paused and let his gaze drift over the grasses. His vision had fully adjusted to the dark. The intermittent light of a quarter moon provided some aid to his aging eyesight. "You see, Dexter overheard you and Brontë plotting. You said that night—the very one in which you took your shot at Petrarch—that you thought the murderer was Bixby Hawsfeffer…In the moment, we misconstrued the statement. We thought you were on to us. It wasn't until your later interview with Dexter as Pimento that we realized you actually thought it was the homosexual Bixby—Pip—from Paris."

Crockett controlled his breath, grateful that the evening breeze and the rush of the river provided cover to his soft exhalations. He had no plan, but he knew he must make a final effort to return the note to the manor. Fear manifested itself in goose pimples forming on his neck and arms. He reasoned he had precious little time before Bixby discovered his hiding place.

"That next bit of the plot was chaotic." Von Bunson ran his arms over the grasses, searching through them. "Dexter had to leave his note and disappear to come back as the detective in disguise. We were planning to proceed with our scheme the next morning, me calling the police and him arriving, but you expedited that with your little shot at Petrarch. You made us pivot very ungracefully, Crockett. We thought we could trap you, you see." Bixby heard a movement to his left and raised his gun frantically; in his haste, he fired one of his three remaining bullets into the blankness of the empty countryside. He was embarrassed that the cause of his alarm was a grasshopper which leapt at an inopportune moment. He cleared his throat and lowered his weapon. It took all his emotional strength to keep the frustration from his voice. "Ah ha! More ungraceful pivoting!" He threw his cape over his shoulder. "We contrived the detective's midnight visit at the last moment as a form of triage. Dexter called up two of his acquaintances to play the parts of the doctor and the policeman, and the game began."

Crockett went rigid after the bullet was fired. He lay, stiff as a piece of driftwood, as Bixby continued.

"You surprised us again, though. You were very smart during the Pimento investigation." Bixby regained his composure and methodically paced through the weeds, down to the riverbank, then back up into the short grass. For the first time in decades, he felt irritated at Dexter's poor groundskeeping; a competent servant would have trimmed this area which was so near the dock. "Dexter thought he could manipulate you, get you to make some confession that would allow us to incriminate you. The house was already indifferent to you—a poor, self-educated street dweller. It would take very little to convince the family you were guilty of *something*."

With each pass down the bank, Bixby grew closer to Crockett's location.

The young man reclined on the ground to keep below the grasses. He knew he had to master his fear, tame his wild, beating heart, and make his move against the evil patriarch. Looking upward at the stars, he breathed deeply and braced his nerves for an offensive strike.

Bixby's thoughts also churned. He reviewed what he knew of Crockett as he spoke slowly of Dexter and his plot. Then it struck him, like lightning—the *coup de grâce* which would draw the boy out of the shadows.

The old man tried to keep the glee from his voice as he spun his web with more earnestness. "Dexter did draw you into his confidences, but we didn't plan for everything, did we dear boy?"

Crockett's breath came faster.

"Dexter didn't imagine the bond you would develop with my granddaughter, the depth of feeling which blossomed between you. How could he think that such a young, fortuneless boy from London would draw the affection of my eldest granddaughter…my lovely Brontë?"

The old man paused. He thought he heard a movement in the grass. This time he wanted to be sure the rustling was a threat before he fired his weapon. Slowly, he let his gaze drift over the waving weeds looking for signs of human activity.

He had been correct in his assumption of movement. Crockett did make the slightest of noises, inadvertently digging his hands into the dirt at the mention of Brontë's name. All schemes of escape ceased as his thoughts turned to Bixby's speech, the possibility that Brontë was tethered to him in some miraculous way, across class and boundaries of titles.

Bixby shivered with anticipation as he continued. He was sure the slight stirring in the dark had been the turn of the tide in his direction. "She saved you! Against all odds, she went into the darkness of the vault and set you free for this final confrontation. Neither of us could have imagined that sudden burst of action." Bixby gained momentum. He continued earnestly. "And imagine the joy Petrarch will feel when he sees you returning, triumphantly, with Lucinda's note in your hands. He said you were 'the brightest young man in London,' and this will only prove it irrevocably. I think when you return home you can expect a very large raise in salary." Bixby smiled to himself, sure the young man was entranced. "All thoughts of your attempt on his life and the subsequent head injuries will be forgotten. How could he hold you accountable when you've won the prize? I would say the sacrifices were well worth the joy of seeing you expose such a grand revelation."

Crockett closed his eyes blocking out the light of the stars. He had never intended to harm Petrarch. The old solicitor knew how much he meant to him—if all were revealed and he exposed the mystery, would this frightful week and its events be forgotten?

"We all make mistakes, Crockett." Bixby's eyes flowed through the darkness looking for any indication of the young man's presence in the tall grasses. He had made three full trips down the bank. Whether he exposed Crockett by convincing him to come to him or by finding him hiding in the grass, he would soon be victorious. "I've made my share of them, and, through you, I hope to make some amends. Come with me into the house. Allow me my own confession. My family may lose their reputation, but at least give me my honor back. Allow me to speak and clear the air—I'll tell them everything."

Bixby then heard a slight rustle, not the wind, but the sound of a body moving in the brush. He was not sure where it was, but he had its attention. His voice rose in pitch as he charged forward; it was difficult to suppress the joy creeping into his words. His pace wading through the tall grass quickened.

"Honor, dear boy," he said. "We often think others have not earned it. You must know—growing up in the streets, stealing to get by, no education. But you have won it now. You have done what you needed to do to solve the case, restore peace to my family, and make amends with your mentor, and," he took a deep breath, "win the heart of my beautiful granddaughter."

Crockett's eyes opened. He lifted up slightly and rested on his knees. He was on the verge of standing upright, moments from raising his hands in the air to submit to the old murderer. Bixby sounded genuine in his desire to be restored to his family. If Crockett began the reparations, could he earn the hand of Brontë in the process?

"Come into the house with me and let them both admire you, Petrarch and my granddaughter." Maniacal glee dripped from Bixby's soft voice; Crockett was too distracted to hear the threat. "They'll be so proud, Crockett. Euphoric."

Crockett rose.

He had been lying only a few feet away, concealed in the brush and shadows. Bixby saw his multicolored eyes shine in the dark. The young man's face was peaceful, almost angelic. Bixby's eyes flicked to the piece of paper held in Crockett's fist. The killer was sure there was still a way to make it all work out. He could kill Crockett, finish Martha, and put them in alignment. Who would doubt that the senile old maid wasn't behind the murder? She could be Crockett's accomplice.

Bixby raised the gun. The expression of calm in Crockett's face fled. His eyes widened.

"Never trust an actor, dear boy," Bixby said.

The old man pulled back the hammer.

But, at that moment, whether sent from some divine being or a magical intervention from the Danube Mob, there was a gust of dramatic wind.

Had Bixby been less garish, less obvious with his theatricality, the cape wouldn't have been problematic. But in the sudden rush of air, it lifted and swept across his line of sight. Already a bad shot, the old man fired up and into the dark, his penultimate bullet lost in the night. The gun roared as he toppled to the ground.

Crockett hesitated as he watched the old man writhe in his costume. He remembered his old days in the street gang, his avoidance of all roughhousing and fighting. Petrarch was his escape from the pugilistic lifestyle of the streets. The life of a solicitor's assistance freed him of the wild, untamed underworld of London. But as Bixby screamed and twisted in the fabric, he knew his time was short. He must be the brute or face the terror of the old thespian again.

He leapt onto Bixby and attempted to hold the man down. Bixby was still covered in the cape, unable to see, but he thrashed wildly.

"Get off me you contemptible, impoverished—"

Bixby bucked and threw Crockett to the side. Lucinda's note fluttered out of his hand. For a moment, Crockett's heart nearly burst out of his chest in fear. The epistle hovered, just out of his reach, like a white moth flapping through the dark. Clutching maniacally, he was able to pull it back toward him. The confusion gave Bixby time to right himself. The cape swirled backwards, and the old patriarch turned the barrel of his gun on Crockett.

Crockett threw his hands up, the note clenched tightly.

"Give it to me," Bixby's voice was feral. "This idiocy ends now."

Crockett stuttered. "It's...don't do it! It's...your legacy! Your family!"

Bixby, mad with rage, reached out hungrily for the note. He again lost his balance; Crockett used the opening to aim a swift kick at his chest. The old man spluttered and toppled backward, the force of Crockett's attack causing him to hurtle down the hill, through the brush, and into the muddy waters of the Tiddlymouth. With a loud splash, Bixby's gun landed away from him, the revolver spluttering into the muck.

Crockett breathed a sigh of relief. He still held the note, and Bixby was in eight feet of water, his gun buried in the depths. He paused for a moment, wondering if he should extend a hand and help the old man out of his predicament.

The internal question was answered, quite outwardly, by the blast of a gun. A spray of red splashed onto the shore, coating the waving brush and weeds in a slick, violent paint.[47]

---

[47] As with most of the violence in earlier drafts, this scene was much more dramatic. There was nearly a page of description on the consistency of Bixby's brain. "The cerebellum detached itself, like a leech being removed from a commodore's foot. It spluttered, ribbons of gore shedding outward in spools of red and gray..."

Crockett turned. His pulse raced as he looked to his right. Beside him was the imposing shadow of the house maid, glaring at the dark of the river. Her weapon was still leveled at the water. The blood from her earlier wound glistened, black against her pale skin. The image of Martha was identical to that of the woman he'd seen in a butcher's apron just a few days before.

She turned to Crockett. He was upset to see that, even in the dark, at a distance, he could tell the odd eye was swiveling around, it's sweeping orb glinting in the dark.

With a sudden movement, she lowered the weapon. Her body shuddered with an immense sigh.

"I have been waiting," she wheezed through the pain of her earlier wound, "half my life to fire that bullet."

Crockett looked toward the water. His scalp prickled. He could add blood to the long list of stains that would need to be lifted from his clothing.

"It was a magnificent shot," he said finally. He was unbearably nervous, unsure if the crazed maid would turn the gun on him.

But when he turned to face Martha, the gun was down; for the first time since he'd known her, she smiled.

26

Martha

When the blood, gore, gunshots, and screams ceased, the night grew quite pleasant. The stars were shining, and the wind, now gusting less dramatically, became a constant, warming rush from the countryside. Crockett turned away from Martha to take a moment of solace and enjoy the world around him, a world that had nearly faded for him into an eternal darkness thrown from the barrel of a gun.

When he was calmed, and certain that the danger had fully passed, he turned toward Martha and expressed his gratitude.

"Thank you," he said warmly.

"It was my pleasure," Martha said, still smiling. "I was under the thumbs of those men for years—he and Dexter both."

"You couldn't escape?"

"Where to?" Martha shook her head. "I had no family, nowhere to run. For Dexter, I was an obsession, so he kept me. They dismissed everyone but me before they killed the real Master Bixby..." She looked anxiously into the dark, "When I did try to escape, they threatened violence."

Crockett's skin prickled. He could only imagine the crazed schemes the two men would have put into motion had Martha tried to get away. "I'm very sorry, Martha. I can't imagine being a prisoner in this place."

"It was a jail, to be sure," she said warmly, "but I believe that the gates are now open."

MARTHA

Crockett did his best to dust the stains off his trousers, but the mud was thick and there was no hope that he could get back to London in any clothing not covered in filth and gore. He resigned himself and caught up to Martha who had begun shambling back toward the house. Gently, he extended his arm, linking it with the old woman's to help her down the track.

"I always liked you," she said. "You've got a good, poor head on your shoulders. When the rest of the rich folk thought the key solved it, you kept going."

"I don't know if that was a rational course of action." Crockett blushed, remembering the thud Petrarch's body had made collapsing onto the floor. "And Brontë was the one who convinced *me* that we should pursue the mystery further. Regardless, somehow it all worked out in the end."

"I should say so." Martha puffed out her chest proudly. "You two gave me renewed courage to fight for myself. I knew something more diabolical was happening even before Bixby Hawsfeffer—or Von Bunson, that is—disappeared; he came back erratic from his meeting with Petrarch in London regarding the will. I spied on both him and Dexter more frequently—Corinthiana was sure we renewed our imaginary affair, but I needed to know what was going to happen." She lifted her head up and breathed deeply as if the death of Bixby Hawsfeffer had changed even the air on the grounds. "Dexter and Bixby kept me trapped for so long, I'd begun to think there was no hope, but you two, putting your noses where they shouldn't be, gave me a fresh sense of purpose. The day you came into the kitchen, I was still unsure. I admit, I helped them…I washed the bloody rags Dexter used to clean up the Beatrice mess with the rest of the laundry, but, after that day when I saw you looking for the truth, I changed. I tried to help. I did my best to give you hints in the bedroom…"

"And you did, Martha. Without you I wouldn't have put it all together. You even helped accidentally, when we awoke you after Beatrice was killed and you spoke of a 'him'…But it was those last pieces—the painting and the back stair—that made all of the little gears in my brain click together. The back stair confirmed Dexter could have been involved in the chaos of the séance, even if his excuse was tending the back lawn."

"I hoped you'd catch on. At first, I didn't trust anyone. I was sure any secret I passed on would get back to him and then…" She shook her head sadly.

Crockett noted she was cringing. Fresh blood still flowed from her shoulder wound.

"One moment, Martha," he said. He removed his overshirt and gently wrapped her shoulder with it. She winced only slightly. "You're a tough, old bird." Crockett smiled. "I can't believe they kept you captive for so long."

"Power and violence," she said casually. "You'd be surprised what those can do. In the end I'd grown so afraid I was even starting to worry about Corinthiana—as much of an ogre as she is—that's why I moved into the room close to her after Bixby faked his death. I was unsure of what was to come."

Crockett pulled the shirt tighter and patted her shoulder. "There now, all fixed, I think."

"It's a shame the doctor left after tending to the homosexual. I suppose we'll have to call him again."

"We really should have made him a bed this weekend."

Martha laughed, a sound which, after hearing it, Crockett thought he'd like not to hear too often. It was an odd mixture of a foghorn and locomotive engine, a more technological version of Corinthiana's "AWRK!"

Progress to the house was slow between the two of them. Martha was more wounded than she initially let on, her steps heavy and short. Her breathing came with visible effort. When they got to the tomb, Dexter was passed out. Blood still poured from his leg; his face was an ashen gray.

"Should we help him?" Crockett asked.

Martha shrugged. "Someone will later. I say we wait a bit. If we're lucky, he'll die."

"You'd be having a very lucky night, then," Crockett said.

Martha's eye spun more quickly with joy.

They were on the track through the garden and to the main house when Martha stopped and turned to Crockett.

"Would you…" Martha hesitated. "Would you read me the note in your hand? I know it will be a big family hullabaloo, but I'd like to know. When you're the help, they never let you know. I'm the one who put it in the tomb before they sealed it—right under the carved hat like she told me to. I never read it, though; I kept my word to her. I never expected it all to end the way it did. I only wish I heeded my own doubts and fled the house with Lucinda and Bixby Hawsfeffer before it was too late."

Crockett nodded, excited himself to see the words on the parchment for which he risked his life. There was a bit of mud on the folded paper, but it was all clearly legible, in the same hand as the note they shared with Corinthiana only a few days before.

Dearest Pipsy,

It is my strongest hope this somehow finds you. It is a wishful link in a gossamer chain that I hope spans from Petrarch's desk, to the tomb, to you, who can finally know the full truth.

Your father's cousin, Bixby Von Bunson, returned to England a few months ago with an American oddity in tow, a Mr. Dexter Fletcher. To be sure, this new guest unsettled me from the start, his blankness a source of terror. I have never met a man who is so instantly forgettable, himself like the impression of a dream you have upon waking.

At first arrival, nothing seemed out of the ordinary. Your father and Bixby Von Bunson got along well. Your father never brought up his successful scheme to kill Bixby's father (that is another story for another time, but you know we never really cared for your great-uncle), but, since Bixby Von Bunson had been estranged from his own family, we thought perhaps the feeling was all very mutual.

After a few months of our gathering, however, Bixby's intentions and his presence grew more malevolent. He demanded more money, more time, more power. When he first arrived, he convinced your father to invest in an expansion of the west wing, an imitation of the American White House. Your father loved the idea, but slowly Von Bunson's claws pushed further in. He solicited outside help and had murals done in his likeness (and the likeness of the perverse Mr. Fletcher). He expanded the plans without input from your father, putting in a secret vault, and signing an initial agreement for an eastward expansion which included a large, gothic tower.

Over the past few weeks things have swelled in intensity. Mr. Fletcher has grown bolder, all but outright threatening me in times we pass alone in the hall. He has taken to reading all epistles entering and leaving the house, perpetuating the feeling that we are living in a jail. Bixby Von Bunson disappears for long stretches altogether. Your father, never one to ask for my counsel, asked me the best course of action to take. I think we need to go away, to run, but your father will not have it. Dear Martha is the one who confessed she heard Bixby and Mr. Fletcher discussing in earnest whispers a plot, the details of which we have no real clarity; however, Martha stated she believes our lives are in danger.

Immediately upon hearing this, I set my plan into motion. It was my desire to protect you, our family, and our fortune to the best of my feminine ability. Petrarch should have the note which will be released upon your father's death. I hope it guided you here. As I said, it may be a fool's hope, but the possibility of it is enough for me to face tomorrow and its uncertainty with more alacrity than otherwise would be possible.

At the last, I must also issue an apology for many things, but the one for which I'm most culpable is not taking a stand against your father in the light of your announced homosexual proclivities. Whilst I do disagree with your inclinations strongly in the face of God and man, you are family, our only son, and I love you dearly. I hope that, should the worst happen and our fortunes are lost, this note finds you, if only for you to be reached by my earnest apology, my deepest love, and my warmest wishes that, whatever life sets before you, you triumph knowing that I am, and will always be, proud of you.

In deepest love,
Mummy

Both Crockett's and Martha's faces were wet with tears. The illumination of a mother's final words to her son leaving them in states of differing, but total, catharsis.

A preternatural calm followed the reading. Crockett took a deep breath and then gently pressed his hand into Martha's.

"You knew," he said softly. "You tried to warn them."

MARTHA

"I was very young," Martha said. "I admired Lucinda very much. The reason I went to that silly séance this week was to…I know it's absurd, but I hoped there was a chance she *would* speak." Martha shook her head, but then the hint of a smile appeared on her face. "I know they are only loosely related, but young Brontë reminds me of her—determined, beautiful, joyful. I had heard…" Here she paused, tears freely falling from her eyes. With her features softened so, Crockett could see into the past, to the young woman who tried to save her beloved matron, whose looks seduced Dexter Fletcher. "I heard Bixby and Dexter plotting. They were such wicked men on the inside—outside, they were pleasant, boisterous, but you knew they were up to something. One morning I cleared the breakfast table and went to the west wing to begin making the beds. That's when I heard them. I'll never forget that morning." Her old hands tremored. "I didn't hear the exact words, but they said they wanted Bixby out of the way. They said in order to truly execute the plot, they needed to clear out the Hawsfeffer family completely.

"I didn't know if that meant murder, scandal, or threats of violence, but I knew that I must confess what I heard to Lucinda." Martha stopped. She pulled her hand from Crockett's and wiped her eyes. "They found me," she said abruptly. "They knew I'd heard. Dexter took me into the vault. He…" she stuttered, "I saw then what he was capable of." She indicated her bulging, spinning eye.

Crockett's heart cracked with grief. "But you told Lucinda anyway…" he said.

Martha raised her head, a resigned smile on her lips. "I told her anyway."

As they approached the mansion, the noises in the house grew louder. Martha took a deep breath and again wiped her eyes. The night enveloped them, protecting them for a fleeting moment from the violence of the past.

"I should think, then, that you're the real hero of this story," Crockett said putting his arm around her. "If it weren't for you, there wouldn't have been anything for me to discover."

Martha said nothing but pulled free of Crockett and began to pace toward the mansion. After a few steps, she turned and simply said, "It usually is the ones like us who save them—the forgotten ones, the simple ones. We see it all." At this her eye twisted quickly, a physiological flourish to her platitude.

Crockett came after Martha following her unsteady steps toward the front door of the house. From inside the sounds of August's bellowing, Corinthiana's vowel-filled caterwauling, and the occasionally staccato reprimand of May, burst from the open windows like a storm. Despite the cacophony, the windows glowed with golden warmth. If anything, the house stood, at that moment, as a formal symbol of family—welcome, warm, and rebounding with noises we'd all eschew under different circumstances.

Just as they approached the front door, it opened quickly. Brontë stumbled out, her hair disheveled; August, steps behind her, called out in reprobation.

But when Brontë saw Crockett and Martha, alive and standing in the dark, she smiled, her whole face filling with light.

Crockett's heart fluttered. For once, a welcoming door illumined his path, making him feel full of love. For the first time in his life, he felt as if he were coming home.

27

The End of the Affair

Brontë's joy faded as August pulled her back from the entryway. The querulous man shoved her inside then reopened the front door to wave Crockett and Martha into the house. Once Brontë's precious presence was removed, Crockett's heart constricted. He ran forward in the earnest hope of meeting Petrarch and setting their relationship right.

It didn't take long to find him. The front entry contained the mansion's whole cast of characters in various states of dress and emotion. Corinthiana held a huge tankard of sherry, her eyes crossed with drunkenness. She was ignoring the protestations of May, who kept screaming intermittently at her mother and sister. June, wearing a robe, appeared ready to pounce on her younger sibling.

Petrarch and Kordelia were engaged in some version of a conversation. Kordelia nodded enthusiastically while Petrarch gazed upward, a look of complete confusion writ on his features. When Petrarch turned his attention toward the door, to Crockett's relief, a large smile appeared on his face. The young man ran toward him, speaking quickly and stiltedly.

"Petrarch—it—I'm sorry, it was chaotic and idiotic...I don't...You must forgive me..."

Petrarch's eyes twinkled. He patted his belly joyfully. "My boy, I have to say the means were very questionable, but it looks like the ends may justify them."

Crockett, seized by emotion, reached out and pulled the old man into a warm embrace. His voice shook as he spoke. "I thought I lost you, old man."

Petrarch, his eyes shining with nascent tears, squeezed his assistant enthusiastically. "Same, my boy." He cleared his throat, in an attempt to quell his emotion. "When I heard you were outside, I assumed the worst."

The two could say little else. August interrupted their emotional moment and ushered them into the sitting room. The rest of the house followed them, the intense emotions transforming from anger to curiosity as their attention turned to the young lawyer and the old maid.

All had heard the gunshots, but the chaos and arguments of the inside outweighed anyone's fortitude to run out and go help whoever was being (possibly) murdered in the night. Brontë would have fled to aid Crockett, however she had been held back by both August and May who accused her of heightened female hysteria. They spent the better part of an hour pouring chilled water on her. May suggested they begin powdering Brontë's breasts with flour (an old trick in the convent to quell female emotion) which was when June grew enraged and stated she would not "have my daughter turned into a pastry!"

Corinthiana was the most contented. She shuffled in her slow, theatrical gait to the sofa and took a seat. As she sipped on her sherry, she stroked a large feather boa she'd thrown about her neck sometime before Crockett and Martha returned to the house.

Pip Hawsfeffer showed no signs of emotion at all. His injuries now cared for, he sat on a chair, leg elevated, humming a French tune to himself. He had evidently fallen back asleep due to his medications after Crockett fled the house and did not share his knowledge of the killer as the family argued about what to do.

The rest of the house hung in suspense, not knowing quite how to behave. May wrung her hands, June nervously bit her lip, and Brontë was forced to sit next to her father, a look of distress on her beautiful face. Kordelia sat dreamily in the seat opposite Pip (whom she had developed an instant, consuming admiration for now that she knew he had written *The Viscount's Ram*).

Petrarch stood by the fireplace, a moony, half smile on his face. Crockett hadn't realized how dazed his mentor remained from the medication and head injuries of the previous night. He sincerely hoped his forgiving heart wasn't due to valium rather than true reconciliatory feeling.

It was after much *hmm*ing and *harrr*ing that Martha and Crockett were finally seated on the sofa. The family gathered around anxiously staring at them. It was August who spoke first, his mustache jauntily leaping, as though it was also uncertain of what emotion it needed to portray.

"Well..." he said softly. "What's the news, then?"

Crockett deferred to Martha, however the older woman returned to her grizzled house personality. She sat with her arms crossed, eye rotating slowly, and said nothing as she stared disdainfully in the direction of the drunken Corinthiana.

Crockett then proceeded to tell the house the story of what transpired at the Hawsfeffer tomb. There was much initial confusion about the sequence of murders and faked deaths (at a certain point Pip took a page from his precious notebook to help illustrate what had occurred). May had the hardest time understanding that her father was not really a Hawsfeffer, but rather a Von Bunson who murdered a Hawsfeffer to take back his family fortune and sired her under the stolen Hawsfeffer name. Pip's picture of a stick figure drowning in a river helped finally hammer the point home.

After initial confusion, however, the family proved to be such a rapt audience that Crockett became fully invested, leaping about atop the sofa, making loud gunshot noises with his mouth and basking in the collected gasps of the family when he revealed Dexter Fletcher had not fled the grounds due to the succession of maiming, ghosts, and murders, but stayed as an auxiliary to the crimes as Detective Pimento.

His only regret was he wished he could have outlined the structure of the story better before telling it to the gathered crowd. He put the revelations about Lucinda near the middle when, really, they would have been more effectively placed at the end.

When he finished, he handed the handwritten note to Pip to read. The family clamored behind the invalid to glance at the text over his shoulder.

A tortured silence settled when it was all out. Pip, reading the final lines, allowed some emotion, a large dramatic tear squeezing from his eye and plopping on the parchment.

"This place is so dusty," he said quickly. "It gets in the eyes."

Corinthiana, although drunk, was the most concerned, her entire well-being having been wiped out with one ancient letter.

"Sooo..." she said, a hiccup escaping. "Whaaat then?"

August cleared his throat dramatically but then said nothing. Petrarch sighed, shuffling to the center of the room.

"Well," he said, looking nervously at Corinthiana, "as the handwriting in this letter matches the other epistle from my records, it would appear that the inheritance of all of the estate would pass to Pip Hawsfeffer. But," he looked at Corinthiana, "if...you want to tell everyone..."

Corinthiana hiccupped again. Huge, sherry-tainted tears ran down the side of her face. "There is nothing aaanywaaay," she said between sobs, her vowels, in her anxiety and inebriated state, becoming like the ululations of a feline preparing to mate. "Bixby, my husbaaand, whomever thaaat is now, tooo beee honest I no longer know, lost everything."

"I believe you married Bixby Von Bunson," Petrarch said conciliatorily, "which means that Pip," he said pointing to the seated homosexual, "is the sole heir of the estate and all its debts, him being the true heir of Bixby Hawsfeffer, who legally took the estate from the Baron."

At this moment, Petrarch staggered, still exhausted, but Crockett was able to grab him and gently drag him to the couch where he was given a seat. June set a pillow behind his back and lovingly patted his bald head.

During Petrarch's spell, the rest of the house slowly turned their eyes on Pip, who looked absurdly nonplussed, as if the events of the house, his own defenestration at the hands of his cousin, and the revelatory letter of his mother hadn't phased him at all.

"Pip," Kordelia said softly, "we all very much want to know if you will make us abandon the house in exile and shame."

"Ha!" Pip said quickly. "You all can keep this disgusting pile of rocks and boards." He shook his head slowly. "I am cheered to know my attempted murder by Bixby Von Bunson was a result of greed and pride rather than simply an assault on *mon amoureux masculins*. I do think that's rather progressive, if it must be known."

All nodded. In the chaos of the night, Pip's inclination for male company had largely been forgotten, and, in truth, amorous pursuits of one's own sex now seemed largely innocuous amidst the fish eviscerations, murders, gunshots, and plots that had apparently been staples of the family for generations.

"Well," Petrarch smiled, "in that case, we can draw up paperwork so that Pip can sign over the estate to Corinthiana. At which time," Petrarch sobered, "everything will most likely need to be sold to pay off the debts."

"Perhaps we could stay with Pip in Paris." Kordelia smiled warmly at her cousin.

"I would rather die," Pip said dusting off his trousers. "You, *mon petit incendiaire*, would be welcomed, but the rest of your clan is not *Parisienne*, if we're being honest."

No one was hurt at this revelation as the Hawsfeffers (now Von Bunsons?) and Winterbournes were proud of their irascible Britishness and would also rather suffer a fate like Beatrice's than spend more than a long weekend in Paris.

By night's end, the house was in a general state of good spirits. Even Corinthiana had sobered up, ceasing her brooding and joining a game of whist with Petrarch, August, and Kordelia.

Brontë took a seat next to Crockett. Gently, she squeezed his hand before drawing it away. The deed crossed some boundaries, but she was uncertain of the course their budding romance would take and desired that he know he was valued.

"We owe you a great deal," she said. "You and Martha ended the vicious cycle that began all those years ago."

Crockett rubbed his hand where Brontë's fingers touched him. "I'm glad we came to the crux of it. I couldn't—" He smiled. "I couldn't have done any of it without you. You were the one who wouldn't give up when the key was found and everyone else celebrated success."

"Well," her cheeks flushed, "the whole thing was very odd. It was brilliant of you to make the connections. I don't know if I would have gotten that far."

"It was a wonderful twist of fate that I saw Dexter's scribblings in the detective notebook and remembered his illiteracy just as the painting came into my view; then I had the revelation that he could have come up the back staircase to play the record during the séance. Fate has an interesting way of guiding things."

"It's put a great deal in motion this week, I should say."

Both stayed silent for a moment. An irrepressible smile had rested on Crockett's lips since he saw Brontë on the threshold of the house. He turned now and looked at her. To his surprise, she looked distressed. She was turned, facing August, who was watching the exchange from across the room. When her eyes averted from her father and rested on the floor, she let out a quiet sigh. Crockett had never seen her so drained of confidence, so listless.

"Brontë," his said, his voice thick with emotion, "are you all right?"

She again looked to her father, who continued to watch them with a look of reproach. Rather than fix her gaze on Crockett, she kept it on the floor and asked, "You'll leave tomorrow?"

"I suppose so." Crockett's scalp was hot. He felt as if something was quickly slipping away from him. "The details of the will came out tonight, so we won't be needed any longer."

"What time do you think you will leave?"

"That depends on Petrarch. If he's fit to travel, I think we should be on the road after breakfast. We've been out of the office far longer than we initially planned."

"You'll have a lot of work, then," Brontë said.

Crockett felt anxious about the impersonal tone their conversation had taken. From the corner of the room, he could feel August's intense gaze still on them. "Yes," he said finally. "It will take us a while to catch up. Petrarch was supposed to be in East Fletchfordtownhampsonvilleshire earlier this week, but we have much to do in London as well."

Brontë's expression shifted. She looked at Crockett, her eyes luminous. "It's ludicrous, I suppose, to think…"

But before she could finish, August appeared before them, his mustache shivering as if attached to an airplane motor.

"Well done, Crockett," he barked. "We have a great deal to thank you for, not the least being that all of us are still alive and we can keep our pride in dying naturally, naturally."

"I'm glad I could help. I suppose it's not a truly happy ending if everything must be sold, but…"

"Oh! It's plenty happy enough. I can return home to my family's estate. My father has an extra house or two we can settle into. We won't have a lot, but Brontë can come and begin to focus on finding a *proper* match. Albeit one wealthier than we were originally looking for. We'll have to make up for this loss in some way. Kordelia will, of course, need to finish boarding school."

Crockett's heart tightened in his chest. He'd forgotten one-half of Brontë's family was not full of murderers, still had money, and died naturally, naturally. The rosy-hued dream of him taking her away to London seemed a child's fantasy.

"It will be exciting for you to return to a new home." Crockett tried to sound happy, but his voice came out in an uneven, erratic string of syllables. Tears dribbled down the side of his face.

"It's…" Brontë searched for something to say.

"I'm very happy for all of you." Crockett rose, trying his best to swallow emotion. "I'll see you at breakfast for, uh, well, for good-bye, I suppose."

He took off quickly in the direction of his bedroom. The string of gunshots and near-death experiences paled in comparison to his current heartbreak. He needed to go to bed and forget it all, let sleep overtake and drown the sorrow of the real.

When he'd returned to his room, however, he did not immediately go to bed on his little couch. He paced anxiously, muttering to himself. The thoughts were incoherent, a patchwork of personal affirmations mixed with harsh denunciations of his belief that he ever dreamed he and Brontë could be together.

"A hero...old Crockett," he blathered as he moved across the room's wooden planks. "Who'd have thought—and a right idiot to believe..."

Petrarch interrupted his muttering.

"Hullo, old boy." He walked into the room in an erratic fashion, still under the influence of his medications. He attempted to shake Crockett's hand but toppled sideways and rolled onto the lumpy bed.

Crockett helped set him upright. He placed his hand on the old man's and smiled warmly. "So good to see you up and about, Petrarch. I'm glad you harbor no ill feelings for my stupidity."

"Ha!" Petrarch snorted. "I know you tend to overreact, especially when a beautiful young woman is involved."

Crockett's ears turned red. "I know you warned me away from Brontë..."

"I still do, although, with the chaos of this house and the state of the family's fortune, it perhaps doesn't matter much." Petrarch gripped Crockett's shoulder. Crockett's thoughts strayed back to Brontë and the explosive joy he'd felt when he'd pressed his lips to hers.

"Are you all right, my boy?" Petrarch asked. "You seem a bit melancholy."

"Just tired, I suppose. It's been a very long night."

"I should say! I'm very proud of you. You managed to put it all together and save the day."

"I had a lot of help."

"Indeed, but, my boy, how *did* you do it?"

"Fate," Crockett said sadly. He thought of looking into Brontë's eyes and saying the same words only moments before. "Fate intervened on my behalf."

"She's a powerful ally."

There was an emotional moment of silence. Crockett shook his head, his feelings a mix of relief and grief. "I just can't believe what a mess it's all been," he said. "Petrarch, I can't apologize enough for my rash actions with the gun."

"Oh!" Petrarch laughed. "As I said, it all worked out. It was quite good fun in the end. It was more the dropping me that did the damage, but I think my head has been restored to some sort of equilibrium. I've stopped seeing peacocks talking to me."

"Well, that's wonderful," Crockett said, allowing himself to smile.

"But how did you know it was Bixby?"

Crockett grew very tired, the events of the day catching up with him. He yawned as he summarized the more precise details of the mystery—the paintings, disguises, the back stairwell, and Martha's insights. He did his best to add more color to the story, providing the context of Bixby and Dexter's misadventures in America.

Despite his growing lethargy, he felt his heart swell with pride. He'd found his rutabaga farmer and solved the mystery—Captain Discord would be proud. Although it was not done efficiently or effectively, it was accomplished eventually, which is the most a junior detective could ask for.

As Petrarch listened, not having his thinking pipe present, he picked up Crockett's hairbrush and pantomimed smoking that. "I suppose Martha was the only one who knew all these tentative links that joined the past and present. She was the only one who could guide you to the resolution."

"She was invaluable. And, once the links were exposed, it being Bixby Von Bunson and Dexter made perfect sense. They both knew every nook and cranny in the house. Bixby had retained a key to the family vault after his fake drowning and could get the sword without Corinthiana's copy. Dexter knew of the back staircase, so he could fix the record player and escape without raising suspicion, and, of course, Bixby wrote his own letter of introduction to welcome their cousin, Robert Edward. That's why he was never under suspicion."

"I see." Petrarch tapped his head. "But how did Bixby Von Bunson find out about Lucinda's note? I kept my word; I never told him."

"Ah! You left the note in the file. He found it while he was perusing his documents when he last visited you." Crockett moved toward his sleeping couch; his eyes were growing very heavy. "After he read it, he returned home and probed Martha about the game they used to play—notes in hats—which led to him understanding the clue about the true, revelatory note's location in the tomb. He also knew you had been ordered never to relinquish the key until after Bixby Hawsfeffer's death. Once he faked his death, he and Dexter did the séance and murdered Beatrice to get Corinthiana to speed the burial ceremony and get into the tomb to destroy Lucinda's revelation."

"But then you tried to kill me…"

"And that's when they had to get *really* creative." Crockett's eyes fluttered.

"So, they created Pimento to frame you and clear their names completely. They'd blame you for all of it, destroy the note, and head off into the proverbial sunset."

"Exactly. But then…" Crockett smacked his lips. "When Pip showed up, who would know what the note meant…"

"They threw him from a window…" Petrarch nodded.

Petrarch followed up with a few more questions, but before he received answers, Crockett was snoring peacefully. The solicitor did his best to tuck in his young apprentice. As he fluffed Crockett's pillow, the young man's eyes fluttered open.

"Oh…Petrarch," he said softly.

"Yes, my boy?"

"Someone should probably go check on Dexter. He's been dying for several hours out near the tomb. Martha and I forgot about him."

Petrarch blinked but said nothing. As he shut Crockett's door, he heard the young man snoring again and, from what the old solicitor could make out, whispering something softly—what he believed to be the name "Brontë."

28

The Danube Mob

Crockett awoke in a stupor. His clothes were still covered in dried mud and blood, and he had nothing to change into. It was still very early in the morning; a light mist was on the house grounds. The events of the previous night still seemed distant and dreamlike. Had it not been for the mud and blood, he most likely would have believed none of it happened.

In his addled state, he was surprised to hear a light rapping on the door. There was a moment of sheer confusion and terror when he stared at the wall, unaware of how to do much of anything. The brief suspended state was followed by a chaotic, rapid firing of his brain cells, which caused him to trip toward the mirror to fix his hair. The tripping built into a falling, the culmination of which sent him sprawling toward the vanity. A sharp crack rang out as his head collided with the side of the small fixture. He was both surprised and unsurprised when he felt his forehead and found that damp blood was dripping down the side of his face.

"Oh, dear," he said.

Since his clothes were all soiled to begin with, he picked up a discarded shirt and wrapped it around his head to slow the bleeding. This, of course, rendered the need to comb his hair unnecessary, so he staggered toward the door and opened it, revealing Brontë.

While Crockett's face broke into a wide, beaming smile, Brontë looked past him, into the room, with a hard, humorless gaze.

"Hullo," she said dryly. Her face twitched slightly when she saw the makeshift turban atop Crockett's head.

"Brontë..."

To Crockett's surprise, she had already dressed for the day. Instead of her usual taupe trousers, she wore a long, green dress. Her hair did not hang freely, chaotically, as it had during the week, but was fixed, held back tight.

"I've come to say good-bye," she said walking to the window. "Father talked to me last night, and we're to leave for Winterbourne House this morning. I'll be packing during breakfast, so this will be our last chance to speak."

"So soon," Crockett's face dropped. "I thought we could go for a walk around the grounds this morning after breakfast. Perhaps you could pretend to be a canary once again."

Brontë's mouth tremored but would not reveal a smile.

"No." She said it haughtily, turning her face away. "We have to go. Grandmother canceled the burial; she decided to just kind of stuff Grandfather in the tomb and forget about it. She is planning a rather nice ceremony for Beatrice, but she says she needs a month to plan for it, so we'll return then. I think she's planning on hiring some of the local circus performers to do a kind of show." Brontë's cold exterior had been slowly cracking, but she suddenly remembered herself. She stood more erect and bowed slightly toward Crockett. "All that aside, it has been a pleasure to meet you, Mr. Cook." She extended her hand for Crockett to shake. He sadly took it, gazing into her eyes for a moment, catching, what he thought, was some distant glimmer of their old connection.

She turned and bustled toward the door, the swishing of her skirts the death knell to Crockett's hopes.

Had this scene occurred a week ago, he would have let her go, said nothing, packed up the shards of his heart and begun the healing process, but since the events of the house, the madness, the life and death experiences, he had changed; he had to speak.

"Brontë," he called out, "Is it...did I imagine it all? The kiss..."

The bustling of skirts ceased. She only half turned to address his question.

"Crockett, it's not worth dwelling on. Father says there's a family with a son and a large sum of money. Ironically, it's the cousin of the man Aunt May is currently courting. But he can offer security." She paused here. Crockett was unable to see her face as she turned fully toward the door and her skirt began bustling again. "Can you imagine you and me? We'd gallivant around London solving herring murders. What kind of life would that be?"

She did not wait for an answer. With little more than a wave good-bye, she disappeared out the door and into the darkness of the hallway.

Crockett's heart broke fully then. Tears dripped down the side of his face. The scene was a sad one, the young man, head wrapped in his white Oxford shirt, staring plaintively toward the window. Around him dust motes and muted light gave the air of a macabre painting, not even done by a great master artist, but, perhaps, credited to his alcoholic failure of an apprentice.

He was just about to collapse back on the couch when there was another knock on the door. For a brief moment, the hope that it was Brontë returning gave his heart wings, but when he turned toward the open portal, he instead saw Kordelia looking past him to some distant object.

"My room has become quite the place for visitors," he said.

"I saw Brontë leaving." Kordelia, despite all that had happened, retained the sound of someone softly speaking from the other side of a wall. "Did she break your heart then?"

"Yes."

"She and father talked for a long while last night. I didn't hear much, although I tried to listen through the air ducts. I assumed it wasn't a pleasant chat, however."

"Not for me."

Kordelia walked toward Crockett and extended her porcelain hand. It rested on his shoulder and then, awkwardly, in a syncopated rhythm, she patted him reassuringly. The girl was not well versed in the art of consolation. Crockett was unsure the purpose of the exercise, but Kordelia's dreamy eyes focused for a moment and attempted to look concerned. He took this to be a friendly gesture and warmly smiled.

"*A Fishtescent Murder*," she said while patting him.

"I'm sorry?"

"That's Pip Hawsfeffer's new play. It's based on all that's happened."

"It's about your family? And," Crockett's eyebrows scrunched together "is…fishtescent a word?"

"No, it's not a word, but Pip takes great liberties with the English language." Kordelia ceased patting and took a seat on the bed. "And yes, it is about the family. He stayed up all night writing. I helped him. He needed assistance capturing the characters just right, you know."

"I've always wondered how artists receive inspiration."

"He said last night it was like 'The sound of a cry of the world's lightning all at once.'"

Crockett nodded his head. "That sounds like something he would say."

"You're in it, of course," Kordelia said playing with the lace on the collar of her blouse. "We made you less horse-looking and wealthier, but it's a very similar character."

"I'm honored."

Kordelia refocused, again, on Crockett. Her blank expression turned warm for an instant. "Thank you," she said quickly.

"Well, I couldn't let the murder go unsolved."

"No." She turned toward the window and nervously itched her ear. "For listening. That day on the river—no one really listened to me, but you did that day, and Uncle Pip is listening now. That's what I'm thanking you for. And," she turned and slightly smiled, "for understanding that sometimes gloves simply get placed in conspicuous places and don't mean anything more."

"I'm glad I could add something pleasant to your return home from Switzerland," Crockett smiled. Everything irritating about the young girl, even her halitosis, had turned to fondness in these last moments together.

Kordelia nodded, then, abruptly, leapt up from her seat on the bed and drifted toward the door. While her hand rested on the knob, she turned around and gazed at him. "I like your turban, but if you're going to be doing a séance, it should be red and pushed back a bit; also, jewels give it more authority."

Crockett laughed. He was surprised to hear it after just having his heart broken, but in the moment, he only remembered the silly séance and, further back, the day Kordelia told him she set the cat on fire.

"Also, Crockett," she continued, "it will be hard, but you'll recover from my sister. At least someone isn't grating all of your favorite cheese in front of you."

This time Crockett tried to restrain his laughter. He bit his lip and nodded emphatically. When he felt that he could speak without breaking, he said, "Thank you, Kordelia. That really means…well, more than you can know."

"*Jiboody kirkegaard*," she said sweetly. "In fortune teller, that's 'I'll always remember you.'"

#

Breakfast was a joyful affair, despite the sad start to Crockett's morning. Even August and June were pleasant, having successfully torn their daughter's affections from the impecunious solicitor's assistant. The most shocking conciliatory event, however, was May asking Crockett to pass the crème for her coffee. Her normally stiff expression broke, slightly, to show a belabored smile.

Corinthiana was the most effusive with her praise and mirth. Having gotten to the bottom of the events and been assured by August and June that, after the sale of Hawsfeffer Manor, they would have the ability to care for her, she was in the highest spirits, as evidenced by the more prolonged vowels that now fueled her sentence constructions—this, of course, combined with the slight hangover from her obscene tankard of sherry she had drunk the night before.

"Hellooo," she bellowed as Crockett and Petrarch sat down to the meal. She was so happy she didn't even mention Crockett's lack of formal coat, his mud-stained shirt, or the dried blood on his forehead. "How aaare yooou?"

Pip Hawsfeffer was even in high spirits when he came down to eat (assisted by Kordelia due to his sprained ankle, bruised leg, and dislocated shoulder). While manic, clearly, from his night of writing, he gave Martha a compliment, noting that the scones she had prepared, "Weren't *très mauvais.*"

Petrarch was feeling his old self as well, leveling one of his usual well-dressed insults at Pip as he took his seat. "Sir," he said to him, passing the toast, "we never met properly, but you have the regal air of Shakespeare and all the talent of his index finger."

By the end of breakfast, Crockett felt slightly better. The blood from his morning forehead wound had ceased; after eating, Martha took time to dress his wound with warm water and a bandage. Crockett returned the favor after, redressing her shoulder injury from the previous night. Brontë didn't appear at all in the morning, which only helped Crockett feel that he could move on freely with his life after the affair at Hawsfeffer Manor. He had done a great service for the family, proven himself to Petrarch, received his first kiss, and, most likely, would have a character based on him in a French play—overall, it was a very successful outing for the young solicitor.

Petrarch seconded this as they made final preparations to leave. He was buoyant due to his mix of high spirits and the last of his medication.

"My boy, it's easy to fall in love. You meet a beautiful young woman with new ideas in a new place, and your heart makes decisions before your head. Trust me, we'll go back to London, and we'll find a better match for you."

"You're very wise, Petrarch. I think I got caught up in the events of the week, and many of my emotions ran too freely."

"A boy as clever as you will find someone perfect soon enough. With my connections, it may even be someone with more money than the Winterbournes. You could be living with a beautiful woman in the middle class very soon."

Crockett smiled. He extended his hand and grabbed Petrarch's, squeezing it warmly. "Petrarch, thank you for everything. I mean it. You have taken a number of chances on me and never given up on me, even when the family was ready to throw me into prison. And," his face flushed, "when I accidentally almost killed you."

"Well, I trust you!" Petrarch thumped his belly once, dramatically. "Your heart was in the right place when you fired that gun, and," he paused with slight drama, "*that* is why I'm sending you ahead to the Mayweathers in East Fletchfordtownhampsonvilleshire. I am going to Winterbourne House to help August and June with a few legal issues there, then I also have to stop in Dunstead village to get a signature from Mrs. Chambers."

"Oh," Crockett blushed with pleasure. "You want me to go ahead and start the final will reading with the Mayweathers?"

"Of course! I'll follow along a day behind, but consider this a promotion. You may now call yourself a junior solicitor."

Crockett couldn't suppress his joy. "Petrarch, you…thank you!"

"If risking life and limb for a client doesn't prove your worth, I don't know what will."

Crockett's joy was dampened by the thought of his bag full of muddy and bloodstained clothing. "Petrarch," he said, "could I perhaps get an advance on my salary. I'll need a fresh suit before arriving at the Mayweathers."

Petrarch winked and handed him a small fist of bills.

"SOLICITOR!" They heard Martha's shriek come from down the hallway. "CARRIAGE IS HERE!"

Petrarch patted Crockett on the shoulder. "That will be my ride with August, June, and Brontë to Winterbourne House. Your coach will be here shortly to go on to the Mayweathers' estate."

The two men, again, shook hands.

Once Petrarch was gone, Crockett took his bag to the main hall and then went for a walk around the grounds. To his surprise, Petrarch had forgotten to report Dexter's situation the night before, and the man had expired outside the tomb. While Crockett was not exactly overjoyed by the corpse, it perhaps was the best outcome, as no one would have been really been safe had the old man survived. Martha helped him drag the body to the Tiddlymouth and throw it in after his master.

"Seems a fitting end," Martha said, her eye slowly spinning. "Glad you found him before the flies and maggots settled in."

When Crockett's carriage arrived, the remaining family, excepting Pip, who was still too injured to move far, all waved good-bye from the front lawn. Martha helped him with his luggage, even going so far as to stiffly hug the young man and slip him a parcel containing a few ghost biscuits. Tears were in her eyes, an uncomfortable situation when one of them spins, sending a light spray of sadness onto those in close proximity.

The carriage driver's assistant was clumsy and spoke in a shrill, bleating voice that made Crockett extremely uncomfortable. He had to help the young lad get the bag onto the carriage before watching him fall onto the ground trying to get back into the driver's bench with his master. Crockett would have normally helped, but he had no desire to be of assistance to someone who, at a base level, couldn't do the most perfunctory parts of his trade.

It was while he was double-checking his bag was secured to the carriage that the last piece of the puzzle fell into place. He realized the reason the doctor who arrived with Dexter looked so familiar was because it was the old carriage master from the day of their arrival. He had worn the scarf to cover the growth on his neck and brought the potato to woo Corinthiana. This revelation somehow struck him as the most absurd, so he was laughing merrily as he gave a final wave to Martha and yelled for the carriage to proceed.

The sound of the horses' hooves signaled their movement forward with great gusto. The manor receded into the distance, the ill-kept bushes and trees passing by Crockett's window. Slowly, as more distance was put between himself and the house, he felt his merriment turn to a profound sadness. It wasn't merely the loss of Brontë but a feeling of letting go and growing up. When he'd arrived at Hawsfeffer Manor he'd simply been a solicitor's assistant, a young man on the edge of a career, still yet to fall in love or be shot at multiple times with a revolver.[48] But now, on the other side of the madness, he couldn't help but feel as if a part of his youth was buried along with Beatrice in the grounds of the old house, as shambled and grotesque as it was.

---

[48] In parts of rural England, one isn't considered a real man until he has had his life put in danger by "a weapon of killing strength."

The carriage wheels creaked happily, pulling them away. Crockett sighed and turned in his seat to take one last look at the tall, pillared front, the stalwart, dark green tomb, and the scattered dead trees, marking Dexter's poor gardening skills. The sky behind the scene was the purest, June blue, a hopeful premonition for the house and its inhabitants.

When Crockett turned forward once again, he was startled to see another carriage approaching. The two men in the front of it waved as they drew near, signaling for Crockett's carriage to halt.

Once they were close enough to speak, a gentleman in the front, wearing a bowler and full black suit, saluted and spoke in a thick Viennese accent.

"Hullo," he said. "You're coming from the Hawsfeffer house?"

"Yes, sir," Crockett said deferentially. The man's jacket lifted exposing a firearm.

"Very pleasant to meet you," he continued. "We're the Danube Mob; we've come to do the last of the fixing up."

Crockett blanched. "The…Dan…Mob?"

"Yes, sir, we've been tasked to go tidy up the ending a bit." The man cleared his throat and looked at a neat list written in precise lettering. "We've got May Hawsfeffer's farmer lover in the back."

At this, a gentleman peeped from the back curtain and waved. "Hullo!"

"Hell-o…"

"For the maid, Martha, we got this secret document that states she's the heiress to some fortune, left by a…" the Austrian gangster squinted at the text, "a…Miss Havisham."

Crockett's heart swelled imaging both Martha and Corinthiana sharing tea, covered in jewels.

"And we got some books for Kordelia's new French school and this…outfit for the Pip fellow." The man withdrew a bright blue suit; it was accompanied by a sling covered in jewels to aid Pip, stylishly, in his recovery.

"Lastly," the man signaled to his assistant in the front of the cart who withdrew a small, fishbowl from under his seat, "we have this for the old woman of the house, of course."

Crockett smiled broadly at the sight of a wriggling baby herring. "Yes,

I think they will very much like all of this. The house is just a bit farther down the road. You're almost there." Crockett felt the compunction to add, "I hadn't heard of you until a few days ago, but you really do great work."

The man nodded. "We do what we can." He consulted his list, stroking his chin. "And are you Mr. Cook?"

Crockett answered apprehensively, "I am."

"Well, I have two things for you then." The man pulled a parcel out first. Crockett snuck a glance into the package and was relieved to see a brand-new shirt and suit tailored to his size.

The second object was a square black case. The mobster passed it to Crockett, after which he saluted and then grabbed the reins and pushed his horses onward. "Cheerio!" he called. Dirt swept backward as his steeds picked up speed and disappeared toward the horizon.[49]

Crockett looked down at the case in his hand. He was about to open it when there was a clatter from outside his compartment. To his surprise, the carriage driver's assistant left the driving stand and leapt by his side.

"Hello!" he said emphatically.

Crockett stared at the young man for a moment. He did look familiar but not fully. The hazel eyes were magnetic, something very memorable in their earnest gaze, but the face and the bristling mustache were not.

"I'm sorry," Crockett said. "I don't—"

"Crockett!" The boy slapped his shoulder. "Don't be daft."

With a quick flick of his wrist, the boy tore off his mustache. Another deft movement removed his cap. In its absence, long, brown hair fell to his shoulders.

"Brontë!" Crockett's face lit up with joy. His eyes grew as large as tea saucers.

"Yes!" She pulled him close, kissing his cheek. "I had to be dramatic and tell you good-bye so that father would believe it. I couldn't have him chasing

---

[49] The editor was very torn about including this scene in the final text as it pushes the bounds of the narrative and is really implausible in a work of (supposedly) historical fiction; however, the inclusion of the baby herring tilted the scales in favor of its inclusion.

after me."

"But you were supposed to have left this morning!"

"Mother, Father, and Petrarch went ahead in one carriage. Petrarch made an excuse for me—he told them I wanted to spend more time with Kordelia before she left for school. He was in on the plot."

"And he gave his blessing to it?" Crockett's heart fluttered.

"Of course. He said he told you a made-up story about finding someone better, but he didn't believe it himself."

Crockett felt a sudden stab of betrayal, but it quickly healed under the warm gaze of the young woman before him.

"You are a remarkable actress," Crockett said, gently touching her cheek. "I really believed it. I convinced myself you were in pursuit of something better."

"What could be better?" she asked matter-of-factly. "And don't think Kordelia and my grandfather were the only ones who can put on a show. I learned from the best…and worst, I suppose, but don't worry, I won't kill you for money."

"Since neither of us have any, I think we're safe on that account."

Brontë pulled him close and they kissed, fully on the lips.

"Oh!" Brontë said reaching into her trouser pocket. "Petrarch said this came for him this morning. It's from the Mayweathers, but he didn't have time to read it. It could be about your arrival."

Crockett took the note and unfolded it. His eyes grew wide as he scanned the lines.

"What is it?" asked Brontë.

Crockett couldn't suppress his smile as he handed over the epistle to Brontë.

Dear Mr. Bluster,

Thank you very much for notifying us of your delay. We are grateful you and your assistant will be joining us in the next week to handle the dealings of Grandfather's estate.

It struck me as important to notify you prior to your arrival that all is not well

BEATRICE

in the house. Our sister Candace has vanished. Right before Grandfather died the two had a terrible row, and she disappeared from the town completely. On top of that, our neighbor Mr. Babcock was, well, to put it as pleasantly as possible, found decapitated in our cow shed earlier this week.

We hope you don't think these kinds of occurrences are common or reflect upon our family's normal state. Generally, we are very good citizens of the crown and all keep our heads, if you'll excuse the pun.

Looking very forward to your arrival,
Alluvia Mayweather

Brontë's eyes looked into Crockett's full of pure joy.

"Poor Mr. Babcock," she said smiling.

"It really is a tragedy," Crockett said taking her hand.

"I suppose they'll need help getting to the bottom of it, then," Brontë took the note and pored over it once more. She then turned to Crockett and asked pleasantly, "What do we know about the Mayweathers?"

Before Crockett could answer, however, he opened the black box provided him by the Danube Mob. Inside the case was a small, silver ring shaped perfectly to Brontë's finger. With little thought, he slid it onto her hand.

She looked at it warmly but briefly.

"I'd be deblighted, of course."

Crockett's heart leapt in his chest. Brontë reached out and placed her hand on his cheek.

"We can worry about the details later," she said.

Her hand lingered a time on his face. The young lovers stared deeply into each
other's eyes.

The carriage hit a rut, which returned them to their senses. Brontë shook her head as if waking from a dream.

"Where were we?" she asked.

Crockett immediately launched into a list of facts he knew about the Mayweathers, the small oddities Petrarch pointed out during their initial review of their will and family background.

The rest of the afternoon the carriage rolled forward and took them to Mayweather Manor, a rather pleasant, Tudor-inspired home on the edges of East Fletchfordtownhampsonvilleshire. The events surrounding their time there were darker, more dangerous, with slightly less animal involvement (aside from a small cameo from a cow named Blundergäst).

But—not to get carried away—that story is a tale for another time.

The most important piece of information to be shared at the end of this novel is regarding the young couple. And, for the sake of completion of this particular narrative, the reader can be certain that, in terms of perpetuity, Brontë and Crockett lived very happily ever after.

An Afterword and Apology

Dear Reader,

The editor hopes that you enjoyed the novel or, at the very least, hated it marginally less than you do federal taxes.

While most authors/editors would append a thank you note of sorts to the end of a book, those that helped get this book to publication stated that they would prefer anonymity (aside, of course, from @badgrrlkinzay47 who says "Sup, bitchez!" and again requests you follow her on Instagram). It's the editor's hope that the request for anonymity is due to humility rather than embarrassment, but we may never know.

It is necessary to issue an apology at this point in time. The story alluded to at the end of this novel regarding the Mayweathers and their cow, Blundergäst, has been lost to time. Earhart kept extensive notes on other stories about Crockett and Brontë, however the tale of the Mayweather murder is gone. The next novel will pick up at the conclusion of that mystery. *The Caddywampus* will be thoroughly edited and reviewed and be available for purchase in 2022.

Along with that apology, the editor issues a plea—he does hope that you will help him sketch in the story of this missing adventure. The notes at the conclusion of this text are largely all the information we have about what happened. Some would say it's a call for fan fiction, but I think it's more fan forensics, piecing together the lost mystery from what we have left from Earhart.

Story submissions can be posted on www.beatriceunbound.com. Having read this book, you know the bar is low, so the editor hopes you'll take your creativity and explore every possible option for what could have happened in those dark days in East Fletchfordtownhampsonvilleshire.

AN AFTERWORD AND APOLOGY

    Thank you in advance for your time and imagination. Earhart, Brontë, Crockett, and I will see you in 2022 for their troubling encounter with the German demon bear, the Caddywampus.

    Sincerely,
    Tedd Hawks

Made in United States
Troutdale, OR
03/17/2024

18542891R00166